Canadian **Dani Col** wanted to write rom years later, after ma having two kids wit office jobs and submitting countless manuscripts, she got The Call. Her first Mills & Boon novel won the Reviewers' Choice Award for Best First in Series from *RT Book Reviews*. She now works in her own office, writing romance.

Amanda Cinelli was raised in a large Irish/Italian family in the suburbs of Dublin, Ireland. Her love of romance was inspired after 'borrowing' one of her mother's beloved Mills & Boon novels at the age of twelve. Writing soon became a necessary outlet for her wildly overactive imagination. Now married, with a daughter of her own, she splits her time between changing nappies, studying psychology and writing love stories.

UNTOUCHED UNTIL HER ULTRA-RICH HUSBAND

DANI COLLINS

CLAIMING HIS REPLACEMENT QUEEN

AMANDA CINELLI

MILLS & BOON

First Published in Great Britain 2019
by Mills & Boon, an imprint of HarperCollins*Publishers*
1 London Bridge Street, London, SE1 9GF

Untouched Until Her Ultra-Rich Husband © 2019 by Dani Collins

Claiming His Replacement Queen © 2019 by Amanda Cinelli

ISBN: 978-0-263-27344-1

MIX
Paper from
responsible sources
FSC™ C007454

This book is produced from independently certified FSC™ paper
to ensure responsible forest management.
For more information visit www.harpercollins.co.uk/green.

Printed and bound in Spain
by CPI, Barcelona

UNTOUCHED UNTIL HER ULTRA-RICH HUSBAND

DANI COLLINS

CHAPTER ONE

BORN IN THE Year of the Dragon, Gabriel Dean was dominant, ambitious, passionate and willing to take risks. He jumped for no one.

His signature detachment, however, was not impervious to his grandmother's ringtone.

The distinctive tinkle of a brass tea bell might have struck some as a sign of affection. And yes, he had seen her shake such a bell on two of the three occasions he had spoken to her in person, but sentiment was not a gene either of them possessed.

No, the bell was a practical choice, being odd enough to draw his attention no matter what was going on around him. Mae Chen's missives were financial in nature, time sensitive and always lucrative. He didn't need more money, but he hadn't joined the eleven zeroes club at thirty by ignoring opportunities to make more.

Therefore, at the first peal, he held up a finger to pause the roundtable discussion of an energy takeover that would make him the de facto owner of a small country. He turned his titanium smartphone onto its custom-made back and touched the sapphire crystal screen.

Transmitted from Luli: Your grandmother has experienced a medical event. Her instructions in such case are to promptly advise you that you are her designated heir. Contact details for her physician are below.

That was new information.

In one fluid move, he tagged the doctor's number, picked up the phone and rose to leave without explanation. He moved with purpose from the room, more disturbed by the label heir than by his grandmother's condition.

For one thing, Mae was far too bellicose to suffer anything for long, particularly ill health. She would be on her feet before this call was picked up.

As for Gabriel being her heir, she wouldn't stipulate such a thing without attaching a symphony's worth of strings. She had been trying to maneuver him into a beholden state for two decades. It was the reason he had kept his interest in her fortune objective and made no assumptions about his entitlement to it. He religiously returned her invitations to invest with equally advantageous opportunities of his own. Tit for tat, scoop for scoop. No obligations incurred on either side beyond reciprocal courtesy.

"A stroke," the doctor advised him seconds later. "It's unlikely she will survive."

Her transfer to the private clinic had been swift and discreet, the doctor continued.

"I expect this will cause ripples through the financial districts when it's announced? I didn't know *you* were her grandson."

While Gabriel's agile brain sifted through the implications of his grandmother being incapacitated, possibly disappearing from his life altogether, the inquisitiveness of the physician's tone penetrated. He could hear the man's thoughts buzzing like an annoying mosquito. Buy? Sell? Were there properties that could be snatched up before they were officially on the market? How could the fine doctor take advantage of this news before anyone else?

Thanks to their mutual exchange of information over the years, Mae had expanded from relatively stable investments in real estate to tech and renewable energy, precious metals and that fickle mistress—oil. None of that could be left without a sitter.

Gabriel assured the doctor he would be there as soon as possible. He messaged his executive assistant to reschedule the meeting he'd abandoned. He also told her to clear his calendar and notify his pilot to ready the jet. As he headed to the elevator, he glanced at the nearest face at a desk and said, "My car, please."

The woman quickly put her call on hold and his chauffeured Rolls-Royce Phantom arrived at the curb as he pushed through the revolving door at the bottom of his building.

The humidity of a New York summer hit him in the face, but it would be monsoon rains in Singapore. His butler kept his jet packed for all climes and occasions, though. His grandmother kept a room at her house for him, not that he had ever used it. Invitations had come periodically, maybe to discuss the fact she was designating him her heir. He also owned a building of flats in that city. The top one was designated for his use, so he never took his grandmother up on—

"Gabriel!" A woman moved into his path and dipped her sunglasses to reveal her fake lashes and waxed brows. "I thought you might like to take me to lunch. It's Tina," she reminded after a beat where he only stared, trying to place her. She splayed her hand on the upper swells of her breasts where they were revealed by her wide-necked blouse. "We met at my father's retirement party last weekend. You said you liked my song."

He must have been speaking out of politeness because he had no recollection of her voice, her father or the party.

"I'm traveling," he dismissed, and stepped around her.

If there was one thing he needed less than more money, it was another social climber throwing herself at him.

He slid onto a cool leather seat and his driver closed him into the air-conditioned interior.

Gabriel glanced at the square face of his gold Girard-Perregaux and calculated the approximate time until he would land.

Such affectations as vintage watches and Valentino briefcases meant nothing to him, but appearances mattered to everyone else. He always played to win, even at "who wears it best?" so he ordered hand-sewn suits in rare wools like vicuña and qiviut. He had his leather shoes lined with the softest materials when they were custom cobbled in Italy. He hung all of it off a body that he ruthlessly kept in peak athletic condition.

He wore sunscreen and moisturized.

And he genuinely didn't care that folding his grandmother's net worth into his own would tip him into the exalted echelon of world's first trillionaire. All it meant, quite inconveniently, was more work—yet another thing he didn't need.

His grandmother was his only relative of note, however, despite being both strange and estranged. He might lack strong feelings toward her or her money, but he did feel a responsibility to preserve her empire. He respected what she had built in her seventy years. He might be progressive by nature, but he didn't tear down institutions for the sake of it.

He flicked back to the original message and brought the phone to his chin as he dictated a text.

Who is Mae's business manager?

Transmitted from Luli: I assist Mrs. Chen in managing her transactions. May I help with a specific inquiry or instruction?

Artificial intelligence was so delightfully passive-aggressive, always deferential when it was being obstructive.

Send me the contact details of the man or woman who carries out Mae's personal banking transactions.

Transmitted from Luli: I perform those tasks. How may I help?

Gabriel bit back a curse. Once this news was released and his connection to Mae Chen made public, a global circus would erupt around her financial holdings. The clock was already ticking, given her doctor had learned of their connection.

He switched gears and began sending instructions to his own team of advisors and brokers to reach out to hers. Once he was on the ground, he would learn exactly who ran things for Mae Chen and firmly take the reins from him.

* * *

"Luli." The butler introduced her last, since she had deliberately positioned herself at the end of the line of staff, after the housemaids and cook. She was practically standing around the corner of the house where vines grew against the wall that ensured the privacy of Mae Chen's colonial-era mansion.

His mansion now.

"You're human."

If she was, Gabriel Dean was the first to notice in her twenty-two years of existence.

Of course, Luli experienced very human reactions as she shook hands with Mae's grandson, bowing slightly and murmuring, "Sir," as she did. Her heart was pounding, her skin coated in cold perspiration, her stomach churning like a pit of snakes.

Aside from the married butler and the gardeners, she rarely saw men. Not this sort of man, especially. His black, glossy hair was precision-trimmed and disheveled with equal precision. He was clean-shaven, his cheekbones a masterpiece, his mouth—she didn't know what to compare it to, having never studied a man's lips before. They weren't the feminine peaks and sensual fullness with corner curls like hers. They were thinner, straighter and as much a statement of unspoken authority as the rest of him.

"Is that your full name? Luli?"

"Lucrecia," she provided, tacking on the other half of a name she had nearly forgotten. "Cruz."

His gaze flickered down her pleated-neck dress. Its straight cut was belted with the same pale yellow cotton and the hem ended just above her ankles, revealing her bare feet in sandals. The maids wore an apron over theirs and looked efficient and smart. Luli wished she had that extra layer of protection, but even a plate of armor wouldn't hide the fact she was significantly more endowed in the chest than the delicately built Malaysian women beside her. On her, the fabric pulled across her hips and required a higher slit to accommodate her longer stride.

Gabriel was taller than she had expected. No wonder Mae was always telling her to sit. It was intimidating to have someone look down on you.

Gabriel's gaze came back to her face, taking in features she knew to be striking. It wasn't just that her skin was paler than the rest of the staff's, or her eyes distinctly Caucasian. Her light brown hair was naturally streaked with ash blond and her nose slender and elegant.

Gabriel's eyelids were distinctly Asian, his irises an unexpected gray-green.

She had seen enough photos to expect him to be beautiful, but she had not expected this radiation of power. She should have. His grandmother possessed a version of it, but this man's force of will nearly knocked her off her feet and all he had done was step out of his car.

Now he relaxed his grip so she wasn't sure if the handshake was over. She took too long to draw her hand from his. It made her feel ignorant and foolish. The maids would be laughing at her later, but she couldn't help this weakness of fascination that overcame her.

"May we offer refreshments, sir?" the butler asked. "Your room has been prepared, if you wish to rest."

"I'm here to work." He glanced toward the front of the house. "Coffee will do."

"Of course." The butler clapped his hands to send everyone filing back to their duties.

Luli breathed out a subtle sigh of relief and started to follow.

"Luli." Gabriel's voice jolted her. "You'll show me to my grandmother's office."

He spoke English with an American accent, not the British one she was used to hearing and copying. He waved for her to join him as he climbed the front steps.

She was disturbed by it. She struggled to find acceptance here as it was. Mae gave her special treatment in some ways, but Luli never liked to do anything that made it seem as though she was *trying* to rise above everyone else.

Besides, her guilty conscience wasn't ready to confess to him what she'd done.

She concentrated on her breathing and maintaining a tall posture. She ensured her expression was serene, her movements graceful and unhurried despite her unsteady pulse and the shakiness brought on by sleep deprivation.

She had had twenty hours to react to this sudden change in her circumstance. It was her habit, through years of boredom and confinement, to mentally plan for every conceivable situation. Thus, she had known from the first call of alarm into the garden what she would have to do.

Executing those actions, however, had taken nerves of steel and hours of careful coding into the night. There was no room for error—and likely no forgiveness from this man no matter how things played out.

Gabriel paused inside the opulent foyer, taking in the mosaic tiles beneath their feet, the inlaid wood in the stair banister, the priceless art and the arrangements of fresh flowers. All his now.

Luli halted as well, waiting until he glanced at her expectantly.

"Mrs. Chen's office is the third door," she murmured with a nod toward the hallway.

In a confusing war of chivalry against her effort to be subservient, he waited for her to go first then fell into step beside her.

"I'm very sorry about your grandmother," she said. "We'll miss her deeply."

"It sounds like it was very swift."

It had been. They'd all known the quick, anxious efforts of Mae's nurse were futile. Even as Mae's helicopter had airlifted her from the garden where it had happened, a blanket of subdued reflection had hung over the entire house.

Luli brought him into Mae's office. The room was designed along spare lines, more staid than the other rooms, but still had feminine touches in the pastel color scheme and the English teapot that Luli filled for both of them every afternoon.

It felt terribly empty in here. Who would she drink tea with now? What was going to happen?

Her future was no longer in the tight, but secure hands of Mae Chen. Luli could kid herself that she was taking her destiny into her own hands, but that wasn't true. The way this man reacted once he learned what she had done would dictate how the rest of her life proceeded.

His hands were long-fingered and lightly tanned. They looked powerful. Deadly.

Luli stood beside the rolling chair at the delicate

writing desk that was her workstation, waiting for him to sit. He took in the room, glancing beyond the windows to the garden, and gave each painting and vase a brief, incisive glance.

She found herself holding her breath, waiting for his assessing gaze to come back to her, hoping for a sign of approachability in him. Approval on some level. Something that would reassure her.

"I thought you were a form of AI, but there's nothing artificial about you. Is there?" His head turned and his expression eased, revealing a slant of something that invited and appreciated, even as it caused her inner radar to tingle with caution.

She had the most bizarre sensation of being chased, breaths growing uneven despite not moving. Her middle filled with fluttering butterflies, but they weren't fear. They were the excitement of the unknown. Of playful pursuit.

This was sexual awareness, she realized with a pressure in her throat that was an urge to both laugh and scream. She understood sexual attraction in a very abstract way. She had been exposed to the feminine tricks of making herself appealing to the opposite sex far too young, but she wasn't trying any of them right now. She was barefaced and the only reason she stood tall and sucked in her stomach was in an effort to seem confident and competent.

And she had been judged on her external attributes from an early age, but hadn't *felt* it, not like this. If anything, she'd been repulsed by older men studying her and assigning her a score. Occasionally, since being here, one of Mrs. Chen's visitors had noticed her and made a remark before she was shooed out of sight. She had been an odd duck, if not an outright ugly duckling.

She hadn't realized a man's gaze could make her stomach wobble and her blood feel as though it fizzed in her veins. That a force field could encompass her like a cup over a spider, so she could be scooped into the palm of his hand to be crushed or freed on his whim.

The butler came in with the tray, breaking their locked gaze.

"How shall I prepare your *kopi*, Mr. Dean?" the butler asked, pouring from the carafe into a jade-green cup with a gold handle that he balanced on its matching saucer.

"Black." His sharp gaze touched on the single cup and swung back to Luli. "You're not having any?"

The butler didn't react, but Luli read the servant's affront in the angle of his shoulders and the stiffness beneath his impassive expression. They'd been at war for years because she had Mae's confidence in ways he didn't. He'd been incensed that he had learned from *Luli* who Mrs. Chen's grandson was—*after* Luli had informed Gabriel.

What could Luli have said, though? *She doesn't trust you. She doesn't trust men.* Mae had encouraged Luli to trust no one but her and Luli had given her the loyalty that Mae craved.

None of which changed the fact that if the butler had to fetch Luli a cup right now, he would *die*.

If she was a small person, she would force him to do it, but she was saving her energy for a greater revolt. A more daunting target.

"You're very kind," she murmured. "But that's not necessary."

"The bell is here if you require anything further, Mr. Dean," the butler said, glancing darkly toward Luli before he closed the door firmly on his way out.

Gabriel waved at the arrangement of sofa and chairs, all upholstered in silk brocade, and waited for her to lower onto a cushion before he sat across from her.

Honestly, this regard he was extending to her was laughable. Her conscience writhed as she folded her hands in her lap. He was going to explode when he realized how undeserving she was of this respect.

Despite the fact she would have to take control of the discussion eventually, she waited for him to lead. There were so many ways this could go, some of them life altering—maybe even life-threatening. Her research had revealed he was a black belt in kung fu. Her morning tai chi in the courtyard with Mae and the rest of the household was no match for the lightning-fast and lethal moves he no doubt possessed.

"After signing papers at the hospital, I met with my grandmother's attorney," he informed her. "My power of attorney was finalized so I could assume the helm during probate. A press release has been issued to announce our connection. Legally and publicly it is accepted that I have taken possession of Chen Enterprises. Yet, when I arrived at the head office, very few of my instructions could be fully executed. I was told that every instruction and transaction goes through Luli."

He sipped his coffee while his gaze stayed pinned on her.

"They couldn't even run me a comprehensive list of her assets and accounts, so I could begin contacting the banks for access."

A coal of heat burned in her center, but she said nothing, knowing that stammering out explanations when he hadn't yet asked a question would betray her nerves.

"You realize I'm not the only person under the impression you're a sophisticated task-management app?"

"I believe that is the impression your grandmother preferred to cultivate."

"Why?" His voice was whip sharp. She had to concentrate not to flinch as it landed on her.

"Among other things, it forces people to express themselves in writing," she explained in an unruffled tone. "It creates a traceable trail. She told me once that when your grandfather died, his business manager attempted to take advantage of her. She wasn't able to prove his wrongdoing and she wasn't able to take control of the wealth she had inherited. Not without a terrible fight."

"Those who don't learn from history are doomed to repeat it. Apparently."

Bam-bam-bam. Her heart threatened to crack open her breastbone.

"Since then, it has been her practice to maintain tight oversight with regard to her finances. She personally approves all but the most routine transactions."

"Does she? Because it sounds like *you* do."

"She didn't care for computers. I work under her direction." And steered her direction, when opportunities presented, but that wasn't important right now.

"Your actions strike me as empire building." He crossed his legs, hitching his pants as he did. "You have made yourself indispensable in a grasp for power. I've seen it before, many times."

"I have no empire," she assured him.

His cynical look said he saw right through her, which

shouldn't cause her stomach to bottom out, but it did. He was nothing to her, but it was taking every ounce of courage she possessed to hold his gaze.

It struck her that she had never had the courage to defy Mae. What chance did that give her against someone like *him*?

"You live here?" The cynical twitch of his mesmerizing mouth called her a parasite.

"A room is assigned to me, yes."

"Where did you come from?"

"Venezuela."

"That wasn't what I was asking, but I hear that in your accent now." His gaze shifted as he took in her features once again. "It's sultry. Exotic."

He sounded vaguely mocking, which stung. Her rudimentary English, taught to her by a chaperone, had been perfected here, where Mae had learned it from a British boarding school. The staff spoke broken versions peppered with Indian, Malay and Pilipino accents.

As he stared at her, the tingle of sensual, elemental awareness shimmered around her again, disconcerting her. Logically, she presumed she could use her voice and looks to charm and distract him, but she had no practice wielding those weapons. Instead, she found herself fascinated by the subtle inflections in his voice and the slightest twitch of his lips.

"How long have you been here?" he asked.

"Eight years."

"Not Singapore. In this house, employed by my grandmother."

"I came to this house when I came to Singapore eight years ago."

He frowned. "How old are you?"

"Twenty-two."

"Were you hired as a housemaid?" He was taken aback. "How did you come to be doing high-level work like this?" He jerked his chin toward the sleeping laptop on the writing desk.

She licked her lips. How to explain?

"As I said, your grandmother found computers tiresome, but she wished to be as hands-on as possible with every facet of her business."

"You're her hands?"

He was skeptical, but it was true. Luli couldn't count the number of times Mae had nudged her in the back of the shoulder and told her, *Go back. Show me that again.*

"I perform various confidential tasks at her direction."

"Bank transfers, stock purchases…?"

"Yes. If a broker or middleman is used, I follow up after transmitting requests to ensure the task has been completed. I compile background information on potential employees and business partners, assist her in reviewing performance reports and run random secondary checks on various budgets and accounts, helping spot discrepancies that could point to misuse."

"People love audits, especially random ones. I bet you're very popular." He was being sarcastic.

"A necessary evil" was probably the kindest thing she'd been called, usually in an email chain not meant for her eyes.

Was she evil? She would have called her mother that, until she had been backed into a corner herself and now had to think about how *she* would survive.

"As you say, most people think I'm a computer program. I've never concerned myself much with whether people *like* me so long as your grandmother was satisfied with my work."

A small lie. She would love a friend, a real one, not an old woman who had forgotten what it was like to be young and curious about the world. One who was scared to let her see any of it, in case it made her leave.

"On the topic of programs," she said, feeling clammy sweat break on her palms. "It might interest you to know that your grandmother requested I switch exclusively to using your operating system. She had reservations about cloud-based so she purchased the download versions. We use all your business modules, accounting and security, the productivity suite… She wanted to know her most important records and cryptocurrency were backed up and protected against intrusion. She liked that you claim it's next to impossible to hack. I'm sure *you* could get in, though. If you had to."

There. She was inching onto the limb she had chosen.

It might hold her or it might snap and send her plummeting to her death.

CHAPTER TWO

LUCRECIA. IT SOUNDED like the Latin name for one of those exotic flowers found in remote jungles. The kind with waxy petals in shades of ivory streaked with lush crimson and mysterious indigo. The kind with a perfume that drew a bee inexorably into her honey trap.

Where she paralyzed and ate him alive.

What a way to go. Gabriel almost didn't see a downside, except that he'd learned very early not to fall for any sort of manipulation. They'd all been tried—threats, flattery, guilt, false friendship and—frequently—lust. Sex was something he enjoyed like whiskey over rocks or a cool swim on a hot day. It wasn't something he needed or succumbed to.

Yet this woman had put a coil of tension in him merely by existing and was notching it with each lift of her thick, curled lashes over her piercing blue-green eyes.

To think, he had only come to the house as a last resort, thinking he would fire up his grandmother's laptop and ascertain exactly what this "Luli" software was all about.

Her wares were soft, all right. In all the right places, despite being draped in the least flattering dress imaginable. The color was wrong for her skin tone, but there was no hiding her catwalk height or her flawless complexion. She didn't need makeup or adornments. In his mind, she only had to remove that dress and the pins from her hair and she would be perfect.

But she was his employee, he reminded himself, in the same way the workforce of any company became his responsibility and resource after a takeover.

Therefore, while he enjoyed fantasizing each time she threw one of those doe-eyed, speculative glances his way, looking ever so innocent as she let the tip of her tongue dampen her lips suggestively, he refused to let her see it was having the desired effect on him, i.e., *Desire.*

He definitely didn't let his carnal reaction blind him to the nuanced threat she was making.

"Why would I need to hack into accounts that belong to me?" he asked, muscles activating as though preparing to face an opponent on the mat.

"You wouldn't…"

If.

She didn't say it, but he heard the lilt of suggestion in the way she trailed off.

He set aside his half-finished coffee with a click of bone china meeting lacquered wood.

She swallowed, eyes shielded by her lashes, but she was watching him through them. Cautious. Scared, even.

He let his lip curl to let her know he was amused by her adorable attempt to extort from him.

"You understand I could have you arrested." Which was a strangely appalling thing to imagine. He had brought charges to bear in the past, when laws had been broken. He never thought twice about protecting himself and always sought justice through due process.

But there were exceptions to every rule, he supposed. Even the rules he made for himself.

"You could bring in the police," she agreed in that same trailing tone. This time the adjunct was *but*. "I haven't done anything illegal, though. Not yet."

Not *yet*? "Ah. You've planted a cyberbomb." He ought to be furious, but he was so flabbergasted by her audacity, he wanted to laugh. Did she know who he *was*?

"May we call them incentives?" Her gaze came up, crystal as the Caribbean Sea. Placid and appealing and full of sharks and deadly jellyfish with stinging tendrils.

His divided mind wanted to watch the shift of color in those eyes as he immersed himself in her even as the other half absorbed the word *incentives*. *Plural*.

"Call them anything you like. I'm calling the police." Even he didn't know whether he was bluffing. He took longer than he needed to bring his phone from his pocket, though, watching for her next move.

"If I don't log in soon, a tell-all will release to the press."

"Has my grandmother been running an opium den? What terrible tales could you possibly have to tell about her?" As far as he knew, Mae Chen's worst crime was being stubbornly resentful of her daughter's choice in husband—and rightfully so.

Luli's face went blank. "I'd rather not reveal it."

"Because you have nothing."

"Because your grandmother's good name would be smeared and she's been good to me."

"Yet you'll destroy her reputation to get what you want from me."

"I'll tell the truth." Her tone was grave, her comportment calm enough to make him think she might have something more than threats of revealing a dodgy tax write-off or a penchant for young men in small bathing suits.

"Something to do with my mother?"

"Not at all." That seemed to surprise her.

"What then? I'm not playing twenty questions."

She pinched her mouth together and glanced toward the door to ensure it was firmly closed.

"Human trafficking and forcible confinement."

"Ha!"

She didn't laugh.

"That's a very ugly accusation." There was a thriving black market in everything from drugs to kidneys, but it wasn't a shop on Fifth Avenue where women in their golden years could drop in and buy house staff. "Who? You?"

She swallowed. "Ask anyone here how many times I've been outside the front door of this house. They'll tell you today was the first time in eight years."

"Because you've coached them to say that? Are you ring-leading?"

"I'm acting alone. I would be surprised if anyone else knows my situation as anything but a preference for staying inside the grounds." Her watchful gaze came up. "As I say, it would damage their memory of your grandmother if staff began gossiping. I'd rather you didn't make serious inquiries."

"You know as well as I do that without a thorough investigation, it's very much *she said*, *no one else said*.

I've weathered disgruntled employees making wild accusations many times. I'm not concerned." He was a
little concerned. This woman was not like the others
here, that much was obvious. Not just in looks and background, either. At twenty-two, she had inveigled her
way into controlling an elderly woman's fortune. She
was infinitely more dangerous than she looked.

Luli's cheeks drew in as she set her chin. "Whether
the police believe me or not, I expect they will deport
me, seeing as I have no legal right to be here. My prospects in Venezuela are dim. I've had to make arrangements for that possibility."

"I bet you have." He couldn't recall the last person
to be so bold in their stalk of his money. He was reluc-
tantly fascinated. "Stealing is a crime."

"Only if I collect it."

"Indeed." He picked up his cup to sip and allow that
lethal threat to sink in.

She might have paled slightly, but the sun had set
and the light was changing.

"You could kill me," she acknowledged. "Or I could
simply disappear. Contingencies have been prepared
for that possibility, as well. The investigation into that
would be very thorough and go on a very long time."

"Hell hath no fury like a woman with a keyboard.
What did I do to deserve this wrath?"

Her hands, so prettily arranged in her lap, turned
their palms up in a subtle entreaty. "I'm aware that my
only value right now is my ability to reverse the incon-
veniences I've arranged."

"I'm confident I can reverse them myself before they
do too much damage. Your value is nil."

"You're probably right." She nodded, not even sweating. Her only betrayal of nerves was the rapid tattoo of the artery in her throat.

Gabriel had a weakness for puzzles. There was a twelve-year-old boy inside him itching to lock the door, put on his noise-canceling headphones and hack his own system until he'd found every Easter egg she'd hidden there. Not because he was worried. Purely for the game of it.

And there was a thirty-one-year-old man who wanted to put his hands on the twisted pieces of this woman and see how quickly he could untangle her and make her come apart.

"If what you say about your circumstance here is true…" He set aside his coffee mug again. "One could argue that by taking control of my grandmother's assets, I am taking possession of you."

There was that intriguing stillness again. The screen of her mink lashes, so ridiculously long and curled like a filly's, hid her eyes while her mouth might have trembled.

"One could argue that," she admitted in a voice that wasn't quite steady. "I've done my utmost to protect all of her assets. Including me. Which wouldn't stop you from unloading me. As assets go, I'm probably at my top value right now. If you were to sell me, for instance."

He told himself she was mistaking him for someone with a conscience that could be played upon, but his stomach clenched in revulsion.

"Of course, if you were to do that, I would make every effort to use what I know of her business interests to my advantage," Luli continued.

Such a cool delivery. He told himself to focus on

that, her complete lack of emotional hysteria despite the topic they were discussing.

Instead, he was compelled to ask, "Is that how she acquired you? Off some auction block?" He would turn the fortune over to the authorities, not wanting a penny of it if it was built on something so ugly.

"No." She shifted the fit of her hands, interlacing her fingers, but her knuckles remained white, telling him she was in a state of heightened stress, even though that was the only visible sign of it. Why? Because her story was true? Or because the lie she was telling had grown too heavy and unwieldy to carry?

"My mother lived in a building my father owned in Caracas. She was his mistress. He was in government, married to someone else. He sold the building to your grandmother without making arrangements for my mother's upkeep. Mae was trying to have her thrown out. My mother cut a deal with her to take me as an employee in exchange for allowing her to stay there. I'm working off my mother's debt."

She named a figure in bolivars that would calculate to about a hundred thousand dollars.

Was that what a human life was worth? Pocket change?

"You were fourteen?"

"Yes."

"Why haven't you left? Even if she deducted room and board, I would think you'd have paid that off by now."

"Where would I go?" Her hands came up empty. "If your grandmother has my passport, it's long expired. I have no right to be here and there's nothing for me in Venezuela if they deport me. I could live on the streets,

I suppose, and work under the table as other illegals do. How is that better than this? At least here I'm safe, fed and clothed."

And now that safety net was gone. He began to understand her motive.

"I'm grateful to your grandmother," she continued. "I didn't fully understand it at the time, but there was a man who had also come to the apartment. If Mae hadn't insisted on taking me, I'm quite sure my mother would have given me to him. My computer work these last years would have been purely as content." Her faint smile was an inscrutable *Mona Lisa* of agonized acceptance.

No. A sharp spike of repugnance slid deep into his gut at the idea of any woman being exploited that way. At fourteen. *Ever.*

"She really doesn't pay you?"

"Please don't be offended when I say this." She angled her head with apology. "I think she looked on me as a sort of daughter. She didn't pay me because you don't pay family for working in the family business."

"If that's how she saw you, why didn't she leave everything to *you*?"

"She said…" Luli sighed toward the ceiling. "She said that when the time was right, she would arrange a marriage for me. I don't know if she was serious, but if I brought up money, she would get defensive and ask me if I would be happier scrubbing pots in the kitchen."

"No one else knows about this agreement?" Could it be called an agreement if Luli hadn't been given a choice?

"I've never told anyone. I don't believe she ever did."

Because, no matter the lofty motives she might have had, holding Luli here like this was a crime.

Or a complete fabrication.

And his grandmother was gone. He couldn't ask her if she had really kept a young woman as an indentured servant for *eight years*.

"Mr. Dean—"

"Gabriel."

"Mr. Dean." Her voice made his scalp prickle, her accent so musical and warm despite her formal address. "I very much appreciate that you've given me this opportunity to explain myself." Her gaze slid to the clock on the mantel, an ornate bronze piece atop a trumpeting elephant, likely from one of the Louis periods.

"If you're willing to continue this conversation, I would like to reset the timer on the laptop."

He was impossible to read. Intimidating with his innate physical power on top of his wealth and influence. She had to continually remind herself to breathe. Inhale, exhale. No sudden movements. Predators were attracted by panic and the stench of fear.

She suspected he deliberately let the seconds tick audibly in the silent room as a small form of torture to her. A test, perhaps, to see how nervous it made her.

Poise was something she had begun cultivating as soon as she understood the word. She made herself hold his gaze, refusing to give up her small advantage until he agreed to her condition. If he thought what she had told him about herself was a complete fabrication, they would discover the hard way that it was true.

His head jerked in an abbreviated nod.

In a smooth, unhurried motion that hid the gallop of

her heart, she went to the desk and opened the laptop with a single minute to spare. She used the opportunity of having her back turned to gather her composure. Her fingerprint unlocked the screen, but she had to enter a code at the same time and she had to get it right in two tries. She managed it, then navigated to give them another thirty minutes of playing chess on a minefield.

As she turned, she found him on his feet. He removed his suit jacket and draped it over the arm of the sofa. His shirt strained across the virile expanse of his shoulders and chest and tucked into the narrow belt to accentuate his lean waist.

"More *kopi*?" She moved to the tray where the urn sat, more to avoid approaching him than a desire to be a conscientious servant.

He brought his cup to the tray. "No, thank you."

A deliberate effort to approach *her*? His jawline was what some might refer to as chiseled. It was a clearly defined, angular structure from corner to corner, quite a fascinating study for an artist's eye.

Or the eye of a woman who'd spent her adolescence in something like a harem, surrounded by women and a few off-limits middle-aged men.

Gabriel's chin went up a degree so his narrow eyes looked down his straight nose at her. "How much do you want?"

She dropped her hands to the sides of her dress, palms gently cupped, fingers pointed, but relaxed. *No fidgeting.*

"This isn't blackmail."

"If it looks like blackmail and smells like blackmail…" he scoffed darkly.

"I don't want it to be," she clarified, making herself

hold her ground despite the twitches of alarm pu[...]
in her limbs. "I've had ample opportunities to ste[...]
enjoy this position of trust with your grandmother because I've never betrayed her. I've worked for her in
good faith, not to repay my mother's debt, but to thank
her for removing me from my mother's power."

"And you no longer owe her that allegiance?"

"I don't owe it to you."

His expression didn't change, but the scent of danger stung her nostrils, making her want to skitter away
out of self-preservation.

"Not yet," she allowed, fighting to keep him from
seeing how unsure and frightened she really was.

"Oh, might I earn the privilege of your holding *my*
fortune for ransom? Do tell me how."

That was sarcasm. She could tell.

Saying nothing, she took refuge in her long-ago
training, tucked her heel into the arch of her other foot
and squared her shoulders. A smile of any kind was
beyond her in this moment, but she kept her expression relaxed, stood tall with a long neck. She tucked in
her butt and did her best to project self-assurance and
limitless patience.

"What kind of person are you, Luli of the deceit-
ful intelligence?" He sounded scathing, but as his gaze
swept down, she thought it caught on her chest, lingered.

She became aware of the weight of cotton across the
swells of her breasts. A prickly, heavy sensation made
her ultraconscious that she *had* breasts. A tight, pinched
sensation hit her nipples, making heat flush from the
pit of her stomach up to her cheeks for no reason at all.

When his gaze came back to hers, something flickered in his expression. Curiosity and something avid. Luli had known about him for years and had studied him online in the same way she read facts about bears and deadly vipers, without quite believing such a creature existed because she'd never seen one with her own eyes. Even so, she knew she ought to be terrified if she ever came face-to-face with one.

She was terrified.

But she continued to stand there. Had to. She held her ground because she had no other options.

"I propose that I work for you in the same capacity as I have for your grandmother."

"Free?"

"More or less." She cleared the strain from her throat. She had known this would be a tough sell, given the anvil she had positioned over all that he was poised to inherit. "I would assist in the transition at no cost to you in exchange for other considerations."

"I have no reason to trust you. Clean up your mess—" He nodded at the laptop. "—and your debt to my grandmother is zero. You'll be free to go."

The floor seemed to fall away from beneath her.

"Where?" She carefully modulated her tone so her fear of abandonment wasn't obvious. "I have no money. If I wanted to live as a refugee, I would have run away years ago." She was so *tired* of being powerless. Of feeling as though she owed her very existence to someone else.

"You want to stay here?" He folded his arms, signaling his refusal. "No. I *will* take control of her fortune, if only to knock your fingers off it. You are no longer needed, Luli."

"*I know that.* Why do you think I'm doing this?" It

came out with the fervent anger she had sublimated for years, emotions flaring so hot, her eyes burned.

"What do you want then?"

The things she wanted were so far out of reach, she had stopped thinking about them long ago. Love, security, a place where she belonged...those were luxuries. She had to focus on what she *needed*—a means to support herself.

"I want to move to one of the modeling capitals. New York, preferably."

"You want to be a model?" He said it with such disparagement, she let her weight shift onto her back foot.

"You don't think I'm pretty enough?" Panic edged in from all sides. This was all she had!

"Why haven't you done it already? Singapore has a thriving fashion district."

"Of Asian models. My look doesn't fit this market. It's not a profession where you walk in a door and get a job anyway. You have to build up to it, provide headshots and find an agent."

He waved at the laptop. "You have options. Why haven't you made inroads?" He sounded incredulous.

"Your grandmother couldn't run her business without me. Not the way she liked to run it." Her conscience grew heavy with the familial obligation she had alluded to a few minutes ago. "And she would never have forgiven me. She was furious with your mother for leaving without her permission."

The sudden flash in his eyes told her that particular topic was off-limits.

She resisted the urge to tangle her hands together and wring them.

"I've been struggling these last few years, aware that

she needed me, but also aware that the two advantages I possess—youth and looks—won't be available to me forever. If I'm going to exploit them, it has to be now."

"Don't overlook that cunning brain of yours."

"Much as I would prefer to be valued for my intellect, who will hire someone without accreditation or even a home and a computer of her own? The work I do for your grandmother isn't transferable to anyone except you. And my use to you has a very short shelf life. *I know that.*"

She sighed, trying to keep hold of her composure as she continued.

"Her passing has forced me to secure my future as quickly and expediently as possible. Models with the right look can work anywhere. They're paid well and agencies help with the travel and residency paperwork."

"You just pointed out that no one walks into that career."

"It depends who escorts me, doesn't it?" She was way out on her wobbly limb now, grip slipping and the whole tree swaying in hurricane-force wind.

His brows went up. She'd watched those raptor wings lift like that several times, expressing his astonishment at the audacious mouse in his sharp-taloned foot, chittering no matter how hard he squeezed her.

He smiled faintly. "I wondered when we were going to get to an offer like that."

The tip of his finger grazed her temple in a caress that tucked a stray hair behind her ear.

Any further words she might have found became tangled in her throat because his fingertip continued that nascent caress into the hollow beneath her ear, then stroked the soft flesh beneath her jawbone, tilting up her chin before she had realized she was obeying his silent command.

"Pleasant as that inducement promises to be…" His voice grated sensually across her nerve endings. "I won't be persuaded to let you handle my grandmother's money. Or me."

He dropped his touch, sending a chill through her whole body.

Dragging his gaze off the temptation of her plump, shiny, parted lips took every ounce of Gabriel's well-honed discipline. He controlled all that he did because he controlled *himself*. Giving in to impulse, especially the sexual kind, was juvenile.

But the flare of yearning and disappointment in his eyes was almost his undoing.

"I wasn't…um…trying to offer s-sex for—"

"The stutter is a nice touch. Most men go crazy for the helpless damsel act. Good on you for trying it." It was her first show of vulnerability amid a nerves-of-steel performance. He wasn't buying it, though. "I'm impervious."

Mostly. His hands itched to drag her against his chest, not only because he wanted to do things to her—carnal, wicked things—but because the tremble in her lashes tugged at something in him. Against his better judgment, he felt an urge to shelter her. Reassure her.

She didn't argue or stammer out more protestations. There might have been a glimmer of injury behind her eyes, but it was gone so quickly, he knew it was only a strategy that was briefly considered before she discarded it. Within seconds, she returned to her true, iron-butterfly persona.

"Sex is firmly off the table?" Her tone gave him the sense he was missing something.

"I never force sex and I never pay for it. I am, however, open to enjoying it anywhere, including on tables."

"I'm willing to offer other acts that might be of value to you, then. Marriage, for instance."

"You want me to marry you? I honestly didn't think you could astound me further. Not my first offer. Thank you, but no." He rejected her firmly even as a voice in the back of his brain reminded that he would have to begin thinking of marriage. Was he going to leave his fortune to those idiot cousins of his father's?

He brushed that aside, needing all his concentration to deal with this surprisingly daring and skillful con woman. Especially when she seemed genuinely taken aback by his words.

"I don't want to marry *you*. You're far too young," she said, as if the idea was ridiculous.

"I stand corrected," he drawled. "I am further astounded."

"I would make an excellent trophy wife. I'm open to considering marriage to a man of advanced years at your direction, provided I'm granted residency in a major center like New York or London."

"You want to marry someone twice your age?"

"Three at least." She frowned. "I'm only twenty-two."

"Now you're trying too hard." He couldn't help it. He laughed openly.

"Marrying an older man worked out well for your grandmother. She was widowed at thirty."

"They say emulation is the sincerest form of flattery." He folded his arms. "But I am not a pimp. Old men may find their trophy wives without my assistance." The idea of lecherous, gnarled hands claiming those curves revolted him to the point of violent rage.

She looked to the window. There might have been a sheen on her eyes and a pout in her lips as she ran out of gambits, but he felt no triumph. He was captivated by the sheer perfection in her exquisite profile, graceful as a cameo carved into ivory.

She was so remote and untouchable in that moment, his abdomen clenched with craving for something he couldn't articulate.

"Very well." She moved to the laptop and glanced at him. "I'll undo everything I've done if I have your word it will square my debt with your grandmother and I'll be free to go. No police."

He heard the defeat in her tone and experienced loss, even though he had won. He wasn't ready for this game to end, but he made himself nod agreement.

She touched the tip of her finger to the sensor.

"Just to be clear…" She slanted a glance at him.

Foreboding filled him—and thrill. He had thought she was giving up, but this delightfully tricky wench didn't seem to know the meaning of the word *quit*.

"Yes?" he asked with deliberate lack of concern that bordered on tedium.

"When I say *everything…*"

"That doesn't exactly clean up your mess, does it?" He let fury lick at him because it was better than allowing her magnificence to blind him.

"If Luli isn't needed, everything under that profile must also be unnecessary," she said with simple logic.

"Come here."

She stayed where she was, but had the good sense to take her hands off the laptop and close the screen.

"Do you realize how dangerous I am?"

"Do you realize," she asked in an even quieter voice, lips white, "how little I have to lose? How much I've already lost?"

Eight years, if she was to be believed.

Her hands were curled into angry fists, but stayed at her sides. "You're welcome, by the way, for all the times I've asked your grandmother, *Is this an opportunity you would like me to bring to your grandson's attention?* You could have stepped in at any time to help her manage her affairs. You didn't. *I* did. For nothing but a roof over my head and three meals a day."

"And you think you can strike back at *me* for that? By deleting a few paper trails? Any database or personnel records you compromise can be rebuilt from backups. It won't take long and the price tag won't be that high."

"I estimate the cost at ten million US dollars, based on penalties for failing to finalize certain contracts on time. Or you could keep me on and not lose a penny."

"Is that what you think you're worth?" he scoffed. "Ten million dollars?"

His words pushed a pin in her back, forcing her to take a step toward him. Anger smoldered around her in a cloud, making her entirely too sexy and distracting when her voice was so sharp and profound.

"I've spent years thinking my value is less than zero. I thought I had to stay here because Mae was the only person who wanted me, and only if I was useful to her. From the moment I emailed you that she had collapsed, my only thought has been that I have to prove my worth to you, but how do I do that when I'm a walking, unpaid debt?" Her hand moved to press into her middle, as though clutching at a knife stuck in her navel. "The debt is my mother's. I am worth exactly what *I* decide I'm worth. If I'm to be exploited, *I* will choose the terms. And if you're going to put me on the street like a stray dog, you *will* feel the bite of it."

A discreet knock on the door had him snapping out, "Busy!"

An older brown-faced woman was already peeking in. "I'm sorry, Mr. Dean. I was told you left instructions I report to you the minute I returned."

"Mrs. Chen's nurse," Luli said, stepping back and letting her hair fall forward to shield how color had risen in her face during their confrontation.

He swore under his breath and nodded at the woman. "Come in."

He swung back to Luli and pointed at her laptop. "Put that on hold for a few hours. Then tell the butler to prepare us dinner." He needed a damned minute to think.

The nurse bounced her gaze between the two of them as Luli moved to the desk and tapped a few keys. Seconds later, Luli closed the door behind her.

The nurse didn't give him any information he didn't already have. She offered condolences; he promised a severance package so she could take her time finding another position. She bowed slightly when he dismissed her.

"Wait," he said. "How long have you been with my grandmother?"

She turned back, expression brightening the way most of his employees did when he gave them the opportunity to prove their value to him.

"Almost twenty years, sir."

"You've known Luli since she came here? How long has she been working here in my grandmother's office?"

"From the beginning, sir."

"That was my grandmother's idea? Was she competent? My grandmother, I mean. Mentally."

"Oh, completely, sir! But Mrs. Chen never cared for telephones or computers." Her hand washed such things from the air. "She thought them unhealthy and brought Luli in as a convenience. Luli spoke Spanish and your grandmother had recently acquired properties in South America."

"Luli was quite young when she arrived? What was she like?" Scared? Angry?

"Quiet." The nurse's expression faltered as she delved into her memory.

"Because she only spoke Spanish?" He seldom thought about his teen years, but recalled adolescent girls traveling in colorful flocks and relentlessly twittering at each other. No matter what the truth was today, Luli must have felt isolated at the time.

"She spoke a little English, but it was the patch that was the problem. I had to remove it from her tongue. I had completely forgotten about that," the nurse said with a distant frown.

"What kind of patch?" he asked sharply.

"For weight loss. It makes it painful to eat solids. She was already stick thin, but young women will do the stupidest things to themselves in the name of fashion. Mrs. Chen saved her from herself, if you want my opinion."

CHAPTER THREE

A CRISP RAP on her door snapped her awake.

Luli glanced at her alarm clock, but it wouldn't go off for another hour. She had set it so she wouldn't over-sleep resetting the timer on the laptop.

"Luli," *he* said. "Open the door or I'm coming in."

She quickly rose and brushed her hands down her wrinkled dress, then opened the door to Gabriel's glower.

He glanced past her to the dented pillow on the single bed, the plain walls and utilitarian night table with only a clock and hairbrush upon it.

"What are you doing?" he demanded.

"Sleeping."

"You're supposed to be eating dinner with me. Why did you tell the butler I wanted to eat with *him*?"

"You said, *Tell the butler to prepare us dinner.* I presumed *us* meant him."

"No, you didn't," he said flatly.

It had been open for interpretation and she'd been dead on her feet. Also, there was no way the butler would believe the new master of the house wanted to eat with her unless he heard it directly from Gabriel himself. He and all the rest of the staff had given her apprehensive looks, everyone asking, *What did you tell him?*

And, exactly as she did when it came to her closed-door conversations with Mrs. Chen, she had given up nothing—earning zero friends in the process.

Now she'd made Gabriel angry. She'd fallen asleep thinking about his nearly kissing her, imagining things she barely understood. What would it feel like to have his lips on hers, his hand moving to her bottom? Her breasts. Between her legs.

Fresh heat pressed there, disconcerting her. How was it that all she had to do was think about him, stand before him, and quivers shook her abdomen and her mouth watered? It was mortifying.

"I'm not hungry," she tried in a voice that scraped.

"I'm not requesting."

His hard tone told her that all the work she'd put into giving herself leverage had left her with virtually none.

"Garden," he said, stepping back to indicate she should lead the way.

She did, self-conscious the entire time that he was right behind her. She arrived to find a table had been set with Mae's best china on a silk cloth. One of the maids brought the first course, a small bowl of curry *laksa* made with shrimp and cockles. Gabriel handled the vermicelli with his golden chopsticks as adeptly as she did.

And noticed the curious look she sent after the maid.

"I gave the butler the night off," he said. "After clarifying he wasn't my date."

"I'm sure he appreciates a free evening." He was going to kill her when he saw her next.

"He didn't offer many compliments when I asked him about you."

It didn't really surprise her that he'd made those inquiries, but it made her squirm inwardly, knowing that no one would have anything very nice to say. She never dwelt on her ache of loneliness, but it was humiliating to have the staff's contempt of her become the center-piece of this already painful dinner.

"I sat in on his meetings with Mae when they re-viewed household expenses and raises. It was my task to prepare the performance reviews and suggest appro-priate wage increases."

His laugh was a single cut of disbelief. "Have you made *any* friends here?"

"Perhaps you'll be my first," she said with a smile of false hope.

She watched for a twitch of humor in his mouth, but it held its tense line while she only wound up thinking about his rejection of her perceived advances.

She lost her appetite and set aside her chopsticks.

"I read your note," he announced.

"Which—? Oh." She realized as she brought her gaze back up to his antagonized one.

He must have tried to hack his way into the network while she'd been sleeping. Of course he had. And he'd found her warning against proceeding further.

"I thought this whole thing a bluff, but those are an elegant few lines capable of doing *so much* damage. I have an idea how to get around it. I've cloned the entire thing to a testing file. I'll crack it before I go to bed," he said with confidence, nipping off the tail of a shrimp and setting it aside as he chewed the meat.

"You realize there's more?" she asked cautiously.

"I'd be disappointed if there wasn't." His smile was as false as hers had been. "Where did you learn to code?"

"We had to design our own website at school. There

were a handful of standard templates to choose from. We were supposed to load basic details and a few photos, that kind of thing. I didn't like the colors it offered and wanted a different layout. I looked up how to hack into the back end and customize it."

"For extra credit?"

"To stand out from the rest. We were also required to have a hobby and volunteer hours. I chose programming and contributed to open-source projects. Since I've been here, I've had time and opportunity to become proficient in several languages. Mae liked that I could manipulate things to the way she wanted them."

"Coding is a skill that's very marketable," he pointed out.

"That's why I'm demonstrating my skills to you." She pushed her bowl away. "But who will take me seriously, without a track record or credentials? Which door do I knock on when I land after being deported and have nothing in my pockets but lint? At best, I'd be recruited for click farms or phishing scams, maybe have to resort to criminal activity for my own survival. As I said before, if I wanted to break laws, I would have already."

"You don't fit the stereotype for coding geeks—I'll give you that." His penetrating look made her want to touch her hair and see if it was falling out of its knot. He certainly was unraveling *her*.

The maid exchanged their soup for plates of barbecued stingray.

As Luli scraped a tiny morsel of meat from the wing and dabbed it in the sauce, Gabriel asked, "Are you concerned about your weight?"

"I don't care for seafood. And these portions were obviously meant for the butler."

"Order something else." He looked for the maid who had already carried their dirty bowls away.

"I don't see how acting too good for the chef's food will improve my social standing. It's fine. I like the chili sauce with the rice."

He tucked into his own. "The nurse said you were wearing a weight-loss patch on your tongue when you came here. Why?"

"For weight loss." He was not a man to be played with, she *knew* that, but she knew where this was going and would really rather not.

"*Why* did you want to lose weight?"

She bit back a sigh.

"Advantage. My mother requested the school attach it and I went along with it. Many girls had liposuction or nose jobs. The tongue patch was nothing." She dismissed it with a twitch of her shoulder.

"What kind of school would arrange such things?"

"One that trains pageant contestants."

"You were training for a beauty contest?"

She lifted her gaze, mildly affronted. "Why is that shocking? I was a front-runner."

"I didn't know there was such a thing. This is the same school where you were making websites?"

"To build our online presence from the earliest age, yes. I was eleven when I started and built it into something that would have been a decent calling card today, but it's long been taken down." She was still annoyed at her hard work disappearing into cyberspace.

"This is why you wanted your site to stand out from the crowd?"

"Everything was a contest." Understatement of the

decade. She tasted another bite of stingray. It was smoky and stringy, but tender and not too fishy. Tolerable.

"Which means no friends there, either?" he guessed.

"Some girls were friendly, but my mother's view was that a consolation sash like Miss Congeniality is for those who need consoling—something winners don't require, so there was no need to aspire to achieve it. She once played a vicious mind game with a rival, though, by pretending she was trying to win that particular title."

"Your mother competed?"

"Won every major title, yes."

"And yet she had no money for an apartment?"

"She has expensive tastes. And she was angry with my father. Me, too, I think."

"Why?"

Luli sighed, hating to face this head-on.

"There's renown in keeping the crown in the family and the prize money I won paid for my school, but how can you claim to be the most beautiful woman in the world if your own daughter is threatening to take the title from you?"

"She sounds like a lovely person. Did no one notice you dropped out and disappeared?"

"She told people I'd gone to live with relatives. A few schoolmates inquired online and I backed her up. The reality was too…"

To this day, thinking of her mother's casual divesting of her sent a lightning strike of agony into her heart. Her mother had been purely self-serving. It was why she'd had an affair with a married man in the first place. Getting pregnant had probably been one more way to squeeze support out of him. One more thing she hadn't thought through and wound up regretting. She had considered her daughter a commodity and certainly never loved her the way mothers were supposed to love their children. It had left Luli with a gaping emptiness in her soul, one Mae hadn't filled, but had at least acknowledged and attempted to paper over.

"I wasn't sorry to be away from my mother," Luli admitted quietly. "I saw no point in telling people what had really happened. The best-case scenario would have been that she was arrested and I would be living as an orphan there, without prospects. Not even at school any longer."

"Did you want to compete? Or did she force you to do that, too?"

"I saw opportunity and applied myself. I only competed in national titles for girls in the younger categories. I left before I moved into the teen contests. I'm confident I would do well in the global pageants if I entered today. It's one of my contingency plans, if I'm deported. There's quite an investment up front, though. You have to win all the feeder pageants. It's a long game." She was talking too fast. "That's the only reason I set up an account for myself in Venezuela. If I'm forced to draw from it, I promise I'll pay you back with interest."

He didn't immediately refuse her, only narrowed his eyes. "Pageants sound like a path to modeling. Would it be so bad to start there?"

"In Venezuela? The minute I gained any sort of publicity, my mother would come back into my life. I'd prefer to avoid that."

"That's the main reason you don't want to be deported? Your mother?"

"Sí." She poked at the stingray flesh, unable to take another bite of it.

"Stop torturing that. It's already dead." He took her barely touched plate and set it atop his emptied one. "I'll finish it if you're only going to play with it."

"I'll clean toilets if that becomes the only option available to me," she told him, clutching her empty hands in her lap. "I *will* pursue programming, which I know can pay well, but it's also a long game. My physical attributes mean I can aim for a higher and faster return if I try modeling or something like it. It only makes sense that I try. Don't you agree?"

She held her breath, waiting for his assessment. So far he hadn't pulled any punches. If he said she wasn't attractive enough, she would rethink her strategy.

His gaze swept across her face in an almost tangible caress, like a cool scarf of silk wafted over her skin.

"I can't deny you're beautiful." The gravel in his tone had her reflexively holding her breath, waiting for a strange all-over ache to subside.

Then he looked away and his expression hardened, making something catch in her chest. She wanted him to keep looking at her, keep sending that electric current through her that held such possibility.

"I'm only asking that you take me with you and give me time to establish myself," she pleaded softly. "I'll continue my work on Mae's investments in exchange for accommodation and meals—"

"Quite the bargain, considering your minimalist approach to both."

"I would need a small loan for clothing and makeup, but I can continue wearing this uniform for office work—"

"Like hell you can."

She closed her eyes, angry with herself for trying too hard. Judges could always smell desperation.

Ignoring the sting behind her eyes, she considered other avenues of persuasion. He hadn't seemed interested in sex in exchange for favors, maybe because he sensed her inexperience in that department? Should she tell him she'd read up on that particular topic? Extensively? She was always willing to put in the work to do better.

Soft footsteps sounded. The maid arrived with braised duck on a bed of colorful, julienned vegetables.

"Take that one back," he said of Luli's plate before the maid could set it. "You enjoy it. We'll share this one. I'm getting full." He sent Luli a droll look as he set the single plate between them.

The maid curtsied and hurried away with her full plate and fresh gossip. Luli imagined she would be accused of sleeping with Mrs. Chen's grandson very soon. Little did they know he had already turned her down.

"Mr. Dean—"

He dipped his chin in warning.

"Gabriel?" She said it softly, not wanting to be overheard when it felt so much like an overstep. She was still the youngest on staff and always addressed others formally or at least with a respectful *auntie*.

"Eat," he commanded. "My turn to talk."

He was the one who had asked so many questions, forcing her to go on and on. She singled out a pale stick of daikon and nibbled the sweet-spicy end of it.

He sat back and regarded her with flinty eyes as he sipped his wine.

"You accused me of neglecting my grandmother—

not stepping in to manage things before today. She dis-owned my mother before I was born. I met Mae for the first time at my mother's funeral when I was seven. I didn't see her again until five years had passed. My father warned me about allowing her to influence me, which seemed paranoid, but he knew her better than I did. I saw her again at my father's funeral and we re-mained in touch—through you, I now realize, but I never made assumptions about whether I would inherit her fortune. As for assisting in managing her wealth… How would I know she needed help? You've done your job so well, I had no cause for concern."

Was that a compliment or a rebuke?

He set down his stemless glass.

"I, however, have no need for your management ser-vices. Chen Enterprises is mine. I'll chew and swallow it the way I would any other company that falls under my control, restructuring where necessary and allow-ing my existing legion of executives to do what I pay them to do."

She kept her expression a stiff mask, not revealing the crumple inside her.

"As to the threats you've made, my life is completely impervious to them. I don't need my grandmother's money and her misdeeds are not mine. I'm not close enough to her for her loss of good standing to affect my pride. You're the one who will feel it if you implode her legacy. I'll walk away unscathed."

She had known that, deep down. She had known she had no real leverage. She had nothing and was nothing. Her throat tightened and it took all her effort to keep the press of tears from reaching the front of her eyes.

"So I'm to be deported?" Her stomach fell while the

flutter of nerves behind her heart became the panicked batter of bird wings against a window.

He wasn't saying anything.

Through the lashes she dropped to disguise her agony, she saw his lips curl, but it wasn't a smile. Self-deprecation, perhaps.

She set down her chopsticks, but she couldn't think beyond that.

"You're not going to eat? Come with me, then." He rose abruptly and started into the house.

She half expected to be shown the front door, but he went up the wide staircase and strode into Mae's bedroom. She trailed him on feet that felt encased in cement, heart dragging as a weight behind her.

She had only been in this bedroom a handful of times. It was the purview of Mae's personal maid and her nurse, decorated in Mae's signature classic style without too much fuss or femininity, if a little dated. Mae never spent money unless she had to.

The mirror over the makeup table swung open like a cupboard. Gabriel revealed a safe and punched in the code.

"How did you—?"

"You can open these older safes by setting them back to their factory default. It takes longer to look up the combination online than it does to actually break in." He removed a leather-bound portfolio. "I was looking for her will and also I found this." He handed the portfolio to her.

"What is it?" She unzipped it to see a handful of her standard reports on some Chinese businessmen. Head shots, the natures of their businesses, net worth, any red flags that might cause Mae to have concerns about partnering with them.

"I don't know why she had this in her safe. It's a very typical—" She flipped past the third profile and found a document that read Marriage Contract.

"Oh, my God!" She threw it all away so the pages and photographs and colored notes with Mae's spidery handwriting fluttered like a flock of startled birds, then drifted to the silk rug to leave a jagged, broken puzzle upon it.

"Why so surprised? You said she was arranging you a marriage," he chided.

"I didn't know she was *doing* it!"

She hugged herself, staring in morbid horror at the papers. What did they say? What had Mae hoped to get in exchange for her? What was she worth *this* time?

"The dowry she was offering was quite generous. There's a decent settlement if you divorce, especially if you stick it out at least five years. Excellent terms if you provide children, especially sons."

"*When?* I thought—" She had thought Mae wanted her. That she was doing a good job for her.

She had told him what she was, but it was pure debasement to stand here before him, proven to be nothing but an asset to be bartered in one more business deal. Chattel.

"The one in textiles is the oldest. Has a heart condition."

Luli turned her head, expression persecuted.

Gabriel's conscience twinged, but he was still processing this discovery himself. He had removed the folder with his name on it, curious to see if she would betray a notice of its absence.

She seemed genuinely shocked by the existence of this portfolio at all. The fact it had been stored in the safe told him Mae had wanted to keep it very private. Her notes on each of the candidates revealed explicitly how she saw each of those older men falling short in her estimation, especially as compared to *him*.

That had been the most disturbing discovery. These other men were fallback positions. Mae had wanted *him* as Luli's husband.

Because she did, in fact, seem to view Luli as a daughter. His efforts to find Luli on any payroll list or other household record had turned up nothing. He had personally questioned the butler who had shown him his own system for tracking staff hours and vacation days, but Luli wasn't on it.

She had her own arrangement, the butler had said with affront. And no, she didn't leave the house, which was a nuisance. Other staff had to pick up her personal items and the cost went against his household budget—a perk not available to anyone else. In his opinion, if staffing cuts were needed, Gabriel should start with Luli.

Gabriel remembered clearly the feeling of his own money, earned honestly and through great effort, going to support his father. It wasn't something he should resent. As Luli had said earlier, family supported family, but his father had abandoned any effort to do his part. It had all fallen on Gabriel at a very young age to keep him and his father clothed, sheltered and fed.

Luli had to be suffering a similar impotent anger. She had put in the time, had done what was expected, but that work had gone unacknowledged. Her reward was the opportunity to do the same for a stranger. Him or some other man.

"I won't do it." Her voice shook with the rest of her. She lifted her gaze from staring through sheened eyes at the pages she'd thrown across the floor. "You can't make me."

"Calm down. I'm only saying that I'll honor her intentions if you want to go through with it." He was testing her, was what he was doing.

"Of course I don't!" She covered her face, visibly trying to take hold of herself.

"You said you would make a good trophy wife. That's what this is." He had never aspired to have any sort of wife—trophy or otherwise. That Mae had thought she could interfere in his life to this degree was a shocking affront.

"I want to marry on *my* terms," Luli said, echoing his own sentiments. She dropped her hands to reveal a raw agony in her expression that made his heart lurch. "I thought she *liked* me. Why would she do this?"

He had his theories, but asked instead, "Was there any indication she was ill? Was she putting things in order because she thought her time was near?"

"I don't think so." She paced a few steps, calming a little as she thought. "She only brought it up a few times. One of the maids left to get married last year. Mae said I wouldn't have to marry some fish-smelling man from the hawker center. She said she'd find me a good husband. But she also told me at different times that she would take me shopping and let the chauffeur teach me to drive and take me back to Venezuela so I could tell my mother what I think of her. It was never a good time for any of those things. 'Another day,'" she tacked on in Mandarin.

Presumably she was quoting Mae. Her accent was spot-on.

"I don't think she was lying to me on purpose," she continued despondently. "She talked about a lot of things that never happened. She wanted to redecorate. Retire. She said when you came to visit we would take you to see the sights."

Gabriel had seen the ones he wanted to see. He'd been here several times and had never once let his grandmother know he was in town.

His stomach tightened in disgust with himself. Had she meant to introduce him to Luli? Oversee their courtship?

So what if she had? What he'd said earlier about having no interest in finding women for other men stood. He had no desire for his dead grandmother to find him a wife, either.

But he ruefully had to admit she had never led him astray with any of the other opportunities she had presented to him.

"I don't want to marry one of those men and be trapped here for the rest of my life." Luli's hushed voice made something grate in the base of his throat. "Why would she do that to me?"

Why had Mae thought she could do this to him? The answer was the same in both cases.

"She was angry my mother didn't abide by the marriage she wanted for her. Good children allow their parents to make them a good match."

"I'm not her child and I'm not doing it!"

He held up a hand. "But this does prove she saw you as a foster daughter. She was taking a personal interest in your future the way she thought a mother should.

She wasn't finding husbands for any of the housemaids. Only you."

In fact, like the rest of the house staff, the maids were entitled to a settlement based on their years of service. Gabriel had shown that part of Mae's will to the butler and told him to begin making plans to take the house down to a skeleton staff.

Luli wasn't house staff, though. Not that it mattered. Gabriel could offer her any amount that he deemed fair out of his own pocket and ignore his grandmother's wishes. He owed Mae nothing.

Except that she had birthed the woman who had given him life. Luli could tell him things about his grandmother, maybe even his mother, that likely no one else could.

He cursed silently and ran a hand through his hair.

"I don't know how to *ask* to be deported." Luli moved to the window where she stared down at the courtyard. Her shoulders seemed very narrow, all of her quite fragile despite her willowy height. "I'm worried they'll put me in jail if I admit I've been here all this time. I can't stay, though. I don't want to and I have nothing to stay for. I have no one to put in a good word to help me get a job or find a place to live. They all hate me for never doing laundry or dusting. They think I'm a freeloader."

Her fingers were digging in to her upper arms, liable to leave bruises beneath her smooth skin.

"I heard men on the other side of the garden wall talking about fake passports once. I should have called out to them, but I was afraid. They were talking about guns and drugs. I would have had to steal money from Mae's purse. They might have decided to come in if they realized—"

"Luli." The other suitors crumpled beneath his feet as he walked across to her. "My grandmother intended you would be looked after. That's proof of it." He pointed back to the billionaires found to be not quite good enough for Mae's surrogate daughter.

"She wanted to hand me to a stranger like I'm a...a thing." Her eyes were bright and angry.

"I don't think that's true." He had taunted her earlier that she was one more asset he was inheriting, though. And he might not need this inheritance from Mae, but if he intended to accept it, he had to take all of it—including the treasure she had confined to this house like an heirloom jewel tucked in a safe.

He took in Luli's ugly dress and flat-footed sandals, her hair rolled into a cinnamon bun at her nape, her hands like rocks in the wide, patch pockets of her dress.

Whatever *she* was, Mae had kept her close for a reason. She had valued Luli highly enough to think her good enough for her only grandson. For that reason alone, he couldn't throw Luli away. Not without a thorough polish and appraisal first, he deduced with dark humor.

"You'll honor the dowry if I marry one of them?" she asked with dread, glancing at the papers with desperation and anguish.

Repulsion gripped him as he thought again of gnarled hands setting themselves against those luscious curves. If anyone touched her, he wanted it to be *him*.

"No. I want you to marry *me*."

CHAPTER FOUR

"WHAT?" HER EYES went round as big blue plates. "Why? *No*."

"It's what she wanted." He moved back to the safe and brought out the pages he'd removed from the portfolio, the one with his own head shot atop it. "I was in there, too."

"No." She shook her head and spoke in a hurried, half-panicked tone. "She often asked me to include you as a comparison when I prepared reports like this. She regarded you very highly, always measuring other businessmen by the standards you set."

"She asked me nine different times in the last year to come visit. How many times were any of those men invited here?"

"They live in the city. She didn't like to travel. She probably wanted you to come so she could tell you she was leaving everything to you."

"She wanted me to meet you. Look." He flipped past the summary of his holdings and showed her the contract with their names already written into it.

Her sharp inhale told him that had been a blow she hadn't expected. He'd been shocked, too. And had wanted to see her reaction, to be sure she hadn't set this up. Her lips were white, her pupils tiny dots.

"You don't want to marry me! Do you?" she asked with trepidation.

"Marriage has not been a priority for me," he admitted, but frowned.

Mae was the only person he had ever listed as his beneficiary because she was the closest relative he had. There were reasons he hadn't pursued marriage and children, one of them being that he would have to wade through a swamp of gold diggers to find someone suitable.

Regardless of how uncomfortable it made him that Mae had plotted like this, there was something very expedient and businesslike in having marriage and progeny sourced and negotiated so all he had to do was agree to the terms. It provided a beautifully simple means of keeping emotions out of the equation.

"You could just give me the dowry," Luli urged with faint hope.

If everything she had told him was true—and he was beginning to think it was—then she was too inexperienced to strike out alone, especially in a major center like New York or Paris, money in her pockets or not. The idea of her disappearing into thin air didn't sit well.

"It's very likely Mae intended to make our marriage a condition of my inheriting." He likely would have refused, but now he'd met Luli and wasn't so sure. He saw so much untapped potential in her. "In the same way I'm honoring her arrangements for the staff, I should provide you what she intended you to have."

"A husband? Lucky me," she choked.

He was both amused and insulted.

"This is a very quick means of gaining you residency in New York, where you said you wanted to go. I'd prefer to get back there without delay." He handed her the contract. "Read it. If you agree it's favorable, we'll sign it in the morning, marry and be on our way."

"New York? Really?" For the first time, an avid flash glittered in her eyes.

It made him cautious enough to add, "And this way I can be sure you're not embezzling to accounts in South America or dropping inconvenient PR bombshells."

She rolled the contract and held it in her fist, cocked her head in suspicion. "Am I supposed to disable everything now?"

"This isn't a trick." He hid a smile at how much he enjoyed the way she held ground and presented a challenge at every turn. "Disable the timer. I'll break in on my own time and assess what you've done. I don't like that you've found vulnerabilities. I'll examine those doors and seal them myself, ensure nothing like this can happen again."

Maybe this was the real attraction to marrying her, he mused as she frowned and left the room. He wanted to delve past her defenses and understand how *she* worked.

It was an opportunity that felt too good to turn down. And Luli had run out of options. Losing Mae had left her bereft in many ways.

The marriage contract *was* quite generous, but he didn't really want to give her an allowance, did he? Not that much? She crossed it out and set a question mark beside it for discussion. What about the settlements for children? Did he expect them to have sex? Or was this a marriage in name only?

She went down early the next morning, wanting to talk it out, but he was much in demand. Solicitors and other officials were literally queued up, waiting their turn while he signed papers, made arrangements for Mae's cremation and held a small press conference.

She finally caught his eye by hovering in the doorway as he was dismissing someone.

"Ready?" he asked, waving her in with a frown at what she was wearing.

He had asked her to put on something for travel, but she didn't own anything except her uniform dresses. She had stolen into Mae's closet for the only clothes that fit her wide hips and ample chest. The pleated skirt was a mustard color, the brocade jacket double-breasted and so dated it had mattresses for shoulder pads.

She smiled a hesitant greeting at Mae's lawyer who sat with a clerk on the sofa, papers laid out before them on the coffee table. Another man rose as she entered.

Gabriel took the pages from her, reading as he said, "Close the door. This is Mr. Johnson from the American embassy. He's liaising with the Venezuelan authorities to obtain your emergency passport and issue your permit to enter the US."

"Oh. Thank you. Nice to meet you." She shook the American's hand.

"I understand you're both very much in love," Mr. Johnson said, making a facetious V with his lips.

"What…?"

"He's officiating our marriage." Gabriel leaned on the desk to affix his signature to the bottom of the contract in a firm scratch. He offered the pen to her.

"Which is, of course, a love match and not a work-around for residency."

She opened her mouth, wanting to say she had come in here to discuss the contract, not sign it. Not *do* this.

But there was Mr. Johnson, waiting to issue her a passport and the right to enter the US. All she had to do was keep her mouth shut.

She pressed her lips tight and took the pen in fingers that felt nerveless and clumsy. Her scrawl was jerky and not the least bit pretty. In fact, she couldn't recall the last time she had written her whole given name.

Gabriel handed the document to the attorney then looked to Mr. Johnson.

Right there in front of Mae's desk, where Luli had stood a thousand times, she spoke vows to create a life with Gabriel, then signed another piece of paper and was pronounced his wife.

"You may kiss," Mr. Johnson said.

Gabriel was suddenly very close. Bigger. His eyes seeming to turn a dark, hunter green. He was asking her a silent question, one she couldn't interpret, let alone answer.

The heat of his palm settled against the side of her neck. The width of his chest blocked out the world while his head came down.

She had wondered about kissing. There had been one, a very long time ago. It had been wet and off-putting and—

Conscious thought disappeared as the smooth heat of his lips grazed hers, once, twice. It caused a buzzing sensation, almost ticklish. Maddening. She found herself pressing into her toes, rising so her mouth more firmly met his, soothing the crazed feeling and suddenly his lips were fully sealed over hers.

Surprise held them both still for one heartbeat. Then his mouth moved in a lazy, curious taste of hers, parting her lips with the movement. Fireworks detonated under her skin and exploded against her closed eyelids.

A gasp caught in her throat, but it was the shock of having so many sensations accost her. His faint taste of bitter, black *kopi*, the scent of his aftershave on his smooth cheek, the sweep of his tongue that somehow sent a wrecking ball into her middle and another into her pounding heart.

She splayed a hand over his chest. His kiss grew more devouring. She found herself squeezed up against the solid wall of his chest. His hard arms felt strangely good, if overwhelming. She was barely aware of what she was doing, moving her mouth against his out of instinct. Her arms unfurled to twine around his neck and she let her weight rest more fully against him as a drugged lassitude kept her in this wonderful place. She wanted to do this forever, mouth sliding against mouth, easing slightly then coming back with a deeper hunger. It was glorious.

He lifted his head and a noise of loss caught in her throat. His hands moved to her upper arms and he set her back a step, expression smoothed to something unreadable. He turned his head to look at Mr. Johnson. "Thank you."

It was like a bucket of cold water. Her head was still swimming, but she figured out that their kiss had been for the benefit of their small audience, not something that had affected him the way it had affected her.

"Collect your things," he said. "We'll leave shortly."

She nodded dumbly, not looking at anyone. It was starting to hit her that she had placed her future into the hands of a man with far more power than her mother's strident urging for her to win prize money or Mae's dictatorial demands.

Gabriel was master of everything he touched, including her. She had used up all her bravado yesterday—and played every card she had. Since then, she had actually discarded and folded a few. She had deactivated most of her insurance policies and had no doubt he would be able to hack into his own system within days. Then what would she be? Useless again.

And once again in a foreign land without a friend in the world.

At least here, she had her feet planted. The moment she left, she would be at his mercy.

Maybe she should stay, she thought with a wild rush of cowardice, hand shaking as she pushed her few things into a bag. Then she stared at the paltry evidence of her life here. With force of habit, her hand went to the front of her skirt, but failed to find the patch pockets where she kept a smooth stone she had found in the garden years ago.

It was on the night table and she dropped it into the bag.

Would the fish miss her throwing a handful of crumbs into the pond each morning? Would anyone miss her once she left here?

Gabriel was at the front door, seeing the men out. She went along to Mae's office where she started to unplug the laptop, but checked first to see if he had made any progress breaking in.

Not that she could tell. She confirmed that this week's payroll figures had been entered by all the department heads, then double-checked them and ensured the balances were available to cover it before she hit the keys that finalized the process.

Then she clicked over to market numbers. The announcement about Mrs. Chen's hospitalization might have caused a sell-off if the news hadn't been accompanied by the identity of her surprise grandson taking over. *That* had caused a rush to buy into some of her ventures, sending their value jumping several points.

Eight years of hard work and Luli hadn't made anywhere near the profit for Mae that Gabriel had by the simple act of connecting his name to Mae's.

She touched the power button, shutting down in disgust.

"What are you doing?" The butler's accusatory tone made her jump.

"I—" Did she have a guilty conscience? Very much so. "I'm packing." She wrapped the power cord around her hand and dropped it into her bag.

"Not that, you're not!" He puffed up with indignation. "You take *nothing*." He came across and tried to grab her bag to see inside it.

She backed up a few steps, distancing herself from his aggression. "Gabe—Mr. Dean is taking me to New York." She couldn't bring herself to tell him they'd just gotten *married*. "I need the laptop to keep working."

"You don't *work*." He made it sound as if she'd never lifted a finger in her life. "Were you on your knees when he said you could go with him? *Slut*." He sounded like one of her preteen fellow contestants.

"If this is about last night, I'm *sorry*." He felt tricked she supposed. "I misunderstood about dinner."

"You're not sorry. You wanted to make me look foolish. You were always trying to be Mrs. Chen's little pet and now you want to be his. Out. Now." He grabbed her by the arm.

Luli squeaked out a noise, so shocked at his getting physical, it took her a moment to dig in her heels and struggle against his hold.

"Let me go!" she cried.

He did—in a whirl of movement so fast she wound up clutching her hand against the thick fabric of her jacket's lapel, trying to keep her heart from leaving her chest.

Gabriel stood before her instead of the butler, but he was bent over and the butler was flat on his back on the floor. Gabriel's hand was pressed to the man's throat, turning the older man dark red.

"*You* will leave," he told the butler, switching his grip to the front of the man's shirt and yanking him to his feet as he straightened. *"Now."*

Swaying in shock, the butler clutched a protective hand to his wheezing throat and hurried from the room.

Gabriel shot his cuffs and adjusted his tie, eyes ashen as he stared at her. "We're leaving." He jerked his head for her to precede him.

Luli was still dressed like a seventy-year-old woman, but Gabriel didn't tell her to change. He just wanted away from this place.

He was furious over what had just happened. He had nearly killed the man—who was in his fifties and no match for Gabriel's deadly training. It hadn't even been self-defense. The butler had been rude and rough, but Gabriel didn't think his intention had been to physically hurt Luli, only to force her from the house.

Even so, a haze of bloodlust had blinded him. He had acted on instinct and was still disturbed by his brief loss of control. Why had he reacted so strongly? He would intervene in any situation where someone was being bullied, but he wouldn't commit *homicide*.

The primal male in him had been roused by a threat to his mate, was the problem. His ears were still ringing from their kiss. He had meant to keep it a chaste peck, but her lips had been so soft. He had lingered, enjoying the tremulous way her mouth flowered open against his. Nothing had prepared him for the impact when she pressed into the kiss. A bolt of pure lust had jabbed through him, tightening his arms around her.

The rush of blood when her soft curves had collided with his frame had left his groin throbbing with the beat of his heart. It had been all he could do to set her back from him and keep an impassive look on his face when he'd wanted to snarl at the men to leave so he could consummate their marriage right then and there.

He was used to being pursued by women. It was a game where he allowed himself to be pounced upon and played with and always walked away when he grew bored.

This situation with Luli was entirely different. He had thought last night, when he had talked her into this marriage, that he had secured the perfect partnership. He could have the sensual wrestling he enjoyed while everything he valued—including detachment from the sort of emotion that weakened lesser mortals—would be protected.

Then he'd tasted a depth of passion unlike anything he'd ever known. It roused a beast that had reacted to the butler's manhandling with atavistic violence.

"Why have you never stood up for yourself with anyone here?" His tone was thick enough with leftover rage she flinched, expression defensive.

"What would I say? Make accusations that would get me thrown out with nothing? He wasn't wrong. I did ingratiate myself with her."

The irony was, her openness about currying favor made her seem vulnerable, provoking the protector in him again. None of this made sense.

He led her down the front steps, still waiting for a miracle where his grandmother came back to life and made clear that he was either correcting her wrong against Luli or told him he was falling for the greatest trick a gold-digger had ever pulled.

"Is that all the luggage, sir?" the chauffeur asked, setting Gabriel's single case in the trunk.

"And that." He nodded at the bag Luli carried. It was the cheap fabric kind the kitchen staff no doubt took to the market stalls for produce.

What had her childhood been like that she thought living like this had been a step *up*? How could such a beautiful, healthy, bright woman be in such a position?

He'd spent half the night reading her code. She hadn't been bluffing about blowing things up, but she'd also layered in fail-safes in case she was also locked out. The most critical functions were being monitored electronically so the many people employed by Mae's various enterprises wouldn't be too badly impacted if no one was at the wheel.

Such a perplexing woman.

"What are you doing?" he asked as he realized she was hovering on the bottom step, balking at coming forward to get in the car. The rain had let up, but the humidity was around 1000 percent, making his suit cling to his skin. "Did you forget something?"

"I'm scared." Her clean features were pale in the flat light of overcast skies, her mouth tense, her brow furrowed.

"Of?"

"You. What I've done. Where we're going."

He was having second thoughts himself, but a clench of barbaric implacability insisted he take her away from this place.

"You can't stay here." He wouldn't let her.

"I know." She looked into the car the way someone facing execution might look toward the electric chair.

He scraped together the pieces of himself that still possessed some civility and held out a hand. "It will be all right, Luli."

It wasn't like him to reassure. He enjoyed the feel of a woman's naked body beside him in bed, but he didn't cuddle or coddle. She was causing all sorts of unrecognizable pangs in him, ones that warned him he'd have to proceed carefully where she was concerned, but he still wanted her to come with him.

Now, more than ever.

She tightened her lips with resolve and her grip was clammy. The way she squeezed his fingers filled his chest with inexplicable pressure.

He settled beside her and reminded her to put on her belt.

"Do you think I could get fish someday?" she asked as he turned up the air-conditioning and the car pulled away.

"Odd question, but I don't see why not. I have several aquariums. They're very soothing."

"You do?" She brightened a little. "Will I see them?"

"Of course." It struck him that she would be living with him for the foreseeable future. There was a reason he chose fish as pets. They were quiet and demanded nothing of him.

What the hell had he done?

"Maybe a cat would be better." She set her elbow on the armrest and tucked her fist beneath her chin, speaking to the window now. "Spending your life stuck in a bowl isn't fun."

CHAPTER FIVE

"Is this the right place?" Luli asked with confusion. "Where are the other people?"

"What other people?" Gabriel rose from the car to stand beside her and accepted the umbrella from the chauffeur.

Airports were busy places, weren't they? Gabriel had brought her to a quiet field where stretches of road cut across acres of green toward the blurry horizon. There was an airplane with Arabic writing on its tail parked toward the other end of the low building that crouched behind them. The chauffeur handed their bags to an attendant and they were carried up the stairs in front of them, into an aircraft that was downright intimidating.

It was designed like the ones folded out of paper, with big triangular wings. Like a fighter jet. The windows were a continuous stripe down the body and the tail was painted with the Chinese symbol for dragon. Luli knew that meant it was Gabriel's. He'd been using that symbol in his logos since developing a smartphone game about dragons when he was a boy.

"Don't I have to show a passport to security?"

"It will be waiting for you when we land in Paris."

"Paris!" She swung around. "You said you'd take me

to New York." She had tried to teach herself French at one point, but hadn't had anyone to practice with.

"A small detour for shopping." He gave her outfit another disdainful glance and waved to the stairs into the airplane.

Everything was happening so fast. She could barely catch her breath. And now she was awestruck as she entered the jet. It wasn't the kind that looked like a bus with rows of seats and an aisle and little round windows. This was a house. The staff was even lined up exactly as she had stood outside Mae's mansion when he had arrived yesterday.

The pilot welcomed her and invited Gabriel to join him in the cockpit to review their flight path.

"May I show you to your room, Mrs. Dean?" a pretty attendant asked.

"Call me Luli." She needed to talk to Gabriel about how real this marriage was before she ran around calling herself Mrs. Dean. It was still bothering her that he hadn't been nearly as caught up in their kiss as she had been. Then he'd been so angry after the incident with the butler.

With her mind whirling with misgivings, she'd stood on that bottom step as if it had been a jump off a high diving board. She probably wouldn't have come this far if he hadn't held out a hand, reassuring her she could trust him.

Foolishly, she wanted him to keep holding her hand as she followed the woman past the L-shaped sofa and reclining armchairs arranged to face a flat-screen television that hung above a *fireplace*.

Not a house, Luli decided as she absorbed the ebony-

and-ivory interior with its glints of chrome and glass. A spaceship.

The attendant took her down a short corridor that ended in a minisuite in grays and chrome. Along with a massive bed, there was a private dining area for two, a sofa, a desk and another television.

"Please use the bell if you need me to bring anything." She pointed at the button near the headboard as she left.

Luli saw her bag hung empty on a hook behind the door. She opened a couple of drawers, finding Gabriel's clothes in them.

Her heart stopped. This was his room.

And there was her underwear in another drawer, looking very paltry in such a big, empty compartment. She closed the cupboard and touched the vase on the night table. It was magnetic, ensuring it wouldn't fall over during turbulence.

She went into the bathroom. Mirrors and subdued lighting turned the powder-blue color scheme silver. The shower had frosted glass and the towels matched the bedspread.

Luli stared at herself in the mirror. Gabriel was right. This double-breasted jacket did her no favors. She had been trying to blend in for so long, she had mostly forgotten how to make the most of her attributes.

There was only soap and lotion in here, no makeup. She washed, then, rather than pin up her hair again, left it loose. The thick, wavy mass had always been one of her best features along with her natural honey-toned skin. She left the jacket on the hook behind the door, even though her plain cotton bra caused unflattering lines against the thin fabric of her knit top.

She paused before she opened the door. Gabriel was on the other side, advising someone on the phone in French what time they would arrive.

She opened the door to see him tossing a pair of bone-colored pants onto the foot of the bed. He noticed her and glanced at the blue shirt on the hanger in his hand. He replaced it on the rack and brought out a red one.

"*Merci.* Au revoir." He ended his call. "These are for you. More comfortable for travel." He pulled the shirt off the hanger and picked up the pants. "And more flattering. Although, that's better without the jacket."

The way his gaze lingered on her made her think of their kiss. Her skin grew tight.

"Thank you," she murmured as she came forward to take the clothes. The linen pants had a wide, woven tape as a drawstring and the shirt was a soft knit with a half dozen buttons at the collar. "We, um, should talk about a few things."

"Sure," he said absently. "I wondered how long it was." His gaze traveled to where tendrils of her hair scrolled against and around the swells of her breast. His hand lifted and she felt a light tug against her scalp, as though he drew a few strands through his finger and thumb, testing its silky texture.

She stood very still, not sure what to make of his curiosity, but liking the tingle that rippled across her scalp and down her nape into her shoulder. It was like their kiss, leaving her feeling shaken, while he had seemed to shake it off.

"I wondered if—" She started to lose her nerve. "We didn't talk about whether this would be, um, a real…

um…" She swallowed, voice almost nonexistent as she squeaked, "Marriage?"

His brows came together like a pair of crashing trains, head-on. "You signed the contract. I thought that meant you agreed to everything."

"I didn't have a chance to disagree, did I? Everything happened so fast. Then, the way you kissed me, I thought maybe it was just for show."

"What do you mean? Were *you* pretending when we kissed?" His voice rang with such foreboding, she shivered inwardly.

"N-no?"

"You don't sound sure."

"I'm sure. But I wasn't sure if you…?" She swallowed, completely out of her depth.

"I wasn't pretending anything. I was trying to keep it this side of X-rated."

There was something in his demeanor that reminded her of the time her mother had been photographed with a jaguar. Luli had been seven or eight. Her mother had insisted she join her. Luli had been fascinated by the power and heat radiating off the spotted cat, but the handler had warned her, *Don't look him in the eye.*

So she knew better, but she did it now with this beast—and instantly understood why it was a mistake. It aroused the hunter in him. He might appear relaxed, but his pupils opened and he bared his teeth, sending swirls of reaction into her abdomen. Strangely, it wasn't terror. It was the opposite. An answering type of excitement? She didn't know what it was, but she couldn't look away, couldn't move.

Another tug pulled against her scalp as he turned his finger, winding her hair to draw her forward, until she stood close enough to feel the heat off his body. He let his gaze wander her face, both lazy and thorough, like he was staking a territorial claim.

She found herself studying his mouth, licking her lips.

His fist rested on her shoulder, still tangled in her hair. His thumb stroked along the artery in her throat, where her blood moved thick and unsteady.

"You have the most beautiful skin."

She didn't know how to respond to that and wasn't given a chance. He dipped his head and opened his mouth against her neck.

This was what they did. They crushed their prey with their powerful jaws.

Except he only breathed hotly against her throat, licked once, sending her pulse skyrocketing. Her breasts prickled and stung inside her bra and a wicked dampness rushed into her loins. She forgot to inhale as he rubbed his lips against her skin. Heat suffused her body and her bones turned to melted wax.

He made a purring noise and scraped his teeth, then sucked lightly, soothing with another lick. The sensation was so enticing, she let her head fall back, fully baring her throat to him.

With another noise of satisfaction, he set a hand on her hip and drew her closer, lifted his head and took her mouth in a kiss that buckled her knees. Hot, thorough, hungry. His arms went around her, pulling her in. Holding her up.

Her arms were tangled in whatever she held, but she didn't care that she couldn't move them. She only wanted more of that raking pleasure of his lips across hers.

The swipe of his tongue against hers sent streaks of

electricity through her. She met it with her own, moaning softly in her throat as a near-painful sting heightened every inch of her skin. As if he understood that, he ran his hands over her back and waist and hips, soothing but inciting, making her wriggle restlessly, wanting more.

Her shirt came loose from her waistband and his palms went under the edge, up and up, arriving to cup her breasts so they throbbed with sensitivity in the firm hold of his hands. It was too much and not enough. She could smell something feral on his skin and wanted to drown in that scent. She plucked at his shirt and drew on his tongue and wished she could breathe, but she only wanted *him*.

With a savage hiss of breath, he jerked his head back. The gray-green of his eyes was jungle dark, filled with mysterious shadows and the secrets of life.

Her heart thudded so hard she could feel it rocking her whole body, pulsing in her nipples against his palms and throbbing in the plump folds between her legs.

"Are you faking this?" he asked in a voice that made her scalp prickle.

She looked down at the way his hands were trapped against her breasts under the taut fabric, the clothes he'd given her rumpled on the floor at their feet.

"No." She didn't have a clue what she was doing, but she was lured by the feel of his palms on her breasts to lean in to his touch.

"Good." The word was a satisfied rumble. His thumbs flicked across her nipples, and even muffled by the cotton of her bra, the caress caused a sharp spear of electric sensation to stab into her abdomen. "I'll close the door."

Consciousness began to seep back into her brain. "I was going to save it," she remembered distantly.

"Save what?" His head lowered so the air between their lips became magnetized, tugging with invisible force.

It took all her efforts to remember what they were talking about and say it before he kissed her and erased every thought she could conjure.

"My virginity."

Gabriel stopped a scant millimeter from claiming that luscious, clever mouth. He balanced on the knife's edge between rational thought and the sweetest, blindest escape he could recall glimpsing in his lifetime.

He made his hands slide down to her waist and swallowed.

"You're a virgin?" he asked carefully.

Her tense stomach muscles quivered against the heels of his hands. Her pouted mouth was still parted with invitation. "Yes."

"And you kissed me like that?"

She blinked and the sultry haze of arousal in her sea-green eyes grew tepid and unsure. "Am I not good at it?"

He was hard as high-carbon steel, his flesh nearly searing its way through the layers of cloth between them to get to the molten center of her. He swore he could smell her arousal like nectar, beckoning him to burrow deep. He would give anything to taste her, to feel her arch with pleasure against his mouth.

But he refused to believe what she was suggesting.

"Back up a step."

She took him literally, drawing back so his hands fell

to his sides. Her shirt stayed loose, her nipples sharp points against her unbecoming top.

He opened his mouth, closed it. Sought out a couple of brain cells and tried to kick them together, force them to spark cohesive words.

"I'm the first person to ever kiss you? *That's* what you want me to believe?"

"The first *man*." She folded her arms defensively. "There was a boy when I was thirteen. It was…" Her nose wrinkled. "Like pushing my mouth into a pile of mashed potatoes. But there were mostly women in Mae's house so he was my only one."

Gabriel folded. If they were playing poker, she won that hand with a wild-card joker that could be a bluff, but at this point, he could only swear and wave at the clothing on the floor.

"Change. Then go to the lounge. I need a minute to collect myself." Maybe a cold shower. He locked himself in the bathroom the way werewolves chained themselves to a tree on a full moon, so they wouldn't have terrible deeds on their consciences the next day.

He ran his hand down his face as if he could physically bank the heat that had risen in him as he'd contemplated starting their flight in the reclined position.

That had been even better than their first kiss. He hadn't seen any reason to stop except to ensure their privacy, the fines for sitting on the tarmac worth every minute. Hell, they were *married*. If they both wanted it, what was to stop them?

But she was a virgin.

How?

And how hadn't he realized it? He wasn't a womanizer, but he'd slept with enough women he should be able to recognize a lack of experience in a kiss.

He'd been too carried away by her responsiveness both times to register how untutored she was, though. He liked to lead and she had let him. He'd thought it was a sign they were compatible. If he'd noticed any surprise in her, he'd put it down to his same delight at the way their chemistry ignited so quickly, feeding into each other's arousal in a way that was exponential.

Potentially mind-blowing.

And how was her virginity such a turn-on? He was a normal man with normal fetishes like pretty underwear and high heels. Virginity had never reached the top twenty in his fantasy playlist, but the idea of being Luli's first drew him taut as a piano string.

He skimmed his hand over his hair, tamping down the prickle in his scalp.

The more evidence he collected, the more he was coming to see Luli as every bizarre thing she claimed to be. But the only way to prove she was a virgin was to sleep with her.

And if she was a virgin, he shouldn't touch her.

That paradox wasn't going to torture him at all.

Luli fought her way out of the clothes she wore, half terrified Gabriel would walk out and see her naked. And reject her again.

Part of her knew he had saved her from being careless and impulsive, but she still felt rebuffed. Like she'd done something wrong. Not morally, although maybe he *was* judging her. She didn't know. But more than that, she feared she had repelled him in some way, out of ignorance.

The drawstring pants hung low on her hips even after she tied them, but they only needed to be turned up twice at the cuff because she was only a little shorter than Gabriel. The shirt seams dropped off her shoulders and the sleeves also needed turning up, but the light knit was soft and comfortable and smelled of him which was disturbing and nice at the same time.

She went to the lounge, sat in one of the armchairs and buckled, then studied the panel in the armrest. Along with several reclining adjustments, there were a dozen massaging options and both heating and cooling settings. She could also control the television, the music, the lights and call the attendant. There were screens of safety instructions and a message from the pilot welcoming them aboard. It showed a countdown to takeoff.

Apparently, they would begin taxiing in seventy-eight seconds.

Gabriel appeared, hair damp as though he'd showered. He removed the shopping bag with twine handles from the other armchair, setting it at her feet before he sat.

"Something for you to play with while we travel."

"Is this your chair? That's why the panel has so many options. I'm sorry." She reached to unbuckle.

"They're exactly the same." He waved her to stay put.

The attendant appeared with a glass on a silver tray that she offered to Gabriel.

"May I bring champagne? Lavender-infused lemonade? Perhaps a cappuccino?"

"Water is fine," Luli said, pressing into her chair.

"Sparkling or Arctic glacier?"

Luli looked to Gabriel, expecting him to make it clear she didn't deserve this level of catering.

"The Canadian spring water for now. No seafood for Luli."

"Thank you, sir. We received that instruction and have arranged alternatives for Mrs. Dean. The pilot is ready to taxi to the runway if you are?"

"Thank you." He didn't correct her on Luli's title.

The attendant disappeared and the view beyond the windows began to move.

Luli didn't know how to bring up what had happened in his room.

Her downcast gaze landed on the bag, which she had to admit made her curious. It looked like it held black boxes marked with Gabriel's golden dragon logo, all still sealed with cellophane along with something in periwinkle blue.

"Go ahead," he coaxed, sipping as he watched her.

She drew out wireless, noise-canceling headphones, wireless earbuds and other accessories she had only ever seen, mostly online, never dreaming she would use them.

"A new laptop?" And a tablet.

"You'll like it. More processing power. Better security. Consider it a thank-you for making me aware of a vulnerability in my own security program. I've discovered how you broke in and locked me out. Innovative, but it won't happen again."

Luli returned all the boxes to the bag, but kept the periwinkle clutch. It was the most buttery suede she'd ever touched. It had a tiny belt with a gold buckle. A wallet over a smartphone, if she wasn't mistaken. Her ancient flip phone had died years ago and she had only ever held Mae's long enough to fix settings, never needing one of her own because she had no one to call.

The attendant reappeared with her water. "I'll be taking my seat for takeoff. May I set your bag in here?"

She touched a button on the box table next to Luli's chair. The top popped up a few centimeters and slid back to reveal a padded storage bin beneath.

"Thank you," Luli murmured, keeping the wallet in her lap.

"Please don't be alarmed if you hear a noise in the rear of the plane as we ascend. Our design reduces the sonic boom to the decibel of a car door slamming, but you may still notice it. It's perfectly normal." The attendant closed the bin and walked away.

"Your plane travels faster than sound?"

"This one does, yes. There are laws as to where they can be used so I have others for airspaces where we have to travel subsonic."

Others. Plural.

The passage of landscape beyond the windows became a rushing blur before it fell away without any bumps or noises to indicate they had left the ground. She listened and thought she heard the clap, but wasn't sure.

Luli fingered the buckle on the adorable wallet, releasing it to reveal it did conceal a phone. A very feminine and pretty phone in rose-gold-colored metal with crystals embedded around a casing designed with a graceful swoop that set it a world apart from every boring rectangle out there. She wanted to draw it from its custom pocket, to examine it from every angle, but was afraid to mar its shine with her fingerprints.

A light blinked once and a modulated, feminine voice said, "Hello, Luli." The words appeared on the screen then faded against the home screen that showed Gabriel's logo and a handful of icons for apps.

"How—?"

"Facial recognition."

"That's why it took so long to take my passport photo yesterday? You were scanning my face?"

"If you don't like it, you can change it in Settings. I don't always want my phone to open when I glance at it so I also require my fingerprint."

"I know you manufacture all of this technology, but it's still very expensive."

"Very," he interjected dryly. "That's real gold and those are genuine diamonds. Kindly take care of it."

"What?" The priceless phone slipped from her fingers and landed in her lap. She scrambled to pick it up again, mortified. "Why would you give me something like this?"

"You're my wife. People will expect you to have the best."

She shook her head, still not clear on what all was expected of his "wife."

She reached for a sip of water, trying to collect herself, and was promptly distracted by the diamond-cut cubes inside her crystal glass. Judging by the weight, they were plated gold if not solid.

Gabriel's drink was poured over similar chilling stones. Each one was engraved with his dragon symbol.

"You're very different from your grandmother. Mae didn't like her wealth to be obvious. She was afraid people would be encouraged to steal from her if they knew how much she really had."

"Which explains why she kept you locked away and allowed the rest of the staff to think it was okay to treat you poorly. She didn't want anyone to know exactly how much she needed you."

What would it say about her value if he let his staff wait on her and she flaunted the fancy telephone he had given her?

"What was she like?" Gabriel asked. "If my mother told me anything about her, I was too young to remember."

"She didn't care to leave the house. Once she realized how much she could accomplish online, she worked from home and only went into Chen Enterprises for meetings."

"Don't make excuses for her. She didn't take an active role in my life because she didn't approve of her daughter running off to marry an American."

"That's true," she murmured, setting aside her glass. "She had strong views on loyalty and didn't trust easily. Someone must have damaged her trust in the past."

"My mother?" he suggested.

"Perhaps." She closed the pocketbook over the sparkling phone. "But she particularly didn't trust men. It goes back to that business manager, I think. She would only employ a man if he was married and she was introduced to his wife. With her female servants, she didn't want them to be married or have boyfriends, thinking it distracted them and split their loyalty. She fired a maid who was dating without her permission."

"Controlling."

"Yes, but she was kind in her way. I caught a virus once and she had the doctor come, brought me soup and sat with me, even though I was just sleeping." She swallowed back the lump of emotion that swelled in her throat. "I'm going to miss her."

"Have you heard of Stockholm syndrome?" The stones clinked in his glass as he drained it. "It's the bond of trust and loyalty a hostage feels for their captor."

"It wasn't like that." Was it?

Was that what she was starting to feel toward him? She had nearly given him free rein over her body a little while ago, even though she didn't know him well at all.

"She never spoke about my mother other than to complain about her disobedience?" He looked into his empty glass, making it seem a very idle inquiry, but she sensed a deeper need for knowledge inside the question.

"Mae wasn't one to confide or reexamine the past. She never admitted to mistakes or regrets. I only learned she had a daughter when she came back from your father's funeral. I sat in as she directed her attorney to rewrite her will to include you. Until that day, I thought she followed your investments for business reasons."

"Many do."

"I do," she admitted, idly opening a pocket on the wallet to find a metal credit card made of actual platinum. It had an electronic chip on one end, his logo on one side and her name on the other. She shoved it back in its pocket, not ready to contemplate that she had funds at her disposal. "I, um, I've learned a lot from you. I like to imagine that one day I'll have my own money and will manage it wisely and create my own fortune, instead of doing it for someone else."

She smiled at the silly dream of it, but she had needed something to get her through the endless days of feeling like the girl in the tower. A fairy-tale fantasy of building her own castle was a lot more fun to dwell on than facing the reality of her situation or worrying there was a darker future in store for her.

Never in her wildest imaginings had she pictured *this*.

"I think your grandmother was proud of you," she said.

His dark brow went up with skepticism.

"I don't mean that as flattery. Maybe I should say she took a certain amount of credit for your success."

"Her DNA made me what I am? Perhaps. God knows I didn't get any hidden talents from my father. But I'm beginning to think she owes *her* success to *you*."

"I would never make such a claim." Not without expecting a sharp rebuke from Mae.

The plane leveled off and the ultrapleasant attendant appeared with a fresh drink for Gabriel and a fresh smile for Luli. "May I bring anything to ensure your comfort?"

"The lavender thing is popular. You should try it," Gabriel advised.

She *was* curious. She nodded.

"There's a lovely iced-mint cookie that pairs with it. I'll bring that, too." The attendant melted away.

"You don't have to be so…nice." Luli wondered what the attendant was going to say to the rest of the crew behind her back. "Do you feel sorry for me or something?"

"You told me what you were worth, Luli. Act like you believe it."

Gabriel came to Paris at least once a year and almost always with a woman. He didn't consider his sexual partners as objects to be "kept," but he liked to think of himself as a generous partner in bed and in boutiques. More than one lover had accused him of offering material items in lieu of his thoughts and feelings, which he couldn't refute. He had developed the habit of keeping both of those things firmly to himself.

If asked, he blamed his martial arts training for his circumspection. Deep down, he knew it was simply his nature to be aloof. He had never cultivated close friendships and had always felt a step apart from regular society. Did it stem from a broken heart after losing his mother so young? From fear of turning into the drunken shell his father had become? That was likely part of it, but people who spoke their thoughts aloud or permitted emotion to rule them only got back more of the same. Physical feelings of hunger and sexual desire were distraction enough. He had no wish to *yearn*.

And sometimes, when he was in a particularly introspective mood, he suspected that the wealth he had accumulated was both a strategy against wanting any of those abstract things that seemed to be so important to other people and a buffer against the world at large. He shouldered immense responsibility for people's jobs and the infrastructure that served their lives and influenced whether the stock market went up or down on a given day, but he employed armies of people to look after all of that. He spoke to very few people in any meaningful way. A professional of some kind or another could be hired to do almost anything that he didn't care to do himself so that's what he did.

But he couldn't do that with Luli.

She didn't fit the compartment of employee or lover or any other label he had previously slotted people under—not even estranged blood relative. He'd gone and *married* her, which made him personally responsible for her. People could be hired to feed his fish, but who would feed *her* if he didn't see to it?

Who would tell her, "It's okay. Go."

She stayed put, only her nose poking out the open jet door like a cat testing the air, sapphire eyes taking in the pale pink clouds of the evening sky, the car on the tarmac below and the people waiting beside it.

"There's someone in a uniform down there," she reported and backed into him.

The feel of her was erotic and enticing and caused a strange sensation to flutter through Gabriel. It wasn't unlike the aggression that had gripped him in that moment with the butler. Protectiveness, he realized as his hands went to her upper arms in both an effort to reassure her and a claim of warning to anyone who might threaten her.

"The customs agent." He made himself release her. "It's fine. Go ahead."

She cautiously went down the stairs before him. His assistant met her with a smile and an envelope. "Your passport, Mrs. Dean."

"Really?" She hurried to look inside.

"If I may?" the customs agent asked, taking the passport long enough to glance at the stamp inside it. "*Merci*. Enjoy your stay." He handed it back to her. "Mr. Dean, nice to see you again. *Toutes nos félicitations*." He tipped his cap and walked away.

"Thank you," Luli said with bewilderment to his retreating back.

"Your birth certificate is in there with your marriage certificate and my contact details," his assistant continued. "Please reach out at any time with questions or concerns. I'm Mr. Dean's feet on the ground here in Europe, but I can quickly direct any inquiries to another party if it's outside my bailiwick."

"Thank you." Luli's eyes were big as beach balls, glossy and bright. She blinked rapidly.

Gabriel nodded his thanks and steered her into the back of the car.

Luli's hands shook as she tried to pull the certificate from the envelope without damaging its pristine condition.

"It is my birth certificate," she said to him with awe. "This is me."

"Good," he commented.

Her hands continued to shake as she took great care folding the document exactly right so it fit into a pocket of her blue wallet. She transferred her passport and his assistant's card and their marriage certificate into the same pocket, then secured the zipper, anchoring the little tab with her thumb.

"Are you cold?" He reached to take hold of her hand, only wanting to test her temperature.

She twisted her hand to squeeze his tightly and turned a wet look on him. "Thank you," she choked, using her free hand to press the wallet into her navel.

"Why are you crying?" Alarmed, he reached for the box of handkerchiefs, each square of ultrasoft bamboo dyed a different shade from ruby to emerald to amethyst.

"Because—" Her voice broke. She dabbed one beneath her eyes, then beneath her nose. "I don't know how I'll pay you back for this, but I will. I promise."

"For what? It was nothing." He had paid a premium to fast-track the paperwork, but the fees were a tenth of what his chauffeur carried in his money clip for incidentals.

"No, *I* was nothing. Now I have the most important

thing in the world. *Me.*" She wrapped both hands around the wallet and pressed it between her breasts, breathing still shaky. "Thank you."

You told me what you were worth, Luli. Act like you believe it.

She *had* been acting. The whole time. Still was, especially as a handful of designers whose names she knew from Mae's glossy magazines behaved with deference as they welcomed her to a private showroom complete with catwalk.

She had to fight back laughing with incredulity as they offered her champagne, caviar, even a pedicure.

"I—" She glanced at Gabriel, expecting him to tell them she aspired to model and should be treated like a clothes horse, not royalty.

"A full wardrobe," he said. "Top to bottom, morning to night, office to evening. Do what you can overnight, send the rest to my address in New York."

"*Mais bien sûr, monsieur,*" the couturier said without a hint of falter in her smile. "Our pleasure."

"Gabriel—" Luli started to protest as the women scattered.

"You remember what I said about this?" he tapped the wallet that held her phone. "I need you to stay on-brand."

"Reflect who you are?"

"Yes."

"Who are you?" she asked ruefully. "I only met you ten minutes ago."

"I'm a man who doesn't settle for anything less than the best." He touched her chin. "The world is going to have a lot of questions about why we married. Give them an answer."

His words roused the competitor who still lurked inside her. She wanted to prove to the world she was *worthy* to be his wife. Maybe she wanted to prove her worth to him, too. Definitely she longed to prove something to herself.

Either way, she made sure those long-ago years of preparation paid off. She had always been ruthless in evaluating her own shortcomings and knew how to play to her strengths. She might not be trying to win a crown today, but she hadn't been then, either. She'd been trying to win the approval of a woman who hadn't deserved her idolatry.

She pushed aside those dark memories and clung instead to the education she had gained in those difficult years.

"That neckline will make my shoulders look narrow," she said, making quick up-down choices. "The sweetheart style is better, but no ruffles at my hips. Don't show me yellow. Tangerine is better. A more verdant green. That one is too pale." In her head, she was sectioning out the building blocks of a cohesive stage presence. Youthful, but not too trendy. Sensual, but not overtly sexual. Charismatic without being showy.

"Something tells me I'm not needed," Gabriel said twenty minutes in and rose to leave. "We'll go for dinner in three hours." He glanced to the couturier. "And return in the morning for another fitting."

"*Parfait. Merci, monsieur.*" Her smile was calm, but the way people were bustling told Luli how big a deal this was. How big a deal *Gabriel* was.

The women took her measurements while showing her unfinished pieces that only needed hemming or minimal tailoring so she could take them immediately.

"You'll be up all night," Luli murmured to one of the seamstresses.

The young woman moved quickly, but not fast enough for her boss who kept crying, *"Vite! Vite!"*

"I'm sorry to put you through this," Luli added.

"Pas de problème. Monsieur Dean is a treasured client. It's our honor to provide your trousseau." She clamped her teeth on a pin between words. "Do you know where he's taking you for dinner? We should choose that dress next, so I can work on the alterations while you have your hair and makeup done. It must be fabulous. The world will be watching."

She would be presented publicly as his wife, Luli realized with a hard thump in her heart.

She still didn't know what their marriage meant. He had remained silent on the topic of their sleeping together after her confession before they left Singapore. They had spent the flight talking about the features of his laptop and some investments she thought she should unload, since their value had peaked and would likely begin to dwindle as the news of his takeover sank in. He had approved it, allowing her to continue ensuring the cogs of Mae's business kept turning while he chewed his way through the wiring into her accounts himself.

They had dozed in their recliners at different times, neither of them seeking the comfort of the bed. He hadn't invited her to join him there, at least. She hadn't known how to circle back to whether he wanted her there.

She wished she knew what he was thinking, now that she had confessed her virginity. She wished she had experience to draw on! Had he kissed her because he found her attractive? Or merely because she had signed a paper that allowed him conjugal rights? She met all the criteria for typical standards of modern beauty, but perhaps that only made her objectively attractive and didn't translate into someone who was actually desirable.

She reminded herself again that he had done her a favor in cutting things short. Along with youth and beauty, one of the few things she possessed that was hers to give or barter was her virginity. She had presumed it might have value to certain men, but Gabriel didn't seem to be one of them.

And yet he must like sex and women. She stood where other women must have stood, buying clothing charged to him. Gabriel was a *treasured client*.

How strange to hate women she had never met, but she did. Instantly and bitterly.

Jealousy is a sign of insecurity and low self-esteem, she could hear her mother cautioning her. But this wasn't a case where Luli could size up her competition and see how many of their qualities she possessed then make adjustments to outshine them.

She could only make the most of what she had—and gritted her teeth in determination, intending to.

"This one," she said of the dress she tried on a few minutes later.

From the back, it was a one-shouldered evening dress in cranberry silk with a filmy chiffon skirt, except half of the skirt was ivory. The front was more dramatic, with its silk bodice fitted to her breasts and the bottom of the dress made of shiny silk and cut to miniskirt height. The chiffon of the overskirt was belted in the pink-red silk, but its ruffled edges opened as she walked, delicate as fairy wings.

"You have a good eye and the ideal figure for Madame's creations," her seamstress gushed.

Luli accepted tall silver shoes with a pop of merlot on the sole then moved to the styling room. Her hair was blown out and her nails buffed and polished. A cosmetician applied cleansers, toners, moisturizer, antioxidants and foundation. When the woman reached for her color palette, Luli said, "I'll do it."

It had been years, but her muscle memory for liquid eyeliner and blending hues to contour her bone structure served her well.

Even so, when she stood dressed and ready in front of the mirror, she saw a stranger. Not because it had been so long since she had seen herself stage ready, but because she was no longer fourteen. Being twenty-two shouldn't have made such a difference when she had been acting like an adult as an adolescent, but it did. Rather than looking like a girl playing dress up, she looked like a woman. A confident, self-possessed, beautiful woman.

Act like you believe it, she silently told the apprehensive face in the mirror.

"Monsieur Dean has arrived," her seamstress came in to advise her. "*Ooh, là là!* He will faint. I may." She fanned her face.

"Thank you," Luli said, accepting the compliment graciously, as her mother had taught her to do. Anything less would suggest she believed herself inferior in some way.

Luli gave herself a final scrutiny, adjusted her posture and ensured she stood as tall as she was able. Then she thought back to the puppy she had played with as a child. She didn't recall whom it had belonged to, but the memory was one she had always used to awaken a feeling of happiness within her. It was the happiest she'd ever felt.

She faltered. Had she really not had a happy moment since then?

"Perhaps you would like to carry this instead?" the seamstress said, offering a Cleopatra clutch in black alligator skin with an ornate silver clasp.

Luli had kept her wallet in her line of sight the entire time she'd been here, terrified that if it disappeared, *she* would. She used the excuse of changing purses to check *again* that her precious identification was still in her possession. She handed off the empty wallet to the woman who promised to bag it with the items going to the car.

Emotion threatened to swamp her afresh as she absorbed what Gabriel had given her with a few legal documents. Options. Possibility. The gift of existence was greater than any haute couture dress or designer handbag or limitless credit card.

It was a miracle.

She *did* have a more recent memory of happiness, she realized. This. As she snapped the clutch closed and turned its tiny lock, she let the glow of gratitude toward him seep through her until joy shone from her smile and radiated from her demeanor.

With every ounce of grace she had ever possessed, she walked to the reception lounge.

Gabriel turned from instructing the couturier to box up as much as possible by morning so they could take it on the jet with them—and all the air was punched from his lungs.

A goddess approached in an unhurried gait that rocked her hips. Her skirt wafted back from her mile-long legs and her breasts bounced lightly above a long, slender waist. Her hair slithered in loose ribbons of caramel with glints of cool platinum against the warm gold of her bare shoulders and upper chest.

Her face was an angel's, luminous and pure. Aside from the dramatic lines that accented her eyes and gave them a hint of tilt, she wore little makeup. Or wore it so well, it was barely noticeable. Her lashes were naturally long and thick. He'd studied them while she had slept on the plane. Her succulent lips were accentuated with a delicate pink and shone with gloss. Her smile was one of exultation. Whatever she was celebrating, he decided she was entitled to it.

He couldn't fault her in that moment for one damned thing.

She halted before she reached him, struck a pose, pivoted to show the back of the dress. It lifted and floated back down before she pivoted again and continued toward him with a playful sparkle in her eye.

The entire move had been executed so smoothly, he chuckled with enjoyment.

"Maximum points for first impression, I hope. Otherwise we start again." She met his gaze without shyness, smiling, utterly composed.

She was sexy as hell.

Virgin, he reminded himself, yet the only thing that kept him from ravishing her on the spot was their rapt audience.

She was waiting for his judgment, he realized, as she continued looking at him and he noted tension creep in around her smile. The flutter of her pulse in her throat grew more rapid, exactly as it had been when she had quietly challenged him in his grandmother's office.

"You broke the scale." He brought her hand to his mouth, wanting to place his lips in far more intimate places than her soft knuckle. "And good thing because I'm too hungry to wait while you start again. This is for you."

He gently splayed out her hand and threaded the ring onto her finger.

It was a performance for their audience and she gasped with appropriate amazement at the fifteen-carat marquise-cut blue diamond. Its split shank was coated in white diamonds to set off the rare color of the center stone.

The women around them squealed with excitement.

"I don't know what to say," Luli said faintly.

"Thank you?" he suggested dryly, and did what was expected, taking her into his arms for a kiss.

Her arms went around his neck and her heart pounded so hard he felt it against his chest, teasing his own to come race with hers. He kept the kiss light, not wanting to ruin her lipstick, but her lips clung shyly to his and she slid her lashes down with awareness as he released her.

He groaned inwardly. Virgin she might be, but her response to his touch was the most erotic thing he'd ever experienced.

"Good night, ladies. Your extra effort won't go unrewarded," he said with a nod.

Voices wished them a lovely evening and he escorted her to the car, for once anticipating the entrance they would make. Women invariably wanted to be seen with him, whether it was an innocent business meeting or a lengthy, more intimate association. He found the quest for attention tiresome, but accepted it.

With Luli, however, he was already smiling inwardly at the stir she would cause. He usually only felt this sense of excitement when one of his personal projects went to market—a niche app or something else he had poured himself into developing.

He was swelling with pride, he realized, but not of ownership. He didn't take credit for this transformation or even for the discovery of her.

No, he was simply proud to be with a woman who shone brighter than the midday sun.

CHAPTER SIX

THE RESTAURANT WAS a converted house in the Sixth Arrondissement, once owned by an art dealer. It brimmed with impressionist paintings and priceless objets d'art. A murmur went through the diners in the main lounge and piano bar as they were shown through to an atrium with only one table that was obviously reserved for the most illustrious customers.

A small fountain and an abundance of ferns provided a modicum of privacy, but the glass walls and ceiling provided none. Luli didn't care who looked at them. She was too busy taking in the fat moon above the glittering Eiffel Tower.

"I've wanted to come to Paris since I first understood what it was. I can't believe I'm here," Luli said, trying not to betray her complete awe.

"We'll come back soon. I have to get back to some meetings I left when you texted about my grandmother."

"Was that a flash?" She looked toward the fountain.

"Outside? Yes."

"No, from—"

A jewel-bedecked customer had crept to the fountain and held a smartphone in the air space behind the streaming water, aiming it at them. One of the servers in a black vest and long white apron hurried to draw the woman away.

"Ignore it," Gabriel said. "My security team will address it."

She couldn't. Glints of light were popping against the wall of shrubbery beyond the atrium's walls and on the rooftop of the adjacent building.

"I used to dream of being so famous everyone would want my photo. It's quite intrusive, isn't it? How do you stand it?"

"Honestly, I'm not of much interest to the paparazzi unless I'm with a woman. Even then, it very much depends on who she is. I met with a married actress a couple of times, years ago. She was researching a part. It was completely innocuous, but she was of a mind that any publicity was good publicity. She tipped off photographers every time and the entertainment sites made it into something it wasn't. The movie did well at the box office and on the award circuit. Perhaps her strategy had some weight." He told her whom it had been. She was quite famous, but old enough to be his mother.

Their wine was delivered and poured. Luli didn't know where to look. Outside at the cameras? At the craning necks in the main part of the restaurant? Looking at Gabriel would only get her tangled up in his gaze.

"I suppose your connection to your grandmother makes you news right now," she murmured, studying the ornate silver stem and the patterns etched into the tulip-shaped red bowl of her one-of-a-kind handcrafted wineglass—or so their server had informed her.

"My grandmother's connection to me affects people who have business dealings with Chen Enterprises.

I'm already so rich. No one could care less that I just got richer."

"But you said the paparazzi only pay attention to you if the woman you're with is famous. They don't know who I am."

"Exactly." One corner of his mouth went up in a cynical curl. "The waitstaff is going to make a bundle in tips from people wanting your name. Joke's on them. I didn't offer it."

"They wouldn't recognize it anyway. I'm nobody."

The waiter brought an amuse-bouche—a spoon that held a deviled quail's egg on a mushroom cap with a glazed baby carrot next to it.

"It seems silly that anyone would care," she continued. "I'm as guilty as the next person for following celebrity gossip. Your grandmother subscribed to overseas magazines and I love royal wedding photos and the like, but—*oh*."

"You've arrived. Welcome." His lingering smile held gentle mockery. "Yes, everyone is trying to be the first to report on my marriage. More pointedly, to *whom*."

"I suppose that is news." *She* was. She sobered as she recalled how attentive the *couturier* and her staff had been. "Was there someone else they expected? Are you *with* someone?" She should have asked that several kisses ago.

"Only you," he said dryly. "A press release goes out at midnight explaining I've been quietly courting my grandmother's business manager and we've made it official."

"No one is going to believe that. Or that I'm a business manager." She thought of the butler trying to throw her out on her ear, first chance he got.

"It doesn't matter what they believe, only what I know. While you were playing dress up, I accessed the backup files and ran some reports for my edification. You make a lot of small adjustments that make a big difference. You do, in fact, manage her business affairs."

"Mae liked me to be vigilant."

"But you did much of it electronically. I saw the scripts you inserted to alert you when something falls outside your parameter sets. You've been playing with my back end for a while."

She had, but he didn't need to make it sound so suggestive.

Their plates were exchanged. A light shell of something that might have been egg white had been quick fried into a lacy web and bent into a basket while warm. It held a leg of squab, a half dozen bright green peas and a dollop of what she learned was whipped turnip. A smear of chili sauce framed it and violets were sprinkled for decoration.

"If you've gone that far," she said, hand going to the clutch in her lap. "You're able to restore from backup and lock me out."

"I could. But I refuse to take the easy way. I won't let you get the better of me."

"Because I'm a woman?"

"I'm competitive, not sexist."

"How did *you* learn to code?" She snapped a strand from the basket and discovered it was made of sharp cheese, rich and salty against her tongue.

"My grade school had three afterschool clubs—computers, arts and athletics. I didn't want to go home, so I had to pick one. I can speak on a stage if I have to, but

I have no talent for performing or other creative pursuits. I was decent in track and field, but have no interest in team sports. The isolation of a computer screen, however, was my dream habitat."

"Why didn't you want to go home?"

"My father was a drunk and not fun to be around."

"I'm sorry."

"It's not your fault."

She couldn't help noticing the strain of his shirt across his chest, as though his muscles had tensed despite the fact he sounded very indifferent and relaxed.

"I read that you're a black belt in kung fu."

"It's a good workout and clears my mind."

"When did you start?"

"When bullies started calling me Kung Fu Kid." He pointed at the tiny overlap at the corner of his eye. "I went to the nearest dojo and offered my computer skills in exchange for lessons. It was another convenient way to avoid going home."

"Did you teach those bullies a lesson?"

"My *sifu* taught me not to care what they said."

"You never fought back?" What was the point in going all the way to black belt, then?

"I threw a boy to the ground once, when he tried to start something. His friends were right there, planning to help. Word got around and they stopped bothering me. Then I sold my app and everyone wanted to be my friend."

"You were twelve? It was a game, wasn't it?"

"This is why I never bother talking about myself. Anything of note has already been documented online." He cleaned the meat off the delicate bone in one bite and set it aside.

"I don't know much more than that, except that you won a national competition for young entrepreneurs and caught the attention of Silicon Valley. They paid you a million dollars?"

"Which caught my grandmother's attention. She came to warn me not to let my father take control of my money. He cautioned me against trusting her. They had a heated discussion and I didn't hear from her again until she came to his funeral."

"She didn't try to help you? Did she realize your father had a drinking problem?"

"Given how furious she was with my mother, I believe she probably did. I didn't want her help."

"Why not?"

"My own version of Stockholm syndrome, I suppose. The devil you know and all that."

She absorbed that, thinking he was onto something. She had rationalized staying with Mae rather than taking the hard road of striking out on her own. Before that, she had tried relentlessly and earnestly to earn her mother's regard.

"Did you keep control of your money?" she asked.

"More or less. I hired a certified advisor and talked my father into paying off our mortgage, which had been my grandmother's advice."

"Real estate has been very good to her."

"And me. I invested heavily in property as I sold more apps. It came easily to me. Felt like a license to print money. When I was fifteen, I hired a private tutor so I had more flexibility with my education. I graduated high school early and completed a business degree before I turned twenty. I predicted the financial crash and was one of those select few who came up roses."

"And your father…?"

"Drank himself to kidney failure, but lived comfortably until then. I supported him, put him in rehab several times. It never took." He used a jagged corner of shell to stab a pea and ate it with a crunch.

"Did he have other family? Do you have cousins?"

"A handful of people who didn't want to know him, but who crawl out of the woodwork periodically to ask me for start-up capital. Some ventures succeed, others have gone bust. It's another reason I've kept my distance from my grandmother. It's hard to say no to family, but it can be foolish to say yes. Do you have family besides your mother and father? Is he still alive?"

"I haven't seen anything online about him since he went to prison for corruption a couple of years after I left for Singapore. I guess his sons are my half brothers, but I've never met them or tried to reach out." She wrinkled her nose in dismay. "I presume they're much like him. My mother's family was very poor. She never spoke of them. I wouldn't know where to begin looking for them and have no reason to."

It was odd to talk about herself. No one had asked about her life or seemed interested in it for years.

Their plates were cleared and bowls of warm, scented water brought to rinse their hands.

"We should dance," Gabriel said when she looked toward the drift of piano notes from the other side of the restaurant.

She shook her head. "I took ballet years ago, but only to help with grace and posture. I've never danced for real."

"With a man, you mean? That's a good reason to do it, then, isn't it?" He rose and held out his hand. "Leave that here," he said of the clutch she would have carried with her. "It's perfectly safe."

She nervously left it on the chair as she rose and placed her hand in his. An electric current seemed to run from the weave of their fingers up her arm to start an engine purring in her chest.

Eyes followed them, but she kept her gaze on the lobe of Gabriel's ear as he wound through the tables ahead of her. Out of nowhere, she wondered what it would be like to nibble his ear. People did that, didn't they? Would he like it? Tendrils of intrigue unfurled inside her at the thought of dabbling her tongue there and sucking. Of him doing it to her. She had to stifle a reflexive moan at the carnal fantasy.

Along with the pianist, there were a cellist and a violinist. It was like being in a movie as he turned when they reached the dance floor and drew her into his arms. She felt as though she floated when they began to move together.

"You're perfect," he said as he led with athletic grace.

Her light skirt lifted and fell against her bare legs in a sensual caress while she absorbed the strength of him, the surety of his touch moving her about so effortlessly. A pleasurable heat suffused her and she knew this would be her new memory for her stage smile. She didn't know if she'd ever felt so light in her life. So carefree and purely, simply *happy*.

She suspected she was actually asleep and would wake in her plain room in the servants' quarters of Mae's mansion very soon.

"The entire place is spellbound," he murmured, making her falter slightly.

"Was that the goal?"

"I can't deny I wanted to see their reaction."

"Why?" She became self-conscious and had to concentrate to ensure she didn't misstep.

"A crowd like this is used to being surrounded by beauty. You're above and beyond anything they will have ever seen."

"Is that what I am? A piece of art you've acquired?" Was that why he hadn't said anything about their kiss?

His mouth was no longer relaxed. "No."

"What, then? A project? A percentage?"

"I have no idea. You're unlike anything *I've* ever encountered."

"But you want to twirl me around and say, *Look what I found.*"

"I want to feel you in my arms." His voice was low and powerful enough to resonate through her.

Somehow he kept them moving without bumping into anyone while she tried to read his eyes. She didn't know what she was seeing in those rocky ocean depths.

"You haven't said anything since I told you," she reminded him.

"Is it true?" he demanded.

"I'm looking to you for guidance because I have no idea what I'm doing." She spoke with a thread of wildness in her voice. The sense of spinning beyond herself was growing as she realized exactly how much she was looking to him—because she was that far out of her depth in every single way.

His cheek ticked. "I wish I knew whether I could believe you."

"What reason would I have to lie?"

"The twenty million I just dropped on clothes and shoes, perhaps?"

"You didn't." She stopped dancing. The world continued to sway and swirl. She thought she might faint as all her lifeblood dropped into her feet. "Please say it wasn't that much."

"With the ring, closer to thirty. It's Paris, Luli. What did you think?"

Sequin-covered bikinis and formal evening gowns were expensive, but they were the price of pageant entry, maybe the cost of bus fare or a flight to get to the competition. They weren't the value of a district's worth of housing. What had she done? She clung to his sleeve to keep herself upright, vision hazy as she absorbed that she had indebted herself to him far beyond anything she could have imagined.

His arms firmed around her, supporting her. "Look at me. Are you all right?"

"I think I'm going to be sick."

If he had wanted to create a sensation, mission accomplished. Speculation about his mysterious new wife would shift to whether she was carrying his child as she paled and leaned into him.

"Come sit down." He led her back to their table.

She took her clutch into her lap and, he suspected, checked for her passport, judging by the furtive movement beneath the edge of the table.

"Have a sip of water," he ordered. "Then tell me why you're upset." She had handled the shopping like a pro. He wasn't complaining about the cost, only pointing out that it made for a strong motive where manipulating his emotions was concerned.

"Why would you do that?" Her hand shook as she

sipped. Tears brimmed her mink lashes. "I'll never be able to pay you back. *Never.*"

"I don't expect you to."

The waiter brought their next course and she turned her face to the window to hide her distress. Gabriel waved him off from pouring fresh wine.

The single braised lamb chop with watercress and candied pistachios was decorated with a sprig of rosemary, pearl onions and dots of orange and mint sauces. Gabriel thought it looked appetizing, but Luli looked at her plate with misery. He didn't dare tell her that the lamb had been flown in fresh from New Zealand this morning and the six vintage wine pairings they would sample with each course were thousands of euros each.

Minutes ago, she'd been incandescent, fully enjoying herself. Her mood had started to dim when she had asked if she was a project for him.

"Luli." He set his hand palm-up on the table, wanting her to look at him. "I told you I don't pay for sex. I don't buy women. You don't owe me anything."

"I keep thinking I'll wake up in my room. I wish I would." She pinched her arm.

That bare cell of a room with not so much as a family photo or a glimmer of vibrant beauty that was *her*? *No.*

"I shouldn't have started this," she said with a despairing shake of her head. "I wanted to take control. I thought I could handle it, even if it was difficult. It was very hard when I arrived in Singapore, but I got through it. I'm a strong person," she insisted, but sounded like she was trying to convince herself. "This is too much."

Her gaze finally met his and the rawness she exposed clawed at his heart.

"Whatever you think you can turn me into, I'm *not*." She looked to the windows, then the other direction, then the ceiling, as though she sought escape and realized she was cornered. Her breasts rose against the binding of her dress, plumping with each shaking breath.

"Luli." He wiggled his fingers. "Give me your hand. This is culture shock. That's all."

"Culture shock!" She blinked and a tear fell to glisten diamond sharp on her cheekbone. Her hands stayed in her lap.

"Culture assault," he corrected dryly. He should have anticipated it. Even his top executives dropped their jaws and bumbled with nerves when they caught a glimpse of how he lived. "Would you like to leave?"

"Does it matter what I want? Why did I think I should fight so hard or reach so high? It's not as though I could make myself matter by wearing new clothes and going outside. I'm still *nothing*."

"We're going all the way to existential crisis? Come on, then. We'll take this somewhere more private." As he helped her into the car moments later, she heard him tell his driver, "Cancel the helicopter. We'll go to the apartment."

"Where were you going to take me in a helicopter?" she asked twenty minutes later, when he joined her on the balcony of his modern penthouse.

The colorful reflections on the Seine were smudged lines through the sparkling cityscape below. The Eiffel Tower was so big before her, she could have reached out and touched it.

She was still overwhelmed, still feeling like she was

on stage, wearing this gown, but the bricked patio was about the size of Mae's courtyard. The darkness turned down the volume on how alien the world had become, giving her a chance to catch her breath and grapple her emotions back under control.

"I was going to take you to my *château*. Do you want anything? I could order take-out noodles and roast pork. That might feel more familiar."

"You have a house *and* a flat here?"

"I've been restoring the *château* since I bought it two years ago. I've never stayed there. It was built in the sixteen hundreds as a folly for the King's mistress and has become one of mine. I have to park my money somewhere." He leaned his elbows on the wall and studied the city below them.

At the word *mistress*, she had to ask. "Why did you want to take me there?" For seduction?

"It's pretty. I thought you'd like it. At least I thought that a few hours ago, when I made the arrangements and you were having fun spending my money."

"Why did you *let* me? I don't understand what you want from me," she said with a throb in her voice. "Am I a white elephant, more curse than blessing? A pretty adornment for your arm? Am I supposed to sleep with you because you saved me? Because we're *married*?"

"One way or another, you were going to save yourself. We both know that, Luli." His voice was firm and strong, if a shade rueful. "All I'm doing is adding accelerant."

"Why?"

"Because you're a riddle. I enjoy puzzles."

"I want to be a woman. My own woman," she said, soft and fierce.

But she was realizing that leaving Mae's house and building a new, independent life were two very different things. There was a wide chasm that had to be bridged and she didn't have the skills or resources to do it.

He sighed. "If I see you as a woman, I'll want to sleep with you."

She hugged herself and rubbed her arms, even though she wasn't cold. In fact, she grew warm. Empty in a way that longed for him to hold her and kiss her and fill her with all those sensations that made the world a magical place.

"What's so bad about that?"

"You said you were saving your virginity," he reminded. "For who?"

"I don't know. You? You're supposed to wait, aren't you? For your wedding night?"

A long, tense silence.

"I haven't," he finally stated.

She sighed, admitting heavily, "I thought it might mean something to whoever it was. Have value. Maybe even if I was desperate—"

"Your virginity is not a commodity, Luli," he cut in sharply. "Your body isn't. Save yourself for a relationship that matters. Someone special."

"So you don't…" She swallowed. "Want me? Because I'm a virgin?"

"Have you looked in a mirror? Of course I want you. I'm saying don't have sex with the first man you marry."

She choked on a laugh, recognizing it as a joke, but *they were married.*

"You talked about becoming a trophy wife and that led me to believe you were experienced. Given that you're not…" His voice became tight with reluctant honor. "I don't know that we should go there. You would want what every woman eventually asks for and I can't give you that."

"Children? I don't want them. Not for a long time, if ever. That's totally fine if you can't make them."

Another pointed silence, then a husk of a laugh.

"I was going to say love, but you continue to confound me." He straightened and leaned his hip against the low wall. "Why don't you want children?"

"I can't even take care of myself!" She waved a helpless hand through the air.

"You're so blind." He reached out and gave a tendril of her hair a small tug. "My grandmother employed two hundred people directly, not to mention the ten or so thousand who work for companies in which she invests. Who looks after all of them? Her? No."

"That was with *her* money and resources. I don't even have pajamas. I'll be sleeping in the clothes you gave me on the airplane." She wondered where they were.

Wondered why he couldn't love her. Far above Paris and freedom and all the other fantasies she had ever had was the dream that one day she would be loved. Was she not worthy of such a thing? Why not?

"Silly girl," he said. "You have six cases of ready-to-wear in the guest room. Didn't you hear the bell when the concierge delivered them?"

"What bell? *Six?* Gabriel, I can't!"

"Don't start hyperventilating again. Come on. I want to show you something. You'll like it." He took her hand in his warm one and drew her inside.

Her heels clicked on the herringbone pattern in the parquet floor of the hall. The penthouse was bigger than the bottom floor of Mae's sprawling mansion, but this was located atop a skyscraper. It was modern, but filled with old-world touches in the wainscoting and crown moldings. A castle in the sky.

"Your room," he said, pushing open a door into a darkened room where a half dozen suitcases stood at the foot of a wide bed. "But come into mine."

Her heart rate picked up.

He didn't turn on any lights as they entered the massive room with the massive bed. She barely looked that direction or took in anything else. She was drawn to the primordial glow of the floor-to-ceiling aquarium.

She gasped, pulled forward by the muted burble to feast her eyes on the iridescent blues and neon pinks, the fierce reds and flashing yellows. Spots adorned long lacy tails that swished in slow motion while striped orange missiles darted into crevices in the colorful fingers of coral and swaying blades of sea grass.

She didn't know where to look and grew dizzy trying to take it all in. She wanted to lean against the glass, breath fogging upon it as she watched.

"You like?" His arm came around her waist and she leaned into him, overwhelmed, but this time in a way that was gentle and full of wonder.

"Your grandmother's pond only had koi. They were pretty, but nothing like this. It's so beautiful."

"Can you see the tub on the other side?" he pointed. "I'll run you a bath and you can watch the fish, then dream all night that you're swimming with them."

She wanted to laugh, but his arm around her felt so nice her own arms reached to encircle him on instinct, needing to cling to him for fear of going adrift.

"No one has hugged me since—" She couldn't remember. A long, long time ago. She welled up and began to shake.

"Shh." His hand offered a soothing caress against her ribs. "Keep it together, Luli. I'm useless with tears."

He wasn't, though. As she began to sob in earnest, he shifted so she was pressed fully to his front. He held her in a firm embrace that kept her from breaking into a thousand disjointed pieces and spoke against the part in her hair.

"It's okay. You're not in there. You're out here. *Breathe.*"

CHAPTER SEVEN

Despite a long bath after her breakdown, Luli didn't dream of the fish. She dreamed of Gabriel's arms around her and his soothing voice and his strong hand rubbing her back. She dreamed he was beside her in the bed, his hands on her breasts and seeking their way into other secretive places.

But he wasn't. And she woke in a sweat, loins aching, embarrassed with herself for such erotic fantasies.

The lingering memory made her self-conscious as she emerged from her room, dreading making eye contact, but Gabriel was on the phone behind the closed door of his office—which perversely made her disappointed.

A servant invited her to a table in a nook that caught the morning sun and overlooked the Seine. She brought her a blessedly familiar breakfast of rice porridge and *kaya* toast with soft eggs. Afterward, Luli took her second cup of French-press coffee to the balcony where she listened to the city noises that were both the same and different from the ones she had heard beyond the garden gate.

"Good morning."

Gabriel's voice sent a rush of startled pleasure

through her, along with a rush of memory at her subconscious yearnings. She blushed.

"Good morning," she said shyly, turning to catch his gaze lifting from her thighs in the jeans she'd put on with a T-shirt, something she hadn't worn in years, but that felt comfortable and right.

The way his expression flickered made her smooth an uncertain hand down her hip. "I thought we were just going to the showroom so it didn't matter what I wore."

"Small change of plan," he said with a humorless smile. He tsked as his phone buzzed in his hand. "The press release is out. This is turning into something I want to drop off that balcony." He held up the phone and nodded at the half wall she leaned against.

"What's the new plan?" She folded her arms, bracing herself.

"Apparently newlyweds go on something called a honeymoon. I have been asked a thousand times where ours will take place."

A pulse of anticipatory heat struck her loins. She blushed even harder, with guilt, as if he could see into her filthy mind and know what she had imagined. Could tell what she longed for.

"What I said last night stands." His cheek ticked and he looked away, mouth tight. "But a week out of the public eye will give you time to get used to all this while the attention dies down."

He wasn't happy. She could tell and lowered her lashes, feeling like a burden.

"I'm s—"

His phone buzzed again and he swore. "I have to take this. They're packing for us. We'll leave shortly."

"Where are we going?"

"Safari." He swiped to accept his call.

"Safari! *Where?*"

"Africa. Where else do you go on safari?"

Eight hours later, his sound-barrier-defying jet landed them in Tanzania. They climbed aboard a helicopter for another hour, but it passed quickly as she kept her nose pressed to the glass, viewing herds of zebras and wildebeests, elephants and antelope and giraffes from above.

Then they were on the ground, traveling by Jeep, passing within a few hundred meters of more animals, pausing beside a waterhole where muddy hippos wallowed and yawned.

Their driver did most of the talking. Gabriel wore mirrored aviator sunglasses and stretched his arm behind her seat, both tense and relaxed. Each time she smiled in wonder at him, she found him watching her and her heart skipped and bounced in reaction.

He must think her so foolish, snapping her neck around as she tried to take it all in, but if she didn't immerse herself in the spectacle around them, she would grow too conscious of his thigh splayed near her own. Or the way she would only have to slide down a little in her seat to nestle into that space beneath his arm.

He had told her they were staying in a camp, but despite the grass-pressed mud walls and thatched roofs, the collection of buildings was as luxurious as his supersonic airplane. They were shown through the main lodge where a dining room was set with china and crystal. A sturdy suspension bridge took them across a wide, shallow stream where crocodiles lurked. Strange birdcalls followed them into the open air of their raised villa. It had three bedrooms, each with a bed canopied in mosquito netting and a deck with a view across the Serengeti.

As she watched the setting sun streak glorious magenta and scarlet, indigo and marigold across the horizon, she heard the noise of ice shifting in a bucket behind her. She turned to see Gabriel in the shadowed lounge behind her, heard him peel the foil from the bottle he held.

"Do you want to put the light on?" she asked.

"Not yet. You make an interesting optical illusion standing there so still. Like a black hole in the shape of a woman cut from a piece of painted paper."

It was an innocuous thing to say, but knowing he'd been looking at her again made wires of tension tighten inside her.

"I'd forgotten what a big place the world really is." She looked out again, watching the last of the light fade. "It's as noisy as the city here, but in a different way, which makes it seem quiet. I feel small and remote and I should probably be terrified to be so far from civilization, but I just feel…calm."

The cork popped.

She chuckled at the incongruous, yet perfect timing. "Maybe not that far from civilization."

"No," he agreed.

She had the feeling his efficient staff packed "civilization" for him the way anyone else remembered a toothbrush.

"We should take this to the plunge pool. Cool off before dinner," he suggested as she came in to take a glass.

"I'd love that. I feel all sweaty. I'll change and join you there."

Not ready to walk out in, essentially, a bra and panties, she chose a tankini. The bottoms were black short shorts, the top a formfitting print that tied behind her neck. Bright swirls of neon twisted over and under the cups, accentuating her bust.

The small pool was situated in a grotto-like private balcony off the master bedroom, which Gabriel was using. Four torches cast flickering light and left a citrus scent in the air that she suspected were meant to discourage insects. Gabriel was in the water, his arms stretched along the edges, hair wet and slicked back from his face.

She tiptoed down the steps into the cool water, sipped her champagne and set it on the edge. And wondered how awkward the next week would be, trying to make conversation with a man who expressed so little.

"You would think they would situate the pool so guests could watch the sun set," she murmured, seeing nothing but bush around them.

"The privacy allows for suits to be optional."

She snapped him a look and he chuckled.

"Your face is priceless. I'm wearing a suit." He stood in a rush of water so she could see the snug band of black.

Not *much* of a suit. The water trickled and slid in silvery trails down every glorious bronze plane and dent in his chiseled physique. A black arrow of hair disappeared into the low band and the fabric cupped—

She jerked her gaze off that bulge and quickly wet her dry throat with a gulp of champagne. She thought he chuckled again, but he turned away to fetch the bottle out of the bucket, which he'd left on the edge near the stairs. He waded across to top up her glass, then refilled his own and settled beside her.

But she sensed his tension.

"Are you angry that we had to come here?" she asked.

"I don't have to do anything." He turned his head to regard her. "Neither do you."

And just like that, she understood his tension was the same kind that gripped her—sexual.

"What if I want to?" It was her *honeymoon*.

He stretched out his arm, setting his glass on the edge and tipping back his head. His chest rose above the water as he took in a deep breath and let it out.

"Do you know where babies come from, Luli?"

"Oh, for— Is that a real question? Yes." She rolled her eyes.

"Being a virgin, I'll presume you're not on any sort of contraception?"

"I've heard of something called condoms?" she shot back facetiously, then buried her mouth against the rim of her glass, admitting, "I'm *curious*."

"Curious is fine." He abruptly gathered her, easily floating her in the water so she was sitting with her knees straddling his thighs. His hands sat against the crook where the tops of her thighs met her hips, hot palms branding her through the fabric of her short shorts. "I'm more than curious. I'm obsessed with finding out how high this fire between us might burn."

That fire was beginning to consume her now. "Okay," she breathed, leaning in.

His thumbs dug in at her hips.

"But slipups happen. I signed our marriage contract thinking you would provide me an heir. If you don't want children, I'm not going to force you, but I will need some. If you don't want them, we'll have to divorce at some point so I can marry someone else who does."

She sat back and bit her lip in consternation.

"You see? I wasn't entirely joking when I said you shouldn't give your virginity to the first man you marry. How involved do you want to get, knowing this marriage won't last?"

"What is my second husband likely to think if I show up a virgin? You're appalled and—"

"I'm not appalled. I'm recognizing that your inexperience makes you vulnerable."

"Then give me experience," she near cried. "I've never had a boyfriend, never done anything. Here I am married, on my honeymoon, and I get nothing? That's so *typical* of the way my life goes."

She started to shift off his lap, but his hands tightened. His cheekbones were like scraped granite, high and hard.

"Stay." His voice was harsh, but not angry. "Kiss me. Take what you want, then."

She wanted to ask if he meant it, but her voice was caught in her throat and her thoughts burned away in the flare of heat in his gaze.

His hands shifted, barely moved really, but the easing of his thumbs at the front of her hip bones and the subtle pressure of his fingertips against the swells over her butt urged her to lean forward.

She started to set her hands on his shoulders, realized she still held her half glass of champagne and put it on the edge. Then she set her hands against the tense muscles of his neck and kissed him.

She kissed him the way he had kissed her, with long slides of her mouth across his, lips parted so they could taste one another. He was delicious. Better than champagne. And the way he kissed her back was pure magic.

She wanted to do this forever, mouth catching at mouth, easing away then sinking back to be devoured by him.

She couldn't get close enough. She shifted, arched under the slide of his hands up her back and—

Oh. She knew what that pressure was, startlingly hard against the tender flesh between her legs. She tensed in surprise, rising slightly as her thighs tried to close.

He didn't disguise the hunger in his expression, didn't flinch from the fact she knew he was aroused. He only quirked a brow in silent query. A tug between her shoulder blades released the tension of the tie behind her neck and relaxed the fabric across her breasts.

She instinctively caught at it, saw the passion in his eyes dim slightly at her reflexive modesty. He swallowed, nodded slightly.

She slowly let her hands drop, taking the front of her top with her.

Her breasts sat partially submerged, nipples thrusting in dark coral peaks above the surface.

For long moments, he simply stared, breath unsteady. Then he said, "I want to taste that."

His voice was a spell, drawing her to dig her fingers into the tendons across his shoulders and lift on her knees, glorying in the way his hands slid all the way to the backs of her thighs and steadied her. Encouraged her to arch and offer herself in a way that had always made her wonder if it could really be all that—

His mouth enclosed the tip in heat and she opened her mouth in a soundless scream. He wasn't gentle as he threw her into the inferno. He was scorching and greedy, filling her with the pound of her own heart so she rocked there gently in the water, hammered by pleasure as he sucked at her. Caught in a net of live wires that pulsed sensations into her loins.

Just when she thought she couldn't take any more, he moved to the other breast.

She speared her fingers through his damp hair, encouraged him to draw harder, only distantly aware that the noises she heard weren't from a jungle animal, but from the one inside her. She was pushing her backside into the hands that squeezed and roamed, and began to sink back down so she could feel that fierce pressure of him between her legs again.

"More?" he asked against her mouth.

"Yes," she moaned, and kissed him with flagrant passion, twining her arms around his neck and tilting her head for maximum submission to his kiss. She wanted him to know what he was doing to her and to keep doing it.

His arms hardened. He lifted her as he stood in a sluice of water, surprising her into gasping. He turned and sat her on the edge.

"How much more? Lie back and let me taste the rest of you?"

Wicked tingles raced from her face to her breasts and deep into the flesh protected by the shorts he began to peel off her hip. She didn't have it in her to be quite so blatant, but he helped her, leaning over and licking at her nipples again so she eased back and let him have his fill.

He picked up the part of the top that covered her stomach and lifted it, kissed her quivering abdomen while his other hand continued easing the shorts off her hips. By the time she had to pick up her hips so he could get them right off, she was screaming with anticipation.

She let her eyes drift shut then, "Oh!"

He poured the cool champagne across the tops of her legs, chuckling at the way she jumped before he leaned down to take a long and luscious taste into the crease of her thigh.

"Still with me?" he asked, sipping from her navel and petting the backs of his knuckles over the fine hairs protecting her most sensitive flesh.

If she could form words, she would tell him he could do whatever he wanted to her. She was a virgin at the dragon's mercy, trapped in his private lair, feeling the heat of his breath.

"Yes," she hissed.

"You're beautiful. So beautiful," he said huskily, wafting the words across her mound. He shifted her thigh onto his shoulder and gently spread the slippery dampness of her response against the petals of her sex.

She made a noise of agony and tried to muffle it with the back of her wrist.

"Let me know you like it," he ordered.

"I do," she moaned, ready to beg if he didn't quit teasing.

His fingertip circled, knowing exactly what he was doing because he chuckled softly and said, "You do." Then the heat of the most intimate kiss arrived. He crooked her knee outward and took his time feasting on her, letting her bask in the sheer magnificence of the experience.

This, she thought, staring up at the star-speckled sky, feeling the hot night breeze sensually caressing her everywhere that he couldn't reach—*this* was luxury. She never wanted or needed anything else in the world except this.

His finger lightly probed, making her clench in reaction and intensifying the sensations.

"Hurt?" He withdrew.

"No. Please." She was panting and had to lick her lips.

His touch returned, making her throw her arm across her eyes and lift her hips as she groaned jaggedly. It was so good, so good, and he kept pleasuring her with unhurried caresses until she thought she would liquefy and disappear.

His intrusion deepened slightly, did something that made the pleasure sharpen and redouble. She bit down on her lip as he focused on delivering her past what she could bear and into a profound climax. She sobbed with abandonment as her stomach muscles contracted and her thighs quivered, the whole of her convulsing in glorious release.

Slowly he withdrew his touch and planted two gentle kisses on each of her inner thighs before he rose to kiss her still-trembling abdomen.

"I have to go shower. Now." His voice grated with strain. "Before I forget my good intentions and take this too far."

She rolled her head on the hard tiles beneath her, still filled with lassitude. "I'd like to touch you. Help."

"Do you realize what's going to happen if you do?"

"In theory." She smiled with her newfound womanly experience. "That's why I want to do it."

He made a noise that was both strangled laughter and defeat. In a lithe move, he settled beside her on the tiles and covered her mouth, kissing her with all the passion in him that had yet to be satisfied.

It made her hungry again and she kissed him with

abandon until he growled with suffering. She cupped his jaw, urging him to back off a little so she could see.

His tiny bathing suit was too small to contain his arousal. Fascinated, she started to reach out, glanced at him.

"Be my guest."

"Show me," she whispered.

He did, wrapping her hand around him and teaching her what he liked. They kissed again as she caressed him. Kissed until the hand he'd tangled in her hair stung and his body shuddered and his feral cries spilled across her lips.

They enjoyed a mellow dinner in the dining room, chatting on and off with the couple at the next table.

Luli almost felt as though Gabriel had deliberately drawn those other people in to dispel the intimacy between him and Luli, which stung. She was beginning to realize what he'd meant about how she needed to be careful how much of herself she gave him. He had warned her that physical closeness would make her long for the emotional kind and it was true. She already did.

What she didn't understand was why he didn't want to give it to her.

"Can I ask why you were estranged from Mae?" She paused on the bridge to take hold of the rope that formed the rails and looked up at the stars. "I know she didn't exactly reach out. She was very reserved. Is that a family trait?" she tacked on lightly.

"To some extent." He moved to stand beside her. "I don't spend a lot of time navel-gazing and paying therapists to tell me my family of origin is the source of all my problems, but what little I remember of my mother, she was very quiet. Regretful, perhaps, but I may be projecting. Given that Mae drove my mother to marry my father, I didn't see a point in pursuing a relationship with her and possibly winding up committing a similar act of recklessness."

"Present marriage excluded."

"Of course."

She smiled briefly, but it faded to sadness. "Your parents weren't in love?" Was that why he didn't feel he was capable of it? He had no example of it?

"My father was. Perhaps my mother was." What she could see of his shadowed expression was inscrutable. "I don't remember them fighting, but I was young."

"How did she die? Mae never said."

"A complication with her pregnancy. She wouldn't let them take the baby and they both died."

"I'm so sorry. That's terrible." She thought of Mae's inexpressive face on the few occasions when she had mentioned her daughter. She must have been containing so much pain.

Much like Gabriel's mask of indifference as he nodded toward the end of the bridge where their villa sat.

She didn't take the hint.

"You lost a brother or sister." He must be terribly lonely.

His shoulder jerked. "I wouldn't wish my childhood on anyone else."

She cocked her head, thinking of what he'd said about being bullied. "Mixed race? I thought America was the great melting pot, accepting of all."

"What does that even mean?" he scoffed. "I'm pig iron, that's true, but I wasn't something anyone had use for until I refined myself into that other American ideal, the self-made man." He spoke with an infinite depth of cynicism.

"I hate that feeling of not fitting." Her heart panged with more than empathy. She was living that feeling even now. "The pageant school was a competitive place, but at least we all looked and sounded the same. The whole time I've been at Mae's, I've felt like a big, sore thumb. Now I'm with you and I'm a square peg trying to fit into a dollar sign."

"Fitting in is overrated."

"I do that." In so many ways, they were so alike. "I convince myself I don't want what I can't have."

His resounding silence made her look up at him. He seemed so remote in that moment, her heart lurched.

"What I mean is, I always told myself it didn't matter that I didn't have money of my own because my needs were always met," she tried to explain. "It works as a coping strategy. Especially when I looked at all the money Mae had and she didn't have what she really wanted, which was her daughter."

Still he said nothing.

"I'm not saying you're wrong," she hurried on. "Mae *was* difficult. I presumed she was controlling and isolated me because she had lost her daughter, but it wouldn't surprise me if that was her nature from the beginning. Maybe your mother felt suffocated and pushed Mae away. I wouldn't think your mother giving birth to you was an act of defiance, though. She probably wanted a family. If she had survived and you had siblings, you maybe wouldn't have felt so set apart."

"It's late. We should both get some sleep." He touched her shoulder.

She hesitated. "Together?"

"I don't think that's wise." His flinty gaze met hers, read the injury she couldn't hide. "I did warn you," he said of his gentle rebuff.

If this was how much it hurt to be close to him, then pushed away, he was right. It was too much to bear. More than she wanted to risk.

Forlorn, she went to bed alone.

He didn't hear her so much as feel her move through the villa as sunrise approached. He rose from the bed where his mind had been too noisy and his body on fire with the knowledge he could have her—he only needed to compromise what few principles he had.

He had taken things way too far by the plunge pool, rationalizing that he was doing a damned public service by granting her the experience she craved.

He had pushed the boundaries, though. He had seduced her and had wanted all that they'd done and more. *Everything.* He was quite convinced she would have gone all the way if he'd guided her there.

Her startled newness to his most intimate caresses had told him she was as virginal as she claimed, however, passionate response notwithstanding. Recognizing that had allowed him to keep his head and take her to dinner instead of keeping her under him the rest of the night.

When she appeared dressed for dinner wearing a dreamy, adoring smile, he had realized his arrogant mistake. He had spent the next hours backpedaling, not wanting to lead her on.

Because he wasn't like other people. He might meet society's expectations by marrying and producing heirs, but only because he saw the elegant simplicity in it. He didn't want or need a wife and family. He wasn't trying to "fit in" or feel closer to anyone.

I do that. Convince myself I don't want what I can't have.

Her words shouldn't stick like a fishbone in his throat, but they did. He was an honest person, especially with himself. And he had always known himself to prefer being alone.

At least, he had managed to convince himself he preferred living solo. It wasn't lost on him that he was clinging to that belief even as he stood here watching her instead of lying alone in his bed.

She wore a pair of loose pajama bottoms and a snug, sleeveless top. She took a moment to look out at the western horizon, still purple and dotted with fading stars, then looked to the moon.

No. She was orienting herself.

She took up a stance facing north and rubbed her palms together, taking her time, taking in the world around her, taking a few deep breaths. Then she slowly drew her hands apart, fingers relaxed. She began to shape an invisible ball.

Chi.

He set his own palms together and began working up his own energy sphere as he walked out in his boxers and joined her.

She glanced at him, but neither said anything. He had taken the odd class in many different martial arts over the years, but hadn't done tai chi in a long time. Even so, it was easy to follow her fluid movement when she stepped her feet apart and began. As she turned west and moved so gracefully, her forms could have been mistaken for a modern ballet, but each move was as much a practice of self-defense as his own lightning-fast kung fu.

He matched his breathing to hers, mirroring the care she took as she moved in and out of block and protect, retreat and strike, gather chi, shield, jab and push, draw in again.

Did he notice the elegant line of her spine? The thrust of her breasts and the curve of her ass as she lunged? Yes. It filled him with sexual vigor and admiration for nature's ability to create perfection. It made him strive all the harder to execute each turn and press as precisely as possible, exactly as she did.

East now. Jab to chest while opponent is down. Twist. Perfectly synchronized, as if they'd been doing this all their lives, they spread crane wings and crept down with one leg extended, like a snake. His mind was filled with everything and nothing, thoughts flitting through to stick or fall as they would. He lived inside his muscles, his bones, his organs, aware of the slide of his blood in his arteries and the air exchanging in his lungs.

And just as his warmed hands had formed a ball of energy after he rubbed them together and held them apart, a similar force of *chi* grew in the space between them. As their bodies warmed and their breath soughed in measured hisses, his life force picked up hers and grew into something bigger, unseen, yet tangible. Energy swirled between them like ocean currents and trade winds and molten lava deep in the earth's core.

This was what it would be like to make love to her. Pure Zen. For a moment, he imagined this feeling could permeate a whole life together.

But that was an illusion. Another attempt to rationalize the sex he ached for. He'd seen the hurt in her expression last night. He couldn't ignore how vulnerable she was beneath that veneer of mouthwatering beauty and heart-stopping bravery.

She pivoted them north for the final scoop, bring feet together, fist into palm and close with a bow.

With his bent body, he thanked her for the practice and he thanked her for the teaching. He was not a man without cravings, only a man who pretended not to have them. But satisfying those cravings at the expense of someone else would put a weight on his soul.

So he would not, and could not, satisfy his craving for her. He would exercise discipline and resist.

He straightened and went directly to the chill waters of the plunge pool.

CHAPTER EIGHT

LULI FROWNED WHEN she logged in and saw a balance had dropped significantly lower than she expected. She popped into the account and gasped.

"You're in!" She flashed a look at Gabriel, lounging indolently on the sofa across from her, feet on the ottoman, his own laptop on his thighs. His amused gaze hit hers.

"Since last night. Took you long enough to notice."

"I haven't had a chance, have I?" They'd been on the savanna all day, then swam and ate and finally settled in with their devices a few minutes ago.

She closed the lid of her laptop, setting it aside. "Congratulations?" she offered.

His brows moved in an infinitesimal acknowledgment, unimpressed with his own prowess. Given this was how he made his living, she had expected him to outmaneuver her very quickly, but she still craved an acknowledgment of the effort it took him to do it. She wanted him to see her as a laudable opponent.

And she desperately needed to know, "What now?"

He already held all the power between them. Even the sexual supremacy. It didn't seem to matter if they were half-naked in the plunge pool, moving within inches of each other through the forms of tai chi or sitting like this, feet almost sole to sole. He indicated no more than casual awareness of her while she was in a constant state of heightened senses. His scent, the heat off his body, the husk of his laugh. It all made her thirst for *more*.

Consent went both ways, she kept telling herself morosely.

His cheeks hollowed. "Come tell me what's going on here." He nodded at his screen.

She moved to perch next to him. "Oh. I didn't agree with Mae on this, but she had a longtime relationship with that company."

Thirty minutes of discussion followed on a handful of other funds and transactions in Mae's portfolio. Gabriel had a higher risk tolerance than Mae, which made Luli feel defensive about the decisions she had made in the past.

Gabriel watched her mouth while she spoke, which distracted her. They were spending nearly every waking minute together. Which was the point of a honeymoon, she supposed, but married couples usually exorcised this tension with sex. Her desire for him was making it nearly impossible to respond to his incisive questions.

She finally sat back with her hands in her lap. By this time she had her knees folded beneath her and was facing him on the sofa.

"I have to know, Gabriel. Are you going to lock me out? I really like doing this."

"I can tell," he said, not mocking her. "And some of my Ivy League executives aren't putting this much analysis and consideration into their decisions. I can't run all these as separate entities for any length of time, though. It's not practical."

"You're firing me?"

"Consider yourself on notice. Keep doing what you're doing for the moment, but discuss all your decisions with me. I'll start breaking this into pieces and farming them out once we're back in New York and I can meet with some of my people."

"You just said I'm good at it!"

"No, I said you're thorough and careful. You're micromanaging, which has its drawbacks."

"You're going to fire me because I *care*? What am I supposed to do if I don't do this?

"Be a society wife?"

"Ha-ha. You don't want a wife. Not me, anyway. Is that why you're planning to fire me from that, too?" she asked on a sudden burst of understanding that his rejection had nothing to do with whether she wanted children. "Because I care too much?"

He turned his head, expression a dark glower. "Yes."

Crushed and trying not to show it, she shifted to sit straight, knees hugged to her chest. Her mind reached and tried to grasp, but only found thin air.

"Luli." He sighed. His elbow nudged hers. "I care enough to want to look after you. Don't worry about whether you're working."

"I want to look after myself," she muttered, feet hitting the floor in a stomp. "Of course I'm going to worry about it."

"Where are you going?" he asked as she started toward the door.

"Where any society wife goes when her husband tells

her to quit her job and stay home. To spend his money at the nearest shop."

"If you come back wearing zebra print, I'll divorce you on the spot."

"I'll buy them out, then." She swung the door shut behind her.

Disappointing a woman was not new territory for him. Feeling like an ass about it was. Gabriel stood by what he had said, though. It wasn't practical to keep her running a separate entity, double-checking and doubting herself, simply to give her something to do. Granted, she'd never been given the chance to take full responsibility. In time, she might prove to be more assertive and successful, but he'd find something else for her to cut her teeth on.

In the meantime, he half expected her to lock him out of Mae's accounts again—or at least try. He plugged all the holes she'd found in his code, but she was wily.

Apparently she wasn't the type to hold a grudge, though. She came back from the gift shop with a bar of specialty chocolate and offered him some.

"I'll find something for you," he promised her.

"I don't want nepotism. No one would respect me—including me." She popped a square into her mouth, chewed thoughtfully. "All I knew was beauty pageants until I worked for Mae. Education is never wasted, but sometimes you need more despite what you have. I'll figure out the next stage for myself. You don't have to give me a job just to make me feel useful."

He respected that desire for independence, but still wanted to look after her. It was a tough line to walk. He really wished he could see her as an employee or a

project or an exotic creature he could pet and pl___
and ultimately set free with smug satisfaction at ___
rescued and rehabilitated her.

But there was no hiding the fact she was a woman,
even when she dressed like a man.

He took her to the office with him when they landed
in New York. She was still caretaking Mae's investments and he had some ideas on how to utilize her
skills, but he needed to put a few more pieces in place
first.

Mostly he brought her with him because he couldn't
stand the idea of leaving her alone in his penthouse all
day. Which was all about her, he chided himself. *He*
could have gone those hours without seeing her just
fine.

With equal parts curiosity and wariness, she took her
cue from his custom-made suit and dressed in flared
pants with a matching pinstriped vest over a crisp white
shirt with a sharply pointed collar. She twisted her hair
up and carried a briefcase that cost as much as the sleek
new laptop within it. She rather cheekily pilfered one
of his ties and wore it loose enough her collar exposed
the hollow in the base of her throat.

She was sexy as hell. If anything, the contrast of
authoritative masculine clothes on her nonstop curves
made her femininity more obvious. Very much more
alluring.

After a week of trying to ignore her round ass in
snug khakis and the way perspiration gathered between
her breasts in her low, round-necked undershirts, it was
taking all his concentration to behave like a civilized
man when the territorial beast inside him wanted so
badly to *mate*.

But he couldn't. He didn't know how he would keep his control in place, but he would.

They turned heads as he walked her through his top-floor offices.

"That's the meeting I left when I got your message." He thumbed toward a glass wall into a boardroom where a dozen faces, stern and concerned and curious, watched them walk past. "Come find me if you need me. I'll be there for a few hours."

He continued along to the open door of the office closest to his own.

"Luli, this is Marco."

"Sir." The good-looking, well-dressed Latino man stopped typing and stood. He was a little older than Luli and eyed her with sharp interest as he came around to greet them. "Congratulations on your recent marriage, sir. And thank you for the promotion. I appreciate your thinking of me."

He shook Gabriel's hand and smiled warmly at Luli as he shook hers. "Mrs. Dean, welcome."

"Nice to meet you," Luli murmured shyly, gaze taking in the view of Central Park behind the sleek desk, the mini fridge beneath the bar and the presentation screen over the meeting table with four chairs. "I'll set up there and check in with Singapore while you're tied up?" she suggested to Gabriel, nodding at the table.

God, she was adorable.

"Luli, we've talked about this," he admonished sternly, enjoying her discomfiture as she widened her eyes and grew defensive.

"I want to make those transfers we talked about on the plane. You said I should continue doing what I was doing until you made other arrangements."

"Do your work at your desk. This is your office." He moved so she could see the plate on the door read Lucrecia Dean. "Marco has everything set up for you. He's your personal assistant. If you need anything—thumbtacks, dry cleaning, tickets to a Broadway show—he'll source it. But make sure I'm free to go with you. Sync our calendars," he told Marco.

"Done, sir."

"Thank you. Marco speaks Spanish," Gabriel added to Luli. "It's one of the reasons I thought he'd be a good fit for you."

"I barely do," she admitted sheepishly to Marco. "It's been such a long time." She pushed her mouth to the side in a look that was both reproving and rueful as she realized Gabriel had been deliberately teasing her, letting her think Marco was her boss or sitter. *"Gracias."*

"De nada. We have plans tonight. Steal a nap on the sofa in my office if you need it." Unable to resist, he kissed her cheek before he walked out.

Wear something dramatic, Gabriel had said when he informed her they would attend a black-tie gala benefiting a museum.

The gown Luli chose was made of stretch lace with subtle dragons embroidered into it. It clung to her arms and flared out at the hem to create the impression ink had been poured down her body and splashed out around her feet. It was lined with nude satin so she wore only a peach-colored thong beneath. The plunging neckline didn't allow for a bra and she applied double-sided tape against her cleavage to avoid a slip.

Her shoes were a glamorous half dozen straps bedecked with rhinestones and a high ankle strap. She straightened her hair to a sleek curtain combed back from her face then drew attention to her eyes with mauve and gold, chartreuse and teal. Her lips received a coat of dark red called Salem.

"Are you trying to kill me?" Gabriel stopped with his drink halfway to his mouth when she appeared.

"Really?" She smiled with shy pleasure and gave him the one-hand-on-her-hip pose. A small weight shift and she changed hands, giving her hair a slow flip along the way, so the curtain gently spilled off the back of her hand. She held her pose, chin high, gaze on the distant future, not a care in the world.

"You're going to put the entire city in the hospital." He pretended to take a phone call. "Yeah, that was my wife. I can't help it if she's that freaking hot. Get a better power grid because she's going to keep knocking it out."

She burst out laughing, flattered, but more bowled over that he would be so silly about it. It helped her relax and pin a smile of lingering humor on her face when they arrived at the chaotic zoo that was the red carpet.

An audible "Whoa..." rose from the crowd. Photographers hurried into position to snap their photo, demanding to know who she was wearing and how was her honeymoon and when had they started dating.

Gabriel drew her inside before she had to answer.

"Are there specific people you need to see tonight?" Luli asked as he handed her a flute of champagne. She wanted to be prepared and help in any way she could, not run away with a case of stage fright this time.

"They'll come to us," he said with careless arrogance. His eyes narrowed as she released a small snort. "What?"

"I'm wondering if you ever go to anyone." After seeing him in several environments now, she was realizing she wasn't the only one in awe of him. From janitor to pilot to executive to governor, people fell over themselves trying to anticipate his needs.

"Not if I can help it," he answered unabashedly. "I hate people. I only talk to them if they make me."

"Hmmph." She hollowed her cheeks and looked across the crowd.

"You don't count," he said.

"Because I'm not a person," she surmised.

She studied the tiara of a matron who passed them. Luli wore a pair of teardrop diamond earrings Gabriel had given her before they left. She hadn't wanted to accept them, but he had said they were a loan—unless she decided to keep them. Which she wouldn't. But she loved them and wished she could.

"Luli." His tone was apologetic. He touched her arm.

She let him see that she was laughing beneath her mask of affront.

He tsked and sipped, profile filling with self-disgust as he turned his face away.

Why that was funny, she didn't know, but it was. She laughed with open enjoyment and he looked at her with so much admiration, he melted her bones and made every other part of her sing. He was so handsome, he hurt her eyes. His chiseled face and keen stare, his barely-there hint of a cynical smile, his mussed hair that she wanted to muss even more, lingering over the feel of those fine strands between her fingers…

Save yourself for a relationship that matters. Someone special.

Did he not realize *he* was special?

"Gabriel!" A woman appeared beside him and

snaked her touch around his arm, smooshing her breasts against his elbow. "Introduce me to your wife."

"Brittany Farris," he said after a brief pause. "Lucrecia Dean."

Brittany offered air kisses and *had* to know *everything* about how they had met.

Luli had met variations of this woman before. Some girls on the pageant circuit were genuinely nice—and scared to be on their own. They did everything they could to make friends, needing bolstering and the safety of numbers. Some, like Luli, were there to win. They weren't mean, but they didn't make friends because feelings got hurt and friendships folded when there could be only one winner.

Then there were these kind—the ones who acted like friends, but didn't have a nice bone in their bodies.

"Luli managed my grandmother's business affairs for the last eight years," Gabriel explained.

"I saw the headlines about your inheritance! You're a *trillionaire!*" Her excitement was quickly schooled into a pout of sympathy. "But I'm so sorry, of course. I didn't even know you had a grandmother, let alone a raging romance with her *business manager*." She gave Luli a once-over. "You must be *very* shrewd if you've kept this relationship under wraps all this time."

Luli did what she had done with every other witch who thought she could backhand her with a compliment.

"Gabriel called me cunning the other day, didn't you?"

Over the rim of his glass, he asked her if that was really how she wanted to play this, as if he didn't think she understood who she was dealing with.

"I did," he admitted after a beat. "And I meant it."

Someone else came up, forcing Brittany on her way. Gabriel held court for the rest of the evening, continuing to introduce her as Mae's manager even when a professor from a prestigious design school asked if Luli had ever considered modeling, providing the perfect opportunity to talk about her pageant experience.

Gabriel squeezed her hand, however, warning her to demur.

"Every tall girl is told they must model or play basketball, aren't they?" she said.

"Not every girl is told as vehemently as I'm telling *you*. I have contacts at several agencies. Gabriel, she needs to be immortalized in the pages of *Vogue*, wearing Chanel. You can't let these cheekbones languish in an office."

"Why not? Mine do," Gabriel said with blithe conceit. "Luli is one of the best programmers I've come across. I'll fight to keep her."

She couldn't tell if he was being sincere, but the man moved on and other people moved in.

"You've been quiet," Gabriel said a few hours later, when they arrived back at his penthouse. "Was it too much?"

"No," she murmured. "It was just a long night of being 'on.' My face hurts from smiling."

"Don't feel you have to. I don't."

She had read that memo in his expression of bored tolerance.

She'd seen his home earlier so she wasn't as agog returning to it, but was still taken aback that he lived in this massive split-level mansion in the sky. The foyer led to a sunken lounge where the exterior wall held another of his spectacular aquariums. It formed the inside wall of the infinity pool outside—which looked down onto Central Park.

She lowered to the sofa, its cushion stuffed with goose down, he had informed her, when her first time sitting caused her to gasp with a sense of sinking into pure luxury. All of his furniture was custom-made for him by an Italian couture house that hand-turned legs and hand-stitched pleats into leather and velvet.

They measure me like my tailor, even ask me which side I dress, he'd drawled.

One of his servants appeared with a pot of Chinese tea, something she had confessed to craving after her breakdown in Paris. It appeared every night now, without her asking for it.

"Thank you," she said with a warm smile for the maid.

The woman curtsied.

Luli sighed. *I'm one of you*, she wanted to say, but Gabriel dismissed her.

"I thought Brittany might have said something to upset you," he said as the door closed. He shrugged out of his jacket and loosened his tie, throwing both on the back of the sofa, gaze staying fixed on her.

"When?" She set aside her shoes and wiggled her toes with relief. Then she picked up her skirt as she walked across to where the tea had been left on the bar.

"She came out of the ladies' room after you did and smiled at me like she had sunk my battleship."

"Please." Luli glanced over her shoulder so he could see her brow crinkled with scorn and pity. "I know a school in Venezuela where she could learn to be a cat with actual claws."

"So she did say something." His voice tightened.

"She told me you slept together." She paused in pouring, glanced at him again and saw by his tense expression that it was true. She ignored the fresh strip that admission peeled off the back of her heart. "Actually, she asked whether *you* had told me that you'd been lovers." She finished pouring and set the pot aside. "I said you probably didn't think it was important enough to mention."

He looked away, but even in the subdued lighting she saw the twitch of his mouth.

"Then she warned me that she could blackball me among the social elite here. I told her I'd never heard the expression, but that she must feel very disappointed things hadn't worked out between you, and maybe it was because she talked about you behind your back." One spoon of sugar. "I said I'd ask you. She didn't like that."

She heard his snort.

"Then I told her I would look up *blackball* so I understood *exactly* how that works." Her spoon clinked as she stirred.

He swore under his breath, head hanging and shoulders shaking. "Every time I worry about you, I discover you're perfectly capable of taking care of yourself."

"Are *you*?" she asked, facetious, but also with tendrils of jealousy still working its poison through her veins in thorny little stings. "Why would you sleep with someone like that? What happened to saving it for someone special?"

"I'm not a virgin."

She turned fully around to see his hands had balled in his pockets. His jaw had hardened. All of him had.

"Is it easier to remain celibate when you know what

you're missing?" A horrifying thought occurred. "Have you been seeing someone while we've been—?"

"No! When would I even— We're together *all the time*. I have been celibate since we met and no, it is not easy."

"Then… How long does this marriage have to last, Gabriel? Are we supposed to wait to have sex until it's over?"

"What are you asking? Whether you're allowed to have sex with other people? No. Neither of us is stepping out. It's gossip we don't need and would jeopardize the believability of this marriage."

"So I'm just supposed to live here with you, wondering what sex would be like?"

He closed his eyes and sounded very beleaguered. "I've told you why we shouldn't have sex."

"Because you might hurt my feelings when this is over. Well, I'll tell you what. It hurts my feelings that you'd have sex with someone like *her* and can't bring yourself to make love to *me*."

"Brittany? That's what this is about?" He shoved a hand into his hair. "People want things from me, Luli. All the time." He spoke with the infinite weariness of a battle-scarred warrior. "Sometimes it seems simpler to sleep with someone who is transparent in their motives. I didn't realize how much she drinks or I wouldn't have gone near her. It lasted less than a week."

He had said his father drank himself to death. She wanted to ask how bad it had been, but the remote cloud around him told her it had been very bad. Her heart tremored, urging her to go to him, but his stillness held her off.

"I don't drink," she pointed out. "No more than you do."

"I've noticed. I appreciate it."

"So...?"

"Luli. You're far too vulnerable."

"You just said you don't have to worry about me."

"Yet I do."

"Well, I'm worried about you! You have sex with people you don't even *like*."

"That was one misjudgment. Just...give it a rest," he sighed. "We can't, okay? I can't let you start thinking this is real."

"How is having sex making this more or less real? People who are married have sex. You're afraid that if we sleep together, I'm going to want you to fall in love with me?"

"Yes."

She folded her arms, aching because she already wanted that. Her marriage already looked very bleak, filled with lust and craving and deep yearning while he felt...nothing.

"I can't say I wouldn't," she admitted. "I've always wanted someone to love me."

His expression tightened as if her words had scored a line through him. "It's not as idyllic as it sounds, trust me."

"How do you know? Have you loved someone?" The world tilted and nearly dropped her off the edge into cold, airless space. "Is that why—"

"No," he said, taking her aback with his harsh tone.

"No? Not even your parents?"

"Of course my mother." He sounded like she was yanking out his teeth.

"Not 'of course.' I have no feelings for my father and terrible ones toward my mother. If you loved your mother and she loved you back, that's good."

"Well, I have grief over the loss of my mother, because I *loved* her. And terrible feelings toward my father. He couldn't handle her loss *at all*. It was a nightmare. Because he *loved* her. He railed and wept and broke things. He told me love was agony and never to let myself feel it."

For once Gabriel had stepped outside his jaded, impervious shell. He was breathing fire, snarling and showing his claws.

"I wouldn't bother taking the advice of a man who was drunk and slurring from ten in the morning on," he continued, "but he would grab me and cry against my chest, fall to his knees and tell me he loved *me*. He made me promise never to leave, never to get hurt or get sick or die. I was seven. I didn't know how to promise that! And I don't know if I loved him, but I do know it was agony."

Oh, Gabriel. She swallowed, thinking of him being confused and grieving, then picked on at school. So alone.

Until he had money. Then everyone wanted to be his friend.

She abandoned her tea and went across to him, took off her earrings and made him give her his hand so she could put them in his palm.

"I love these. They're beautiful. But I don't want to keep them unless you want me to have them. You've given me things I *need*, Gabriel. You've given me someone who listens and draws me a bath and calls me intelligent. That's far more valuable to me than anything you could buy me."

She closed his fingers over the earrings, then ran her thumb across the hard bumps of his knuckles. She wanted to kiss his fist, which felt silly and too impactful. Emotions suffused her that she didn't know how to express. There was gratitude, definitely, but other nameless things that urged her to reach out and offer, search for something in him, but give up to him at the same time.

"I have nothing to give you that equals any of that." Her voice creaked.

His mouth opened in protest, but she squeezed his hand.

"Only me," she continued. "And I *want* to. It's okay if you don't love me. But I want to touch you and hold you and feel those things you make me feel. I want to know what it might feel like if someone *did* love me."

His breath hissed in and he pulled his hand from her touch, thrusting his closed fist into his pocket.

She set her hand on his chest. "I don't want you to protect me from you or myself. I want you to let me become the woman *I* want to be."

He made a strangled noise and pinched the bridge of his nose, eyes clenched shut.

"Please?"

"I'm only a man, Luli," he said in a rasping voice. "When this all goes to hell, I want you to remember this moment. I tried to be honorable."

CHAPTER NINE

"REALLY?" EXCITEMENT AND TREPIDATION and anticipation all came together in a war inside her.

"I've been wanting to tear that gown off you all night." He opened his eyes and there was such atavistic light in his gaze, her heart stuttered.

"Don't! I love it." She looked down at her cleavage. "Plus there's tape that will sting so bad if you pull it too fast."

"You were put on this earth to drive me crazy. Go. Lock yourself in your room or meet me in mine. *Now.*"

She picked up her skirt and ran up the stairs, hearing him take them two at a time behind her. She let out a wild laugh, riding an adrenaline rush. She went straight to his room where she whirled to confront him.

He came in behind her, shirt open and pulled from his tuxedo pants, edges wafting like wings.

She gasped in awe at the sheen of his burnished skin stretched taut across lean muscles. He stalked her on panther feet and grasped her hips, dragging her into a soft collision with his bare chest. His mouth came down on hers in a blatant claim of ownership. His lips were hard. Devouring. Insatiable.

Her body responded in a flowering throb that made

all of her hurt. She moaned at the pleasure-pain of it and he immediately dragged his head up.

"No?" he asked through gritted teeth.

"Yes," she breathed. Groaned. She tangled her hands in his hair exactly as she had wanted to and urged him back to kissing her. She pressed her tongue to his and cried out with excitement when he sucked on her.

Wet, fiery kisses went down her to her throat. His arms folded all the way around her narrow waist and he held her tight and still, teeth against the straining cord in her neck.

"Tell me you want this," he said against her skin. "Because I'm barely hanging on to control."

"I do. So much." She pushed her hands beneath his open shirt, freeing his shoulders, wanting to touch all of him.

He straightened to throw off his shirt and she saw his eyes, feral and ravenous. It sent a dangerous spire of hunger into the pit of her belly. Lower. Liquid heat pooled between her legs and she clenched with emptiness and longing.

"Take it off, then." He nodded at her dress.

She swallowed and ran her fingertips along the inner swells of her breasts, watching him watch her lift the strap off her skin. She turned and gathered her hair onto the front of her shoulder, revealing the zipper at her spine.

He released it. Slowly. The lace relaxed and his hot hands took possession of her bared waist. He kissed the top of her spine and his humid breath fogged near her ear.

"The way you smell drives me insane. I want to lick every inch of you." His teeth nipped her lobe and her nipples tightened so hard and fast, they stung. She pressed her thighs tight together, trying to ease the ache that shot high and hot between.

She eased the dress down off her shoulders, but before she had it fully off her arms, his hands stole forward to claim her breasts. She stilled, head falling back against his shoulder as he fondled her, filling her with lassitude. Her backside instinctively pressed into the firmness behind his fly and his breath hissed at the way she writhed against him. His hands tightened on her and she felt his teeth again, scraping the tender place where her neck met her shoulder.

"Keep going," he demanded, pushing into her butt, confusing her a little when he added, "I want to see you."

She kept herself snug against his fly as she turned her sleeves inside out peeling them off. He stepped back then, just enough to let her push the clingy dress off her hips. She stepped out of it and turned.

His gaze claimed her in a lazy exploration that was nearly tactile, taking his time and leaving a burn of awareness at each curve and swell. He only held her one hand in his own, wasn't even squeezing, but somehow he kept her in place for his leisurely inspection. His free hand came out and his finger hooked into her thong at the hollow on the front of her hip.

And finally, his gaze lifted to meet hers.

She only licked her lips, waiting. His heavy touch eased the one side down her hip, then skimmed across, grazing her mound on the way.

She jerked and the corners of his mouth deepened with satisfaction. He slid the other side down an inch, teased her again with the back of his knuckle against the humid seam of her folds.

"Gabriel," she whispered in a helpless throb.

"Is this what you want?" The thong cut across the tops of her thighs while his touch traveled back to center and barely touched her, petting ever so lightly.

She bit her lip, embarrassed by the release of moisture there, but so wanting him to stroke into it.

"Say yes."

"Yes," she obeyed in a thready voice.

He traced the center line of her, slowly deepening the caress, driving her mad so she was biting her lips, eyes clenched tight, waiting and waiting.

There.

Her mouth opened in a soundless scream as he found the swollen knot of nerves that craved his touch.

He made a noise that was a growl of satisfaction and a snarl of torment.

"Please," she whispered and blindly reached out.

"You're okay." He stepped closer, folding her arm behind the small of her back as he kept her hand in his and embraced her. Held her up. His other hand kept torturing her while his mouth found hers. "Feel," he said against her lips, and continued his delicious torture.

She curled her free hand around his neck and kissed him back, lost in a sea of sensation as he dragged his mouth across hers and her twisting scraped her nipples against the hair on his chest. And his hand, oh, his wicked, masterful hand found a wonderful rhythm that she met with abbreviated thrusts of her hips.

She tried to tell him she wanted him, all of him, filling that ache. She wanted that hard shape she could feel so implacably against her hip, but she was drowning in this kiss and the pleasure and suddenly she was showered in the spell of climax, shivering and clinging and gasping.

And Gabriel was laughing softly. "I knew," he said against her lips. "I knew we would be like this."

She went bonelessly onto his bed like a gift. Her hair pooled in ribbons of brunette satin, framing her face. Her gaze was soft, her mouth pouted and swollen from their kisses. Her limbs splayed weightlessly and her curves beckoned.

His mouth watered as he stripped the last of his clothes. Somehow he remembered a condom when the only thought in his head was that he had to be against her. Over her. In her. He noted the hint of apprehension as she watched, studying his engorged shape, and knew he would die if he had to wait.

But wait he would. As long as it took.

He settled over her and cupped her face, letting himself burn in the fire of need and craving and anticipation of relief. When he kissed her, he tasted hesitation. He felt the tension in her thighs as she nervously made room for him.

He kissed her chin, the heavy but slow pulse in her throat. She wasn't nearly as frantic as he wanted her. Her collarbone, so delicate, reminded him that all of her was fragile, whether she realized it or not.

Ah, these breasts. They were a fantasy unto themselves and he gave himself free rein to pleasure both of them, teasing and sucking and licking until her nipples were turgid beads against his tongue.

"Gabriel," she gasped. The fingers in his hair began to clench with desperation, but she wasn't yet near the level gripping him.

"Soon," he soothed, drawn by her scent to rub his face across the trembling muscles in her abdomen and here. *Here* was the magic and the sweetness and the way to fully prepare her for the hard thrusts of his body.

He tantalized, glorying in the honeyed perfection of her until she moved without inhibition, making exquisitely helpless noises that shredded his control. He longed to take her over the edge like this, but she was in such a delicious state of surrender.

Now, finally, her body held the same frequency of tremble, the same throbbing agony of desire that echoed his own.

He rose over her and braced himself on an elbow while he sought her center. Somehow he made himself command, "Say it again." He had to know they were perfectly aligned.

"Yes," she told him, eyes opening to slits that were glazed with passion. "I need you. Please."

He tried to be gentle. She was tight and the heel of her hand pressed into his shoulder. She caught her breath. He stopped. Gritted his teeth.

"It's okay," she murmured, biting her lip as she shifted.

He withdrew a fraction. Kissed her. Slowly she relaxed and feathered a caress in the base of his spine.

He let his weight sink the rest of him into her, all the way, until his eyes nearly rolled to the back of his head with sheer ecstasy.

Mine, he thought, knowing that to think it was to take something from her, but in this moment it felt like a fair exchange.

Because she possessed him. Utterly and completely.

* * *

Luli was trembling in what she thought might be shock, but Gabriel lifted his head and just that tiny shift of movement caused such a wave of heated pleasure to wash over her, her scalp tingled and she was suddenly on the verge of climax again.

This was acute arousal holding her in its grip, she realized. She was quivering with desire.

Her loins stung where he intruded, but she loved it. *Needed* it. Restless frustration guided her hands as she ran them over his back and hips, claiming tense muscles and hot, damp skin.

He kissed her, the rake of his mouth drugging, but inciting. Her knees lifted on instinct, ankles crossing in the small of his back.

He made an animalistic noise and sank a fraction deeper into her. Then he gathered her beneath him, withdrew slowly and returned in a steady thrust, all the way until he had pressed a cry out of her at the reverberation of sensation he rocked through her.

He stiffened and she frantically caught at him. "Yes, Gabriel. *Yes.* Keep going."

His rhythm became elemental and primitive, yet sumptuous. It wasn't a destination, it was a place, a glorious place where they existed together. Where her entire being was filled with light. Any shadows that remained were the long, sweet shadows of summer evenings. The kind cast by a full moon when darkness reigned but pale white shapes existed.

On his skin she smelled earth and fire, metal and rain. She embraced him and pulled him deeper into the well of herself. He growled and tipped up her chin and licked at her neck, said things she didn't understand, but knew in her soul to be true.

The friction burned intimate places, the impact was nearly unbearable in its intensity, but she couldn't get enough, couldn't touch enough of him, hold him tight enough. She made her own wordless noises, primitive and feline, clenching in ecstasy while his strength held her in place for that relentless, thrilling pleasure. It was exquisite and agonizing and she wanted it to go on forever.

But she couldn't subsist in this state of tension and acute sensations. She was going to suffocate or break or her heart would explode.

And then it did. Her entire world contracted to a fine dark point, then burst. She was flame and gold and joy. Naked and pure and new.

As the most powerful release of his life receded, and Luli's sobs of culmination settled to soft, ragged breaths, an incredible sense of peace fell over him.

Gabriel somehow managed to withdraw and discard the condom, then pulled her across him, damp and sweet-smelling as the sheets beneath them. She made a contented noise and her lips touched his chest before she sighed and relaxed into a doze. He was aware of warmth and the pressure of her against him, the tickle of her hair against his naked arm, the weight of her thigh on his and an encroaching sense of regret.

His *sifu* would berate him for losing focus and letting his discipline lapse, for allowing his ego and bodily hungers to rule him. He was guilty of all those things. He'd been desperate to feast upon her. He had wanted the smug satisfaction in knowing *he* had initiated her to these pleasures and had done it *well*.

It had come at a cost. The walls he kept so impermeable around himself were weakening. The first knock had come when she had locked him out of his own software. Sections of mortar between the bricks had disintegrated under the tears she had shed against his chest that night in Paris. The winds of Africa had eroded those bricks further, as her joy at the beauty of the earth and earthly pleasures had reminded him that this world was more than greed and users and privilege.

Now she had rocked his foundation with such power he could feel the fissures extending through him.

Because she had wanted to know what it would feel like if someone loved her.

He worked his fingers into her thick hair and turned his mouth to press a kiss into the fragrant mass, wanting to shelter her even as he wanted to ravish her again.

For this privilege, he would give her almost anything.

Except his heart.

He hoped like hell it would be enough.

Luli lingered over her morning routine, feeling shy. Gabriel had woken her a few hours before dawn with kisses and caresses that had had her reaching for his turgid shape, so fascinating with velvety skin over hot iron. She had gloried in knowing how to touch him in a way he liked. They had fondled and kissed until she was burning and molten.

Then he'd slid sweetly into her and stayed there, rocking lazily.

Each time she climaxed he asked, *More?*

And she had greedily said, *Yes.*

The fourth time he had shattered with her.

She was sore, but not sorry. She felt languid and pleased and filled with mysterious knowledge.

She suspected she was in love.

It was such a new emotion, she had to pause and examine it, try to understand how its rough edges fit inside her and why it felt heavier than the ring he'd given her.

Most of all, she tried to understand how love was something she had wanted all her life and now, as she glimpsed it, it wasn't something that nestled into her and made her feel safe. It wasn't a state of being, like contentment. It was something to be given away. It was an active emotion, flowing outward, striving to reach the man who had sparked it, wherever he was at this moment.

She wanted him to love her, but strangely, even more than that, she wanted him to let her love *him*. She wanted him to welcome this overwhelming spill of feeling she wanted to pour over him.

She had tried that once, though. Her mother hadn't had a use for her heart. She'd put it on a plane to Singapore and never asked for it back.

A wrenching pain went through her as she thought of Gabriel rejecting her love. Given his childhood, she understood his reservations. It made her want to throw herself further into the fire with him. Somehow heal his pain.

But she also understood that she had to be strong. She couldn't be the girl who had become a pawn because she was afraid to be on her own. She could love him, but she couldn't be a slave to that love.

Drawing a shaky breath to bolster herself, she went down to breakfast in her robe.

"I wasn't sure if you'd still be here," she murmured, joining him at the table. It was almost ten.

"Why is Marco making you a lunch appointment with that professor from last night?" He glanced up from his tablet, took in her light makeup and the hair she'd pulled into a clip. His gaze lingered on her mouth until her lips tingled.

Then he seemed to gather himself behind an invisible wall. He looked into her eyes, seeking an answer to his question.

"Pardon? Oh, um, he wants to talk to me about modeling opportunities. I said he should get in touch with my assistant. I didn't think he was serious. Do you mind?"

"No." He spoke abruptly, sounded like he minded. "Don't rush into anything, though. He might know people, but he might just want to be seen with you. Make sure he knows you don't need the money and you're doing him a favor by showing up."

So cynical. She bit back a sigh.

"Then I should let him buy my lunch because I don't actually *have* money?"

"You have a credit card and a generous allowance. If you want to carry cash, send Marco to the bank to withdraw some."

She shook her head as she drew her napkin onto her lap. "I crossed out the allowance on the contract and put a question mark beside it. I expected we would discuss it, but we got married and here we are."

"I wrote it back in with an extra zero. Pay attention to what you sign. This lunch is a bad idea if you won't even do that much."

"Gabriel, you know that makes me uncomfortable! I

don't want *things*—" She cut herself off as she turned over her coffee cup and discovered the diamond earrings on the saucer.

All their intimacy came back in a rush. Her uninhibited clinging to him, begging for more. She had offered him her soul last night and he was giving her... crushed carbon.

Because he thought that was all he was worth? All he *had* to give?

Her mouth felt wobbly as she picked up one platinum shank. The diamond caught the sunlight and winked rainbow sparks.

"I said only if you want me to have them." The words scraped like sandpaper in the back of her throat. She had wanted to know what it felt like to be loved and instead she felt cheated.

"I do." Something in his guarded tone put a sharp vice around her heart.

This was a warning, she instinctively recognized. He would give her diamonds and limitless credit cards, but nothing more. That was the deal.

Meanwhile, she had given him her passion, her virginity, and wanted to give him so much more.

He hadn't said she couldn't, she realized.

"I'll accept them," she decided, swallowing the lump in her throat. Her voice stayed husky. "Do you know why?"

His brows went up in cautious inquiry.

"Because someday, long after our hideously civil divorce, when I'm old and gray and feeling sentimental, I'll put them on. My daughter will ask me where I got them and I'll say, *Your father would never let me wear them while he was alive. He knew it made me think of my first husband with deep fondness.*" Love. So much love. Her whole body ached with it. "But I won't tell her why that memory was such a good one, because there are some things children don't want to know about their mothers."

His expression didn't change, but his cheek ticked. "I thought you didn't want children."

She shrugged. "I'll still think of last night every time I wear these."

She put them on and deliberately met his gaze, confident that now, so would he.

You have violated our terms of service. Your access has been revoked. Join me in the tenth-floor conference room.

"What? Why? *Argh.*" She knew immediately what had happened. She had run an update this morning and Gabriel's software had overwritten all her code. She couldn't restore from backup, either. She didn't have access.

Devastated by the white screen and the stark note, she gave her useless keyboard a few more random stabs with her finger, then picked it up and rattled it in frustration.

"Mrs. Dean?" Marco appeared in her door like one of those cartoon characters that defied time and space, conjuring himself from thin air in time to say his line. "I'll call IT."

Good luck.

"No. Show me where the tenth-floor conference room is, please. And *please* call me Luli."

"Mr. Dean is the only one who calls you that. I presumed it was an endearment." He cleared his throat, then tacked on, "Ma'am."

An endearment? Gabriel had just nuked her ability to do the only job she had ever had—after picking away at it until it was down to bare bones. In the week they'd been here, he'd had her unload several investments, moving the cash into his own coffers. He'd had all the payroll records moved to his central accounting department. The property managers of Mae's various complexes now answered to someone else and even Luli's emails were cc'd to others.

"Will you go with me to my lunch tomorrow?" she asked Marco while they were in the elevator.

"Of course."

"I'm not sure how to get around the city. You could show me how the subway works."

He chuckled, then sobered with a start. "I'm sorry. I didn't realize you were serious." He shot out a hand to hold the elevator door while she stepped out. "You have full use of Mr. Dean's car. Why would you take the subway?"

Because she had to learn. She might love the man, but this marriage wouldn't last and she refused to be dependent on him.

"This is it." He paused at the first door and placed his hand on the latch and opened it.

"We'll talk about the lunch when I get back upstairs," she said over her shoulder as she entered. "Oh." She checked as she discovered at least fifty people in the room. "Hello." She took refuge in her stage persona, pasting on a smile.

They all stared at her with mouths hanging open, tracking her as she proceeded in a graceful walk down the aisle against the wall. They were seated theatre-style facing Gabriel. He stood in front of a projection screen that showed the note he'd placed on her screen to bring her here.

A public dressing down? Really?

"Why so shocked?" he asked the room. "Beauty does not preclude brains. Thank you for coming." He took her hand as she arrived beside him. "Luli, meet my software-development team. Or rather, the lead technicians for the various modules and apps. These men and women oversee between fifty and a hundred coders each, but you're looking at my best and brightest."

His tone held an edge that made the entire room sink down in their seats.

Luli eyed him with suspicion as she made herself smile warmly and say, "Good afternoon."

"I've been showing them how you tailored our software for my grandmother, the entry points you used and some samples of the code you wrote."

He tapped his laptop and she looked over her shoulder at the string of script she had used to lock him out.

"We've been enjoying a little team-building exercise here. It took this room's collective intelligence two hours to get past your gatekeeper and lock you out."

"Your grandmother was very cautious," she prevaricated, drawing her hand from his and clasping hers lightly together before her. "I was protecting her interests, not hacking into your system."

"No, but you could. And there aren't many hackers at your level, but the fact you got this far means every one of our customers is vulnerable." His words left a resounding silence. "I wrote some rough and dirty patches while we were in Africa. That's what we pushed to the update this morning. It's going to impact functionality until it's cleaned up and tailored. I'd like you to over-see that."

She actually looked to her left to see who he was talking to because he couldn't possibly be speaking to *her*. A couple of people snickered.

"Um…" She touched the fine hairs at the back of her neck. Oversee three or four thousand people? Wasn't there an expression about trees and barking up wrong ones?

"And when people suggest I made my wife the new VP of software development because she's my wife, what will you say?" he asked the room at large.

Silence, then a lone voice said, "Actually she's a ge-nius and made us all look like tools."

"She did, indeed. But she'll soon make you look like rock stars," he promised. "See how good she makes me look?" He held out his arm.

She went to him, pulled by forces greater than her-self to press against him, but she tilted an admonishing look up at him. Smiled brightly.

"Can I speak to you?"

CHAPTER TEN

GABRIEL BROUGHT HER into his office and closed the door.

"I realize I blindsided you with that," he acknowledged, appreciating that she had kept her cool in front of the team. That roll-with-the-punches ability of hers was one of the reasons he'd decided to give her this level of responsibility. "They needed to be humbled, though. I wanted them to accept you by your work before they knew who had outsmarted them."

"How you run your business is your business, but don't drag me into it without asking me first." She didn't balk at revealing her flustered reaction now they were alone, which was oddly endearing. He liked being privy to the woman behind the goddess she presented to the world.

"You wanted a job," he reminded her. "This is a good one."

"It's a huge one! Gabriel, you heard me this morning with the maid. I have a hard time asking someone to iron a wrinkle from my skirt. I can't supervise a *department*."

Gabriel had enjoyed eavesdropping on the power struggle as Luli attempted to pry the location of the iron from the maid while the young woman had earnestly, politely and vehemently insisted she be allowed to do her job.

"You're uniquely qualified for this position. You know the vulnerabilities and will be creative and thorough in fixing them. When you know what you want, you have no problem going after it. You even stand up to me to get it. You'll be fine."

"Yes, well, that's the issue. I don't want it."

"You don't want this exceptionally good job I'm giving you."

"Giving," she repeated. "So this *is* nepotism."

"No." He took a firmer grip on his patience. "I just explained why I chose you."

"Do *I* get a choice? Is it an offer or an order?"

"It's an offer with a salary of a quarter million dollars attached to it." Why was she fighting him? Did she not realize they would work together every day?

"Oh, that does stink of nepotism."

"Call a headhunter." He pointed at the telephone. "It's competitive, not outrageous."

"You call a headhunter," she muttered. "I can make twice that staying home with my feet up, waiting for my allowance to roll in."

He threw up his hands, truly baffled by this woman.

"In Singapore, you said you were proving your skills to me," he reminded her. "You have. You just proved them to a roomful of top-notch programmers. I'm offering you a job in this field and you're refusing it?"

"For how long, Gabriel?"

The barb of sadness in her voice caught in his heart, pulling him up short.

"Will I be able to finish before our marriage is over? Will you still want me here when we're divorced? Will you trust me not to move on to some competitor with what I know? You don't want me that deeply entwined in your livelihood. I know you don't. That's why you've spent every day since we met prying me out of it."

He squeezed the back of his neck. Had he thought that far ahead? Only insofar as to think that maybe, if enough incentives were offered, she would stay here. In his office, in his home, in his bed.

"We could have a successful marriage, Luli."

"Provided I give you babies and never expect anything more of you than having my physical needs met. I have other needs, Gabriel." Her soft voice and the quiet torment in her gaze were too much to face.

He turned to the window.

After a moment, her footsteps padded toward him. Her arms came around his waist and the weight of her head settled between his shoulder blades.

"I'm always going to wonder who I'm supposed to be. Not the person my mother or Mae or you turned me into. The person I make of myself. I have to do that."

"By turning yourself into an object in front of cameras?"

"Maybe. At least it would be my choice."

He looked at her hands folded across his middle, his ring bright on her finger. He could give her his heart or her freedom.

He swallowed, picked up her hands and brought them to his mouth, kissing the inside of each wrist.

"Do what you need to do, then," he said, even though the words burned like acid through his torso. "I'll find someone else."

"Thank you. Oh, shoot." She drew back and brushed

her fingers in the middle of his spine. "I got lipstick on your shirt. You'll have to change it. Sorry."

He turned and looped his arms around her lower back, pulling her in again to ease the line of pain still burning down his center. "You know what people are going to think if I change my shirt after a private meeting with my wife in my office."

"That I threw my coffee at you?" Her lips tilted into the seductive smile that tightened his skin all over his body.

She twined her arms around his neck, crushing her breasts to his chest, growing more self-assured in her feminine power by the day. He thrilled at this brazen side of her. It allowed him to unleash his appetites to the fullest, confident she would slow him down if he became too aggressive.

He slid his hands under her ass and lifted, swelling with invincible strength. Her skirt rode up and she wrapped her thighs in a squeeze around his waist.

He could have taken her to his sofa, but he took her to his desk. It wasn't as comfortable, but as he pressed her onto her back against his blotter, and her earrings winked at him, he knew he would think of her every single time he sat here.

It was foolish and sentimental and self-destructive to want her memory to infuse his private space, but he did. He wanted her everywhere. Her scent on his body, her long hairs on his sleeve, her teeth marks in his shoulder and her hot breath against his ear.

He needed all these things because one day it would be all he had.

That realization slowed him down.

Much as he wanted to strip her naked and drive

into her and *make* her his, he was suddenly gripped by a deeper need. One that demanded he take his time, immerse himself in every caress, wring the furthest reaches of pleasure from her with each kiss and tantalizing touch.

He smoothed his lips across her nipples through her shirt, making her writhe, and made her turn her head so he could unpin her hair, then ran his fingers through the mass that made him crazy, every single time he came near her.

He kissed her tenderly and smiled with satisfaction when she tried to urge him along, driving her tongue into his mouth and reaching for his belt.

He wanted to tell her how beautiful she was, how much pleasure he wanted to give her. Words tangled into a fiery knot in his throat while flames continued to lick inside his chest, branding her deep behind his breastbone where she would stay imprinted forever.

He hurt. Deep inside, he ached with emptiness. The only way to assuage that ache was this. Touch her, bare her, hold her. Cover her and press into her and stay there, unmoving while he kissed her long and slow, drugging both of them with this potent magic they created.

And when she quivered on the knife's edge with him, when the borders of reality smudged and time ceased to exist, he gathered her up so they were eye to eye as the fire consumed them in a golden shimmer that, he knew, would bind him to her forever.

Three weeks later, with great excitement, Luli sat for a test shoot. Not wanting to spend Gabriel's money, she gave students from the professor's school an opportunity to build their own portfolio while starting hers. A handful of designers, stylists and photographers had given her a taste of the grueling work that was the inside view of modeling.

The end result was a selection of photos from classic perfume ad fare to an avant-garde shot of her in smeared makeup with a roller still stuck in her hair and a tinfoil robe hanging off one shoulder.

Gabriel didn't say much beyond, "The clamor to represent you won't have anything to do with me. You're very photogenic."

She hadn't expected him to gush, but she had hoped for more. A deep chasm had begun opening since the day they had made love in his office. He swore he wasn't angry that she hadn't taken the job he'd offered. He agreed that he would prefer to keep his business separate from her, now that Mae's holdings had been absorbed into his own.

Luli kept trying to bring them closer with lovemaking and it worked temporarily, but always made the separation afterward more painful than if they'd maintained their individuality in the first place.

It was becoming clear to her that his prediction was true. She wanted his love and he couldn't offer it. It was agony to be denied his heart and for that reason, she had to begin building the life she would have when their marriage was over. At least a demanding schedule of working away would give her some distance from the pain and provide an excuse for the inevitable publicity when the time came.

"I've decided to take the job in Milan," she told him as they dressed to go to a Broadway premiere.

She saw his hand check as he reached for a shirt on

a hanger. He wore only a towel. His lean back was a study in animal beauty, flaring upward from his hips to wide shoulders and muscles that twisted as he pulled the shirt free.

"I'll leave Saturday morning so I'm well rested and ready to work on Monday."

Please tell me not to go, she silently pleaded. *Tell me you can't live without me.*

"You're not flying commercial."

"First class. They're paying for Marco to go with me." Among Marco's many talents, she had learned he also ensured her physical safety. Gabriel had never been a target for kidnapping or other threats, but given his position, he took precautions. She and Marco were becoming friends so she didn't mind that he was her constant companion when Gabriel wasn't with her.

"Take the jet."

At a million dollars per nautical mile?

"They've already made the arrangements. There's no reason you should be out of pocket."

"I don't care about the money."

"What *do* you care about?" she blurted, and regretted it immediately.

Especially when he dragged in a breath that hissed.

"What do you want me to say, Luli? You've put me in a no-win situation. If I ask you not to work, I'm holding you back. If I let you go, I'm abandoning you."

"It *is* a win for you, though," she insisted with a spark of temper. "You didn't want me in the first place. I'm leaving, giving you the solitude you prefer and you're not even *thanking* me." Her voice started to break.

She walked out of the closet and strode down the hall to her room. She might sleep in his bed, but all her clothes were in here. Not even her dental floss had made it into his treasured private space.

"I told you," he said, following her to brace his arms in the open doorway of her room. "I told you this was how it would be."

"Yes, you tried to be *so* honorable and save me from my silly romantic notions that you might actually come to care for me." She took a shaky breath and flipped her hair back behind her shoulder. "You're right, okay? It is painful to have feelings for someone. No matter how loved you make me feel when we're in bed, the pain comes back afterward when I remember you don't. That's why I'm leaving. And I'll take every job they will throw at me to keep from coming back here and... *wishing.*"

"Luli—" He hung his head.

"Don't worry about it, Gabriel. You can't *make* someone love you. I accepted that a long time ago. But I do have to stop trying." She swallowed. "I'd rather not go out if you don't mind. I'm going to have a bath and an early night." She locked herself into the bathroom.

He stirred, aching with arousal, and reached for her.

She wasn't here.

Gabriel snapped awake and groaned like an injured animal, wondering how he was going to cope with even one more day of this. It had been six and he was dying.

Withering.

It wasn't just sexual hunger, although he missed the physical release. Everything about the act. Everything about her. He missed *her*—the feel of her skin against his own, her weight on the mattress beside him, her smile across the table and her laughter echoing from far down a hall.

You can't make someone love you. But I do have to stop trying.

The anguish that had gripped him as she said that had been nearly unbearable. He didn't want her to stop trying. Did she think he didn't notice when she stroked her fingers across his shoulders, simply because she was passing behind where he was seated? Or that she wore those damned earrings at the most ridiculous times, most certainly to get the best possible rise out of him? She flirted and cuddled and kept him on his toes.

It was painful to have feelings for someone. He had always known that love hurt. But was he making both of them suffer just to prove he was right?

He sure as hell hadn't spared himself any pain by holding her off. She had acted like she was doing him a favor by leaving and he had tried to convince himself he didn't want her to stay.

But he did. He needed her. Like air and water and sunlight.

Throwing off his covers, he picked up his phone, trying to think what he'd say to her if she answered. It was midmorning in Milan. She was probably already working.

He tapped to wake the screen and read a text from Marco that stopped his heart.

CHAPTER ELEVEN

IT HAD ALREADY been an impossibly long day, but Luli dug deep and conjured a sultry expression, lips parted with invitation only a hair's breadth from her fellow model's. He was a gorgeous Italian whose smoky stare drifted toward Marco every time they took a break, but he made his passion for her seem real as he clutched her close and bent dominantly over her.

"What the *hell*?"

Gabriel's voice jolted through the studio, halting the rapid click of the camera shutter. Her partner tightened his hold on her, helping her straighten and catch her balance. Then he angled her away from Gabriel as he strode toward them looking like he would take them both apart.

"Sir!" Marco raced forward to intercept him.

"Gabriel!" Luli extricated herself from the Italian's hold. "What are you doing here?"

"What are *you* doing?"

"Working. Obviously."

He gave the Italian a filthy look that suggested he didn't care for her type of "work," but only asked, "Why?"

"What do you mean, why?"

"Sir—" The photographer was taking a tone. Even worse, he was glaring at Luli as though he blamed her for the interruption.

"I'm sorry—I texted him," Marco said, holding up his hands. "This is my fault. I was worried," he added in a gentle apology directed at Luli. Then he smiled placatingly at Gabriel. "They're almost finished. We can wait outside."

"I'll wait right here." He crossed his arms and stood with his toes mere inches from the carpet of the set.

Luli shouldn't have been surprised Marco had told Gabriel that her mother had died. For years, she had set alerts to pick up her mother's name, but yesterday's had been the first in ages to ping a headline about her. Her death after a medical complication had been noted by the Venezuelan press because she had once been a renowned beauty, but details had been scant.

Luli had mentioned it to Marco, though, and asked him to prepare a statement in the unlikely case the connection was discovered by an overzealous reporter. He had pointed out her contract allowed for family emergency and bereavement leave, but she was too early in this new career of hers to be anything but unrelentingly reliable.

Besides, the news changed nothing.

She should have realized Marco would warn Gabriel of the potential media storm. Had something leaked into the press? Was that why he was stomping in here, breathing fire?

She couldn't think about that right now. She had to do what she was paid to do.

Thirty minutes later they wrapped. As she changed,

she heard Gabriel ask Marco, "What the hell are they even selling with all that sex?"

Marco cleared his throat. "The handbag on the chair."

The resounding silence that followed that statement told her what Gabriel thought of *that*.

Marco apologized to her again when she rejoined them.

"It's fine. We both know who pays your salary." She freed her hair from the collar of her light coat.

"Mrs. Dean." He put out a hand in a plea. "You were upset. I could see it even if the camera couldn't."

And he thought she and Gabriel had a relationship that included endearments and a deeper caring than it did.

"I'm fine," she assured Marco with a faint smile. "Take the evening off. Enjoy the city." Enjoy the Italian.

She went back to her hotel with Gabriel, the silence between them thick as gelatin.

As the door closed behind him, Gabriel was the first to speak, asking tightly, "Why are you angry Marco told me?"

"Why are *you* angry?" The hollow sensation in the base of her throat was spreading into her chest cavity, growing too big to suppress or ignore.

"Because you didn't tell me yourself. Why didn't you?"

Something broke inside her, sending a flood of anguished emotion through her. Not at the knowledge her mother was dead, but at the other knowledge that had struck like a blow when she had considered telling Gabriel.

"I didn't think you'd care."

He closed his eyes in a way that suggested she had run him through.

"I'm not trying to make you feel guilty," she muttered, biting her lip. "I'm not trying to make you feel anything."

"And yet I feel like hell," he bit out. "She doesn't deserve your grief, Luli."

"I know that." She realized she was convulsively opening and shutting the clasp on her purse. She threw it into a chair.

"And yet you still grieve."

"That's why you're angry? I can't help how I feel, Gabriel!"

"Neither can I! That's why I'm angry. At myself. I knew immediately that you'd be hurting and I wasn't here for you."

"*You* hurt me," she reminded wildly, instantly plunged back into the despair of their last conversation.

"I know that," he thundered. "I stood there and saw that I was turning a knife in you exactly as you are turning one in me right now. I hate that we can do this to each other."

Her eyes grew wet. She turned away, thinking that she had known this was coming, but she couldn't bear it. "Please don't say it," she begged, agonized.

"Say what? That I love you? I do. I *love* you, Luli."

Her heart swerved. "What?"

She came around cautiously, dizzy, certain she had misheard. "I thought you were going to say it's over."

"Like hell. This will never be over." He dragged in a tormented breath, face contorting with pained acceptance. "I have never wanted to say those words to anyone. I knew it would be pure torture to feel it."

She inhaled at that gut punch.

He closed the distance in a few strides and picked

up her hands, holding on to them when she tried to pull away.

"Love forces you to feel that other person's heartbeat. When they cry, you cry. When you hurt them, that pain comes back on you tenfold." He drew her closer, so he cupped her hand against his heart and cradled the side of her face with his other palm.

"But when they're happy, you're so happy you can't contain it. When they give you their heart, there isn't enough room in your own body for both. You have to give up yours or the imbalance will break both of you."

"You have my heart."

"I know. It's better than the one I had." His thumb grazed her cheek in a tender caress. "Lighter, softer. God knows it's prettier. Take mine. Fix it. Make it shine."

She had to bite her lips to steady them. Her eyes were so wet, she could hardly see the light gleaming in his gaze, but she felt it beaming through her, filling her until she glowed. "It's just rusty," she choked. "But it works."

"You make me happy, Luli. Too happy. If I ever lose you, I'll become the emotional cripple my father became. That terrifies me." His expression spasmed with deep emotion. "But pushing you away is killing me. I cannot bear the pain of hurting you."

It didn't escape her that he was giving her the one thing he had never wanted to give up. She was awed by the gift of his love and could only return it with the embrace of her arms, the press of her lips to his, the promise of forever that pulsed in her heart.

"Say it," he whispered against her cheek.

"I love you, Gabriel. I love you with every breath in my body. I always will."

"I love you, too. Infinitely."

Their words seemed to infuse the air around them, gaining strength from the whispers and friction of their two bodies embracing. From the meeting of their soft gazes across the narrow space, and the unspoken desire that had them moving to the bedroom in perfect accord to celebrate their union in the most ancient and exalted of forms.

EPILOGUE

"SHH…" GILLY SAID, holding her stubby little finger against her pursed lips.

"That's right. We're quiet when we feed the fish," Gabriel said in the warm, patient tone he always used with their daughter.

"Gen-tow," Gilly said, and carefully pinched the food from his palm and released it into the tank he had placed in her room days after she was born.

Luli hung back at the door, heart so full when she watched them, she nearly cried over it, every single day. Gabriel teased her if he caught her, but if he happened to walk in on tai chi practice, when their toddler tried to follow her mother's moves with her still clumsy, yet determined little limbs, he was as likely to grow misty as he was to step in and join them.

They were both utterly enamored with their little girl, in a state of perpetual wonderment that they had made something so exquisitely perfect from the earthy, greedy hunger that never let up between them.

"Mama!" Gilly noticed her and beamed her teensy white teeth.

"Hi, baby." Luli moved to catch the sprite as she

threw herself from her father's arms and squeezed Luli's neck with exuberance.

Gabriel dropped a smiling kiss against her lips.

"She's been asking for you. I was about to send a search party."

"Blame your coders."

"Anything I should know about?"

"No, I can handle it." She had kept up the modeling for a year, sticking with local shoots unless Gabriel had been able to travel with her. When her pregnancy started showing, she quit and stayed home for almost a year, taking a lead role in some of Gabriel's charities before beginning work on an app to make donations easier to request, track and disperse.

Gabriel had talked her into developing it with his team and she'd been working with them ever since.

"Pwetty," Gilly said, drawing back to touch one of Luli's earrings.

"Let's wash your hands," Gabriel said, catching her fishy fingers. "Those are special."

"Why?" Gilly was at the age when she liked to ask that question *a lot*.

"Would you like to field this one?" Gabriel invited Luli with a knowing smirk as he took their daughter from her.

"Daddy gave them to me the night I fell in love with him," she told Gilly.

"Is that what happened that night?" Gabriel teased. "I remembered something else, but okay."

"That you fell in love with me, too?" she guessed with a sly smile.

"That was it." He dropped another kiss on her lips. "That is exactly what happened that night."

* * * * *

CLAIMING HIS REPLACEMENT QUEEN

AMANDA CINELLI

For Emily

CHAPTER ONE

'I'D RATHER DIE than be your wife a moment longer.'

Khal opened his eyes, clean cool air filling his lungs with painful force. His surroundings were a jolt to his system, the sleek interior of the royal jet's main cabin so far apart from the angry red sands and fathomless black water of his dream. It had just been a dream. He sat back, looking up at the ceiling as his heartbeat found its rhythm once more.

His subconscious had long ago stopped tormenting him with every detail of his last conversation with his wife before her death. Or so he had believed.

He unbuckled his seat belt and stood, stretching out the painful tightness in his shoulders. He could have chosen to sleep in any one of the three luxurious bedrooms on board, but sleep had not come easily of late. The dreams were back with a vengeance. The same dreams that had plagued him for an entire year after his wife's death. Stress seemed to be a trigger and the past few weeks had most certainly not been a relaxing time.

He pressed a button on the panel by his side and, as if by magic, two flight attendants emerged from the end of the cabin. A tray bearing hot towels and fresh ice water was placed on the nearest table without a word.

His chair was returned to the upright position and a pot of hot coffee set down within reach.

'That will be all, thank you,' he said, his voice unintentionally gravelly from sleep. He glanced up just in time to see one of the women visibly flinch as he waved one hand in dismissal. He fought the urge to roll his eyes with irritation. Without another word, they hurried back behind the curtain and he was alone once more. Just as he preferred it.

Most of his staff knew him well enough to disregard the rumours that had spread upon his wife's untimely passing. Disgusting, slanderous rumours that he had worked hard to dispel even while in the first days of his grief. But still, whispers spread and somehow the idea that he was a man to be feared had stuck.

People believed him to be a villain and it suited him to keep it that way. He was not forced to make idle conversation, to pretend to care. He did not throw social functions nor did he attend a great many.

Or at least he hadn't until recently.

Khal opened his laptop and scanned an assortment of international news articles that his press team had collated from the past week. *The Most Romantic Royal Love Story of the Decade*, one headline proclaimed. It was any news reporter's dream, Princess Olivia of the tiny European kingdom of Monteverre turning her back on her lofty title to marry a man her family deemed unsuitable. One picture showed Khal's close friend Roman Lazarov as he walked hand in hand with the beautiful redhead. What a cruel twist of fate it was that the woman he had finally chosen as his second wife, the answer to all his economic woes, would be snatched up at the last moment. And by his best friend, no less.

Remarrying had never been in his plans for his reign as Sheikh. He had been a young man on his first wedding day, filled with naïve hope for the future. That version of himself was long gone. He had no desire to find a woman to mend his broken heart, or any of the other schemes he had heard whispered by his mother and sister when they thought he could not hear. Thanks to his sister, he had two strong nephews that would carry on the Al Rhas bloodline and therefore he'd believed he had absolutely no need for a wife.

But he could no longer deny that the rumours surrounding his wife's demise were affecting Zayyar's international image. His country had been peaceful for over two decades, his father and grandfather before him credited with having brought their small Middle Eastern kingdom back from the brink of complete ruin. Khal had no wish for fame or a place in the history books, but he refused to be remembered as the Sheikh who had ruined all of their hard work.

Known for his careful planning, he had spent months drawing up an arrangement with Monteverre, one of the oldest and most financially troubled kingdoms in Europe. It was a deal that would solve all his problems in one fell swoop. He would provide the Monteverrian economy with a very healthy injection of capital and in return he would gain a loyal alliance in the form of the perfect bride with the perfect amount of political influence and public appeal.

By now the whole world knew that the Princess had given up her formal title to be with her scandalous Russian lover. There was no mention of a failed engagement to the Sheikh of Zayyar in any newspaper, nor would there ever be, thanks to his team. His name rarely graced any of the world media sources, nor did paparazzi images. He paid handsomely for his privacy. And a good thing too, considering he was about to arrive unannounced into a foreign country to retrieve his replacement bride.

He knew nothing of the youngest Sandoval Princess, only that she had been studying abroad in England for many years and had agreed to his offer of a royal marriage of convenience with very little hesitation. She had even agreed to sign a formal engagement contract without first meeting in person. He should feel relieved that his plans had not been completely derailed, and yet something seemed off.

He had amended the terms of the agreement from its original form, limiting the deal to five years of marriage in name only, followed by an easy divorce settlement. With such a solid link to European royalty provided by his bride, five years would be more than enough time for him to repair the bridges that had been burned by his reputation. Divorce was a common occurrence across the globe; Zayyar was no different. Still, he knew he would not truly rest until he had spoken to his fiancée in person.

He spent the remainder of the flight in quiet contemplation, barely noticing that they had landed until his pilot announced the incredibly low temperature in the city of London. It was the middle of May and yet he felt the need to pull up the collar of his impeccably tailored wool coat as he made the short trip from jet to limousine, grateful that he had chosen to change into Western-style clothing mid-flight. His usual flowing white robes were perfect for the desert heat, but not designed for the chilly, wet weather so common in this part of the world.

His Chief of Security sat waiting in the car, his expression stressed—Sayyid never looked stressed. Immediately Khal's instincts stood to attention.

'There has been a small problem,' Sayyid said solemnly.

Khal kept his features expressionless as his trusted servant outlined the events of the past twenty-four hours' surveillance operation. Finally, he closed his eyes, fighting the urge not to slam his fist into the door panel. 'You believe she is a flight risk?'

'She shows all of the signs of it, Sire.' After a prolonged silence, Sayyid cleared his throat quietly. 'If you give me the order, I will have the Princess collected immediately and delivered to the jet.'

'Your men are currently in pursuit?' Khal spoke with quiet control, hardly believing history was repeating itself so blatantly.

'She is safely surrounded and unaware of their presence.'

Khal nodded, running a hand across the light stubble on his jaw. He had already taken King Fabian's word once and been burned, but this time it was different. He had sent his personal secretary to London with official documents and ensured that Her Highness signed them herself in person. He had done everything within his power to ensure her complete consent before entering into a legally binding engagement to protect his investment. If she walked away from their engagement now, the repercussions for her kingdom were grave.

Surely she realised that?

But of course he had to be prepared for the fact that

maybe she did not care. Nonetheless, at this moment in time she was his fiancée. And in Zayyar that was as good as already being his wife. He had a duty to ensure her safety. Princess Cressida might be having second thoughts about their marriage, but he'd be damned if he would send anyone in to talk her round this time, other than himself.

'I'll handle this myself.' He spoke with a calm he did not feel. 'Take me to her.'

The exclusive club was a secret to most Londoners, hidden away behind the rather nondescript black door of a Georgian townhouse in Mayfair. The chilly breeze brushed across her skin as Cressida Sandoval stepped out onto the pavement and looked up at the building's dimly lit facade. The urge to abandon her plans and retreat to the warm interior of the limousine was strong. Frank, her loyal chauffeur of five years, was not happy with her insistence that he remain behind and he'd made his disapproval known by slamming the door audibly behind her.

'Your Highness, are you sure you don't want me to escort you inside?' He spoke quietly, worrying his black tie with one hand.

Cressida stiffened at the honorific. The title that set her so far apart from every other twenty-four-year-old woman seeking a night of freedom. She inhaled softly, reminding herself that her freedom relied entirely on the driver's discretion. 'I have never asked for a favour before now.'

He shook his head, leaning back against the car bonnet. 'Five years of driving you from home to Oxford,

Oxford to home, like blimmin' clockwork. Last night on the job and you've decided to give me heart failure.'

'Two hours alone, Frank. That's all I want.' She understood his worry; his job would be on the line if anything happened to her on his watch. If she'd had any street sense she would probably have taken a cab, but princesses did not take cabs, nor did they sneak out unaccompanied to secret clubs in the dead of night. She'd had to dodge her two bodyguards and beg Frank, just to get him to agree to drive her and wait outside. Once the time was up, she would return to reality. Or at least the suffocating reality of what her life had recently become.

Her father's voice rang in her ears.

'Politically advantageous...royal duty...for the good of the kingdom.'

Tomorrow she would become Princess Cressida Sandoval once more, returning to her kingdom after five years of self-imposed exile. Her father, the King of Monteverre, had barely listened to her weak argument about the European languages doctorate she had signed up for or the assistant teaching position she had been offered. 'Princesses do not *teach*, Cressida,' he had boomed in his usual way. 'I'm sure the Sheikh will have plenty of dusty old books for you to bury your nose in, or whatever it is that you've been wasting your time with for the past five years.'

The Sheikh. Her future husband.

She should not feel so nervous about something that was essentially just a business arrangement. Five years of service, her father had said. How utterly romantic. Not that romance had ever played a part in her life so far, but still... She had been comfortable here in London, away from the watching eyes of the public. Was she truly ready to become a queen?

A fresh wave of anxiety fuelled her with adrenaline as she met the eyes of the burly man guarding the door to the club. She quietly spoke the code word she had overheard three nights before from one of her bodyguards. The door was opened without comment, revealing plush red carpeted stairs with sleek chrome handrails descending downwards. She paused for a moment, fear of the unknown snaking around her chest and pulling tight. The low hum of music and conversation drifted upwards like a siren's song.

This was her last night in London, she reminded herself as she took the first step downwards. She owed it to herself to experience at least a taste of the freedom she had stupidly taken for granted before her face graced the front of every newspaper on the globe.

She had felt the walls closing in on her as she'd signed her name on each document that had been presented to her, precious control slipping through her fingers. Perhaps that was why she was acting on impulse for the first time in her life. She was overcome with the need to go somewhere new and be someone anonymous for just a few short hours before doing The Right Thing.

Because, when it came to royal duty, she always did what was asked of her. Whether she liked it or not.

She had felt on edge from the moment she'd ended that fateful phone call with her father. Knowing that she would do as he asked, even if it was not what she wanted. He knew it too. He knew that she always felt the pressure to measure up to her older sisters. It was so much more than simple sibling rivalry. He had always made it clear that she was his least favourite, the daughter he simply tolerated. Her thoughts turned dark, thinking of that fateful day when, as a twelve-year-old, she had finally found out why...

Pausing at the end of the stairway, Cressida took in the image of a sultry blonde in red and took a deep breath as she realised it was her own reflection. Her dark blonde locks fell in soft waves around her face, free from their usual tight ponytail. Her plain black glasses had been replaced by contact lenses. Her jeans and sneakers gone, in favour of a stylish red dress and heels slightly too high for comfort. She had devoted more time and research to tonight's outfit than she'd given to her most recent thesis. She was good at research. It was the practical application that made her insides shake. But suddenly, standing looking at this strange, almost pretty version of herself, the bands around her chest loosened a little and she felt a hint of that freedom she so craved.

The club was deceptively spacious inside, much larger than it seemed from the narrow building facade. The décor was a modern monochrome with a hint of old world glamour in the large sparkling chandeliers that hung from the ceiling at various points. A small stage with a live jazz band dominated one corner of the large space while a double-sided bar with floor-to-ceiling mirrors glittered in the middle. It was like walking into an old black-and-white movie.

Cressida walked towards the bar as confidently as she could muster, ignoring the painful beat of her heart high up in her throat.

The music was fast paced but sensual, accentuated by a husky-toned singer in a scandalously short dress and elbow-length gloves. As she slid onto a bar stool she spied a line of strategically roped-off areas towards the back, some filled with very beautiful but rather bored-looking people. The nameless secret basement club was known for its A-list clientele and its air of anonymity, according to the conversation she had overheard between her two bodyguards. No paparazzi allowed.

Even though it was a weeknight, the club was filled with people dancing and moving to the music as the lighting curved around them. As she looked on, a famous blonde singer stood up on a table and began to pour a bottle of expensive-looking champagne over the people around her. The group of men and women began dancing and gyrating under the spray, laughing and singing along to the music.

She found herself smiling in wonder at the sight of such ridiculous behaviour. If she were to truly enjoy her freedom, she would just stand and join in with the dancing and no one would look twice at her... The thought came and passed as she took a seat at the end of the long bar, comfortably on the outskirts of the action.

Soon she would probably need to ask for permission before doing something so daring as dancing in public; she felt her mouth curve downwards.

She could refuse the match, of course. This was not some medieval drama where she would be bound and dragged down the aisle, whether she agreed to the union or not. She adored the simple life she had begun to carve out for herself here in London but of course she knew it was not allowed for a member of royalty to take a paid job. She was not meant for such blissful normality as being a teaching assistant, much as she had been delighted to be offered the position. She had a duty to serve the people of Monteverre.

She ordered a white wine, not feeling confident enough to order anything else. She occasionally drank a glass with dinner, but never more. Alcohol dulled her senses in a way that simply did not appeal to her orderly nature. She sipped slowly, feeling slightly at sea amidst the raucous dancing and groupings of people. Mingling had never been a forte of hers. The word itself made her feel twitchy. She remembered herself as a young girl, wishing she was more confident, more natural at being a princess. She had always felt so different to her older sisters, the stereotypical mousy wallflower to their flame-haired beauty. And then one day everything had changed and she had simply stopped trying. She had found comfort in blending into the background where it was safer, where no one looked too closely at her...

You came here to feel free and here you are, hiding in the corner feeling sorry for yourself. She bit her lip hard, swirling the golden liquid in her glass and watching the light play on the surface. She became suddenly aware of a shadow in the reflection of the glass and the delicious scent of a warm, distinctly male cologne.

She looked up.

Goodness...

Tall, dark and handsome simply did not describe the man standing a mere foot away from her. This man was broad, exotic and breathtaking. She swallowed hard as dark, hooded eyes met hers. He didn't make a move to speak and after a long moment her awkward nature interfered, her voice trembling slightly as she asked, 'Can I help you?'

His expression changed fleetingly to one of mild surprise, making her wonder if he had mistaken her for someone else. His gaze moved down to take in her long legs crossed on the high barstool before returning to her face. She half hoped he had made a mistake, then perhaps he would leave and she might be able to breathe normally again.

'Are you expecting someone?' He gestured to the empty barstool beside her. His voice was a deep accented rumble.

'No. I'm here alone,' she said quickly, then worried if that made her seem a little bit needy. 'I mean, the seat is yours. If you want it, that is. It's…not mine, either way.' She felt her cheeks heat. She was a babbling idiot.

A tension-filled silence followed and the stranger's eyes narrowed slightly as though he were waiting for her to say something more. A strange bewildered expression crossed his face as he moved to sit back onto a barstool, leaving the seat between them empty.

Cressida frowned, one hand idly tracing the edge of her glass as she shot a sidelong glance towards the mysterious hunk. Nipping at her bottom lip with her teeth, she took a slow sip of her wine to cool her suddenly dry throat. He was handsome, there was no denying it, with warm mahogany-toned skin and jet black stubble shadowing his jawline.

The shadow that began on his jawline continued down a strong throat to disappear into the open collar of a perfect white shirt. A white shirt that covered the broadest shoulders she had ever seen…

She moved her gaze back up to find a pair of dark eyes watching her. Startled, she inhaled sharply and promptly breathed in a mouthful of wine. Her throat convulsed in a series of loud embarrassing coughs and she was vaguely aware of a napkin appearing in her peripheral vision. She prayed her eye make-up hadn't run and silently willed the dark stranger to disappear so that she didn't have to continue her embarrassment any longer.

She froze as he placed a glass of water into her hands, the heat of his fingers scorching her skin for a few short seconds. The cold water calmed both her raw throat and her overheated brain.

Cressida looked up to find he had moved to the seat directly beside her. This close, she could see tiny flecks of gold in his deep brown irises. The way he was looking at her so intently made her feel as though she had walked under a spotlight. She was too warm, too exposed.

'Thank you,' she blurted, forcing herself to meet his eyes. 'For the water.'

'It's my pleasure.' His eyes did not leave hers. 'However, I believe it is now irresponsible of me to leave you unsupervised while you finish your drink.'

'I must seem quite ridiculous, really.' Cressida half laughed, feeling rather blinded under the intense spotlight of his attention.

'That's the last word I would use,' he said silkily, tilting his head to one side.

She managed a slight smile, wondering again why he had chosen to sit with her. Men like him did not show interest in women like her; it was hard not to be suspicious. Not that she was here seeking male attention; far from it. Tonight was simply about freedom, she reminded herself with a firm shrug of her shoulders.

'I find myself wondering…' his dark voice rumbled somewhere close to her ear '…what might have brought you here tonight to this particular club?'

Cressida felt the vibration of his deep voice travel

down to her toes. She shifted in her seat. 'The same reason as everyone else, I assume. It's an escape.'

'You are looking to escape something?'

'If I say the outside world, is that rather a cliché?' She grimaced with a half laugh, feeling herself relax slightly. 'I must go back eventually, of course.'

He seemed thoughtful for a moment. 'While you are here, what do you plan to do?'

'I hadn't really thought that far ahead.' She laughed, shocked at how feminine she sounded. 'I'm trying to be spontaneous for once. Perhaps I might dance?'

'Alone?'

'If no one asked me, I suppose I would have to dance alone.' It was hardly a suggestive statement, but still she felt herself blush a little, knowing she suddenly wanted him to ask her to dance. What on earth had come over her?

She had never flirted with a man before—she wasn't even sure if this qualified as flirting—but it definitely felt different to any previous conversations with a member of the opposite sex. What was she even doing? She was promised to another man, both morally and legally. She might not have met her fiancé yet, but she still knew where the boundaries stood. But a simple dance…that was hardly improper. Maybe it was the wine, though she knew herself that two sips could hardly provide enough stimulant. It was becoming intoxicating, feeling so free. That was the only explanation. It was making her feel different, bolder.

'By all means, then. You should dance,' he said.

'Yes, I would love to.' She smiled, feeling the sense of bravado heighten further. She slid off the barstool, biting her lower lip as he made no move to stand.

You should dance, he had said, not *we*. Silly girl.

She smiled a little too widely before turning to take a few steps towards the crowded dance floor. Throwing a final look over her shoulder as she walked away, she found herself momentarily pinned by a dark gaze. Heat sizzled through the air, seeming to settle somewhere in the region of her solar plexus.

Her painfully shy nature and workaholic tendencies had stopped her from ever having a dating life. So much so that the opposite sex might well have become a foreign species altogether, apart from her interactions with her bodyguards and driver. She could read and write fluently in eight languages and yet she could not formulate a simple sentence in English to ask a man if he wanted to dance with her. It was so utterly ridiculous that she laughed. Her laughter caught the attention of a blond-haired man nearby and he moved to dance beside her.

She smiled back briefly and continued dancing, distracted by wondering if *he* was still sitting at the bar, watching her. It was a ridiculous thought, that a complete stranger might feel the same hum of attraction after a moment of idle conversation. It was not as though she planned to do anything about it, but she had to admit it felt nice being noticed.

In the background, she registered the beat shifting seamlessly into a soft, seductive ballad. She let her gaze drift around the dance floor just as a handful of couples moved close and began moulding their bodies together sensually. She looked away for a moment then looked back, transfixed by the sight of a couple melting together in a haze of locked lips and intertwined limbs, all the while maintaining a perfect rhythm.

Without warning, the blond man moved close. A chunky arm snaked around her waist and she froze. She took a step away, trying to think of a kind way to decline the dance without hurting his feelings, but he moved with her, not forcefully but still determined to get close. Needing to be free of the situation, she placed her hand calmly against the man's chest, shaking her head to show that she was leaving. Worried he wasn't going to take the hint, she turned fully and took a few steps away from the dance floor, only to be blocked by a wall of warm, hard muscle.

'Waiting for me?' The stranger's deep voice was like a balm to her nerves as he extended a hand towards her. To her surprise, she instantly placed her hand in his, allowing herself to be drawn into the delicious warm scent of his cologne until their bodies were mere inches apart. She was vaguely aware of the other man disappearing into the crowd, but it was becoming increasingly harder to form a coherent thought as a strong male arm moved slowly around her waist.

The smooth, steady rhythm of the music seemed to pound through the wall of her chest before joining her own erratic heartbeat. He pulled her close. So close that the smooth dark skin of his open collar was directly in her eye line, mere inches away. The tips of her breasts pressed momentarily against a wall of warm hard muscle before he moved back slightly. Her free hand hovered uncertainly for a moment before she bravely moved it upwards to link around his neck, her fingers resting between warm skin and the thick dark hair of his nape as he led her into an easy rhythm.

She had been given the finest dancing lessons as a young teenager to prepare her for the many occasions that a princess was required to perform a simple waltz or foxtrot. Nine times out of ten she tripped over her own feet, of course, but she knew the basics. But none of that could have prepared her for this moment. They seemed to dance for hours, moving in perfect unison. He was an excellent lead, confident and strong. He held her in such a way that she almost felt graceful for the first time in her life. His hands did not wander from their place on her waist; he didn't even try to pull her too close against him. She felt safe, she realised. What a strange thing to feel in the arms of a man she barely knew.

Her dark stranger bent his head and for a moment she wondered if he planned to kiss her. She held her breath, relaxing when instead his mouth stopped somewhere just above her earlobe.

'In my country, dancing like this is considered a very intimate act.' His voice was a soft rumble that sent an earthquake of shivers down her spine.

'Is that so?' Cressida breathed, hardly believing that such a husky murmur had just escaped her own suddenly dry throat. 'I can't imagine why.'

A mischievous smile played on his lips. 'You can't?'

'People dance all of the time. It's hardly dangerous.'

'I'm not so sure,' he murmured. 'Swaying like this… pressed so close… I can see how it would be seen as temptation.'

'Temptation for what…?' Her feverish brain wondered momentarily at his choice of words before realisation dawned with all the grace of a sledgehammer. She clumsily missed a step but her dancing partner barely reacted, correcting her misstep with graceful ease and continuing as though nothing had occurred.

'It is usually only married couples who might dance like this,' he continued, oblivious to her embarrassment. 'Or perhaps those who are engaged to be married.'

She barely registered his words as her mind focused on the heat of his hand as it began to move higher on her waist, resting ever so slightly on the bared skin of her lower back. It was as though the movement of his hand shifted some kind of invisible barrier between them. She looked up, meeting the visible heat in his eyes for a long silent moment. The air seemed to pulse with heat along with the slow seductive crooning of the jazz in the background.

Suddenly it felt as though every inch of her front was glued to a wall of warm hard muscle. Her body felt heated and loose in his arms, her mind telling her to move closer. A tiny fragment of her logical brain warned her to walk away. She ignored it.

'I doubt anyone else in here considers slow dancing to be such an important act.' She kept her tone even, trying to maintain some level of worldly composure in the face of her body's ridiculous reaction.

'I had quite forgotten that there was anyone else here at all,' he said softly.

Cressida looked up to meet his eyes; they were dark and earnest, no trace of humour or sarcasm. She felt her cheeks heat, her eyes lowering to rest comfortably on his chin. This was it, she told herself sternly—this was the moment where she should thank him for a lovely dance and make a calm and graceful exit.

The dance had been perfect, she told herself sternly—exactly what she had needed. She had sought a little excitement on her night of freedom and now she would leave London tomorrow and go happily to her duty. She could forget about this night, forget about this handsome stranger and easily go on for ever without wondering…

Suddenly she became aware that they had stopped dancing. The music had got faster and the other couples moved around the spot where they stood, entirely still in their embrace. She looked up. He was still watching her with that impenetrable gaze in a moment that seemed to stretch on as though separate from time entirely. His fingers flexed slightly at her waist, sending tingles up her spine.

What would it be like to feel his mouth on hers and his hands roaming over her body? The thought caught her by surprise, her cheeks heating as she ran the tip of her tongue along her suddenly dry lips. Her sister had described a kind of madness that had taken over when she'd met the man who was now her fiancé, an attraction that had overcome logic and reason. She doubted she could ever harbour such a passion. All of a sudden she despised the calm, rational Cressida who lived in fear of straying too far from her comfort zone. What would it feel like to simply have a thought pop into one's mind and act on it? To be a different version of herself, even for just a moment?

He cleared his throat and she felt the moment slipping away; the small window of time she had been granted seemed to be disappearing, leaving nothing but the promise of tomorrow. Of the life being forced upon her. The choices she would no longer be free to make. *But not yet*…a small voice inside whispered.

She looked up into the deep brown of his gaze, catching her breath at the blatant heat she saw there. Madness indeed, she thought as her breath stopped completely, realising what she was about to do. Letting impulse take the lead, she flexed her body upwards and pressed her lips to his.

Soft, firm lips remained still under the clumsy touch of her inexperienced kiss. The hands on her waist applied pressure, holding her where she stood as his lips began to move against hers, hard and fast. Suddenly the kiss was demanding and filled with a hunger that took her breath away. It was intoxicating and overwhelming and…utterly perfect.

Was this what everyone felt when they kissed a man for the first time? Was this what she had been missing out on all these years? It felt as though she was waking up from a deep sleep and feeling her body come to life for the first time.

When he pulled his mouth from hers all too soon, she felt the loss keenly, as though going from the warmth of a fire to the bitter cold.

He uttered something harsh and guttural in a foreign language before she felt herself being unceremoniously hauled away from the dance floor towards the private area at the back of the club. Still dazed by the earth-shattering kiss, she didn't think to protest, allowing herself to be steered into a semi-private booth shielded partially from view by a thick red velvet curtain.

'I didn't mean for that to happen.' He spoke harshly, his breathing slightly laboured. 'I didn't intend to—'

'Please, don't apologise,' she blurted, not wanting his regretful words to taint what had been such a wonderful moment for her. One half of her prayed silently that he would leave, while the other half wanted nothing more than for him to take her in his arms again. 'I kissed you, after all.' She forced a smile. 'And I'm glad that I did.'

'You might not feel that way if you knew who I was.' He spoke evenly, but his expression held a trace of darkness that had not been there before.

'Maybe it adds to the sense of mystery.' She attempted a smile.

'Is this what you were seeking tonight, coming here?' His voice was a low rumble as he took a step closer. 'Kissing strangers on a darkened dance floor?'

Something in his eyes brought gooseflesh to her exposed skin. She couldn't put her finger on it but the atmosphere no longer felt warm and anonymous; she felt suddenly exposed and thoroughly out of her depth. The realisation of what she had just done came crashing upon her like a cold shower and she took a few slow backwards steps.

'Thank you for the dance,' she murmured, avoiding his eyes. 'It was…wonderful.'

He raised one brow, leaning against the side panel on the wall. 'Time to return to reality already?'

Cressida nodded once, feeling a strange pull between needing to get away and desperately wanting to stay. She wondered what his name was, where he came from. So many questions would be left unanswered once she left.

And still she walked away.

She left the club and its swaying music behind as she emerged into the night, the sharp wind making her wish she had brought a jacket. As she looked around to find where her chauffeur had got to, a trio of men in dark suits seemed to appear from nowhere.

'Your Highness,' the tallest one said in accented English, 'do not be frightened. We are ordered here to assure your safety.'

'My safety?' she breathed, looking around the street wildly. 'Where is my driver? How do you know who I am? Ordered by whom?'

'Ordered by me,' a familiarly accented voice rang out in the silent night from the nightclub doorway.

Cressida whirled, inhaling hard as she was met by the sight of the dark stranger from the dance floor walking towards her. Wordlessly, he draped a heavy woollen coat across her shoulders, guiding her a few steps away from the small army of what she presumed to be bodyguards.

His accented voice rang in her ears, intensifying the sensation of unease along her spine that warned her she had made a grave mistake tonight. She had overlooked something important. Her heart beat frantically in her chest as she met his dark gaze. 'Who *are* you?'

'I am Sheikh Khalil Al Rhas, ruler of Zayyar.' He held her pinned with his dark gaze. 'And you, Princess, are in a world of trouble.'

CHAPTER TWO

CRESSIDA FELT THE weight of his words settle somewhere
in her chest. His accent, the way he had looked at her
when they'd first spoken—it all fell horribly into place.
'You can't be him,' she breathed.

'And yet I am,' he said smoothly.

Disbelief held her body frozen for what felt like an
eternity. Gone was the warmth from his eyes, replaced
by a hardness that sent prickles along her skin.

She had sourced a few photographs online of the
notoriously private Sheikh Khalil but the images she
had seen had shown pictures of a man who seemed
older, dressed in traditional white robes, his features
obscured by a headdress and sunglasses. Not smooth
shaven in a sleek open-collared suit, practically vibrat-
ing the air around him with a dark virility that made
her knees weak.

This was her *fiancé*? The man her father had described as old-world and ruthless? She thought of all
the anxiety that had plagued her, worrying what to say
when they first met or how she should behave...

'Was this a game to you?' Her voice was suddenly
ice-cold. 'Was it some kind of test to see how I might...
perform?'

'No,' he said simply, a strange look crossing his features. 'This was most definitely not a part of my plan for our first meeting.'

Cressida swallowed hard. 'Did you know who I was from the start?'

His jaw seemed to tighten before he answered. 'Yes.'

'Well, then, I fail to see how you weren't toying with me.' She shook her head, unable to stand still a moment longer. She had taken no more than two steps towards the street and he was by her side. A muscular hand encircled her wrist, stopping her progress.

'Let me go,' she gritted, snatching her hand from him with force.

'You will not walk away from me, Princess,' he said softly. 'We have not yet finished our conversation.'

'I most certainly am finished. I never want to see you again.'

His mouth hardened into a thin line. 'You can come with me calmly so that we can resolve this privately, or you can make things needlessly difficult.'

As she watched, his eyes drifted to the handful of men surrounding them. She felt the distinct sensation of being caged in and it was not pleasant. 'Where is Frank?' she asked quietly, suddenly worried for her loyal chauffeur.

He raised one dark brow. 'Your driver has been relieved of his duties, along with your incompetent bodyguards.'

'You can't do that,' she breathed, aghast. 'They are not at fault for my actions.'

His head cocked to one side. 'It's a little late for remorse now, don't you think? If a driver can be persuaded to overlook protocol by a pair of fluttering lashes, then he has no business being entrusted with the responsibility.'

'You can't do this.'

'Oh, I most certainly can,' he purred, encircling her wrist with his strong hand.

'For tonight, at least, your safety is my responsibility.'

She did not know why, shock perhaps, but she put up virtually no fight as he guided her into the limousine that lay in wait by the roadside. The team of guards retreated into their own imposing vehicles to the front and behind. Even when it became clear that they were driving in completely the opposite direction to her apartment, she could not speak. She felt cold, the skin on her arms prickling with gooseflesh.

If her driver and guards had truly been dismissed, then that meant they would have already alerted King Fabian. Her father had already made it clear that he was depending on her to ensure this union went ahead at any cost. Guilt gnawed at her stomach as she closed her eyes, focusing on the gentle sway of the car to distract herself from the many reasons why, once again, she was an utter disappointment to her parents. This was the first and only thing the King had ever asked of her directly, the first time he had spoken to her since…well, since he had decided she was no longer worth speaking to. She had finally been given an opportunity to prove herself, to save her kingdom. And, as per usual, she had failed spectacularly.

'Are we to travel in silence?' The Sheikh was facing her, one long leg propped over the other, making him seem larger and more imposing in the small space.

'I fail to see how making idle chit-chat with you

will make this situation any easier.' She purposefully directed her gaze out at the passing blur of streetlamps and shadows.

'You seem quite indignant for someone who chose to run away from her guards for a wild night out.' His voice held only the smallest hint of impatience.

'I am not the one who did anything wrong here.'

'Aren't you?' He met her gaze evenly.

Before she could retaliate, the car came to a stop outside one of the most exclusive hotels in London. They were escorted inside by the Sheikh's entourage, who shielded them both from view until they were safely inside a private lift.

The Sheikh's suite spanned the entire top floor of the building, offering a breathtaking view of the London skyline. She was instantly drawn to look out at the majestic sea of lights of the city she had spent virtually no time exploring in the past five years.

She was aware of the bodyguards moving around as they performed a thorough check of the rooms. A handful of other men and women appeared briefly, speaking to the Sheikh in a language she assumed to be Zayyari. Her studies had included most European languages, along with ancient Greek and Latin, but she had no experience of Middle Eastern tongues. The way the syllables cut and rolled off their tongues was fascinating; it was a struggle not to turn and observe the conversations.

After a while she became aware of the lack of noise in the open-plan living space. She turned just as he reached her side.

Sheikh Khalil cleared his throat gently. 'Have you

spent all of this time appreciating the view or plotting on ways to escape, I wonder.'

She turned to face him fully. 'At what point did I become your prisoner?'

'Despite how others may portray me, I am not a tyrant. I assured your family that I would escort you to Monteverre personally and I will not go back on my word, even if you choose to end our arrangement.'

His gaze travelled briefly to her mouth before returning upwards. Did she imagine the slight dart of his tongue to moisten his lips before he spoke again?

He took another step so that he was by her side, one hand braced on the glass. 'I came to London to meet my future Queen on neutral ground. To ensure that we might begin our union on equal footing and avoid history repeating itself. It seems I'm destined to fail on that point.'

Cressida lowered her gaze, knowing he was referring to his failed engagement with her older sister, Olivia. The fact that she was a replacement bride should offend her, but she couldn't blame him for wanting Olivia as his first choice. Her sister was graceful and beautiful with a flawless talent for public speaking. Who wouldn't want her as their Queen? The arrangement between Monteverre and Zayyar had been in negotiations for months until her sister had chosen to walk away before accepting the proposal.

'You are our last chance, Cressida. Make me proud.'

'Tell me why you didn't reveal yourself straight away,' she said, ignoring the echo of her father's voice in her mind and firmly throwing down the gauntlet between them. She simply could not go ahead with the deal if tonight had been some kind of practical joke.

She had *some* pride. But could she truly return to Monteverre a failure?

'It was interesting to find myself meeting you without the complication of my own identity in the way,' he said simply.

'You see yourself as a complication?' she asked quietly, mulling over his words.

'When seeing a person as they truly are, yes.'

She raised her brows at his honesty. She knew all too well how the world changed once people knew you had a title in front of your name. Sometimes for the better, sometimes for the worse.

'I am not in the habit of using women as toys to amuse myself—was that what you accused me of?' He raised one brow in challenge. 'However, I will admit when I am wrong. I should have immediately announced my identity once I realised you had no idea who I was.'

'Yes. You should have.' She bit her bottom lip, trying not to look at him directly lest she be overtaken by another flashback to what it had felt like to be in his arms.

'But perhaps none of that matters, as you have said you are finished with all of this and never wish to see me again.' There was no playfulness in his words as he moved across the room to take a seat in the living area. 'Truthfully, this entire deal has been a fiasco from the start, with your father's lies and manipulations. It's clear to me now that you can't have been entering into this marriage willingly if this is how you choose to spend your free time.'

Cressida felt a prickle of irritation rise within her at his easy reclined posture and flippant judgement. There was no way she was going to beg this arrogant man to honour their agreement. And yet she was not quite ready to return to Monteverre if that meant her father lost the deal that would salvage their kingdom's failing economy.

She settled for a nonchalant shrug of her shoulders. 'This is an unusual situation for me, Your Highness, not that it's any of your business.'

'Perhaps both of us acted on impulse, Princess. But still, now I've met you I can't see how you will be happy away from the freedom and thrills of this kind of life. I have a duty to my people to give them a Queen who will be fulfilled by her role.'

'Why not just leave me here, then?'

'I am taking you back to your kingdom, just as I promised I would.' He watched her, his expression entirely unreadable. 'Your father made it very clear that your time in London had come to an end. But, considering recent events, I also made sure to consult my own sources. They told me that you are no longer enrolled with the university and the lease on your apartment has been cancelled.'

Her father had been quite busy this past week. He had not been happy when she'd told him of her wish to accept the teaching position, even before Olivia had walked away from the deal with the Sheikh. Cressida swallowed hard, moving to take a seat directly across from him in the luxurious living area. She had been fully prepared to return to her home country right up until approximately two hours ago. Why all of a sudden did it seem more favourable to walk through hot coals than to set one foot on Monteverrian soil?

She straightened her shoulders, making direct eye contact with the man across from her for the first time since they had entered his suite. 'I know that you have spent months on these negotiations. My father told me that you had already begun to invest millions, according to the deal, before my sister walked away from the arrangement.'

His eyes narrowed slightly, the rest of his expression utterly still. Clearly he'd had practice in holding his reactions in check.

Cressida crossed one leg idly over the other. 'It's clear to me that both our kingdoms stand to lose if we walk away.'

He was thoughtful for a long moment. 'There is much at stake. But tonight has made me question some things. I did not expect you to be a saint, Princess. You have clearly lived a life of…freedom…during your time here.' He looked at her pointedly. 'But a man in my position requires one hundred per cent loyalty from the woman by his side. To project an image of stability and unity.'

She chewed on the inside of her lip, fighting the urge to shout that she had never even kissed a man before tonight, but she resisted. 'I would like to propose that tonight should not have any bearing on our arrangement.'

'And yet it does.' He cleared his voice, angling his face away from her. 'There was something between us tonight—an attraction. A political agreement such as this one does not mix well with emotional involvement.'

'You think I am emotionally involved after one kiss?' she asked.

He tensed. 'I mean that sometimes people tend to read more into simple physical chemistry.'

And by *people* he meant *women*, clearly. She fought against the urge to roll her eyes. 'I am not one of those *people*,' she said pointedly. 'I don't particularly do emotional connections. I have always been perfectly happy with my own company.' She didn't tell him that it wasn't really her choice to be so cold, simply a part of her make-up.

The Sheikh stood, pacing to the sideboard at the corner of the room and pouring himself a glass of iced water. 'So if I am willing to go ahead with the arrangement, you wish to uphold your end of the bargain?'

Cressida took a deep breath, mulling over her words carefully before she spoke. 'I think I would be willing, but only once I know that the terms will remain the same. That it will not be a…a true marriage.'

Khal paused at the slight tremor in the young Princess's voice. She sat perfectly poised on the low-slung sofa, long slim legs tucked demurely to one side. One would never guess she had been virtually plastered to his front less than an hour before. He cleared his throat, pushing the images from his mind. 'The legal agreements you have already signed state the general terms of the union. What they do not overtly mention is that absolute fidelity is required, along with every effort to maintain the perfect image. So while we might not be sharing a bed as man and wife, I assure you that I would still expect a true marriage.'

A strange look crossed her features. She took a moment of pensive silence before looking up to meet his gaze head-on. 'Are those rules the same for you?'

Khal let a moment of silence hang in the air. 'In my country, the act of marriage is not one that is entered into lightly, even one of a political nature. So yes, the terms of the union would apply equally to both parties.'

She stood, pacing towards the window and wrapping

her arms around herself before turning back to him. 'Well, then, I suppose I don't have any other questions.'

'You sound very eager to become my Queen, I must say.'

'It has always been part of my duty to my kingdom to marry advantageously, if required.' She shrugged.

'And abandoning your studies? That does not bother you?'

She frowned, looking away for a moment. 'It's almost as though you are trying to talk me out of this.'

'I'm making sure you won't bolt at the last minute,' he said plainly, seeing no need to mince his words considering the turn the night had taken.

Understanding dawned in the depths of her blue eyes. 'You are concerned that I will act as my sister did.'

'I am protecting my own interests, yes.'

She nodded, biting her lower lip. 'I don't think that my sister intended to behave as she did. The Olivia that I know was always true to her word.' She shook her head once, a frown marring her brow. 'I understand that you have a vision for your future wife. That Olivia fitted a certain mould. I must warn you that I have not been a part of public life for many years—'

'My team are aware of this and are prepared to help you in your new role.' He watched as she moved back to sit delicately on the sofa once more. It seemed as if she were unable to be still. 'You seem quite eager to perform your royal duties; it surprises me in someone who has not set foot in their kingdom for such a long time.'

Her shoulders stiffened slightly at his words. 'Of course I have personal reasons for agreeing to this marriage, Your Highness. They are my own, not ones forced upon me or held over me. All I can do is assure you wholeheartedly that I'm here because I choose to be.'

'That's more than enough for me,' he said smoothly as he stood and took the few steps to close the space between them so that he stood over her. She inhaled sharply, freezing as he reached into the pocket of the coat he had draped across her shoulders earlier. He withdrew a small black box and sat on the seat alongside her.

'I understand that this is the tradition in Monteverre?' He opened the ring box, revealing a delicate vintage ruby ring set in the finest gold.

'Oh…' Her eyes widened. 'There is really no need for…'

He took her hand, cutting off whatever she'd been about to say as he slipped the ring onto the correct finger and surveyed his handiwork. 'A perfect fit.'

She cleared her throat, frowning slightly as she blinked down at the sparkling gem nestled against her pale skin. 'Thank you.'

Khal was suddenly very aware of the intimacy of their position. He stood, clasping both hands together. 'We will stop first in Monteverre for a brief press conference, followed by an engagement party. The wedding will take place as quickly as possible, but likely will be in a few months' time to allow for planning and invitations.'

Cressida frowned. 'Oh… I hadn't realised the wedding would be a big event.'

'There is usually some fanfare when a King takes a woman to be his Queen.' Khal fought the urge to laugh.

'I was under the impression from your secretary that we would be married quickly, that's all. That time was important to you.'

'You have an objection to the timing of the marriage?'

'No, not at all. The sooner the better, really.' She shrugged. 'I just thought there would be some kind of spin put on it. A secret elopement or something.'

'You do not want a big public wedding?'

'Well, it's just… No offence, but you are hardly the most public of figures and I clearly have not lived in the spotlight. It might seem odd if we suddenly announce a big wedding. I don't even know who I would invite, other than my family.'

Khal frowned, considering the logic in her words. The plan had originally been formed to account for his first bride—it was true that Princess Olivia was much more of a public figure in the media than her reclusive sister. Once again, it seemed his plans were being thrown to the winds. But perhaps, this time, a change in direction might benefit him and help him to make up for lost time.

Cressida noticed that the Sheikh seemed suddenly distracted as he called for one of his assistants to show her to her room. She barely had a moment to bid him goodnight before she was swept away and shown into a luxurious bedroom. A fresh silky towelling robe and slippers lay draped on the bed and she wasted no time in stripping out of her tight dress and heels before flopping onto the giant bed in the most un-princess-like manner possible.

The events of the night seemed surreal in her exhausted state. Almost as if she was living in some alternate reality of her own life. She raised her hand into the air above her head, staring at the ruby glinting on her finger. He had slid the ring on her finger with such businesslike finality, and yet the touch of his skin on hers had set her pulse racing.

She closed her eyes against the onslaught of memories from the hours before. The feel of his hands on her waist as they'd moved to the music, that first electric touch of his lips against hers. She would never let him know that he had been her first kiss; that would make it matter somehow.

Which it didn't. It had just been a kiss. She closed her eyes, repeating the words silently to herself and letting the tiredness take over.

She was awoken before dawn and told that they would be travelling to the airfield immediately. The sky was still jet-black and the air frosty as she ascended the steps to a luxury jet bearing the Royal insignia of Zayyar. The Sheikh was already on board and conversing with a team of men and women in traditional Zayyari attire. He had changed into white robes and the elaborate headdress she had seen in pictures.

She was thankful that he'd had the foresight to have a small case of her belongings collected and delivered to her room during the night so that she didn't have to wear the red dress again. She had not expected him to think of her comforts. Or, more realistically, it was his assistant who had thought of her. She took a seat near the front of the plane, swiping through the news on her phone as she waited for the meeting to end.

'Cressida,' a familiar deep voice called to her from within the cocoon of staff.

She stood, making her way down the wide aisle to the long conference table in the middle of the aircraft.

The men and women of his staff bowed their heads, moving away and revealing their King, seated at the top of the table surrounded by official documents and paraphernalia.

'I had not realised you planned to fly to Monteverre at first light,' she said breathlessly, fidgeting with the hem of her simple white blouse. She felt ridiculously underdressed in her blue jeans and worn sneakers. Her more expensive royal attire was sadly out of date, considering she had not attended anything as Princess Cressida in years.

'Change of plan.' He looked up for the first time, pausing to sweep his gaze over her briefly. 'We fly directly to Zayyar.'

'You are not taking me home first?'

'I thought it best to take you home after we are married. Which will now be in two days' time.'

CHAPTER THREE

'Two days? As in forty-eight hours from now?'

Khal had kept his tone deliberately neutral, taking in her pleasantly flushed cheeks and tied back hair. She looked younger without all the make-up from the night before, her ash-blonde hair was now swept neatly back from her face in a tight elastic band. The austere style only served to draw more attention to her wide-set blue eyes and porcelain skin. Of course, the red dress of last night had been more expertly cut to show off her curves than the plain blouse and casual jeans she now wore but he could still see the delicate dip and flare of her waist. If he thought hard enough, he could remember how good those curves had felt under his hands only hours before...

Redirecting his wayward thoughts, he cleared his throat and focused on the papers in front of him. 'That is correct,' he said coolly. 'I ran your suggestion past my team last night, after you went to bed, and they took it quite to heart. It seems you may have averted us from a mistaken course of action indeed.'

'My suggestion?' she breathed, her eyes growing wider still.

'The change in PR operation, of course. You alone

spotted the likely backlash in public opinion. You were absolutely right to question it.' He nodded in her direction as though congratulating her on acing a project rather than bumping forward an entire wedding. 'You did say that you would prefer to get married as soon as possible.'

'Yes… I did say that.' She moved to a nearby seat and sat down heavily. She looked ashen all of a sudden, small and fragile in the large leather chair that cocooned her.

'You have an entire bedroom to yourself for the duration of the flight,' he said, motioning to a set of doors at the end of the main cabin. 'You can't have got very much sleep last night.'

She pursed her lips slightly. 'Thank you. I could do with some more rest.'

Khal felt a momentary flash of conscience as she disappeared through the doors but pushed it away. He had done what was necessary in bringing forward the date. He had made the best decision to protect his deal. The sudden sense of urgency he'd felt—to take her far away from the life she had led in London and back to his kingdom—was purely down to expediting matters and avoiding any more risk of her going back on the agreement. The sooner Princess Cressida was his wife, the sooner he could get back to the business of growing his kingdom's influence and doing what he did best.

Khal took the time alone to gather his thoughts, trying to shift the uncomfortable sensation that had settled in his gut. He felt completely unhinged, as though everything he had believed of himself was being challenged. This entire marriage debacle had done nothing but challenge him from the moment his advisors had suggested it as a solution to their problem with European trade.

From the start he had not been able to deny that an alliance with Monteverre made sense. The global perception of his country was vastly outdated, harking back to their war-torn history. Zayyar had enjoyed an age of peace and prosperity for almost a quarter of a century and still they hit wall after wall when it came to foreign politics. Monteverre was one of the oldest nations in the Western world; it had influence and sway and, best of all, it desperately needed help in the form of cash investments, due to years of spending far beyond its means. It was simple mathematics.

What was not quite so simple was the old Zayyari law that demanded a marital alliance between two highborn members of aligning kingdoms. His advisors had already been fighting a backlash from the older generation, who disagreed with their country's changing landscape. He needed a bride if he wished to avoid public uproar. Thankfully, King Fabian had assured him that arranged marriage for the royal descendants was still a firm practice in his kingdom. Khal was not overly fond of the King, but he had not believed him capable of coercing his own daughter to the point that she would run away to avoid a proposal.

Cressida had assured him that she was not being coerced as her sister had been, yet still he wondered what personal reasons drove her to accept a political arrangement. Clearly she had a strong sense of loyalty to her kingdom and her family. It did not take much imagination to picture her by his side, swathed in silks and jewels, hosting lunches and balls in the Zayyari grand palace for hundreds of guests from all over the globe.

The trouble was, he had imagined a cold marriage. So far, his response to his fiancée had been far from cold. He'd had a true marriage once, built on the foundations of love and companionship. He had no desire to try to recreate that, for many reasons.

But the attraction between them was a complication he had not foreseen. Five minutes with her in his arms and he had practically pulled her to the nearest private area, needing more. She had felt so good in his arms. Too good.

The moment that he had realised she was completely oblivious to his identity he had felt something awaken inside him that he had long buried. Suddenly his quiet political marriage had seemed a lot less straightforward. He had planned to sit and keep watch until she decided to leave of her own accord. Then someone had tried to dance with her and that small primitive part of him he tried his best to suppress had roared to life, moving in to claim what was *his*.

So much for changing his image of ruthless desert King.

He had not expected to be physically interested in the woman he married; it was not necessary to the arrangement, after all. His head was not usually turned by long legs and a short dress. But the moment he'd had her body pressed against his, he had felt his libido emerge from its self-imposed hibernation with a vengeance. He'd been possessed by the mad urge to press his lips to the soft parts of her neck and continue down… It had shocked him, the need.

The wedding would take place in two days. This time he had made sure of it. An iron-clad contract of law bound Princess Cressida to their agreement. If she went back on her promise, his financial investments into Monteverre's failing economy became null and void. Perhaps it was severe, but he couldn't take a chance on her backing out of the marriage just like her sister had. Not when the future of two countries lay in the balance. He was not a patient man, quite the opposite. He liked things to be done precisely when he planned. Soon he could get back to more important matters in his own kingdom.

Cressida tried to stifle a gasp as the helicopter lowered swiftly to the ground, depositing them on a crop of barren flatlands on the very outskirts of the Zayyari desert. Despite her attack of anxiety at the news that she would become Queen so soon, she had surprisingly managed to sleep for almost five hours before waking with a ferocious hunger. The rest of the flight had been spent nibbling on snacks and perusing some of the books she had found on board about her new home, the desert kingdom of Zayyar. It had been a smooth trip from the private airstrip and she had presumed that they would arrive directly at the palace in the centre of Zayyar's capital city of the same name. Her Internet research had provided her with some basic facts of what to expect from her new home, but nothing could have prepared her for the heat. Her blouse already felt damp on her back as Khal helped her out of the SUV and into the direct glare of the burning hot sun.

She had covered her hair with a pale pink scarf before they exited the jet, provided by one of his many assistants. In general, Zayyar was rather cosmopolitan for the Middle East; they did not enforce modesty among the women of its population. But apparently where they were going for their wedding ceremony was a sacred place. It was all very mysterious.

'We continue on horseback from here.' Khal's voice was gruff and sleep-worn as he gestured to where his guards had already begun to mount impressively large dark steeds. 'You will ride with me.'

She gulped, taking in the sheer size of the animal before her. She had never been one for horseback riding as a girl. But, before she could object, strong arms gripped her hips tight and she felt herself being swung up onto the saddle as though she weighed nothing at all. The hard warmth of the Sheikh's chest pressed tight to her back as he settled behind her and she felt her body tense. The effort of keeping her eyes on the horizon was a welcome distraction as they began a swift gallop across the sand. There was no sound around them other than the beating of hooves on the dry desert plain. Gone was the hustle and bustle of city life she had grown used to, the noise she had used to distract her just as much as the books she lived inside. The air she breathed in was warm and fragrant, reaching deep within her and calming her raging heartbeat.

The thought that she had spent the past five years in one city was suddenly ludicrous. There had been a whole world outside her self-imposed cage, waiting to be explored. They crossed the endless expanse of sand for almost an hour; her thighs ached from stopping herself from relaxing back into the warmth of the hard male chest behind her. She still thought of him as the Sheikh, she realised. Surely one should be on first name terms with the man you were about to marry? He shifted his body behind her in the saddle, keeping the horse in pace. She felt gravity press her backwards until every inch of her back was plastered to his hard torso. All at once she felt the heat of him seep into her skin, sending goosebumps down her arms. It took all her strength not to dart away from the sensation, away from the overwhelming urge to sink further into it.

Clearing her throat, she turned her head to dart a quick look up at him. Her throat dried at the vision of his hard jaw in profile as he focused on guiding the powerful stallion up the dunes. Clearly he was not as affected by the ride as she.

All thoughts of him were momentarily curbed as their small party crested the last dune and a vision of beauty spread out in the valley below them. Golden sands gave way to the lush green paradise of a small oasis. Nestled in the middle of trees and ancient stone pillars were colourful Bedouin-style tents and temporary structures.

'Welcome to the sacred ground of Old Zayyar,' the Sheikh announced beside her ear. One strong arm snaked around her waist to hold her in place as they began their descent down the steep rocky hillside. They were greeted by a crowd of men and women in traditional robes and clothing, the men in elaborate headdresses and the women adorned in beautiful paints and jewels.

Men banged drums as the Sheikh dismounted and lifted her down to the ground in one powerful movement. She felt entirely out of place in her T-shirt and jeans combo.

'This is your bridal party,' the Sheikh said softly in her ear over the sound of the music and babbling. 'My young cousins speak a little English. You will be taken care of.'

A young woman stepped forward as if on cue, bowing low. Cressida shook her head and raised her hand, preparing to tell the woman not to make such a fuss.

'You are to be my Queen, Cressida.' He spoke once more. 'Be prepared to be treated as such.'

She nodded, straightening her shoulders as the rest of the women in the crowd bowed low in the same fashion. Her chest tightened with anxiety, feeling so many eyes on her, but she forced herself to take a step forward and then another, following the young woman into a large tent and leaving the rest of the crowd, and the Sheikh, behind.

Evidently it was customary for her to meet and join hands with every single woman in the tribe, each one offering what she hoped were kind words in their native tongue as they inked delicate patterns of henna on her skin. The women seemed warm and welcoming, despite the language barrier between them. She was acutely aware of her own plain Western clothing amongst their colourful draped fabrics. She caught more than one woman staring or whispering behind her hand when they thought she was not looking.

Her self-appointed assistant, Aisha, was a young woman of around twenty who had begun studying English only the year before. In between the courses of their evening meal, Aisha told her how she had sourced books and studied alone for a time before applying for a scholarship to university.

'The Sheikh's first wife was a great patron of female education. I thank her in my prayers each morning and night,' Aisha gushed before biting her lip suddenly. 'Oh, how thoughtless of me to mention such a delicate matter on the eve of your wedding!'

Far from being offended, Cressida's curiosity was piqued. She had already seen from her online research that the Sheikh had been married once before. That his wife had died in a tragic car accident four years previously. He had not mentioned her in any of their conversations so far and she did not see the point in bringing up what was likely to still be a delicate subject. 'I confess that I don't know very much about the late Sheikha. I have read that she was much beloved?'

'Sheikha Priya.' The young girl nodded, a wistful smile crossing her lips. 'She was…truly beautiful. She helped many people…' Tears filled the young woman's eyes and she wiped them away, apologising profusely.

'Please, don't apologise. Her death must have come as quite a shock to everyone.' Cressida felt her chest tighten as she offered a napkin to the young woman.

'It was a terrible time for Zayyar. Her Highness was so young. And of course His Highness was the victim of such scrutiny afterwards…because of the rumours.'

Cressida nodded, not wanting to admit that she had no idea what these rumours entailed. She felt the urge to press further, to find out exactly how many secrets lay buried under the facade of her simple marriage of convenience. She allowed the temptation to pass, exhaling as the conversation flowed amongst the women around her and the meal was served.

After dinner she was inundated with gifts of vibrant fruit baskets, decorated sweet cakes and fragrant teas, flowers and little bottles of oil as traditional music floated on the air. Aisha dutifully explained the symbolism behind each of the gifts, how they strengthened

the couple's love for one another or brought fertility
to the marriage. Cressida tried her best to ignore her
discomfort at the thought of accepting such beautiful
gifts, as neither love nor fertility would play a part in
her marriage. She wished she could just tell them all
not to make such a fuss, that she was not a real bride.
That this was not the romantic fairy tale elopement
that it seemed. She had always hated being in the spotlight and it seemed impossible to avoid as the women
argued over her hairstyle and made final adjustments
to her wedding clothes.

As night fell across the encampment, Cressida was
finally left alone in her bridal tent. She could feel the
strain in her cheeks from the polite smile that she had
kept plastered on her face all afternoon. Her reflection
in a nearby mirror showed dark shadows under her eyes,
making her already pale skin seem even more translu-
cent. She exhaled slowly, removing the pink scarf that
covered her hair and combing it out with her fingers
while ignoring the rising anxiety within her.

She had not been aware of any scandal in Zayyar's
past when she'd committed to the marriage, but it made
sense if that was the reason why Sheikh Khalil would
go so far for a bride with Western ties. She had known
from the bare facts available on the Internet that he
was a widower, but, apart from a few vague news articles, that seemed as far as the information went. There
was no further mention of the Sheikh's activities in the
years since then. But she had noticed the way his staff
hurried around him on the plane…as though he was a
man to be feared.

So why did she not feel that same fear when she
looked at him? She thought of the shivers that had run

down her spine as he'd held her close on the horse ride across the desert, mere hours before. She had felt the opposite of fear; she had never been more excited in her life. She closed her eyes, placing one hand on her chest to feel the steady beat of her heart. No, she most definitely was not afraid to marry the Sheikh. She was more afraid of the intense attraction she felt every time he came close. Five years was a long time to spend trying to maintain her distance. He would find it easy, no doubt.

She straightened her shoulders, meeting her own gaze in the mirror once more. This was a job, she reminded herself. This was her duty. She would prove her loyalty to her family once and for all and make up for the mistakes she had made in her youth. Then she would be free to live her own life without guilt. She would be free of constantly feeling like a failure.

She moved to her bed, burying herself under the silk coverlet and closing her eyes tight. He had been her first kiss—it was only natural that she would be slightly affected by that milestone. She was not made of stone, much as she had tried to pretend she was. But she would not fail at this. If a cold, distant marriage of convenience was what the Sheikh of Zayyar wanted, then that was exactly what he would have.

The royal events team had worked quickly under pressure, creating a simple space that mixed elements of Western and Zayyari wedding cultures. Already the PR officials were drafting articles for the handful of magazines and newspapers who would be 'leaked' the news of the secret nuptials. The Princess had been right.

A large wedding would not have had half as much impact as this would.

Their marriage was to be a seamless union of east and west, a romantic desert fairy tale…or something like that. He had stopped listening to the event planner after she had begun talking about using sand as symbolism for their everlasting love. Little did they know how very far from the truth that was.

Khal stood in the heavy stillness of the desert air, watching as the sun began to dip low in the sky as evening fell upon them. The sand burned orange outside the intimate wedding tent and on the light breeze he could smell the fragrant pink flowers that had been arranged in vases and overflowing baskets all around the encampment in celebration. He picked one from a basket, simply to have something to do with his hands while he waited.

Priya had ordered similar flowers for their wedding day, he mused, the thought catching him off guard. He had ordered thousands of the blooms to celebrate their first anniversary. He crushed the delicate blossom in his hand, letting it fall to the ground as though it burned him. Of all the places for this farcical ceremony to take place, of course it would be here—they were in the very spot his parents had married. The sacred heart of his tribe and all the beliefs they held dear. A grand statement to the people of Zayyar, according to the team of advisors who had planned everything.

Priya had wanted a grand event, opting for a lavish three-day celebration in the Grand Palace. He steeled himself, willing his mind to change course. He could not think of his first wife, not when he was set to marry another at any moment.

Once they had arrived in the camp the day before, he had not wasted time in dispatching his fiancée to the women of the tribe, simply to put distance between them after the torture of the journey from the jet. In hindsight, opting to have her soft warm curves cradled between his thighs on horseback for an hour had not been his cleverest idea. He'd spent the afternoon riding across the desert to clear his head, cursing the lack of freezing cold lakes in their vicinity. He was not a teenager. He would not have his position made weak by his physical desire for the woman set to become his wife.

It was his own fault, for not taking a mistress in the years since Priya's death. He had always found an excuse not to move on—there had always been some battle to fight. Whether it was trying to find out the truth behind his wife's death or working against the economic repercussions of the rumours that had plagued him in the aftermath—that he had somehow been responsible for his wife's sudden demise.

He exhaled hard. He was a man. He had needs. And this was clearly the result when one suppressed those needs for too long. His fiancée was the very last person he could afford to desire right now. And the duty their marriage was based on made his situation even more difficult. He had demanded fidelity of her for the duration of their marriage; it was only fair that he offer the same loyalty himself. He would not risk the credibility of their union simply to slake his lust elsewhere.

His jaw felt as if it was made of stone as he heard a hush fall around the small gathering inside the tent. The event planners signalled that the bride was about to arrive. Khal stepped directly underneath two pillars swathed in snow-white gossamer fabric and watched as the small congregation of people appeared over the dunes. The single photographer who had been granted press access to the camp stepped forward, lens primed to catch the story of the year.

Khal kept his breathing steady, determined to play the part of calm groom. The people believed this to be a true marriage, after all. A romantic elopement between their King and his beautiful Western Princess. She was somewhere in the middle of the women, walking the same path that this tribe had walked for centuries. His jaw tightening painfully, he turned away and waited.

She reached his side with a whisper of silk flowing in the breeze, bringing the scent of jasmine and vanilla to his nostrils. Khal looked down and felt his breath catch for a moment. She was beautiful; there was no doubt. Pale porcelain skin offset by a shimmering golden wedding robe and heavy bejewelled veil. Was it a trick of the light or did her blue eyes seem to glow as she met his gaze?

Inhaling past the sudden tightness in his chest, he took his bride by the hand and began repeating his vows, his eyes never leaving hers. Part of the vows included a short sentence in Zayyari; he watched the concentration on her face as she vowed to be his for the remainder of their lives, a strange feeling within his chest as she did not stumble over the thick syllables of his native language. Their eyes met as the celebrant spoke of loyalty and devotion, of sharing a lifetime with one another. He looked in her eyes as the weight of their vows hung heavy in the air. And yet, as she promised to be true, he knew she spoke the truth. A strange feeling of calm came over him as he slid a wedding band onto her slim finger. A sense of complete victory.

Kisses not being customary at Zayyari weddings, they sealed their vows with a symbolic touching of foreheads. All too soon, he left the wedding tent with his new wife by his side to the rapturous applause of the small crowd. He watched as the new Sheikha bowed her head in delicate thanks as men and women complimented her beauty and good fortune in a language she did not understand.

Sayyid appeared by his side, clapping one hand on his back in solidarity. 'You seem happy, my King.'

'Do I?' he murmured, keeping watch as Cressida bent to take the hands of a group of children gathered around her. Security was tight and the people of the camp were peaceful, but still he resisted the urge to drag her away to privacy.

'You have barely taken your eyes away from your new bride. Am I to assume your concern is that she does not run away?' Sayyid smiled good-naturedly.

Khal smiled at the joke, brushing it off. He watched her because she was in a new country, entering a new life. He wanted her to feel at ease. And if he seemed happy it was because everything was going to plan, the lightness in his chest was a result of sealing a deal months in the making and securing the political future of his kingdom. Nothing more. He ignored his Chief of Security's raised eyebrow and returned to his wife's side as they continued to the celebration.

She had been told that celebrations in the camp usually lasted well into the night but not long after they had finished dining Khal leaned into her ear. 'Now it is time for us to make our exit and move to the ceremonial wedding tent.'

Her eyes snapped up to meet his. 'Just the two of us?'

'Don't look so excited, my Queen.' He made a motion with his hands to his guards that they were leaving before extending his hand to her. 'We must at least appear to be newlyweds who cannot wait to tear each other's clothes off.'

Cressida cleared her throat, staring at his outstretched hand and willing herself to stop being such an absolute coward. 'Can the King not make an exception to tradition?'

'Tradition is important to me,' he said simply. 'And it is even more important to the people of this sacred tribe. My family's tribe.'

'Of course.' She nodded, looking around at the small gathering of men and women, seeing how they looked towards their Sheikh's every move. And hers too, she realised with a sudden jolt. She had not thought much of the responsibility that came with her marriage. She was the Queen now, Sheikha of the realm.

Gulping, she stood as gracefully as she could muster. Khal bowed his head to the crowd once and she copied the motion, trying not to jump as the men suddenly shouted their approval in guttural tones. Raucous applause and what she presumed to be words of encouragement followed them across the sand as she followed Khal, flanked by four silent guards. The jewels on her veil tinkled gently as she moved forward, her skirts gathering around her legs with the effort of trying to keep up with the pace of the men and their much longer legs. Thank goodness she had not been forced to wear heels as well as the intricate dress.

From the outside, the tent had seemed just like the one she had stayed in the previous night. But as they stepped through the entryway Cressida went completely still.

If she had ever been the kind of person to hold romantic notions about her wedding night, this would probably be a fairy tale come to life. Swathes of jewel-toned fabrics cascaded from the intricately patterned roof, softly lit by traditional lamps and coloured lanterns. More lanterns provided a glow at strategic points around the space. Warm, luxurious Persian-style rugs carpeted the entire floor and the sensual scent of incense wafted through the air. But what drew her eye most was the enormous canopied bed of luxurious shimmering golden cushions that dominated the room. Filled with satin tasselled throw pillows and covered in bright red rose petals, it was as though it were created simply for the act of deflowering one's new bride. The thought made her gulp audibly.

'Leave us,' Khal commanded after two of his men performed a sweep of the tent's surprisingly large quarters. Once again, she felt slight unease at the level of security that preceded every move they made. She wondered at the reason for it; Zayyar had been at peace for almost a quarter of a century. But, before she could think too much of it, two things suddenly stopped her in her tracks. One, they were completely alone in the most romantic place in the entire world. And two, her new husband had removed his headdress and was shrugging out of his robe with surprising speed.

CHAPTER FOUR

Naked from the waist up, the man was like one of the statues she would stare at in the palace gardens when she lived in Monteverre. He had the body of a warrior, not a pampered king. He wore his hair long and unruly under the traditional head covering. Cressida whirled to put a few more feet of space between them, pretending to be suddenly interested in the array of fresh drinks and fruit laid out in the small dining area.

When she looked up once more, he had changed into a simple robe and loose drawstring pants, leaving only part of his chest bare. She gulped, looking away from the smooth mahogany skin and wondering when on earth she would regain control of her mind again.

'A robe has been laid out for you as well, and a private area for you to change.' He remained facing away from her, of which she was thankful. She moved quickly behind the screen, immensely grateful that her Zayyari bridal gown was nothing like the Western million-buttons-down-the-back variety. One simple zip ran down the side seam and she was free, stepping out of the pool of fabric and hanging it carefully.

It was a beautiful gown, so simple and elegant that she had almost felt beautiful for the first time in her life.

She had spent a lifetime being the ugly duckling, always comparing herself to her more attractive sisters. Eleanor and Olivia had vibrant red hair like their famous grandmother, the late Queen Miranda, who had once been named the most beautiful woman in the world. Cressida hadn't even inherited her mother's pale blonde locks, instead ending up with an in-between shade of ash-blonde that was entirely forgettable. But the shade of her wedding gown and the sparkling amber jewels that adorned it had made her glow from head to foot.

A standing mirror faced the screen; she angled her body sideways, hardly believing that the woman in the glass was her own reflection. Her lingerie was the same dusky golden shade as her dress but stitched with shimmering embroidery that drew the eye to the illusion of her much fuller breasts. Closing her eyes firmly at the thought, she pulled the buttery soft silk robe over her shoulders, crossing it at the waist and noting that it was significantly shorter than the male version. No drawstring trousers were provided for the bride, it seemed, leaving her legs completely bare from mid-thigh downwards.

Perhaps it was the sensually charged décor of the tent or simply the overwhelming romance of the day in general, but suddenly she felt flushed and hyper-aware of the silk material as it moved against her skin. She felt a strange tightening in her solar plexus at the thought of stepping beyond the screen and revealing her ensemble to the man who was now her husband. She wanted him to see her, she realised with sudden heat in her cheeks.

She wanted him to look at her like he had in London and she wanted to find out just what it felt like to have his hands on her again. But it was unlikely that whatever madness had existed in the dark in London would be present now. He had made it clear that they would not have a true marriage, had he not? With a shake of her head she pulled the robe as tight as it would go, successfully covering most of her cleavage but still leaving much of her legs on show. Opting to leave her hair down, she took a deep breath and stepped back into the open space of the tent, only to find Khal standing opposite her, the ridiculously sensual bed spread out between them like a battlefield.

If only she could have simply turned tail and ducked back behind the screen, just to avoid the treacherous pang of heat that ran down her spine. His eyes raked over her, moving slowly to take in her hair, her breasts, then finally resting upon her bare legs.

Unable to stand still under his scrutiny, Cressida willed herself to move past the bed, turning her back on him on the pretext of pouring herself a glass of water.

'If you plan to continue skittering around me it is going to be a long night.' He sat down and sprawled back on the bed, hands interlocked behind his head as he surveyed her.

She moved forward, stumbling over her words as she nervously twisted the tie of her robe between her fingers. 'I can sleep on the futon if you'd like to take the bed.'

'And have all of the servants know we spent our wedding night apart?' He sat up, both hands braced on his knees. 'We will share a bed for tonight.'

Cressida nodded once. 'Of course. I didn't think...'

'Am I so frightening?' He watched her, waiting.

She placed her glass of water on the table, still twisting one ribbon of her robe around her finger. 'I am not afraid of you. I suppose I'm a little overwhelmed by all of this.'

His brow furrowed. Without warning, he stood and walked to a low table in the middle of the tent where an elaborate tea service had been laid out. He poured the steaming dark liquid into traditional cups and handed her one. 'You seemed to enjoy the festivities this evening. I had worried the Old Zayyari style might be a little far from what you are used to.'

Cressida smiled. 'I adored every moment. I have not travelled much before so this is all so new, but in a good way.' She took a sip of the strong brew, feeling it warm her through. 'I'm impressed at how quickly your team arranged everything.'

'The clandestine photographs will probably be making their way into the wrong hands as we speak,' he mused, one corner of his mouth lifting.

Cressida noticed a tiny dimple appear in his cheek, but it was gone almost before it appeared. He never smiled fully, she realised. It was as though he did not allow himself to. She pushed the thought away, realising that he was still speaking of the ceremony, oblivious to how her thoughts had wandered.

'They simply made some modifications where needed. This tent in particular was redesigned to be larger but the sanctity still lies in the markings on the cloth itself.' He pointed upwards to the domed roof.

She looked up, squinting at a jumble of blurry shapes on the cloth. She could not make out a single thing at a distance without her glasses.

'Looking for these?' He extended the blurry outline of her glasses towards her. She took them quickly as though any prolonged contact might ignite the spark that she was quite happy to ignore.

Cressida adjusted the frames on her nose, craning her neck upwards. Sure enough, the pattern was made up of more than just an arbitrary design. Spread out above them were thousands of intricate symbols and markings painted in burgundy-coloured ink on the raw canvas material. An ancient language. Her mind soared to life, all other thoughts abandoned as she kneeled on the edge of the bed to get a closer look. 'Fascinating…' she breathed. 'What do they all mean, I wonder.'

'I have absolutely no idea,' he said, shrugging. 'The markings are very old; they can be traced back to the first Zayyari tribe that made their settlement in this exact spot. Spending the wedding night here is an ancient custom that goes back to the very dawn of my people.'

'Absolutely fascinating,' she said, mostly to herself.

'Yes, you've said that already.'

She brought her gaze back to him. 'I'm sorry but this kind of stuff is exciting for me. I'm trying my best not to get out my phone to research ancient symbols on the university library database.' She paused, realising with a pang of sadness that she no longer had access to the database as she was no longer a student. Still, she forced a smile. 'Don't worry, I won't.'

'I'm thankful. What would my guards think of me if they walked in here and you were on your phone on our wedding night?'

'Oh, I doubt the signal is strong enough in the middle of the desert, anyway.' She smiled, hardly believing that they were having light conversation after the hyper intensity of the past two days. He still did not smile but his eyes seemed warmer at least, more invit-ing, like they had at the bar the first time they'd spoken. It seemed like another life, rather than mere days ago.

'I can assure you the signal would be perfect,' he said, offhand. 'Zayyar trades in technology; it is the lifeblood of our economy right now.'

'I read an article that called you an economic genius.'

'The success of this kingdom is a result of the strength and knowledge of the members of govern-ment, the money that is put into educating our people and ensuring their quality of life. I believe that when you spend time on nourishing the foundations, growth is inevitable.'

'My father seems to have a very different idea on the measure of economic success,' Cressida said, tracing a circle on the embroidered bedspread. 'When his advi-sors warned him that economic crisis was forecast, his answer was to buy a new fleet of tanks for the military. A show of wealth, he called it. As though pretending debt was not a problem would simply make it true.'

'There are many leaders who think this way. My great-grandfather was one of them.'

She knew a brief history of the kingdom and the wars that had been waged two generations before. She could see it on his face, the tightness that settled around his eyes at the mention of his ancestor. 'It must be hard, having that history to work against.'

'Not as hard as it must have been for those who lived through it.' He became quiet then, his features turn-ing hard.

'You care a lot about your kingdom,' she said simply.

'The same must be said of you, to have agreed to a marriage in order to save it.'

Cressida shrugged, studying the markings on the ceiling to avoid his knowing gaze. 'There are not many things that third in line to the throne is expected to do, except remain free of scandal and marry according to the King's wishes.'

'And now King Fabian finds himself with only one direct heir...' Khal mused.

Cressida looked up, surprised that she had not thought of that fact. Now that Olivia had given up her place in line to the throne the duty fell entirely upon Eleanor to ensure there was a new generation of Sandovals to carry on the name. And the throne. 'My father is not known for his excellent decision-making skills.'

'Your sister will make an excellent queen,' Khal said earnestly. 'I do not doubt that the future of Monteverre is in competent hands.'

'They just need to survive the remainder of my father's rule.' Cressida smiled ruefully, worrying at her bottom lip. 'But thank you.'

She felt something bloom in her chest at his kind words. She had always looked up to her oldest sister for guidance as a child but she had never envied her position one bit. She had never harboured a desire to become Queen, knowing her strengths lay happily in academic work and keeping a low profile. Just look where that had got her.

'I must point out that you said that it was your duty to remain free of scandal, and yet in London...'

'I was not seeking scandal,' she said, her shoulders straightening. 'I just acted on impulse for the first time in my adult life. It made sense at the time.'

'And now?'

She felt it humming between them again, that sizzle

of awareness that she wished she could ignore. But the events in London had made that entirely impossible. She could not tell herself that the attraction was one-sided any more than she could tell herself that the earth was square. It was simply a fact, heavy in the air between them. Ever present in the tension that seemed to coil tight in her abdomen whenever she was in his presence.

'Now it is irrelevant.' She shrugged. 'I am…your wife.'

Something darkened in his eyes at her words. 'Indeed.'

The large bed suddenly felt too small, her body restless under his heated gaze. She turned her head away, murmuring a hasty goodnight as she tried to relax into the pillows. She was vaguely aware of him moving to extinguish some of the lamps in the tent before returning to the bed but she didn't dare open her eyes. Feigning sleep soon became effortless as the activities of the day caught up with her and sleep claimed her.

It was too hot, Cressida mused, turning over onto her stomach and feeling a sheen of sweat on her skin. The air in her nostrils was white-hot and strangely heavy in her lungs, almost painful. Her eyes snapped open, seeing a strange glow illuminating the room like dancing lights through a fog. Not fog, she corrected herself, smoke.

She felt drunk, consciousness sliding away from her like desert sand through her fingers. Sleep pulled her back, the strange dream melting away.

A man's voice shouted nearby in a language she could not understand, jolting her once more. Then she was being lifted from the bed into strong arms and carried at frantic speed. The strange fog suddenly became recognisable smoke in her lungs, the dancing lights the visible flames of a red-hot fire that was burning up one entire side of the tent. Suddenly the stars were above them and fresh oxygen filled her lungs, making her eyes water. She looked up and found herself eye level with Khal's strong jaw, his powerful body carrying her in a zigzag path through the encampment to where a trio of black dune buggies lay in wait. He deposited her onto the back seat, taking her face in his hands.

'Are you okay?' he breathed, his voice hoarse from smoke and exertion. 'Speak to me.'

'I'm… I'm fine, I think.' She coughed, shivering as realisation of what had just happened began to seep into her consciousness. The look on his face said it all—this was no accident. 'Are we in danger?'

He did not answer her question. 'We will be travelling under darkness but I will protect you. You will not step from my side until we reach the palace, understood?' He turned but did not remove his hand from where it lay on her forearm, waiting for the guards to catch up before he began issuing quiet orders. The men simply nodded, obeying their leader and preparing to depart. Khal slid into the seat beside her, draping one arm over her as they set off, a guard at the wheel. His face was only visible for a few moments before the complete darkness of the desert engulfed them and she couldn't help but grip him tighter. *'I will protect you,'* he had said. And she believed him.

He stayed by her side as they moved from buggy to helicopter, holding the woollen blanket around her the entire time. Preserving her modesty. She tried a few more times to ask what had caused the fire and was met with stony silence from both Khal and his guards. She was not to worry about that, they said. The lack of information only served to heighten her unease. The people of the tribe were peaceful; surely the fire had been accidental? And yet the look she had seen in Khal's eyes as they moved away from the desert was not one of annoyance at someone's foolish mistake. It was a look of absolute rage.

Soon the inky blackness of the desert below gave way to a sea of lights, main roads winding towards a large city. Once they had touched down within the old palace walls she felt Khal visibly relax beside her. Knowing that he had been worried the entire time gave her a sharp pang of anxiety.

An elderly servant appeared and offered, in perfect English, to settle Her Highness in the Sheikha's apartments. The sudden noise that came from Khal's mouth startled her. He gave a few commands in his native tongue and the servant nodded once and disappeared with quiet efficiency.

'Where will I be staying?' Cressida asked, surprised that her voice did not shake after the panic of their ordeal.

'With me. Where you will be safe,' he said simply. His hand was gentle but firm as he gripped her elbow, motioning for her to walk. The first pink fingers of dawn were beginning to snake across the darkness above them. She had barely got a glimpse of the courtyard of her new home before she was being led at speed along winding anonymous stone passageways, deeper into the heart of the palace.

Khal never let go of her arm. She was immediately aware when they entered a more modern wing, more refined and luxurious in its décor. The guards performed a quick sweep of the rooms around them before Khal motioned to dismiss them. He spoke one phrase to his own personal bodyguard; the large man nodded once and closed the door behind him with a soft thud.

'They need to clear the rest of the wing,' he said wearily, running a hand along the stubble on his jaw. 'I would like the doctor to see you before you rest.'

'I'm fine, Khal, honestly.' She shook her head. 'All I need is to sleep.'

'You called me Khal,' he said with surprise.

'I suppose *Your Highness* just seems a little too formal now that we're married. And you did just carry me out of a burning tent.' She felt laughter bubble in her throat, along with the irrational urge to burst into tears at the realisation that this man had probably saved her life tonight.

'You need to be seen by a doctor,' he repeated. 'There was a lot of smoke.'

Cressida nodded, remembering the thickness of the smoke filling her lungs, the burning heat prickling at her skin. Then she remembered how quickly she'd felt safe once she was in his arms, enveloped in his strength. Tears filled her eyes and fell down her cheeks before she even realised what was happening. She turned her face away quickly, not wanting him to see her weakness. But hiding was useless; he was by her side almost before the first tear fell, gathering her in his arms and holding her tight. A few choked sobs escaped her throat; she stifled them with her hand, embarrassed at her complete loss of control. 'I never cry,' she half sobbed, half laughed at herself.

'It's the shock,' he murmured. 'Just breathe.'

She obeyed his command, focusing on the warmth of his arms and the steady beat of his heart somewhere near her ear as she inhaled and exhaled. When she finally felt strong enough to step away, he surprised her by holding her still.

Cressida's stomach flipped at the look in his eyes as strong muscular fingers cupped her jaw. He considered her eyes with such fierce intensity that for one crazy breathless moment she wondered if he might kiss her. No sooner had the thought crossed her mind than his lips were on hers, hot and demanding. His hand fisted in her hair as he angled her to deepen the kiss while the other snaked around her waist to gather her against him.

Perhaps it was the adrenaline still coursing through her veins, or the reminder of her own mortality, but his touch was like kindling to a fire. She wanted to fall into the oblivion of desire and forget all the reasons why it was a bad idea. All she cared about was that there should be less robe between them and more touching. Much more touching. He pressed his thigh between her legs, pinning her to the wall as he kissed her so hard she was light-headed. But no sooner had she begun to sink into him than he was gone. He took two steps away, bracing one hand against the door as he got his breathing under control.

'We have both been through a lot tonight,' he said quietly, not meeting her eyes. 'You should go and get some rest. There are three guest rooms to choose from in my wing; choose whichever you wish.'

Cressida did not trust herself to speak, nodding once as she readjusted the front of her robe to cover herself. Clearly that kiss had just been the result of shock; she knew not to read too much into it. He had been more than clear that they would not behave as man and wife. But it seemed that her body had not received that message. She raised a hand to her face, feeling the blush creep as far as her forehead. The enthusiasm with which she'd kissed him made her blush deepen even further.

Her heart pounded furiously, the remnants of such a sudden flare of passion ebbing slowly away. He, on the other hand, seemed to have regained his composure with complete ease. Anger crept into the corner of her vision. How dare he be so cool and collected while she felt completely turned inside out? It wasn't fair.

A firm knock on the door dissipated what was left of the intimate moment and Cressida spun on her heel to pull her robe tighter around her. She didn't dare to look to see if Khal showed any physical signs of unfulfilled lust, focusing her gaze downwards to take in the patterns on the tiles under her bare feet.

'The adjoining rooms have been cleared.' Sayyid's voice came from behind her, in English for her benefit. 'Come with me, Your Highness.'

Khal made no move to speak or meet her gaze as she passed him; she tried not to feel hurt or rejected at his distance. He probably had many things to attend to other than escorting his new bride to her room. He was King, after all.

Steeling herself, she followed Sayyid to her bedroom and tried to ignore the sense of loneliness that rose in her with each step.

CHAPTER FIVE

'WHAT ON EARTH was His Highness doing sleeping in a tent in the first place? It's utterly ludicrous!' exclaimed the Minister of Defence. 'That encampment was likely filled with thugs and ruffians.'

'It is tradition. Part of the family legacy,' someone at the back of the room added.

Khal made his arrival known by clearing his throat, the sound seeming to cut through the unusual din in his official chambers. The emergency dawn meeting had been assembled by Sayyid, his Chief of Security, who currently looked as though he might like to tear a chunk out of the rather elderly Defence Minister.

'Gentlemen, take your seats,' he commanded, in no mood to deal with the squabbling that ensued with this many egos in one room. He hadn't slept since the encampment; the stench of smoke still clung to his skin, even after showering.

'Your Highness, we are deeply troubled to hear of this unfortunate incident,' the Chief of Police offered respectfully. 'I have assembled a team to investigate the site; they are en route as we speak.'

'Do we really need the police involved?' the minister intervened. 'I mean, we aren't sure of the origin of

the fire. For all we know, it could have been a tribes-
man tripping over a lamp.'

'The King has expressed his wish for a thorough investigation,' Sayyid said loudly.

All eyes moved to him. Khal nodded once to confirm
and watched as the men's attitudes changed instantly to
rapt attention, some even taking notes as Sayyid outlined the security measures taken and the times of guard
check-ins throughout the night.

'Your Highness, are you worried that there is unrest
amongst the old orders?' An elderly man, one of his father's long-time advisors stepped forward. 'You once
expressed the belief that they were behind the death of
the late Sheikha Priya.'

'His Highness made those statements while experi-
encing enormous grief,' another advisor said pointedly.
'The Sheikha's death was deemed accidental.'

Khal felt the casual mention of his wife's death like
a punch to his gut. He stood before he had the sense
to rein in his anger. 'The investigation into my wife's
death is still ongoing,' he hissed.

The elderly man shrank back visibly, realising he
had overstepped the mark.

The Minister for Foreign Affairs spoke softly, ad-
dressing each of the men around the oval table in an effort to calm matters. 'Have a care for the language used
in this chamber, gentlemen. All it takes is one whiff of
scandal to cause an international spectacle.'

Khal turned from the table, unable to stand one more
minute of their so-called politics. 'This meeting is over.
Any questions about the incident will be addressed to
my personal security team.'

He didn't know where he was going, anger powering

him along the ancient passageways until he finally felt the sun on his face. Tension filled his veins, the effort of holding back memories threatening to undo him. He changed direction, moving towards the stables with sudden intent. He demanded his prize stallion to be readied and wasted no time in switching his traditional robes for tight-fitting jodhpurs and well-worn boots. He did not speak to the boy who handed him the reins, impatiently launching himself up into the saddle and taking off in the direction of the sand.

With the wind on his face and the pounding of hooves under him, he finally allowed his spine to relax as he moved with his horse, their bodies in tune as he pushed the great beast to the limit. Takaa was a demon, the fastest horse he had ever owned, and right now he had never been so tempted to test his limits. Knowledge made him slow down as he got close to the boundaries of the old palace lands, veering off down the hill to where an almost dried up ravine formed a small oasis of sorts.

Takaa drank deeply and Khal splashed water onto his sun-warmed face, feeling the midday heat begin to claw at him through his thin shirt. His fists were almost white with the effort of suppressing the rage that had begun to unravel inside him in the chambers. They spoke her name as though it were a trivia, not a bomb that had the ability to tighten his gut with emotion. Grief was an obvious one; he most definitely had allowed grief to sink its mighty claws into him more than once in those first months following Priya's sudden death. She had been his wife for five years, his rock during his father's death and his ascent to becoming the leader he was today.

Everyone had offered him condolences and comfort and in time he had moved past it to the point where he could return to normal life. But the anger was another issue entirely. How did one resolve anger that was soul-deep when the woman who'd caused it was being lamented by their people so much they built shrines to her in the streets? Poetry was written about her beauty, her grace.

He had been left virtually alone with the knowledge of who his wife truly was. How she had betrayed him and everything their marriage stood for. How he had driven her to that betrayal with his own over-controlling measures. How did he resolve the guilt and the regret that ate away at his very soul—that things had not been different?

He growled, throwing the nearest rock at the water so hard that Takaa startled and began to pull back at the reins. He placed his palm flat on the horse's neck, crooning low in his throat until the animal stopped resisting and leaned down to drink once more.

The memory of seeing the smoke last night, of rushing to get Cressida to safety while he was sure his heart would burst through his chest. It had brought him right back to the moment he had been told of the accident. It was as though, for a few moments of madness, both incidents had been one and the same and he was trapped in a nightmare of sorts. And then, when the danger had passed and he was sure she was safe and alive, holding Cressida in his arms while she fell apart had been almost more than he could bear. She was not a woman who lost control of herself easily; that much was painfully evident. And yet she had shown him her weakness. And how had he responded? By ravishing her at the first opportunity, beast that he was.

He had never felt such a challenge to his self-control

than when he was around her. With each encounter, it felt as though he were losing his grip on a cliff face one finger at a time. She was getting under his skin and it simply could not continue. The physical attraction between them was more than inconvenient. It was a risk to the business arrangement of their marriage. They needed to keep their roles clear so that the next five years passed without incident. She would be the perfect Queen as he required her to be and he would break down the various political walls that stood in the way of his development plans with ease. Then, once their time was up, they would part without difficulty or complication.

He mounted Takaa swiftly and kicked off back to the palace, a plan in place. He would resolve this situation just as he did every other area of his life, with careful management and the complete absence of emotion.

While the dramatic details of the reasons behind their late-night arrival were kept carefully under wraps, news of the new Sheikha spread through the palace quickly. Cressida was awoken at dawn by a handful of servants and a young dress maid, who set about draping her in traditional silks and jewels. Zayyari was not one of the languages taught in her university and she found it incredibly frustrating not being able to make out a single word of what the women said as they spoke to one another in low tones, avoiding her gaze. She had the strange feeling of being a new statue on display at a museum.

She made a mental note to begin studying as soon as possible. The thought of having something even remotely connected to her previous academic accomplishments made her feel slightly less at sea in her new life. She had always felt most comfortable when she planned her goals for each term and ticked items off one by one. As she was dressed and styled with hair and make-up, she mentally listed out the materials she would need to get started.

Just as she had begun on the prospect of brand-new stationery, an older woman entered and announced herself in English as her new assistant.

'You are expected to breakfast with the esteemed Sheikha Amala and Princess Nia this morning,' the older woman said, scrolling down the screen of a sleek tablet as she spoke. 'Your new mother and sister-in-law, as they are called in the West.'

'Where will that be?' Cressida asked, trying to conceal the sudden rumble of her stomach along with the fact that she had no knowledge of anyone in her husband's family.

'They live in the palace grounds,' Rana said simply. 'Then this afternoon we will commence your etiquette lessons, followed by cultural and language tuition.'

'Etiquette lessons?' Cressida repeated, her mind stumbling over the sudden weight of having an itinerary handed to her.

'His Highness has arranged for an intensive month of tuition to make you more comfortable in the run-up to your celebration ball.'

She was to be given a ball? As in, an entire event to celebrate her? She fought the urge to flap her arms at the woman currently applying make-up to her eyelids. This was too much to absorb while sitting completely still. Taking one deep breath, followed by another, she waited for the make-up artist to move away for a moment before narrowing her gaze on her new assistant. 'You said the Sheikh has arranged all of this?'

'Along with his team, of course. The priority right now is for you to feel as prepared as possible in your role as Queen.'

Or did the Sheikh himself simply wish for her to be kept as busy and out of sight as possible? Cressida wondered. She didn't know why she felt a sense of rejection that he had not chosen to at least eat breakfast with her in order to inform her of his plans. They had not spoken at all of what the day-to-day workings of their arrangement would be. He was not breaking any promises.

So why did she feel so utterly alone of a sudden?

She simply wished to ask for further news on the fire at the encampment, she told herself. She did not like being left in the dark on the matter. She would seek him out, perhaps. She would ask him for an update and perhaps clarify what was to be expected of her from this point, other than the ridiculous ball and the lessons he and a team of servants and tutors had apparently deemed necessary.

Finally, the make-up artist finished her work and stepped away. Cressida barely even glanced at her own reflection; she needed to stand and move and have a few feet of space to herself for the first time in two hours. The fact that it had taken two hours to get dressed was utterly ridiculous; she had always just put on an outfit, brushed her hair and gone about her day with minimal fuss.

'Is everything okay, Your Highness?'

Cressida looked up from the stifling weight of her thoughts to find all three women looking at her worriedly. She straightened, remembering herself, and plastered on the most serene royal smile she could muster in the face of her inner turmoil. 'I'm fine. Let's get started on the day, shall we?'

* * *

Khal's mother and sister turned out to be surprisingly warm and inviting. Their family apartments were smaller and slightly less formal than the Sheikh's wing. They made their introductions and she was hugged warmly by her new mother-in-law before they sat together to enjoy a warm breakfast of spiced breads, fresh fruit and hot Zayyari tea.

The Sheikha Amala was younger than Cressida had expected, a beautiful woman with perfectly applied make-up and eyes that shimmered with kindness. Princess Nia was only slightly older than Khal, with a family of her own. She spoke fondly of her two young sons, who attended an elite boarding school in Scotland for much of the year but returned to the palace for holidays. Khal's mother did not speak any language other than her own but the Princess conversed easily in both French and English and talked wistfully of her time abroad in Paris when she was younger.

After a time, the Sheikha's mood seemed to change as she began to speak with her daughter as translator, asking for details of the secret wedding ceremony. Cressida described the welcoming environment of the encampment, leaving out the details of the heavy security presence and the fire that brought the night to an abrupt close. No sooner had Cressida begun to describe her fascination with the symbolism on the wedding tent than the older woman stood with a loud sniff and excused herself from the room.

'Did I say something wrong?' Cressida asked the Princess, her worried gaze following her as the door snapped shut, leaving just the two of them.

'My mother is deeply unhappy that Khal did not

allow us to attend the wedding,' Nia said, taking a sip of her tea. 'He explained that it was necessary—it was to be an elopement, and none of the royal family would be present.'

'I am sorry.' Cressida bowed her head. 'It all happened very fast. I'm sure he would have preferred to have you there.'

Nia smiled sadly. 'I think she is upset because she knows that is not the case.' She pursed her lips. 'I have two sons. I know my heart would break to find one of them had shut himself off from me. My brother has been like a stranger to us these past few years. He grieved for a long time. I know it well, such grief. I lost my own husband after only three years of marriage. A loss like that leaves a hole in your soul.' Nia sighed. 'Grief can be so destructive…it takes a part of you with the one you lost.'

The young woman's eyes filled with tears and Cressida felt the urge to reach out and embrace her. Thinking that might be a tad too familiar for a first meeting, she settled for a single solemn pat on her hand. Nia smiled, wiping away the single tear that had escaped her heavily made-up eyes.

'I imagine it is not enjoyable to think of your husband when he was so entwined with another.' She winced. 'I did not think before I spoke.'

'Love is not a fundamental part of this particular marriage,' Cressida said carelessly, regretting the words as soon as they escaped her mouth. 'What I mean is…'

'It has not been disclosed by my brother, but I had a feeling that this had something to do with politics.' The Princess smiled. 'Don't worry; your secret is safe with me.'

'Thank you. And I'm sorry for your loss.'

The older woman shook her head gently. 'I am grateful for my position. I have my brother to watch over my sons as they grow into young men. I have time to spend with my mother, though she can be a little dramatic.' She laughed good-naturedly.

Cressida found herself smiling, a real smile. She liked Khal's sister very much and it was nice to know there was someone here to talk to who was not employed by Khal to watch over her or transform her into the perfect Queen. All too soon, their time was up and Nia rushed off to attend to her mother.

Cressida left the family apartments and trailed behind her assistant for an extensive tour of the palace grounds. The historical Grand Palace compound was almost three hundred years old but showed clear signs of renovation in certain places. Her assistant pointed out the renovations as scars of the wartimes when the palace had been damaged by rebels. Cressida thought of Khal and his determination to have his kingdom accepted by the world despite the violence in Zayyar's past. How many other areas of this beautiful kingdom had been destroyed and rebuilt?

In the cavernous portrait gallery, she was shown depictions of Zayyar's past rulers. Fierce-looking men with long beards and swords sheathed by their sides. As the paintings became more modern, she instantly recognised the face of Khal's mother, by the side of an older man. The old Sheikh had kind eyes, not too different from those of his son. The family resemblance was quite strong.

The next picture portrayed a young Khal alongside a beautiful raven-haired woman. Cressida paused, looking up at the picture of her husband and his original

Queen. She was a stunning beauty, all dark features and effortless grace. He was entitled to still be in love with his dead wife, she reminded herself. Theirs was not a marriage built on the pretence of love or even affection. If anything, it should make things easier knowing that he was emotionally unavailable.

She forced herself to move away from the shadow of the woman who had captured her husband's heart, knowing that such a matter should not concern her. She was an instrument of political influence, not a true wife, and she would be a lot happier if she kept that thought front and foremost in her head.

Learning a new language was her favourite pastime in the whole world, so when she sat down to her first Zayyari lesson with her personal tutor, naturally she expected to feel the same passion and excitement that always came over her with a new academic challenge. But after half an hour she still could not pull her thoughts away from her talk with Nia and the mysterious scandal of the late Sheikha's death. Seeing the picture of Khal with Priya had got under her skin. Why did she feel the urge to compare herself to the dark-eyed beauty? To wonder if Khal compared her too. She had already known that she was second choice to her sister Olivia to be his bride. She had been able to rationalise that as Olivia was older and more famous than she was.

But she could not rationalise how she felt in this moment. A sensation prickled in her chest, peculiarly like jealousy, and she pushed it away, throwing herself into her lessons for the day and determined not to think of the Sheikh at all.

Or his beautiful lost love.

CHAPTER SIX

THE NEXT DAY, once again, the Sheikh was nowhere to be found. Still, he made his presence known by ensuring she had meetings with various advisors whose sole purpose was to groom her to become his perfect Sheikha. She took another more detailed tour of the palace and grounds, accompanied by guards, of course, and tried not to be completely overwhelmed at the prospect of memorising the various winding mile-long corridors.

The royal compound had to be at least twice the size of the palace in Monteverre and it was filled with a history that fascinated her. To her delight, her request for a few books on the history of Zayyar led to her being introduced to an entire wing of the palace filled with the royal collections of art, sculptures and, best of all, books. Thousands and thousands of books.

Still, she spent the afternoon looking over her shoulder, expecting to find him standing in a doorway or walking towards her with that dark unreadable gaze. Not that she was waiting for him, she told herself. Really, she was quite glad to have the time to adjust to her new surroundings without feeling as if he was scrutinising her every move. She dined alone in her suite, a simple meal of traditional slow-cooked meats and fragrant rice. Afterwards she took an idle stroll down the corridor towards the Sheikh's wing, casually slowing as she passed the large gilded double doors.

'His Highness has gone to Valar for meetings,' her bodyguard said quietly.

'Of course.' She nodded, as though she knew exactly where her husband was and what he was doing. 'I thought this was the way to the garden terrace.' When she was kindly redirected to her destination she spent barely a moment looking around the exotic plants before returning to her room, feeling utterly foolish for leaving in the first place.

Valar was the new city on the coast; she had read about it in her studies. It was where her ball was to be held at the beginning of next month. She felt her mild irritation grow into a more solid simmering displeasure at her new husband's disappearing act. Was it so unrealistic to expect a single conversation with one's husband? She set to practising in her mind what she would say when she eventually saw him.

The next day passed in exactly the same fashion; meals were taken alone in her suite, except for a pleasant mid-morning tea with Nia. Aside from that, the only company she had were the various people in the Sheikh's employ, all of whom called her 'Your Highness' and did not make eye contact. Still, she took it in her stride, taking advantage of the pool of knowledge at her fingertips in the library and enjoying the heat of the sun on her face on a leisurely walk in the gardens.

After only two full days at the palace, she found herself longing for the calm of the evening when she could close the door of her private apartment and be completely alone. There were guards outside and a maid came to check in occasionally but, for the most part, she was left to her own devices. So far, that meant immediately changing into her pyjamas and camping out by the open balcony doors to read the books she had found on Zayyar's fascinating history and traditions. Occasionally she would look up and catch sight of the sprawling desert laid out beyond the palace walls, further than the eye could see. It took her breath away every time, the raw beauty of this place and how completely untouched it was. She had not expected to feel so calmed by the desert, or so drawn to it.

Her current reading material consisted mainly of books on the history of Zayyar and its customs but she had also taken time to learn the language of her new home outside the formal tutor-led lessons. She had always enjoyed exploring a new language on her own terms, finding the true rhythm of it by herself. As Sheikha, she would be expected to be knowledgeable and respectful of her nation's traditions but she did not necessarily have to become fluent in their language. She simply could not resist the idea of an entirely new tongue to perfect and actually have the chance to use it on a daily basis. It was something to keep her mind busy, she told herself, as her husband seemed to have zero interest in her company.

Despite her best attempts to fill her time, she felt loneliness begin to set in. She had always been comfortable with her own company, but suddenly being alone with her books didn't feel the same. Perhaps it was the fact that she was in a new country, in a new routine and surrounded by people who barely spoke to her. It was as though she had stepped into a glass cage surrounded by people. She was alone.

Her mobile phone seemed strangely unable to pick up a signal since they had touched down in Zayyar. It felt like a lifetime ago since she had stepped off the jet in the heart of the desert, but in reality it had only been three days. She was by no means a techno junkie but still, it was very isolating not being able to just pick up her phone and send an email or call one of her sisters on the odd occasion. After a few minutes investigating, she discovered it was most likely that the number was no longer in service. Probably, her father had cancelled it, a passive aggressive punishment for disobeying his orders to return to Monteverre for the engagement announcement. She presumed he knew by now that she had eloped with the Sheikh, rather than follow his plan for a grand wedding. That would have been a sight to behold.

It was no big deal; surely she could simply ask Khal's team what the protocol was for obtaining a new phone? A small laugh escaped her throat at the realisation that she was the Queen of an entire kingdom and she couldn't even obtain her own phone without permission. The restlessness that had plagued her all day intensified and she stood, stretching the muscles in her back and looking towards the clock on her bedside table to check the time. It was almost midnight, local time.

She calculated the time zones for a moment. Last she had heard, her sister Olivia was in New York. It was still a semi-reasonable hour there... She hadn't spoken to Olivia at all since recent events had begun to transpire. There simply hadn't been an opportunity. Unable to resist, she took a quick peek into the corridor outside her apartments and bit her lip as she found it deserted. Perhaps the guards switched shifts at midnight. She knew there was a phone in the small office beside the library. She could wait for permission…or she could just go. She was an adult, after all.

Not able to shake the sensation that she was a naughty teenager breaking the rules, she set off quickly for fear she might change her mind. Heart beating fast, she moved soundlessly in her bare feet, so eager she made a few wrong turns and wound up hopelessly lost. She cursed her own sense of direction, wishing she had paid more attention to the corridors in daylight. Still, it was a rather nice change from the monotony of the past few days. She actually felt a little bit free, wandering unchaperoned in the semi-darkness.

By the time she found her way back to the library, she had a little bounce in her step. She had forgotten what it felt like to walk around without guards following her every move like shadows. Even in university, she had been free to move about the campus by herself for most of the time.

Disappointment coursed through her when Olivia's phone number also turned out to be cancelled. Not wanting to waste her time alone, she turned on the computer on the desk. It had always been occupied by a guard on her previous visits to the library. Miraculously, she found the option for guest mode with a decent Internet connection and hurriedly set about signing into her email server. To her surprise, her inbox was flooded with concern from some of the members of her research team at university. With horror, she realised she had never said goodbye before unenrolling from her courses.

She made quick work of finding the number of the head of her research team in London and breathed a sigh of relief when he answered on the first ring. He brushed off her hurried apology at the late hour and seemed genuinely relieved to hear that she was well. He told her of the rest of the team's efforts to get in contact with her; naturally, all of their enquiries to the palace in Monteverre had been met with silence.

After a few minutes she learned that the team was coping quite well in her absence; it seemed she wasn't quite as indispensable as she had believed. She ended the call with a fond farewell, promising to try to arrange a trip to London in the future, although deep down she knew that if she did return it would be so far in the future that they would probably have all moved on further in their careers and forgotten her completely.

She turned to exit the office, stopping with a squeak at a looming figure leaning against the doorway.

'Thought you were all alone?' Khal drawled.

She was just as beautiful in her pyjamas as she had been in her wedding dress. That was Khal's first thought upon finding Cressida sneaking gracefully through the library in semi-darkness. It had been late when he'd returned to the palace so he had opted to wait until morning to alert his new bride to his presence. He had been sitting in a corner alcove, taking in the mountains of books she had been studying, when she'd entered, oblivious to his presence. He'd had every intention of leaving to allow her to complete her phone call in private... Until he'd realised the person she was speaking to in such hushed tones was another man. He had found his fists clenched tight as he'd stalked soundlessly closer to the office doorway.

'You startled me,' she breathed. 'I didn't know you had returned.'

'Do you usually wait until the middle of the night to call your friends?' he asked calmly, ignoring the knot of tension in his abdomen.

Her eyes widened slightly at his tone. 'I never said goodbye to some friends in London. I was just checking in…with my research team.'

'You are the Sheikha of Zayyar.' His voice clipped each word out like a gunshot.

Cressida's eyes widened with surprise. 'I am quite aware of my own title by now, thank you,' she said tightly. 'You sound angry. Why do I feel like I'm being scolded when I have not done anything wrong?'

'Perhaps you mistake anger for simple confusion as to why I just walked in on my wife having a hushed midnight conversation with an unknown man.'

'I will not be told who I can or cannot speak to. Especially when I have been here for days without anyone to speak to at all.'

Khal was silent for a moment, his jaw tight. 'This man. He is a close friend?'

'I've known him a few years through my work at the university,' she said. 'But no. I don't have many friends.'

Silence fell between them and Khal saw a flash of sadness in her eyes before she quickly turned her face from him.

'If that's all you want to ask, I've got an early start in the morning.' She took a couple of steps towards the door.

Khal moved sideways to block her way. 'Being Sheikha is a full-time job, Cressida,' he said, noting the way she tilted her stubborn chin upwards in answer to his tone. 'I need to know that you are prepared for the responsibilities of this life.'

'I've been feeling a little isolated so I made a phone call. I suppose I did miss my old life for a moment.' She half laughed. 'I always felt such happiness in the corner of my small apartment, working at my computer or reading. It keeps my mind working. Makes me feel like I'm achieving something, maybe. But anyway, I needn't have bothered because it seems my departure has not left any lasting impression.'

A faraway look crossed her delicate features, the barest sheen of moisture seeming to brighten her eyes for a split second before she hastily blinked it away. She took a deep breath, pinning him with a brave smile. 'I'm hardly planning to give up and run away after one difficult week.'

He took a step towards her. 'I'm sorry that you felt isolated here. I did not mean to…'

'To leave me completely alone in a new country less than twelve hours after our wedding?' she finished helpfully.

Khal winced, knowing her words were entirely true. He had abandoned her to his staff, believing she would find comfort enough in a busy routine while he dealt with the aftermath of the investigations into the tent fire, among other things. Perhaps there was also a small part of him that wished to put some distance between them after the familiarity of their wedding night. She was his wife. It was only natural he would feel some level of protectiveness towards her. The memory of the kiss they had shared in his suite after the fire had plagued him, sending him to bed each night in a sweat, sleep the furthest thing from his mind.

Almost as though she heard his thoughts, her tongue darted out to moisten her lips, leaving a glistening sheen along the plump pink flesh. He felt his body react instantly, heat rushing downwards. Clenching his fist, he cleared his throat. 'I have not been very attentive so far, it seems.'

'No, you have not,' she agreed, moving past him in the doorway to walk into the library beyond. 'But I understand that you had sudden matters to address that could not be ignored. Have you any update on what caused the fire in the encampment?'

Khal pursed his lips, trying and failing not to notice the gentle sway of her hips in her loose-fitting pyjama bottoms. 'It has been deemed accidental. I was just informed this afternoon, in fact.' He watched as her face visibly relaxed; she had been worried about the fire then. Of course she had.

He wished that the news had given him the same relief. The fact that his security team and the police had no idea who had been behind it and had no leads was frustrating. But he could not think of it now, not when she so clearly needed reassuring.

'You enjoy reading books about Zayyar,' he said, changing the subject, gesturing to where he had found her little nook in the corner.

She smiled, walking over to straighten the small mountain of books with an almost lover-like caress. 'It's a beautiful kingdom.'

'You weren't lying when you said that you consider reading a sport. I'd bet you've made your way through a quarter of my collection already.'

She blushed, turning away as she flicked idly through a volume on Zayyari etiquette and traditions. 'I suppose I just like to feel prepared in a new situation. To arm myself with as much knowledge as possible when I'm feeling out of my depth.'

Of course she was feeling overwhelmed. He had rushed ahead with their wedding without a second thought, put her life at risk in the encampment and then abandoned her at the first opportunity. As far as husbands went, he was already a spectacular failure.

'That is to be expected. Not many people would be quite so composed in the face of such upheaval in their normal routine.' He met her eyes. 'You may brush off my compliment but know that I mean it earnestly. And I would like to make this transition as easy as possible for you as you find your feet here. Starting with your own personal phone line in your suite, perhaps?'

'Thank you. That's very kind.' She smiled. 'My father had my mobile phone account cancelled at some point since we eloped.'

'King Fabian is not known for making direct statements when he is displeased.' Khal spoke thoughtfully. 'I will also have a top-of-the-range device delivered to your suite tomorrow.'

'Really, a simple landline is fine,' she argued.

'You are the Sheikha of Zayyar now, Cressida. If you want something, anything at all, it will be obtained for you. You need only ask.'

For a moment, he thought she might argue. He watched the delicate play of emotions cross her features as she bent to retrieve a book from the pile at their feet. When she stood up straight again, her face was a polite mask of control. Something inside him briefly wondered what lay underneath that mask, what she was truly feeling about her situation, but he brushed away the sentimental thought.

He escorted her back to her suite, making idle conversation about the various parts of the palace she had seen in his absence. As he listened to her genuine appreciation of his ancestral home, he found himself inwardly making plans to show her the hidden gems that few knew about. To play tour guide in his own kingdom and show her the true Zayyar.

He simply wanted her to feel at home here, he told himself, but a strange sensation seemed to envelope him in her presence. The physical attraction was there, of course, but something else had joined it. He wanted her to feel at ease with him, he realised.

After he bade her goodnight at her door and returned to his own adjoining suite, he sat at his desk and idly shuffled through official papers. His mind was not with his work tonight, nor had it been for the entire day. He had been eager to return to the palace almost from the moment he had left it. The chemistry between himself and his new bride was an unwelcome complication and until now he had not known how to manage it, except to keep a distance between them. But perhaps all he needed was a simple redirection. It was not weak or emotional to wish for an accord with the woman who would stand by his side for the next five years. It was practical and far more realistic than his original plan.

Humming to himself, he made a neat, concise list of plans and felt the dark mood that had plagued him begin to lift. Everything was still perfectly in order.

Cressida dreamt of her father, his face contorted with anger as he shouted down at her. She was small in the dream, afraid to speak but feeling his words pierce holes in her delicate skin. She woke with her throat parched dry as though she had been screaming. Dawn had just begun to break over the city; she could see the first flickers of pink light spreading out over the desert in the distance.

She took pleasure in dressing herself without an audience, much to the confusion of her maids, who entered her sitting room to find her fully clothed in one of the loose silk kaftans that had been provided as part of her new wardrobe. The material was a jade-green chiffon with satin lining, decorated with sparkling beads and tiny stones around the collar and cuffs. She had showered and allowed her long ash-blonde hair to dry naturally so it wasn't quite straight but still fell in pleasing waves down her back.

When she entered the dining room of the royal apartment she was surprised to find Khal already seated. He stood while she took her seat at the opposite end of the table, offering a pleasant good morning before returning to his coffee and newspaper. She ate quietly, glancing up every now and then to watch with fascination as he switched between his tablet computer and the broadsheet spread out across the table by his side. Taking notes, by the looks of it, she mused. It should not surprise her that his working day would begin the moment he opened his eyes.

When she had finished eating, he was still absorbed in his reading so she stood up quietly, intending to leave him in peace.

'My apologies for being so distracted; I'm not used to sharing breakfast with anyone.' Khal stood, neatly folding his paper and folding up the cover of his device before tucking it under his arm.

'There's no need for you to change your morning

rituals simply because I am here,' Cressida said earnestly. 'I have a morning packed full of lessons and dress fittings and goodness knows what else. I'm kept quite busy around here.'

'Yes, that's what I wanted to talk to you about. My advisors told me that so far you have been using the main library for all of your studies.'

'The library is wonderful. I'm happy to continue there.'

'I wanted to show you something, before you start your day.' He motioned for her to follow him out of the main door of the apartment, a strange lightness in his usually austere expression. 'It's just something I thought of after our conversation last night.'

Cressida kept her expression neutral as she followed him down the halls of the royal wing of the palace in the direction of the Sheikh's formal offices and library. She had been given a tour of this area of the palace but told that it was for official use only.

'This is my office and official rooms through here,' he said idly, gesturing to a door that led onto a room as big as a basketball court. She had not been permitted inside, but she had been told that many more rooms spread out from there, a library, secretarial offices and such. The Sheikh walked across the large sunny vestibule to a door tucked away at the end of the hallway. He hesitated for a moment before pushing it open and allowing her to enter first.

At first she wasn't quite sure if it was an office or a library. Books lined three of the four walls but there was also a working area on one side with a large cherrywood desk, complete with a computer, phone and pens. A long plush sofa occupied the other side of the room, facing a large arched window that overlooked the gardens beyond.

'I decided you needed a place of your own for your studies,' Khal said matter-of-factly. 'It used to be my office when I was the Crown Prince.'

Cressida walked over to one of the bookcases and ran her fingers along the spines. A place of her own. Her own little sanctuary. She had made one comment to him about missing her tiny study space back in London and he had gone and given her an entire office of her own. She darted a look over her shoulder to see him still standing in the doorway, watching her with hooded brows.

'You can have it redecorated to your own personal taste, of course. I won't be offended if you don't like the décor. And I will arrange to have whichever books you prefer transported here from the main library if the selection here is lacking—'

'It's perfect.' Her voice sounded surprisingly calm, in contrast to the alarming burst of emotion swelling in her chest. 'Thank you.'

He waved off her gratitude good-naturedly before glancing at the watch on his wrist. 'I must start my working day officially, but feel free to stay here and settle in if you wish. If you need anything at all, there is an intercom on the desk and an assistant assigned to you.'

'An assistant?' Cressida gasped.

'The Sheikha always has a personal assistant once royal duties commence,' he replied easily, as though it should have been obvious to her. 'You have three weeks until you officially enter into public life. The calendar of a Sheikha can be quite demanding.'

They were interrupted by two palace officials, seeking the Sheikh's urgent attendance in his office. Cressida motioned for him to go, thanking him once more before he disappeared through the door and closed it behind him with a gentle click.

She wandered over to the desk and sat slowly into the buttery soft leather swivel chair behind it. He had thought of her. He had put thought into her comfort beyond what was necessary. It was a strange feeling, having someone else looking out for her.

Placing both hands on the wood, she glanced down and smiled as she noticed the slim mobile handset that had been placed on top of a sheaf of papers. She lifted it, finding it had already been pre-programmed for her ease of use. She sighed with pleasure, hardly knowing where she would begin with all these wonderful gifts. She wondered if he even considered them gifts.

A wind blew gently through the open window, shuffling some of the papers across the desk. She gathered them back, noticing for the first time that they were stamped with the royal Zayyari crest on top in their signature wine and gold leaf design. But when she noticed the signature underneath, her breath caught completely. A feeling strangely like pride filled her chest as she ran her fingers over the ornate lettering, feeling the weight of the words press much further than just her fingertips.

From the desk of Her Royal Highness,
Sheikha Cressida Al Rhas of Zayyar

CHAPTER SEVEN

KHAL MADE A point of eating with Cressida each morning, inwardly congratulating himself as he noticed her mood lightening with each passing day. He told himself that it was simply in his best interests to ensure that she was comfortable at the palace, but truthfully he looked forward to their morning conversations. Soon, he began to forget to take his usual notes from the political broadsheets, abandoning the task to one of his secretaries in favour of occupying his time hearing about Cressida's progress in her studies. She showed a remarkable aptitude for retaining information, relaying some of her difficulties with the Zayyari language with humour and a total lack of self-consciousness.

On the rare evenings that he did not have meetings or functions to attend, they dined together in the apartment. It was far from an effort to keep his mind focused on the conversations that flowed with surprising ease between them; he enjoyed the new perspective of seeing his beloved kingdom and all of its traditions through her eyes. But still, beneath the iron of his control he fought the urge to let his gaze wander over her tempting curves or to linger when he bid her goodnight at the door to her room.

It seemed that married life made the time pass quickly and he found himself thinking less of his investigations into the fire at the encampment or his suspicions about who might have started it. Exactly two weeks had passed since their wedding when Khal found his good mood completely thrown off course by a single piece of information let slip by one of his secretaries. He called for his Chief of Security immediately, sitting behind his desk with clenched fists as he waited for Sayyid to arrive.

'You wished to see me, Your Highness?' Sayyid entered, a heavy look in his eyes.

'Close the door.' Khal spoke slowly, taking every ounce of his effort to control the temper that threatened to spill over at any moment. He gestured for the other man to take a seat before he stood and paced to the other side of his desk.

'Is there a problem, Sire?'

'One might say that, yes,' Khal gritted. 'If you would describe finding out that there has been yet another incident a *problem*.'

'If you mean the small situation that was contained last week…'

'I will decide what situation is considered small,' Khal growled. 'What makes you believe that your King should not be informed of any kind of threat in his own kingdom? That I should find out a week after the fact that there was an intruder apprehended in the middle of the night, scaling the palace walls?'

'With the utmost respect, Sire, there have been instances of people trying to climb the palace walls in the past. The man did not breach the security fences and did not carry any weaponry; therefore it was classed as a non-dangerous incident.'

'Was he questioned? Did he have ties to any rebellious factions?' Khal felt pressure build in his temples as he noticed Sayyid's mouth tighten.

'We questioned him and ascertained that he was a youth on a foolish dare. Even Lazarov agreed that it was best not to make an incident of something so mundane.'

'Roman was informed of this incident, was he?' Khal fought the annoyance that rose in his chest at the mention of his friend's name. Roman's security firm had trained the entire palace guard; of course they would go to him if there had been an attempted breach. No one dealt with high profile risk assessment and security better than The Lazarus Group. Khal had called upon Roman himself within hours of the fire in the encampment. It had been Roman who had informed him that the private investigation had been classed as one hundred per cent accidental, with no sinister or deliberate intention.

In that same phone call his friend's tone had become concerned as he had reminded Khal of instances in the past where his need for heightened security had been extreme. Of how he needed to trust his team to do their job and stop looking for threats where none existed.

Khal felt anger rise within him once more as he heard that same tone of concern in Sayyid's voice.

'Sire, I can assure you that the Sheikha is safe—'

'I have not mentioned the Sheikha once,' Khal fumed. 'This is about your complete insubordination in not reporting a potentially dangerous matter to your King.'

Sayyid stood suddenly, open defiance on his face.

'There was no danger; that is what I am trying to make you see. What many have tried to make you see.'

Khal turned and took a few steps away, feeling the anger within him reach its peak. Truthfully, perhaps he'd been thinking of Cressida's safety when he'd imagined the unknown intruder scaling the walls in the dead of night. But this was not just about possible danger to his wife. This was about Zayyar.

His father had always made a point of reminding him how quickly rebellion could resurge when one rested in a state of peace. It was his duty to ensure his staff did not take that peace for granted and make mistakes. He inhaled deeply, his jaw pulsing with the effort of keeping his tone measured. Of keeping his control. 'You will take a leave of absence from your duties to account for this error in judgement. One week, effective immediately.'

Sayyid's eyes narrowed. For a moment Khal wondered if the line was about to be crossed. If the other man would openly defy his King's orders.

'As you wish, Your Highness. I'll make the arrangements,' Sayyid finally said. He bowed low before turning and exiting the room without another word.

Khal paced the floor of his study for what felt like hours in the aftermath of the confrontation with his trusted employee, feeling the pressure in his head pulse and thrum with every step. He sat down in a high-backed armchair, resisting the urge to fling the nearby coffee table across the room. He would not allow his staff to decide what he could and would not be told. He had the right to know everything that happened within his own palace. Roman's calm voice popped into his head once more. Was this one of those situations he'd referred to? Was he seeing danger where it did not exist? Should he simply trust his security team to do their job and stop trying to control every single thing in his orbit? He did kick out in frustration then, his foot making hard contact with the heavy marble leg of the coffee table in front of him.

'Having a tantrum?'

A quiet voice shook him from his brooding; he silently hoped it was not Cressida but at the same time knew that it was. She stood a few feet away, wrapped in a pale pink silk robe. He leaned his head back, allowing himself a moment to take her in before he spoke. 'Sheikhs do not have tantrums. We have momentary losses of composure.'

'Ah.' She hovered nervously in the doorway. 'I came back down to get a book and I saw your light still on. Am I interrupting?'

'Come in. Though I might not be the best company.'

He stood up, taking a long languorous stretch and covertly watching as her gaze rose to follow his movements before darting away. Khal felt the beginning of a smile tease his lips. It dawned on him that this was the first time she had set foot inside his office.

Her eyes wandered to his desk, where a handful of professional photographs of their wedding ceremony were scattered. Khal had just received them that morning and hadn't quite decided what to do with them yet. She moved closer, her fingertips trailing over the images delicately.

'I look…completely different,' she said in that same quiet voice. Her brow was furrowed as she picked up a shot of them both with their foreheads touching.

'You don't like them?' he asked, genuinely eager to know the answer.

'They are very well done.' She smiled.

'That is not what I asked.'

'I suppose they're quite convincing. Romantic and dreamy. But when one knows the truth, the illusion is spoiled a little.' She placed the photo back down and arranged the others in a square formation, avoiding his gaze. 'It's a strange feeling, being married but not actually being married, isn't it?'

'We are married,' he said with a hint of irony. 'I have photographic evidence.'

'You know what I mean—we have this arrangement.' Cressida sighed, moving over to inspect the collection of tiny ships in bottles that adorned the shelves of his study. 'I never understood how they got such detailed works inside these things without breaking it,' she said absentmindedly, running a fingertip along the glass that encased a large rare Marlin.

'It's a hobby of mine,' he said idly, wondering why her comment about not actually being married stuck in his mind.

'You made all these?' Her eyes widened as she took in the wall of shelves. 'How on earth do you find the time?'

'It calms my mind.' He shrugged, not quite sure why he'd shared something so personal. A king did not struggle with an overactive mind. A king had complete control over his thoughts at all times.

'It looks incredibly complicated.' She was still peering at various models, genuine appreciation on her features.

'It's simple enough once you approach it from a point

of logic. My father introduced me to it at a young age.'
A smile teased the corner of his lips as he remembered
some of the tantrums he had thrown when he'd continued to fail at lifting the mast of the tiny ship. His father
had always remained seated, never raising a hand or losing his temper. 'Go over your plan and begin again,' he
would say calmly. Now, as a grown man, he could see
that his father had given him the tools to harness the
anger and uncontrolled nature that he had shown even
as a young boy. There was no place in Zayyar's future
for another king without self-control. For another king
ruled by his own selfish desires.

'I was just about to order some tea,' he said brusquely,
walking away from her to gather his thoughts for a moment. 'You are welcome to join me.' He kept his tone
light, telling himself he was inviting her to stay because
he was simply not in the mood to be alone with his own
thoughts. She was a good conversationalist. He had no
ulterior motives for wanting to be alone with his wife
in his study at night...

Clearly, she was having a similar thought process,
considering she took a full two minutes to come to a
decision before lowering herself into the armchair opposite his own. He had not been lying; he had been about
to order tea. It was the only thing that calmed him in a
mood such as this one.

His staff were efficient, laying out the perfectly polished pots and utensils between them, hot steam rising
from the ornate copper teapot.

To his surprise, Cressida began the service, performing the Zayyari ritual with seemingly effortless movements. It was only because he studied her so closely that
he noticed the slight tremble of her fingers, or the way

her brow creased momentarily as she focused on her performance. He reached out to accept his cup from her fingers, deliberately brushing his thumb across her skin.

'And you say that you do not feel like you are truly married?' He sat back, savouring the taste of the sweet traditional brew on his tongue. 'This seems like very wifely behaviour to me.'

'Well, you would know more about that than I do.' She focused on stirring her tea, taking a moment to re-alise what she had said. 'Oh, I'm sorry. I'm so thought-less...'

'Don't apologise.' Khal shook off the comment, but still he found himself fighting the sudden sharp jab of discomfort with the reference to his first marriage. Perhaps because, since they'd sat down, he had been acutely distracted by the woman who sat across from him. Or maybe it was because his ring now lay upon her finger and so to think of another time seemed inap-propriate somehow. Truthfully, he'd thought of his first wife less and less as the years passed. And, even then, only to ponder a new lead in his investigations into her accident. It had been five years, after all. He knew he could not feel the same intense emotions for ever, but still it brought guilt to realise he had truly accepted her death and moved on.

'It seems morbid to ask if you sat like this in the past.' Cressida spoke softly. 'You have never spoken of your first marriage. I'll admit that I am curious.'

'My first marriage was very different for many rea-sons,' Khal said simply, taking another sip of his tea. 'I was very different.'

'Your sister told me that you grieved for a long time. I got the impression that you were both very much in love.' She met his eyes, a strangely guarded expression on her usually open features.

'We were.' He flexed the tightness from his fingers, laying his palm down flat on the arm of the chair. 'In the beginning, at least.'

'Oh.'

One syllable was all she needed to portray that she understood. She did not push the subject further and for that he was grateful. It was only the beginning of the myriad secrets of his seemingly perfect marriage to Priya. He had never spoken to anyone of the fact that all was not as it seemed. But now he felt strangely lighter having spoken of it, never having considered that there might be weight to carrying secrets.

'My parents' marriage was arranged,' Cressida said after a while. 'My grandmother always said they were lucky to have fallen madly in love as a result.' She pursed her lips, meeting his eyes for a moment before looking away. 'Seeing what falling out of love has done to them, I have always been of the opinion that it was better to have a marriage free of emotions.'

Khal frowned at her admission, picturing King Fabian and his cold, uninterested wife. He had been in their company on a number of occasions, and each time he had become more aware of the deep well of problems in the royal marriage. He was of the opinion that the issues ran far deeper than simply falling out of love, but he kept that thought to himself.

'Is that why you agreed to marry me?' he asked. 'Other than your extreme devotion to your kingdom, of course.'

Cressida seemed to shift in her seat slightly, one hand

adjusting the material of her nightgown. 'I had many reasons for accepting this…arrangement.'

'This is a marriage, *habibti*. Make no mistake.' He did not mean for the hardness to creep into his voice but all of a sudden the idea that she saw their union as some kind of cold business arrangement was not palatable to him, for reasons unknown. After all, political marriages such as theirs were essentially built on business, were they not?

'I'm not saying that we each aren't bound by the same rules as usual marriages,' she said hurriedly. 'I just mean that, behind closed doors, we both know different.'

'Do you feel bound by the rules, Cressida?' he said silkily, feeling a pang of irritation at the feelings her words evoked. The memory of a similar conversation in the past came to the surface, another woman's voice.

I have never been good at playing by the rules, Khal. I'm sorry.'

'I have no desire to enter into a verbal sparring match at midnight,' Cressida said, standing up and shaking out the fabric of her nightgown. 'You were clearly aggravated by something before I came in here and I think it's best that I say goodnight.'

'Oh, no, you don't.' Khal stood, moving so that he blocked her way. 'You see, I like to finish conversations, not walk away from them if they get a little uncomfortable.'

'I don't feel like this is a conversation any longer. I feel like you are putting words into my mouth.'

She'd mentioned her mouth and, sure enough, that was where his eyes wandered, the perfect pink flesh teasing him. 'Do you feel bound by the rules of this

marriage?' he asked again, softer this time. The air between them thrummed with awareness.

'Sometimes.' She half whispered the word, her breath
seeming slightly laboured all of a sudden. 'But perhaps
not quite in the way that you think.'

'Do you feel unhappy here with me, Cressida?' he
asked, feeling the sizzle of something dangerous in the
air between them. He wanted to know the answer to his
question, the honest answer. To allow him to see beneath the facade she always wore around him.

He wanted something real.

Cressida shook her head once, her eyes meeting his.
'I don't feel unhappy when I'm with you. I feel…frus-
trated.'

He wasn't sure who leaned in first, but suddenly
their mouths were locked and it was like the first drink
after weeks in the desert. He feasted on her, taking
every ounce of the longing that he could feel in her kiss
and giving back in equal measure. He felt the weight
of her arms around his neck, her chest pressed tightly
against his, and yet it still wasn't enough. He pressed
her back against the bookcase, ignoring her sharp intake of breath as he raised her arms above her head and
began a slow trail down her neck.

Her groans sent the blood rushing straight to his
groin, not that he hadn't already lost control of that particular piece of his anatomy. She moved against him,
consciously or unconsciously coming into contact with
his arousal and giving a slight gasp. Khal looked down
into her widened eyes, tension furling and unfurling in
his lower abdomen.

'Tell me to stop,' he commanded. 'Tell me that you
don't want this.'

'I can't,' she whispered, lowering her face into the curve of his neck and pressing a hot kiss to his skin. 'I think I have wanted this from the first moment I saw you.'

The kiss undid him completely, along with the words. He waited a moment as she kissed along his clavicle, running her hot tongue along his skin. Unable to cope with the torture of standing still, he ran his hands over her shoulders, gently spreading the delicate vee of her robe wide enough to lower the neck of her nightgown and expose the porcelain skin of one breast. He let his hands explore one hardened peak until she leaned her head back in sensual abandon. Then he leaned down to replace fingers with lips and tongue. He thoroughly pleasured one delicate breast before moving on to afford the same attentions to its twin. Each movement of his tongue brought forth groans of pleasure, which Cressida tried to stifle with her fist. They were in his study, after all.

She moved against him again, more impatiently this time, as though she knew exactly what she wanted. Her pelvis fitted in line with his so perfectly. It would be so easy to just wrap her legs around his waist and slide himself inside her. He would take her rough and hard, sliding in and out of her moist heat until neither of them could remember their own name...

'Don't stop, Khal.' Her hushed plea threatened to undo him. 'Please.'

Spurred on by the raw need in her voice, he continued his explorations, removing her robe and letting his fingers gather her nightgown up until it bunched just under her hips. Pinning the fabric with one hand, he found the lace-covered centre of her and applied a gentle pressure.

* * *

Cressida's attempts to remain quiet were short-lived; soon her loud gasps and stifled moans filled the room. She had never felt such unbearable pleasure as she did with his hands on her, touching her. It was as though he knew exactly how she liked it, exactly how she touched herself in the dark of night when no one was watching. Khal let out a deeply male groan of pleasure as she moved herself against his hand, wanting more than he gave.

He pulled the lace down over her hips, watching her eyes the whole time. Perhaps he was waiting to see if she had finally come to her senses and decided she didn't want this, after all. She did not falter. She had made her decision the moment he stood in front of her, all male sexual energy. Perhaps tomorrow she would remember why this was such a bad idea but in this moment she had never wanted anything more in her life.

She became impatient with his slow movements and kicked the material off the rest of the way, enticing a husky laugh from his throat. She smiled, amazed that this felt so right all of a sudden when moments ago they had been talking about practicality. There was nothing practical about what they were doing right now and they both knew it.

His fingers came into contact with her bare flesh and within seconds she could feel her body begin to pulse and tighten as it began to ascend towards climax. He must have sensed it too because, just as she had almost reached the peak, he stopped.

'What are you—' Her stunned words were stifled by his kiss as he gathered her up into his arms and carried her a few steps across the room to a long sofa. The cushions were soft underneath her but the fabric of her nightgown bunched uncomfortably around her waist.

As though he read her mind, he helped her to be rid of the pesky layers. All of a sudden she was completely naked, spread out before him while he was still completely clothed. He paused for a moment, eyes darkening with pleasure as he drank her in, then he set about removing his own clothing. By the time he was completely naked, Cressida's throat had gone dry. He was… magnificent. There was no other way to describe the hard expanse of copper-toned skin on show. He was well built in a suit but nude, he was powerful. Muscles rippled along a trim abdomen, leading to trim hips and… She gulped, wondering how on earth that was going to fit anywhere belonging to her.

'I have dreamed of doing this,' he murmured, moving over her so that their bodies were entwined. She could feel the heat of him pressing between her thighs, her own excitement slightly embarrassing now that no clothing was between them.

She was nervous but definitely ready. As he poised himself over her, she was struck by the weight of this moment. He moved against her with such slowness, she felt a lump in her throat. She could feel his hard heat as he slid the first inch inside; there was only slight pain as he moved further, stretching her to accommodate him. His eyes widened for a moment as some of her discomfort must have showed on her face. He made to pull away but Cressida gripped his hips with her thighs, holding him tightly against her. Keeping their bodies joined.

He uttered a curse under his breath, his breathing laboured as he gently pressed his forehead against hers, holding his body still with impressive control.

'Don't stop.' Cressida breathed. She arched herself against him and felt the join of their bodies pulse pleasurably. To her relief, he moved once more in response, then twice, placing one hand between them to slide his thumb against that part of her that drove her wild. What little pain there had been soon receded completely and only pleasure remained as her body quickly got the hang of what to do. She felt pleasure like nothing she had ever experienced building deep within her with every thrust. Her body seemed to move against him of its own volition and she noticed Khal hiss between his teeth.

'Oh, yes, *habibti*, just like that,' he practically growled as he spread her legs wider, moving even deeper, increasing his pace.

She felt him begin to lose control, his neck straining as his own climax approached. The sight of this powerful man at her mercy seemed to spur her on, bringing pleasure like she had never experienced crashing down upon her and sending her body into waves of absolute bliss. Cressida felt a moment of confusion as he pulled away from her at the last moment then bit her lower lip as she realised that he had only withdrawn just in time before his own climax hit him.

Khal fell back against the cushions of the sofa, head arched back in the pose of a man completely exhausted and satisfied. His chest rose and fell in a steady rhythm, the barest sheen of sweat glistening on his dark skin. Cressida could not look away, wanting to remember every detail of this perfect moment. She had never imagined that her first time would be quite so intimate and filled with passion.

Not only had she just made love for the first time, she had made love with her husband. The thought brought gooseflesh to her skin and she cursed herself for having such a sentimental reaction.

Truthfully, Cressida had absolutely no idea what one was supposed to say in this situation. Should she make small talk? Should she tell him that she had enjoyed it, they should do it again some time? It was insane, she had stood in front of a crowd and pledged her devotion to this man and he to her. The entire world now believed them to have had a secret love story worthy of movies and magazine spreads. And yet, in this moment, as the silence stretched onwards, she realised that they were just two people who had finally given in to a passion that neither of them quite understood.

Khal felt as though he had just run a marathon, but in the best way possible. He lay back on the sofa, eyes closed, but sleep was the furthest thing from his mind. He was avoiding the woman who lay alongside him, delaying the moment when he would have to confront the reality of what had just transpired between them.

First, he had not used any protection. Second, his wife had clearly been an innocent and he had crudely deflowered her on a sofa.

Suppressing the urge to growl at his own loss of control, he stood up and began to gather up their clothes.

There could not be a child. He could not bear the thought of history repeating itself… He paused for a long moment at his desk, his body seemingly frozen. He felt such an acute loss of control it was as though his thoughts swam away from him every time he tried to grasp them.

'Could you hand me my nightgown?' a quiet voice

came from the sofa. He turned, not knowing how long he had stood immobile and silent while she waited.

Guilt engulfed him as he saw the uncertainty on Cressida's features as she accepted the nightgown and hurriedly shielded her naked body from him.

'You were a virgin,' he said softly, sitting alongside her and turning her cheek so that she met his eyes. 'I would have taken more time, had I known. Made it better for you.'

'We didn't exactly plan for this, either of us.' She spoke with quiet sincerity. 'But it was quite pleasurable...for me, anyway.'

Khal looked down at the bare skin of her thighs, which had been wrapped around his waist mere minutes before. God, but he wanted her all over again. He exhaled a long breath, astounded at the complete deterioration of his adult mind to that of a lust-crazed youth.

Suddenly, Cressida stood up and pulled her arms through her nightgown, shielding her body from view. Khal fought the urge to pull her back down.

'I understand that you might be worried that this... that tonight would complicate matters between us.' She spoke with a strange coldness in her voice.

'Do you believe that it won't?' Khal asked. 'Tonight was irresponsible on my part, in more ways than one.'

She busied herself by pulling her hair back from her face, twisting it around itself in a neat trick that kept it secured atop her head with no clasps or ties. Next, she retrieved her robe, slipping her arms into it quickly.

Khal stood, quite aware that he had not yet bothered to put on his own clothing. He watched as she lowered her gaze for a split second before hurriedly looking away to focus on the wall behind his head as she spoke.

'We were both irresponsible. We are both adults. We got carried away tonight but we can simply agree that this need not happen again.'

'When I say irresponsible, I mean that I didn't use protection, Cressida.' Khal took a step towards her.

'That won't be an issue.' She straightened her shoulders, lifting her hand almost as a barrier between them. 'Presuming that you are…healthy?'

'Of course I am healthy,' he growled.

'Good. Well, I take medication to regulate my cycle,' she said matter-of-factly, tying the sash of her robe with an almost vicious precision. 'So it seems we have nothing else to worry about.'

She made to step away from him. Khal grabbed her by the wrist. 'Just like that? You've forgotten about what just happened in here?'

Her sharp intake of breath was loud in the silence of the night. 'We both agreed that this marriage was to remain free of complications.'

'And you immediately feel confident that you can go back to that plan?'

Cressida frowned. 'Did you not make it clear to me in the beginning that you were not seeking a true wife?'

Khal stepped back as though burned. 'Of course.'

'Then I think it's probably best for us to go back to our rooms…separately. Perhaps take some distance from each other over the next few days.'

'Yes, of course. Retreat and regroup,' Khal murmured, confused at his own irritation at her calm approach. He did not wish to have to dampen down the hopes of an overly sentimental virgin. He should be thanking his lucky stars at his good fortune. She nodded once, bidding him a very civilised goodnight before disappearing through the door of his office with seemingly effortless composure.

Khal waited until her footsteps had disappeared completely before leaving the office himself.

His feet seemed to know where to take him even before his brain registered where he was going. The open courtyards past the eastern wing of the palace led out onto a long tropical garden. Khal followed a marble path inset with aqua-blue stones that sparkled in the light of the full moon. The path sloped downhill to where a small stone fountain took precedence. It had been many years since he had come here. For a long time this had been his preferred place to sit and brood. Perhaps brooding was the wrong word to use—sorrow was the real emotion that one felt at this fountain.

A small marble square adorned the front of the fountain's stone facade. A single aquamarine stone glittered in the centre of the square. Khal placed his hand over the stone, feeling the warmth of it seep through his skin. He had chosen this spot because the sunshine was uninterrupted here during the day. At the time, that had seemed important. There was no name inscribed on the stone, no words to mark the sorrowful reason this fountain stood on this particular spot.

His son had never taken his first breath, and in Zayyari culture that meant that he had not existed. There was no grave. No tomb at which to kneel and pray.

But he had prayed.

He had prayed for the infant son he would never know, and for the wife who had changed for ever. Something had died inside him the day he had been told that Priya had lost their child. He had been on the other side of the world, and protocol had meant he was not able to return for days after. By the time he had finally reached her bedside, the woman looking back at him was not his Priya any longer. Her own death had come less than a year later.

He had not discussed with Cressida the reasons why he had no desire for an heir of his own. For those brief moments, imagining that she might carry his child had made his insides turn to stone. He'd told himself time after time that a leader did not show his fears. This was a half-truth—just because he did not show it, did not mean that he didn't harbour fears that ran deep into his soul.

CHAPTER EIGHT

CRESSIDA GASPED AS the helicopter swooped low to give them a panoramic view of the spectacular coastline of Valar. The city's skyline was impressive, dominated by silver and glass high-rise buildings and ornate hotels. Further down in the distance she could see the swimming pools of the beach-side resorts, tourists no more than tiny black dots on the white sand. They set down on top of a building so high Cressida felt every muscle in her body clench. Reminding herself not to look down, she was jolted when Khal's warmth slid closer to her on the leather seats as he spoke to the pilot, his voice barely audible over the roaring din of the chopper blades slowing to a stop.

She had barely seen him in the week that had passed since the night in his study. He did not eat breakfast with her, nor did he make any impromptu invitations to dine together in the evenings. She had missed the ease of their conversations but told herself it was for the best. He would never want a relationship with her beyond the sexual chemistry between them. A casual sexual relationship was simply not an option for a woman who was already married to the man in question. It would be utter madness to expect things to remain free of emotions, no strings attached.

She was escorted down from the helicopter by two of the security team but it was Khal who took her hand in his and guided her across the blustery rooftop to the lift. Once inside, she released a breath she hadn't realised she'd been holding and heard a rumble of quiet male laughter erupt alongside her.

'Did you fear I would allow you to fall off the rooftop?' he asked, his hand still holding hers captive within his own. He spoke idly, his gaze fixed on the numbers on the display panel as the lift came to a stop and the doors slid open to reveal a square windowless hallway.

'I'm glad you find my fear of heights entertaining,' she quipped, a reluctant smile crossing her own lips as she looked up into a pair of dark brown eyes filled with mirth.

As usual, part of the security detail had already performed a sweep in preparation for their arrival. They were escorted into a spacious foyer and promptly left alone.

All thoughts momentarily left her brain as she was greeted with the most spectacular view she had ever seen. The large open-plan space was sumptuously decorated in bright modern monochrome and sky-blue, but the main attraction was the double height wall of curved plate glass that offered an unobstructed view of the entire city skyline, beautifully framed by a glimpse of the Arabian Sea on one side. The window was so wide and so clear, it was as though the marble tiles simply ended on a precipice, leaving the viewer at the risk of toppling over the edge. It made her stomach tighten, but still she could appreciate the view.

'This city is…breathtaking…' Cressida murmured, still making sure that she remained firmly in the centre of the room.

'This city will soon be the future of Zayyar, thanks to you,' he said, warmth in his eyes. 'News of our marriage has already opened doors that once were firmly closed. Tonight's celebration will solidify many new connections for us.'

Cressida had already been told by her advisors of the progress that had been made since their marriage had become public knowledge. Tonight's formal celebration would bring politicians and foreign dignitaries from across the world here to show their support. However, there would not be a single member of her own family at the event. A fact that did not surprise her in the slightest. Her older sister, Eleanor, was on a charity mission in North Africa but had promised to come and visit soon, while her middle sister, Olivia, was busily setting up the headquarters of her literacy foundation in New York.

Her parents had openly refused the invitation, stating a scheduling conflict. They had half-heartedly organised an event to be held in Monteverre over the coming week and invited her and Khal for an official visit. A pathetic attempt at a show of power by her father, but still Cressida knew that his alliance was vital to Khal so she would dutifully attend.

She was to be on show to the world tonight for the first time as Sheikha. The thought terrified her almost as much as being up at this height did.

'Come and see the view. The window is bulletproof, shockproof—very safe, I assure you.' Khal moved to knock one hand against the glass pane.

Cressida raised one hand instinctively. 'There is *really* no need to demonstrate!'

A dimple appeared in the corner of his mouth again, that mischievous half smile that made her stomach flip. He braced one hand on the glass wall, shifting so that his weight leaned against it as he looked out into the distance. 'You get a much better view of the coastline over here than from all the way across the room. Just a suggestion.'

He was utterly mad; that was the only explanation for it. Who on earth could manage to look so serene and relaxed while seeming to hover on the edge of falling to their death?

'Is this your way of proving what a fearless leader you are? It's really not necessary.'

'I am simply trying to show you that you will not fall.' He spoke with surprising softness as he turned to face her. 'The danger exists only in your mind.'

In a few long strides he was beside her, taking her gently by the wrist. Her breath caught painfully in her throat at the heat of his skin on her own. She did not resist as he gently pulled her, step by torturous step, across the marble-tiled floor until she stood in the exact same spot as he had. He took her hand and placed her trembling palm against the cold glass. Cressida felt her insides tremble as she tried not to look down, focusing on the sensation of his hand still pinning her own in place.

'Open your eyes.' The command was gentle, but a command nonetheless. She gingerly fluttered one eyelid open, feeling as though her heart was about to beat straight out of her chest. He had not been lying when he said the view was better over here. On one side she could see the entire coastline stretching out into the distance, the sun sparkling on the water like a thousand diamonds. They were otherwise surrounded by a sea of sleek modern buildings and hotels, with the barest glimpse of unspoiled desert peeking out in the distance.

'Just don't look down.' Khal's voice came from somewhere near her ear as he removed his hand from hers and stood alongside her.

'You just reminded me that there is a down to look at.' She exhaled a little harder but resisted the urge to step back.

'Your composure is effortlessly regal, Your Highness.' She could hear the smirk in his voice as he placed one hand on the glass and faced away from her.

She couldn't help but let the corner of her own mouth turn up. 'I think all these brave masculine displays of royal window-leaning have reassured me.'

He turned to face her, a strange expression on his face. 'Now, you see, describing it as brave and masculine strokes my ego. Why lessen the effect by making it a royal activity?'

'I doubt most people would think that being royal lessens anything at all.'

'Ah, but we know better, don't we?' he said softly, his gaze travelling down her body for a split second. He swallowed, a frown creasing his brow.

The way he used the word 'we' so easily, she could almost imagine for a moment that they were a normal couple sharing a quiet moment of intimacy. She looked away, feeling the acute sting of awareness that she was looking for something that would never exist. Strange that, no matter what situation she was in, this feeling was always familiar, like an itchy blanket. The feeling of wanting more from someone but knowing she would never have it. Feeling as if she should be grateful for whatever small sliver of attention she had been given. The old pain threatened to overwhelm her until a silky voice invaded her reverie.

'Your mind has wandered away.'

Pulling herself back to the moment, she nodded, avoiding his gaze. 'I must be tired,' she offered, knowing she was lying but just wanting to retreat to her own space and analyse whatever she was feeling.

'You should rest, then. We leave for the ball at eight.'

Cressida nodded, making a mumbled show of thanks as he escorted her to her bedroom door before practically darting from his side. With the door firmly closed between them, she leaned back against the solid wood and waited for her heartbeat to return to normal.

Suddenly she longed for the solitude of the palace and the comfort of not being in such close proximity to the man who set her heartbeat racing and her stress levels rising. It was just simple chemical awareness, she told herself. He was the only man she had ever been close to, the only man who had ever kissed her or touched her. She had been married for less than a month. There was still another four years and eleven months to survive.

Unsurprisingly, she spent the following few hours in a less than restful state. As the sun began to dip in the evening sky, Cressida forced a smile as she took in her reflection in the floor-length mirror of her dressing room. The dress her team had chosen for the ball was a deliberately Western-styled design of midnight-blue lace, elegant and figure-hugging. If she could have chosen a gown to wear upon her first formal occasion as Queen, she could not have chosen one more perfect than this.

The silhouette made her appear more womanly, without making her feel self-conscious. The delicate capped sleeves were adorned with tiny seed pearls and the tiniest glints of sapphire. The same gems adorned her ears and her wrist, designed in Monteverre she was told, which was a nice touch. East meets West, she thought wryly as she gave a little turn in the mirror. She looked up, noticing that the door had opened, and was met with the dauntingly attractive sight of her husband in his formal robes. The King, she corrected herself sternly. The more she thought of him as her husband, the harder it was to forget what she wanted to forget. Taking a couple of breaths before she turned, she steeled herself for the onslaught of simply being in his presence. They were not alone in the room by any means, surrounded by the remnants of her wardrobe team, her assistant and members of her security detail. And yet she felt overheated and on edge.

'You look…beautiful,' he said, sincerity in the deep baritone of his voice.

'Thank you.' Cressida bowed her head slightly, clasping her hands in front of her. 'I thought we were meant to meet in the foyer?'

'I thought it best that I escort you down myself.' He extended his hand. 'That is, if that is all right with you?'

Cressida fought the urge to roll her eyes at the strained formality of it all. Instead, she straightened her spine and placed her hand in his.

Apart from a near miss when her heel got caught in the train of her dress coming down the stairs, their entrance to the ball was utterly flawless, as planned.

Cressida bowed and curtsied to various foreign dignitaries as needed, projecting what she hoped was an air of calm regal elegance when internally she felt far from it. Khal remained by her side as they were met with a queue of guests waiting for introductions to the new Queen of Zayyar.

As she'd expected, most of the guests commented on her appearance while choosing to compliment her husband on his most recent accomplishments. With her, they gushed over her designer jewellery and fawned over how utterly flawless her skin was. As though she had any control over the fact that her skin was pale and clear.

After a time, the smile she had pasted on her face began to hurt her cheeks so she simply stopped smiling. Apart from noticing Khal staring at her on a number of occasions, no one else seemed to notice. She was grateful when they sat down finally, having not eaten since breakfast in preparation for the event. Apparently it was customary to starve oneself before wearing a designer gown in order to achieve maximum leanness and avoid bloating. She had developed a new appreciation for what her sisters must have gone through in the past while she had avoided occasions such as this.

The menu was a mixture of traditional Zayyari meats and spices arranged in various European-style dishes. It was an ingenious incorporation of textures and flavours on the part of the Michelin star chefs who had been employed for the occasion. But, honestly, she could have been eating plain porridge and it would have tasted like sweet ambrosia.

'I see you have found your appetite.'

Cressida looked up, trying in vain to hide the gigantic mouthful of chicken she had just placed in her mouth. It was entirely impossible to appear ladylike or delicate when one's mouth was full of food. Khal smiled, stifling laughter with his hand as he leaned close.

'You will start a rumour that the King of Zayyar routinely starves his new bride.'

'I forgot to eat,' she said quickly, grabbing a napkin to dab the corners of her mouth. The man had barely spoken two words to her since escorting her into the banquet; of course he would choose now to begin a conversation. 'I had hoped nobody was looking.'

'I sincerely doubt that is the case. The entire gathering is captivated by you,' he said in a low voice, leaning in so that it seemed perhaps that they were having an intimate moment. 'You look...exceptionally regal this evening.'

Cressida felt a shiver run down her spine, having him so close, having his delicious scent invading her senses. The way he was looking at her, the depths of his dark eyes seeming to bore deep into her soul, she could not decide if he was continuing the show for the benefit of their guests or if perhaps he was feeling the same pull that she did, considering what had transpired between them a week ago. Or perhaps her hormones were simply not getting the message yet, she thought wryly.

Before he had a chance to dazzle her with any more of his flowery compliments, they were discreetly interrupted by one of Khal's assistants. A quick conversation passed in hushed tones before Khal turned back to her, a crease furrowing his brow.

'We are needed for a moment outside—nothing to worry about, just formalities.' He extended his hand to her, making quiet apologies to the handful of guests at their table before escorting her out through a set of double doors and into a sitting room of sorts.

There were a handful more assistants waiting for them, each of whom began talking in Zayyari so quickly that Cressida found it difficult to even catch a single word she recognised.

'English, please, for the benefit of your Queen,' Khal said briskly.

Cressida's eyes widened slightly at the tone he used. She had never heard him sound so impatient.

'There has been a report in the media...' one of the female assistants began, averting her eyes from Cressida's worried gaze as she spoke.

The chief of the team, a man with greying hair and beady eyes, moved from the side of the room, a large file in his hands. 'Your Highness, I apologise sincerely for disturbing your dinner, but protocol demands that you be alerted immediately to a report of this nature. When it is in the national interest.' He extended the black file to Khal, who took it immediately, opening it and scanning it.

Cressida felt the slight ball of tension in her stomach turn into a full-blown quake as she watched Khal's features turn from mild concern to disbelief before his gaze slowly rose to settle pointedly on her.

'Leave us,' he said quietly, his eyes never leaving her. It was the kind of quiet, firm voice he used when he was barely controlling his temper. The staff around him bowed their heads and left the room immediately, obeying their King's orders.

Cressida fought the urge to turn tail and run. 'What is it?' she asked, hearing the tremor in her voice.

'Why don't you read it for yourself?' He placed the file in her hands and turned his back to her, walking to the window, allowing her a moment.

Cressida scanned the file. It held an article dated that morning from an American publication, outlining very clearly a witness account to a royal scandal in the mysterious European kingdom of Monteverre. The royal scandal that had shaped her entire life.

Cressida felt a lump form in her throat as she took in the salacious headline in bold black ink.

Newly Crowned Queen of Zayyar's Illegitimate Past: the secret behind the scandalous Sandoval family revealed.

The tremor in her stomach turned to full-blown nausea as she felt her breath leave her lungs. Well, here it was, the moment she had prayed would never come to pass. Perhaps it was simply a gossip article; perhaps it was one of those rare cases where the media actually got quite close to the truth by accident but didn't actually have the evidence.

But, as she scanned through the rest of the article, she saw the name that haunted her. A name that she had found by chance at twelve years old, unknowingly setting the cogs in motion that would lead to her feeling ostracised and unwanted for evermore. She could still remember the smell of alcohol on her mother's breath the day she had told her that she was the product of an affair. Unwanted. A shameful reminder of her own mistake.

'Is this true?' Khal asked, still facing out of the window.

'Am I the shameful secret of the Sandoval royal family?' she heard her own voice say, as though from far away. 'Yes, unfortunately it's true.'

Khal turned around, reaching up to pinch the bridge of his nose. 'You did not think to disclose this information upon our marriage?'

'This information was never to be disclosed. My father... King Fabian, I mean, he and his team took extreme legal measures to ensure that it would never see the light of day.' She felt cold, her skin prickling, her insides shaking. She couldn't look at him; she couldn't see whatever expression might be in his eyes as he looked at her.

'Legal measures?'

'As far as I understand, a very large amount of money has been paid annually to this man to keep his silence on the matter.'

'Your biological father?'

Cressida nodded, the discomfort on hearing those words far too much for her to keep eye contact at all.

'You read the article?' A strange note had entered his voice. 'The last paragraph in particular?'

Cressida picked the file up from where she'd laid it on the coffee table, scanning down to the end of the article. 'Posthumous request?' she said numbly. 'He's dead?'

'The interview was released by his family, who are in control of his estate since his death, it seems.'

'It says here that he passed away four years ago.' Cressida shook her head. 'Why release this now? If they were able to break his nondisclosure upon his death.'

'Four years ago you were not the Queen of Zayyar,' Khal said with cold derision.

Cressida took a deep breath, feeling it shudder into her lungs. She closed her eyes, trying to calm the panic that was rising swiftly inside her to a raging storm. 'What are you going to do?'

Khal did not answer; instead he walked to the door and instructed his team to re-enter. The men and women filed in one by one, each one avoiding her eyes, but Cressida could feel them watching her. Judging her. All of a sudden the air was stifling in the sitting room.

'I need to go to the restroom for a moment,' she mumbled quietly, Khal barely looking her way as she slipped out of the door into the hallway beyond. Once alone, she lifted her dress up from the floor and moved quickly. She had no idea where she was going; she just had to get far away from the room full of knowing eyes that lay behind her.

CHAPTER NINE

'WHAT IS THE PLAN?' Khal addressed the head of his team. 'We have a room full of foreign dignitaries and politicians. They each have assistants and smartphones and instant updates. It's a fiasco.'

His head of PR spoke first. 'I think you need to speak on the matter as soon as possible, Your Highness. The longer it is left unaddressed, the weaker our position.'

'And what you propose I say, exactly?' Khal half laughed. 'This information comes just as much of a surprise to me as it would to them.'

'Yes, but the world cannot know that. We must act as though the Sheikha's parentage was known to you. That it was a matter of delicacy that you chose not to disclose for your wife's privacy.'

'And what is Monteverre's position on the matter?' Khal asked, feeling his fists clench at the thought of King Fabian and his underhand measures. It was likely the man did not care one ounce that his daughter had been publicly humiliated in the media. She was no longer a Sandoval, after all.

In the short time that he had been acquainted with Cressida's father, the man had shown him nothing but dishonesty and a ruthless greed that turned his stomach. King Fabian was not the kind of leader who put his people first. He was not even the kind of man to put his family first, given recent events.

And yet, when he had been contacted with the news that the youngest Princess was willing to accept the marriage, he had not hesitated to accept. Khal thought of the first night that he had met Cressida, once she had realised who he was, and he remembered her words. 'It has always been part of my duty to my kingdom...'

He had asked her numerous times if she had been forced into accepting this marriage. He had wanted to make sure that she was not entering into their union under duress...

Ignoring the sudden niggling feeling in his stomach, he looked up just as one of the junior assistants entered the room.

'The Sheikha has retired to her suite,' the young woman said.

Khal raised one brow. 'Retired? We are in the middle of a function.'

The young woman winced. 'Her Highness was quite adamant that she would not be returning, Sire. I was simply asked to convey the message.'

'I see.' Khal stood, walking towards the door before he even knew what he had planned to do. 'Keep the guests entertained. It seems I must retrieve my wife.'

Long strides and a rush of adrenaline had him at the door of Cressida's room within minutes. He did not knock, entering and closing the door with a thud behind him. She had been standing at the window but whirled around at his sudden entrance.

'I will not be abandoned in the middle of dinner.' Khal spoke evenly. It was taking all his self-control not to let his voice boom across the room with the force of his irritation. 'I understand that this situation is un-comfortable—'

'I can't go back in there.' Cressida's voice cut across him, loud and clear. 'I cannot sit and eat my dessert, knowing that the entire room is whispering about my secrets.'

The slight tremor in her voice unwound some of his irritation. She was upset; of course she would be. She had not known that her biological father was dead, that much was clear. But, apart from that, he realised that he had absolutely no idea what the rest of the story was. He had been too preoccupied with the scandal, and how to contain it. He had been Khal, Sheikh of Zayyar. While right now his wife had just needed sup-port from her husband.

'The whole world will know within the next twenty-four hours, *habibti*.' He was surprised at the softness in his voice as he spoke. 'It is not going to go away. And it is definitely not going to get any easier just by hiding yourself away in your rooms.'

'I'm not cut out for this; I told you that before you married me. I was not given the same training to live in the limelight that my sisters were.' She inhaled deeply, turning her face away from him to look out at where the sun was setting on the horizon of the desert. 'Nothing about me is the same as my sisters, and now you know why.'

'How long have you known the truth of your parentage?'

'On some level, perhaps I always knew. Physically, I never inherited the famed Sandoval beauty. I always had the feeling that my father looked at me differently.

Almost like he held me in disdain, no matter how I behaved.' She moved towards the window, her long skirt
blowing slightly in the breeze that drifted in. 'When I
was twelve, I found a box hidden away in the back of my
mother's dressing room. It was filled to the brim with
letters and some photographs of a man I didn't recog-
nise. My father found me trawling through these love
letters and images. Nothing was particularly graphic or
inappropriate, of course; my mother is a queen, after
all.' A cruel laugh escaped her throat, or perhaps it
was a sob.

'What did your father do?' Khal asked.

'Oh, he never punished me, if that's what you're
thinking. He's not one for physical punishment or
outward displays of aggression.' Her eyes narrowed
slightly. 'I wonder if perhaps a good spanking might
have left less scars; I don't know. He grabbed the box, he
took me by the hand and he brought me to my mother. I
remember she was sitting drinking brandy in the salon.
She smiled at me after he made her tell me the truth. It
was the saddest smile I have ever seen.

'And then I just stood there, twelve years old, and
listened to my father spout rage and venom while my
mother stared blankly out of the window. At one point
he turned to me, photograph in his hand, and he said,
"I am not your father. He is." I will never forget that
moment as long as I live. His eyes were almost black
with rage, spittle flying out of his mouth as he spoke. I
remember flinching as he held the photograph inches
from my nose, screaming at me to look at it, to look at
him. Him being the man my mother had betrayed our
family with.'

Khal let the silence fall between them, amazed at the

lack of emotion on her pale features as she recounted such awful memories. For a moment he felt the urge to close the space between them, to reach out and take her in his arms. It was too intimate, too much emotion tangling up the logical side of his brain that he knew was the priority right now. But his wife was hurting, that much was clear. She might not show her pain, but he could see it in the way she held her shoulders pulled straight, in the way she held her chin high but her lip quivered slightly.

Making his decision, he moved to her side and took both of her hands in his own.

'When you said that you were marrying me as part of your duty,' he began, tilting her chin up so that he could see her face, 'did this secret have anything to do with it? Were you blackmailed?' He did not know what he would do if the answer was yes.

She met his eyes for a moment, the sadness he saw there so profound that he felt his breath catch.

'I was not blackmailed, Khal. My father was already planning to cancel my research work and call me back to Monteverre, whether I agreed to this marriage or not. I made the mistake of sending him a letter around the same time that Olivia had run away from your engagement offer. I told him of a job offer I had received at the university. He was furious. I might not be a Sandoval by blood but I still held the name and title. By agreeing to marry you…he said it would make him proud.' Her voice broke on the last word.

Khal felt his chest constrict, his arms surrounding her as she finally melted into him and let the tears fall. Hearing the evidence of yet more emotional manipulation by such a cruel man made the primal beast within him growl even louder. To use his daughter's love against her, to manipulate her... He took a breath, loosening his hold on her and creating enough space between them so that he could look down into her eyes.

'I will make an excuse for you; there is no reason to force you to return to the function in this kind of emotional state.'

'No.' She shook her head, standing up straight and blotting her eyes lightly with the tips of her fingers. 'It was childish of me to run off like that. Tonight is about taking my place as Sheikha. It's better if we maintain a united front, like the team said. I can hold myself together for another hour or two.'

'You are sure?' Khal frowned at the sudden change in her posture, the way she seemed to so easily switch off such deep pain and anguish.

She nodded, all the weakness from a moment before gone. Aside from a slight smudge at the corner of one eye, it would take very close scrutiny to know that she had been crying at all. She was practised in hiding her pain, he knew now. It made something inside him clench to know that she was now hiding it from him too.

The rest of the dinner passed in a blur. Cressida did not know if perhaps the news had not broken as quickly as they expected it to, or perhaps their guests were simply putting on a very convincing front. But it was a relief that no one seemed to be looking at her differently, no hushed conversations seemed to occur in her vicinity. Or perhaps her inner turmoil was such that she simply did not notice or care.

It felt as though all the energy in her body had been depleted, leaving her weak and tired. So, so tired.

The news that her biological father was dead had shocked her, even though she had never met the man. She had only ever seen his picture, and read the beautiful letters sent to her mother. Vincent was his name, a humble chauffeur. How utterly clichéd that her mother would have a sordid affair with her driver. This really was the media's dream scandal. Most likely, there would be books written. Hollywood probably had someone penning a script as they spoke.

She kept her polite smile in place as the guests began to filter out, taking the chance to slip quietly away. She had fulfilled her duty, she had sat and eaten and listened to speeches and applauded at the correct times. Now, she wanted nothing more than to collapse in her bed and bury herself beneath the covers until the rest of the world was no longer talking about her.

Khal had not spoken to her since they'd returned to the banquet; clearly he was far too preoccupied in ensuring that they retained the power in this awful situation she had created. Poor him, having shackled himself to such an unworthy bride. Heaven only knew what the Zayyari public would make of this scandal. Perhaps there would be call for an annulment of the marriage, now that it was public knowledge that her parentage was illegitimate. She was polluting the royal image of the kingdom with her scandal and secrecy.

Once in her room, she went about the ritual of allowing her maid to assist her with the more difficult garments, then dismissed the young woman for the night so that she could take her time getting ready for bed. She removed the pearl earrings from her ears, placing them delicately into the small box on her dressing table. Next, she removed the heavy necklace from her neck,

taking a final moment to admire the glitter of the sap-
phires in the lamplight.

Standing up from her table, she took a moment to
take in the designer lingerie that had been paired with
her evening gown. Apparently a dress like hers required
a specific cut of bra and underwear to achieve maximum effect. She had just been grateful that she wasn't
forced to wear some sort of medieval corset.

The bra was definitely designed well, she smiled to
herself. A movement in the mirror caught her eye, and
she looked up to see Khal standing in the doorway. They
both stood frozen for a moment, Cressida with one hand
awkwardly cupping the lace of her bra.

'I came to talk.' He averted his eyes, seeming suddenly transfixed upon a spot on the floor. 'I'll wait in
the living room.' With that, he turned around and closed
the door behind him.

Cressida exhaled slowly, dropping her hand from her
breast to rest at her side. A bubble of nervous laughter rose in her chest. If he didn't already think she
was odd, after walking in to find her examining her
own bra…

Not wanting to keep him waiting, she threw on her
dressing gown, making sure it was closed tight at the
front, and tied a double knot at her waist. Slipping on
her silk slippers, she contemplated tying her hair into a
loose bun but decided against it, considering that it had
been pinned up already all evening. Most likely Khal
simply wanted to give her an update on the media situation and he would be gone, leaving her free to fall into
bed alone as usual.

He sat in an easy repose on her small settee, long
legs casually crossed one over the other as he flipped

through the fashion magazine that had been left on her coffee table.

'I just want to clarify that I don't usually stand and examine myself in the mirror like that, in case you think me awfully vain.' She kept her tone light in an effort to appear easy and unaffected by the fact that he had just witnessed her half naked. Not that that exactly mattered, considering that he had already seen her fully naked once before, but she wouldn't dwell too much on that thought if she planned to get through this conversation.

'And here I was thinking I had stumbled upon another little secret of yours.' He attempted a smile.

Cressida appreciated his attempt at humour, considering he was not usually one for jokes. She took a seat on the other side of the settee, carefully keeping the folds of her dressing gown together. For a moment she thought she saw his eyes scanning her body slowly, then he blinked and looked away.

'You disappeared tonight before I had the chance to talk further,' he said. 'I wanted to express my admiration for you this evening. Returning to that dinner could not have been easy.'

'It's easier than sitting alone with my thoughts at the moment.' Cressida shrugged.

'Why do you do that?' he asked quietly. 'I offer you a compliment and you shrug it off as though it makes you uncomfortable.'

Cressida fought the urge to squirm in her seat, feeling as though he was doing that thing where he saw right through her. He had always seen her, the real her, so much more than anyone else had. 'Okay, how about I go back in time thirty seconds and I simply say thank you?'

One corner of his mouth raised slightly, his gaze never leaving hers. 'What else would you do if you could go back in time, I wonder?'

'According to my lessons in royal interview tactics, that is the kind of question the Sheikha must never answer.'

'Never has a question been deflected with more skill.' Khal half laughed, giving her mock applause. It was strange, laughing with him after the strain of the past few hours, but at the same time it was just really nice too.

'Why did you come here?' Cressida asked. 'I mean, of course you are welcome to come here whenever you like. I just meant tonight in particular. You must have something specific you wanted to talk about.'

'I did come here to talk further about the plan for the next few days, the strategy to contain the story in the media...' He met her eyes, uncrossing his legs and sitting forward with his hands on his knees. 'My team want us to lie low for a couple of days while they assess the situation and make plans with the relevant team in Monteverre. Then we will travel over for our official visit and address the matter.'

Back to Monteverre. To confront the truth. Cressida felt anxiety rise swiftly within her but she pushed it back down.

'Are you okay? Honestly?' His eyes held hers as he reached between them to grasp her hands. 'It is all right to show me your weakness, Cressida. I won't judge you.'

Cressida felt her heart pump in her chest, hearing the gentle tone of his voice. 'I'm sorry I didn't tell you. I understand if you see me differently now. If you regret our marriage.'

His grip on her hands tightened. 'Is that what you think?'

'You seemed angry all evening. Agitated. It's an entirely valid way to feel, finding out that your wife is even less perfect than she already was.'

'I do not expect you to be perfect, Cressida. This news has come as a shock but, more than anything, I am angry for you, not towards you,' he said passionately. 'And as for regretting our marriage...' He shook his head.

She inhaled deeply, hardly believing, as a rueful smile crossed his lips.

'Some of my agitation likely stems from how utterly beautiful you look tonight and how frustrated I am at not being able to touch you. I haven't been able to take my eyes off you all evening,' he said evenly, his gaze locked on hers. 'It has been a week since I had you in my arms and I still remember every single moment with painful clarity.'

Cressida took a deep breath, the intensity of his gaze on hers making her heart skitter uncomfortably in her chest. She felt restless and yet glued to the spot all at once.

'We said that we would stick with the original plan. But I think that my plan changed the moment I danced with you in the club in London.' His voice seemed lower all of a sudden...huskier. 'I held on to my plan because that's simply what I do. I keep things under control. But it seems that my control does not exist when it comes to you, Cressida.'

'What are you saying?' she asked nervously, not exactly sure what she wanted to hear. She wanted him to want her, but not just as a sexual distraction until they wore each other out or got sick of each other.

'I'm saying that the tidy little red line that I drew around both of our separate circles has been blurred and broken to a point where they seem to be melding into one, whether we will them to or not. So now it seems we face a choice. We can choose to completely separate our lives in such a way that we are very rarely in each other's presence at all. Or we can ignore the red lines completely and see what happens.'

'A world without red lines...' Cressida said slowly, seeing the tension in his body as he awaited her response. 'It seems very uncertain for a man who loves certainty.'

'The only thing that I'm certain about at the moment is that if I don't have you in my arms in the next five seconds I may very well burst out of my skin or erupt into flames where I sit.'

Cressida smiled, a shiver of anticipation running down her spine. 'Oh, don't do that. I've grown quite attached to this sofa,' she said, her voice taking on a sultry tone that shocked her.

A slow smile spread across Khal's lips, 'Well, it seems your choice has been made.' He closed the distance between them in record time, his body covering hers at the same moment his lips moulded against her own.

CHAPTER TEN

THE KISS WAS filled with every ounce of tension and frustration that she had felt herself. She had dreamt of his kisses, had tried her hardest to remember what it felt like to have his lips on hers in case she never felt it again. And yet now that his lips were on hers once more she wondered how she had ever forgotten the feeling. It was so familiar now, like coming home. Dangerously comfortable and yet feverishly exciting all at once.

Cressida felt as though her heart might beat completely out of her chest. What was it about kissing this man that sent every single hormonal impulse in her body into chaos? And not only that, she wanted to say things to him. Do things that made her shocked. She reached out to run her fingers down the bared skin of his chest, spreading his shirt collar wide so that she could touch him just as he had touched her.

Khal's hands encircled her wrists, moving her backwards until she lay back on the sofa, her nightgown spread wide to expose her partially clothed body. He pressed his mouth to the skin above her navel, moving inch by tantalising inch lower, all the while maintaining eye contact. The heat between her legs heightened to a blazing fire and she could not help but reach her fingers towards him, not sure if she wanted to stop him or tell him to move faster to his destination.

'What do you want me to do, Cressida…?' He spoke each syllable with a caress of his lips against her sensitive skin, his large muscular hands gripping her hips.

She breathed hard, hardly able to control the small movements her pelvis made as his lips reached the edge of her lace underwear. 'I want your mouth to touch me… there.' No longer able to be embarrassed by her own words, she moaned as he drew his fingers up along the thin material.

'Right here?' he asked, repeating the movement and groaning as she arched herself against his touch. He stopped speaking then, pulling her underwear down over her hips and throwing them over his shoulder.

The first touch of his tongue along her bared flesh was like nothing she could have ever expected. It was as though her entire body lit up from the inside, warmth spinning upwards along her nerve endings like fireworks. The second touch was even more intense as he drew his tongue slowly along the very centre of her, knowing exactly where would give her the most pleasure. She arched her hips, needing to move against him rather than lying flat and limp. She could not have stayed still if she'd tried, especially once he moved into a smooth rhythm. She had thought the first part was amazing, but it seemed he had more tricks up his sleeve. After a moment, he shifted, looking up at her while he slid his index finger down and slowly into her tight heat. Cressida tilted her head back as he resumed his tongue mastery now with the addition of moving his finger against a spot inside her that she had not known existed. When he added a second finger she thought she might combust on the spot, the feeling of fullness was so intense. Her heart began to pound and she was sure the tension could build no further, the slow tremendous build up like nothing she had ever felt before.

When she finally shattered, she thought she gripped his hair so tightly she was sure it must have been painful. But she was much too busy being overcome by wave after wave of devastating pleasure to care too much. Eyes closed, she was vaguely aware of Khal moving up over her, his mouth laying kisses along her neck.

'You are even more beautiful when you climax.'

She smiled, unable to feel embarrassed after the earth-shattering bliss of what she had just experienced. She felt beautiful when he looked at her this way, as though he could devour her in a single bite.

She reached to his waistband and unzipped the front of his trousers quickly before she lost her nerve. She wanted all of him. It seemed unfair that she was completely nude while he was still dressed. As though reading her thoughts, Khal pulled his shirt over his head and helped her by pulling the trousers off the rest of the way.

She began her exploration on his bare chest, feeling the strength of his pectorals under her fingertips and moving lower to where his abdomen dipped in at the hips. It was the body of a leader, a warrior. Her protector, she thought with a quiet ferocity. She wanted to show him the same care and pleasure that he had shown her, but fear of her own lack of practice made her settle for encircling his length with her hand instead. He thrust forward into her palm, a low hiss escaping his teeth as he exhaled hard. She stroked him, slowly at first then increasing her pace.

'I need to be inside you,' he growled low in his

throat, pulling her hands above her head and moving over her to crush her mouth against his.

She luxuriated in the feeling of all that powerful bare muscle pressed flush against every inch of her. She could feel the heavy heat of his arousal pressing against the top of her thigh and she rocked against him, showing him with her body that she had never wanted anything more in her life.

Khal willed himself to take it slow when all he wanted to do was plunge hard and fast into the delicious heat he knew awaited him. She moved against him again, sliding her slippery heat against him. She was trying to kill him.

He placed one hand on her hip, stilling her as he entered. Her body grasped him so tightly he seriously doubted his ability to last longer than ten seconds.

He wondered if anything on earth was as perfect as the sheer pleasure of being buried fully inside her molten heat. Her body gripped him like a vice, such an absolutely perfect fit it took every ounce of the patience and skill he had to hold himself still and allow her a moment to adjust. The torment of waiting heightened every nerve ending in his body, so much so that he could feel his climax building almost immediately. He leaned down, taking one hard nipple in his mouth and grazing his teeth along the pink flesh. She gasped, her muscles relaxing and tensing as she took him deeper, squeezing him tight.

'You drive me to madness, *habibti*,' he gritted, burying his face in the hollow of her neck as he moved slowly against her. Taking his time to let her catch up, urging her body upwards to join him. He felt her pulse quicken under his lips, her skin salty with the barest sheen of sweat. She was lost to it just as he was, the storm of sensation dancing and growing in the delicious friction of their bodies.

He groaned as his climax approached, moving harder against her and reaching down to caress the sensitive spot he knew would tip her over the edge. He knew the very moment she began to fall, her eyes meeting his for a split second with nothing but raw, primal need in their depths. That was all it took—one look and he could hold out no longer.

Mine, the demon inside him growled. With a hoarse cry he gave in to the pleasure and fully lost himself in Cressida's heat.

There was a man in her bed. Cressida smiled to herself, taking in Khal's glorious muscular form spread out alongside her. Her body felt stiff in places she hadn't known she could strain but nothing could ruin this for her. They had made love once more last night after Khal had carried her to the bathroom and showed her the hidden pleasures that could be found in the shower.

Sex was so much more than she had ever imagined it to be. It had felt like a meeting of their bodies, like two parts joining together in a mutual dance. And what a dance it was with Khal...

She remembered his words the first time he had taken her into his arms on that nightclub dancefloor, about dance being a temptation. The thought made her smile quietly to herself.

He stirred alongside her and she closed her eyes, not quite brave enough to admit she had been awake and ogling him while he slept. A hand splayed across her stomach, sliding across her skin for a moment before she felt his lips touch the delicate skin of her breast.

'Keep your eyes closed,' he murmured. 'We can pretend that you are still asleep and haven't ruined my very specific plans to wake you.'

Cressida shivered, opening her eyes just as he moved over her, kissing a path down the valley of her breasts and over her stomach. His lips were like hot silk moving over her skin, familiar and tantalising. He paid special attention to each hip before deftly bypassing the place she ached for him most in favour of laying a trail of kisses down the insides of each thigh.

'That's not fair.' She tried to laugh but the sound came out a breathy moan. She hadn't even known she was capable of making such feminine sounds until Khal.

'Never let it be said that the great Sheikh is not a fair man,' he teased, moving down to settle between her thighs with dark promise. She did not tense at all as one finger slowly entered her, closely followed by a second. She gasped, feeling him hit just the right spot and begin to work it in a perfect rhythm. Her hips bucked upwards, the pleasure so acute it was almost painful. Spreading her wide, his tongue darted over her sex once, twice…three times, but not quite allowing her to move towards climax.

Cressida sighed, looking up at him just as he moved over her. She pressed her hands on his chest, rising up from the bed so that they both kneeled facing each other. She looked down at his impressive length, running one fingertip along the silky-smooth skin before encircling him with her hand and meeting his eyes purposefully.

'I want to return the favour,' she said boldly.

Khal raised one brow, lying back on the bed in silent invitation. He was not submissive in bed. He was controlled and knew exactly what to do to drive them both over the edge. She wanted the chance to learn how to drive him crazy, just like he did to her. She leaned over him, taking him into her mouth with one smooth movement. He tasted like sex, the action so utterly erotic she felt herself grind her hips a little. One strong hand moved to slide up the outside of her thigh, dropping a light smack on the curve of her behind. He repeated the action and she bit her lip, amazed that she enjoyed it.

'That's it. Just like that.' He exhaled hard.

Typical Khal, she thought, still trying to maintain control. Not this time. She took him deeper into her mouth, feeling his taut stomach muscles shudder beneath her hands.

'I could have you do this all day,' he growled, letting his hand coil into the length of her hair, stopping her movement but still not withdrawing entirely. 'But I cannot wait another moment before I can be inside you again.'

She sat back, running her fingers down his powerful thighs and trying to take a mental photograph of this moment. She did not know how long this mindless passion between them would last. But right now it felt as though they were the only two people in the world and she wanted to savour every moment. His hand encircled her wrist, gently tugging her so that she lay draped over him. She kissed him, softly at first before letting her arousal take over and taking the kiss deeper. Her mind no longer intruded, her body recognising his and knowing just what lay in store.

Strong hands gripped her hips. He thrust upwards, and both of them filled the room with the kind of throaty moan that only came with that very first joining. He thrust deep, filling her to the hilt, and withdrew halfway before he let his hands drift to his sides and went still.

'Show me how you like it,' he said, lying back to watch her with a look of deep male appreciation.

She bit her lip, feeling momentarily vulnerable with his eyes devouring her, but the delicious slide of him inside her was enough to move her thoughts elsewhere quickly enough. She moved over him slowly, finding her rhythm and gasping at the sensation of being filled so very deeply.

She trusted him completely, she realised, suddenly unable to look at him as the force of her emotions began to build, along with her climax. He moved, sitting up so that their chests were only inches apart; his hands on her hips kept her rhythm in check as he thrust in time with her. After the mind-exploding pleasure of their orgasms had passed there was only silence, and then the sound of their laboured breathing. Khal moved away first, darting a quick glance in her direction before lying flat on his back.

Something in his eyes told her that he felt it too, this painful closeness. She inhaled, feeling a lingering tightness in her chest from the force of keeping her emotions in check. She stood from the bed, moving to the bathroom on shaky legs and closing the door gently behind her.

This was so much more than feeling overwhelmed by sex, she thought, biting her lip at her own naiveté. She had known she was in danger from the moment he had looked into her eyes in that wedding tent. He had started out as the man she had been forced to choose and somehow wound up being her perfect fit. Her lover. The word seemed to caress something deep inside her, a tiny speck of romanticism that she would never have dreamed existed within her cynical heart. But there it was, clear as day. And, just as that speck began to glow and blossom, realisation dawned that she had done what she had vowed not to do.

She had let her emotions get involved. She had fallen in love with her husband.

Khal woke with a start, a light sheen of sweat on his chest as he sat up in the unfamiliar bedroom. It took a moment to realise where he was. He stood up, walking to the long terrace doors and opening them a few inches to take in a breath of fresh air. The city of Valar spread out before him in a glittering blanket of lights. The dream had been much the same as it always was. Priya's voice haunting him, reminding him of his unworthiness, only tonight she had not been alone. Beside her, Cressida had appeared, tears falling from her eyes.

He contemplated slipping out to his own room, but immediately disregarded the idea as cowardly. He was not some kind of lothario who slipped in and out of bedrooms in the darkness. He splashed some cold water on his face and went back into the bedroom. The light beside the bed was on and to his dismay he found Cressida was sitting up, waiting for him.

'I had not meant to wake you.' Khal lay heavily back down onto the bed, turning on his side to take in the beautiful sight that greeted him. Cressida lay back against the pillows, ash-blonde hair spilling around her bare shoulders and the satin sheets tucked demurely under her arms to cover her chest. The innocent display of modesty was a delicious distraction from his troubled thoughts; he could think of no better way to redirect his mind than by peeling away those sheets, inch by glorious inch...

'You were talking in your sleep...' Cressida disturbed his train of thought, a nervous tone to her quiet voice '... I was debating whether or not to wake you but then I heard you get up... I wasn't sure if perhaps you were sleepwalking.'

'I hope I at least said something entertaining,' he joked easily, but still he wondered how much she might have gleaned from his night-time ramblings.

Cressida did not smile. 'I believe that you...you were dreaming of your wife.'

He could hear the sadness in her voice, the uncertainty. 'You are my wife. Let us not get mixed up on that fact, *habibti*.'

'You were saying her name.' She took her lip between her teeth, worrying it slightly, weighing up her words before she spoke. 'Priya. Do you dream of her often?'

Khal exhaled, deeply uncomfortable with the turn this conversation had taken. He had never spoken to a soul about the dreams that'd plagued him since Priya's death. How their final conversation seemed to haunt him so heavily. And even now, four years later, the dreams would come back every now and then. It tended to happen at very inopportune times, like when he slept in a jet surrounded by staff or the first night that he slept beside his new wife after making love... He silently cursed himself.

'I'm not exactly sure what triggers the dream, maybe

stress or lack of sleep. It just kind of happens every once in a while.' He curled one arm behind his head and studied the ceiling for a moment, knowing the conversation had only begun, judging by the curious look on Cressida's face.

'No one ever seems to talk of how she died,' Cressida said slowly. 'It's as though it's some great big secret. Ironic, coming from me, I know.'

Khal attempted a smile but found the muscles in his face seemed suddenly tight. He did not speak of Priya's death to anyone. He never had. Other than to aid in the investigations into her accident, no one addressed the subject and he certainly did not bring it into conversation. It felt as though every comfortable boundary in his life had begun to slowly erode from the moment he had met Cressida.

'You don't have to speak about it,' she said quickly, feigning a sudden interest in the pattern on the sheets that covered her abdomen. 'It's probably quite presumptuous of me to even ask. I'm sorry.'

Khal felt like an utter ass, seeing the look on her face. Of course she had the right to ask; they were married and he had just been speaking another woman's name in their bed. The rules surrounding their marriage were still blurred at present, neither of them knowing exactly what was okay or not. The initial agreement for a marriage in name only had most definitely been broken, but it left them in a kind of limbo. They were not man and wife in the truest sense, but neither were they the kind of formal arrangement he had originally envisioned. He knew that right now was most definitely one of those moments where he needed to do the difficult thing.

'It's not something I'm usually comfortable talking

about,' he said slowly, watching as her eyes raised up to meet his. He reached out and laid his hand over hers on the sheets. 'But you spoke through your own discomfort; therefore perhaps it is only fair that I do the same.'

'You don't have to…' Cressida began quickly.

'I want to,' he said, surprised to realise that he was speaking the truth. 'I told you once before that my marriage was not all that it seemed. To the public we were untouchable. I was the picture-perfect husband and she the perfect wife.' He shook his head, a cruel laugh escaping from his lips. 'Not a single soul knows the last words she ever spoke to me… The words that haunt my dreams at night. She told me that she would rather die than be my wife a moment longer.' Khal turned his head, expecting to see disgust in Cressida's eyes. But what he saw there instead was more uncomfortable. Pity. Oh, how he had despised that look of pity on people's faces in the months following his wife's death.

'Couples have arguments all of the time,' Cressida began.

'It was not the first time that she had spoken in that way.' Khal shook his head. 'I was not the best husband, by any standard.' She didn't understand; she didn't realise that when Priya had said those words she had truly meant them.

'How awful, to have that memory in your mind,' Cressida said softly, covering his hand with hers.

Khal inhaled deeply, wanting to recoil from the pity he could hear in her voice. 'You wanted to know how she died. I'll tell you, but you must forgive me if I still hold some anger.' He had unconsciously begun to tap his foot at some point, a nervous gesture that he constantly tried to overcome since teenage years. Kings did not fidget, he remembered his father telling him. Control—it was always about showing control.

'There has never been a definitive answer on how she came to be on the road that she was, at the time that she was. One point of view is that she was on her way to meet her lover. I was aware that she had been unfaithful to me on a number of occasions in the later years of our marriage.' Khal saw a look of shock cross Cressida's features, followed by a brief hint of anger. 'Another view is that she purposely drove her car over the side of the ravine at a high speed in order to end her own life.'

Cressida winced, her grip tightening on his hand.

'In Zayyari culture, both of those possibilities spell out shame. I was not prepared to have her name sullied, so the nature of her death was never disclosed. The perceived secrecy led to speculation and rumours. Most of which involved various theories of how I was a ruthless barbarian who had arranged his wife's murder. Or worse, that I had killed her myself and had the truth covered up.

'I was assured that her death was instantaneous. For that I was grateful.' He closed his eyes for a moment, trying to ignore the onslaught of memories. The smell of burning rubber in the air as he had moved down the side of the sandbank, his guards shouting at him to stop. He remembered watching as one of his sports cars was hoisted from the shallow water. Priya's lifeless body had already been transported to the morgue where he had identified her, but for some reason Khal had needed to see the car. He had needed to see the place where it had happened, to make sense of it all.

'Nothing about it made sense; that was the worst part

to accept. The investigators told me that there was no way to prove if the car had been tampered with, considering it had to be destroyed upon transportation to be impounded.' He shook his head, sitting up straight. 'The idea that her anger at me led to her driving dangerously never sat well with me. I have spent years trying to find evidence that someone deliberately caused the accident other than Priya herself. It's only now…saying it out loud… that I realise maybe that's just my way of coping with my own guilt and sense of powerlessness.'

Cressida leaned forward, pressing her cheek against his bare back and sliding her arm around his abdomen. The gesture was so intimate and so comforting that for a moment he felt himself tightening, the urge to pull away strong. But then the warmth of her skin seeped into his own and he found himself accepting her comfort, grateful for the fact that for once he was not alone in his recollection of these painful memories.

They sat in silence for a while, Cressida listening to the beat of his heart thumping in rhythm with her own. 'I find it hard to believe that you were ever a bad husband.'

To her surprise she felt him tense beneath her skin, pulling away from her slightly. She sat back, wondering if perhaps she had touched a nerve even after all he had just disclosed.

'We had a son,' Khal said, a strange emptiness to his voice as he spoke. 'He never lived, stillborn in the eighth month of pregnancy. But we had a son.'

Cressida felt something inside her break as the words hit her with full force. She had no idea what it was like to bear that kind of tragedy and pain in one's life. The very idea of Khal going through such a loss was unbearable.

'When I say that I was a bad husband, I don't mean that I was a bit selfish or that I forgot to put the toilet seat down. I was a bad husband because my wife's needs were never taken into consideration. All that mattered was ensuring that my need for tight security and safety was prioritised. I overreacted to everything. She got swarmed in the markets once, early on in her pregnancy, and I decided that I needed to keep her under tighter security, even if it meant keeping her confined to the palace. Priya told me on numerous occasions that she was unhappy but the final straw was when she was rushed to hospital, pregnant and terrified. I was halfway across the world being the grand Sheikh of Zayyar. And when I was finally given the news a day later, there was absolutely nothing I could do. We had only been married a year at that point.'

'You blame yourself for so much…' Cressida began, not quite knowing what to say in the face of such an admission.

'I'm sorry. I said that I don't like to share and yet here I am, unable to stop.' He turned, taking her hands in his and looking deep into her eyes.

'There is no need to explain yourself to me,' Cressida said firmly. 'I am simply grateful that you trusted me enough to share what you have.'

He nodded once, taking her in his arms. The embrace began innocently enough, but then the sheet slipped down between them and suddenly she was being swept away on another wave of passion. Their lovemaking this time was slower, a tentative sliver of intimacy seeming to show in the way he held her face in his hands as he kissed her and looked deep into her eyes. Afterwards, he fell into a deep sleep with impressive speed, leaving Cressida staring up at the ceiling, physically satisfied but emotionally distracted.

She found herself absolutely livid that he had been subjected to such harsh scrutiny in his time of grief.

The world lauded her own father, a man who had held his wife and daughters to emotional ransom their whole lives, and yet Khal was shunned, based on rumours and gossip. She felt something within her changing, a strange protectiveness of this new life she had entered into. It scared her, to think that she felt such loyalty to a man she had only known a matter of weeks now. But she did trust him with all of her heart. It was keeping that heart protected when it was becoming more and more in danger of being broken...that was the real problem.

CHAPTER ELEVEN

AFTER THREE FULL days of an impromptu honeymoon spent mostly in bed, Cressida mourned the arrival of their departure for the official visit to Monteverre. They spent a large portion of the flight hidden away in the master bedroom. While Khal might have introduced her to the pleasures of the mile-high club, she had the pleasure of giving him a tour of her home town through her own eyes once they touched down.

Her decision to leave Monteverre at the age of nineteen to study abroad had held no bearing on her love for her kingdom. She had simply needed freedom from the oppressive disdain of her parents and the effort of hiding her secret from her siblings.

Even as their limousine moved slowly around the main square and she pointed out her favourite ice cream shop and the library where she had spent many an afternoon hiding away, she felt anxiety rising steadily within her. The thought of speaking to her sisters now that they had been made aware of the great family secret was daunting. At least, with her parents, she knew what to expect. She didn't know if Olivia and Eleanor would be upset, hurt or even angry at her for keeping such a secret.

Truthfully, she did not know if Olivia would show up at all. Last she had heard, she and her fiancé Roman were sailing around the Caribbean after becoming formally engaged shortly before Cressida had moved to Zayyar.

'You are very quiet, *habibti*,' Khal said as they shared a speciality Monteverrian vanilla ice cream on a narrow side street. 'Don't think I haven't noticed that you are delaying our arrival at the palace.'

Cressida bit her lower lip, hating that he seen through her so easily but also enjoying the fact just a little. 'I'm delaying the unknown. My sisters were always kept in the dark when it came to the secret of my parentage. As far as they knew, there was nothing different about me other than the obvious facts that I have poor fashion sense and a strange attachment to books.'

'I disagree, your fashion sense is no longer poor since you met me.' He jabbed, smiling as she reached out to smudge ice cream on his nose in retaliation. 'Your sisters may be a bit hurt at being kept in the dark, but they will not love you any less.'

'I hope you are right.' Cressida sighed.

They finished their ice creams and finally there was nothing else to do but make their grand arrival at the palace. Usually a high-profile guest was welcomed in grand style, with all the staff lined up at the foot of the wide concrete steps while the Royal family stood waiting at the top. Today, the steps were empty save for a single butler, who stood at the end. Cressida recognised him as Hansel, the second most senior member of the royal house staff. A harsh laugh escaped her throat at the thought that her father had not even deemed her arrival home after almost five years away to be worthy of the head butler.

'Your Highnesses, allow me to be the first to congratulate you on your recent nuptials and to formally welcome you back to Monteverre.' The older man bowed, escorting them inside and down the long familiar corridors to the grand salon.

Inside, the Sandoval family waited, her mother and sister sitting down while her father stood poised at the mantelpiece, just as she'd expected. It was his usual show of force, he was a tall man and he liked to stand in the position of power in a room when welcoming guests.

She had almost forgotten that Khal was by her side until her father stepped forward, greeting him before he greeted his own daughter.

'Welcome back to my humble kingdom, Sheikh Khalil,' King Fabian said loudly. 'I believe you have already been introduced to my eldest daughter, Crown Princess Eleanor.'

Khal glanced uncomfortably from Cressida to her father, before stepping forward and making his introduction to her older sister.

Eleanor was thinner than she remembered; that was the first thought Cressida had before her sister stepped forward suddenly and embraced her.

'Cress, it has been far too long.' Eleanor did not gush; there was nothing false about the way she held the embrace for a long moment before pulling away. For a moment it almost felt as though they were children again, before anything had ever changed.

The moment did not last long, however, her father booming across the little interlude in his usual fashion.

'And here she is, the woman of the hour,' he pronounced with mock pride.

Cressida felt Khal stiffen beside her, his hand tightening on hers.

'Father, I hope you are well.' She opted for the polite approach, ignoring the urge to simply speak her mind and address the very large elephant present in the room.

'I'm quite well, considering the stress that I and the royal team have been under for the past three days.' His lips tightened in what she supposed was an attempt at a smile. 'I doubt you've been put under much pressure, hiding out there in the desert.'

He looked to Khal in a very male attempt at camaraderie, clearly expecting her husband to share in his joke. Khal did not.

'Perhaps we should take things to a more business setting. Leave the women to catch up. It has been such a long time since Cressida has seen her family.'

Cressida tried not to react to the way the King referred to her mother and sister as her family, not his. He had no need to hide his true feelings now, she supposed. She had never been a Sandoval by birth but now she was no longer even a Sandoval by name. He could pretend that she had never existed and never feel the difference.

'This matter concerns your daughter just as much as it concerns our kingdoms—' Khal began, his shoulders straightening.

'No, you should go. You are much better at all of this.' Cressida squeezed her husband's hand lightly. 'I trust you to speak on my behalf.'

'You are sure?' He dipped his head, speaking quietly near her ear.

Cressida nodded, smiling as he placed a delicate kiss

on her palm and left the room with a few long powerful strides, her father at his heels.

'So you found love, after all.' Her mother's voice drifted across the room.

Cressida had almost forgotten that her mother was there at all, considering she had not stood once since she had entered the room. 'We have a comfortable arrangement. It's more than I could have hoped for, considering the circumstances.' Cressida spoke evenly.

'What your father and I had... Sorry, King Fabian and I...' Her mother cleared her throat suddenly, the first sign of emotion crossing heavily lined features. 'Our arranged marriage was comfortable at best. Dangerously passionate at worst.' She took a long sip of her brandy, rising to her feet and swaying slightly. 'What you want is something in the middle, something warm that will last, not burn itself out before you've even had a chance.'

Eleanor cleared her throat, ever the peacemaker of the family. 'He seems quite fond of you,' she offered kindly. 'I'm happy for you, little sister.'

'I was nervous about coming here today, considering what has been said.' She met her older sister's eyes, feeling her voice quivering slightly. 'You must know that I would have told you, had I been allowed to.'

'Yes, yes.' Queen Aurelia sighed heavily, making her way slowly across the room towards the sideboard and the brandy decanter that stood upon it. 'We would all have done a great many things, had we been allowed to.'

Something within Cressida seemed to stretch thin and snap apart. Years of hurt and emotional pain rose to the surface, her temper rising with it.

'Your attitude is appalling, Mother.' Eleanor spoke

first, surprising Cressida with the backbone in her voice. Her elder sister had always been the strong, silent one. Never sharing the details of her own seemingly perfect marriage. Always simply moving forward with her duty and not getting involved in any of the family politics that might have arisen.

'My attitude?' Queen Aurelia laughed, filling up her glass almost to the top with amber liquid, not seeming to care that it was barely midday. 'At least I did not run away the first chance I got. At least I put my family first.'

'Is that how you justify your actions to yourself?' Cressida asked quietly. 'I have often wondered if you were entirely oblivious or if you simply never cared about your children or the consequences that your selfishness had on them.'

'Selfishness?' Her mother's eyes widened, her hand abandoning the brandy glass entirely as she swung around to face her two daughters across the grand salon. 'I gave up everything for my children. Don't you dare speak of things when you have no idea of the truth.'

'What have you ever given up?' Cressida shook her head, amazed at the vitriol and the energy in her mother's voice all of a sudden. The woman had been a living ghost for as long as she could remember, now all of a sudden she seemed full of life as she defended her own poor choices.

Queen Aurelia shook her head, emotion seeming to overtake her momentarily as she turned her back to them and walked towards the window. Her pale blonde hair caught the rays of sunlight as she stood silently for a moment and looked out at the sea in the distance.

'Did you know that he had died?' Queen Aurelia

finally asked, turning slightly to meet Cressida's eyes for the first time.

Cressida did not need to ask who she was speaking of; the emotion in her mother's eyes spoke clearly enough. By her side she could see Eleanor begin twisting her hands together, a rare show of discomfort from the Crown Princess.

'I think perhaps I will go and sit in on the meeting,' Eleanor said quickly. 'Perhaps you would both like a moment alone.'

Before Cressida had a moment to respond, Eleanor swept from the room. Her mother turned fully to look at her, still waiting for her answer.

'No, I did not know. The newspaper article was the first I had heard of it.'

Silence fell once again in the room, the only sound a gentle sniff as her mother took out a handkerchief and gently dabbed her eyes. 'I did not have lovers, despite whatever poison Fabian may have put in your mind. I had one true love and I never had the chance to say goodbye to him.'

Tears streamed down her mother's face in earnest now, though she tried to turn away.

Cressida took a handkerchief from her purse, walking to her mother's side and offering it.

'You hated me for it. I saw it on your face the day that he dragged you into my room with my letters in his hand.' Pain was evident in her mother's tight features as she reached out to take Cressida's hand in her own. 'I have never been good at communicating with my children. I have never been good at communicating at all. I have wasted so much time.'

Cressida could hardly believe what she was hearing.

This was all she had ever wanted as a child . For her mother to sit her down and explain it to her. To show her that she wasn't the awful mistake that her father saw her as. Even if one of her parents truly loved and accepted her, it would have been enough. It would have made her feel less alone. But seeing her mother now, so broken and lonely, she did not say any of that. Instead she simply embraced her and held her while racking sobs filled the air around them.

'I loved Vincent with all of my heart, you see. He was the only one who listened to me, who made me feel protected. I never told him that he was going to become a father. I think, had he known, he never would have allowed me to stay here. I thought that I was doing what was best for you and your sisters… I thought that I could fix things with Fabian. But he never forgave me, despite me knowing that he'd been taking mistresses for years. He had left me feeling unwanted and abandoned in our marriage long before I strayed. But my mistake carried a lasting consequence, one that he could use against me and hold me to ransom with, and so I drank to avoid the misery. I slowly retreated from my life.

'When you found out the truth, I tried to contact Vincent, fearing what your father might do. I found out that he had married. He was happy, so I stayed away. I dreamed of him coming back for me, fool in love that I was. But I had broken his heart when I refused to go with him before, and so he took the money your father offered and we never heard from him again.'

Cressida fought the lump of emotion in her chest at the pain that spilled from her mother after decades of withheld emotion.

'You could have talked to me,' she said quietly. 'If

anyone in this family would understand feeling alone and unwanted it is me.'

'Cressida… I stayed in Monteverre to give you a better life and it seems as though I achieved the exact opposite. I was selfish. I let my own pain distract me from being there as a mother. You look so much like your father… Every time I looked at you for the first few years I cried. The weight of it was too much for me so I ran from it. I was a coward. I still am, really.'

'You don't have to be,' Cressida said simply. 'Your children are adults now.'

Queen Aurelia shook her head slowly. 'I have no-where else to be. Not any longer.' She stared out of the window for a moment before turning back. 'I just needed you to understand… I could never regret the choice that resulted in the happiest time in my life, de-spite the fact that I knew it was wrong in so many ways. That love resulted in you, Cressida.'

They were interrupted by staff coming to ask the Queen for instructions for that evening's dinner. Cres-sida took the opportunity to slip away under the guise of retrieving her older sister so that she might have a moment to breathe and gather her own thoughts in the aftermath of such a tumultuous conversation.

As she wandered through the halls of her childhood home in search of Eleanor, she found her mind linger-ing on the first words her mother had spoken to her. *'So you found love after all,'* she had said. Knowing now what her mother had been through in her own pursuit of love, the statement stuck in her mind. She desper-ately wanted to go back and ask what she had meant. Had she seen something in Khal's face? A gesture per-haps, or the way his eyes lingered on her? Did she know how to tell if a man was falling in love, even if he had sworn against it?

There really was no point in pretending any longer that she was any different to her mother when it came to seeking acceptance and love. And it seemed she had just the same knack for getting herself into trouble.

She had fallen madly, deeply, irrevocably in love with a man who would never feel the same.

'I see no further point in avoiding the reason why we are here. You invited us here to discuss strategy, did you not?' Khal spoke coolly from where he sat in King Fabian's large study. The man had been blathering on in detail about the extremely positive financial reports that had just been published in the Monteverrian parliament. Khal did not have time to soothe the King's fragile ego at present and found his patience had worn utterly thin since entering into his presence.

'We are still awaiting members of your team, I believe,' one of King Fabian's chief aides said in his monotone voice.

'My team will jump in when they arrive.' Khal opened the large black file that his personal secretary handed him. 'I will begin with a report on what Zayyar has done since we received first notification of this breach. Since this story broke my team and I have received minor retractions from three of the major global news sources. We have released intimate photographs of our wedding in order to redirect media attention and we have also initiated investigations into the nature of Queen Cressida's rights with regard to the legal agreements that were signed twelve years ago.'

'Have you indeed?' King Fabian's eyes narrowed.

'I'm glad that you are assuming responsibility for your *Queen*. I had half expected you to try to shirk off the duty to me.'

Khal flattened his palms on the table, inhaling deeply against his sudden urge to resort to physical violence. 'As this matter preceded our union, Cressida was insistent that your government have their say in the PR, considering that it is the Sandoval name being dragged through the mud. Believe me, had the decision been solely mine, I would not have been so merciful.'

'Merciful?' King Fabian's eyes bulged. 'You seem to have developed quite a *tendre* for your convenient bride, considering she was a poor replacement for the one you truly wanted. How is Roman Lazarov these days?'

Khal smiled at the obvious barb. 'If this is how you conduct political meetings, I can see how you brought your kingdom to such a spectacular ruin in such a short time.'

Both men stood up from the table just as the door burst open and the remainder of Khal's team entered.

'Apologies for the delay, Your Highness,' said the chief of his foreign affairs team, out of breath. 'There has been an urgent development from Zayyar.'

'Well, spit it out. We've been waiting long enough,' King Fabian said impatiently.

Khal nodded once to the man. 'If it is urgent and it involves Monteverre, go ahead.'

The man looked momentarily unsure of himself, adjusting his collar as though it was too tight around his neck. 'It seems…that the marriage agreement between Monteverre and Zayyar has been called into question,' he said slowly, drawing a sheaf of documents from his briefcase.

'That agreement has been signed and done with,' Fabian exclaimed, the rims of his eyes turning an angry red. 'Whatever underhand treachery this is, I won't tolerate it for one moment. Not one!'

'Called into question, how, exactly?' Khal ignored the other man's outburst, feeling a strange floating sensation in his solar plexus.

'Well, Your Highness, Zayyari law demands clear and truthful reporting of parentage. Both biological and legal. Parliament has proposed to nullify the marriage on the grounds that your bride forged her documentation.'

CHAPTER TWELVE

'Nullify,' Khal repeated, the word tasting sour on his tongue. 'Even if the marriage has been consummated?'

'If you rule in its favour, yes. You hold the deciding vote, Sire.'

'I called this meeting in order to reach an agreement to manage a scandal, not create an entirely new one,' King Fabian's voice growled from the other side of the table.

'Do you deny that you deliberately withheld vital information in order to expedite my marriage to your daughter?' Khal met the King's eyes.

'I am her father by law,' Fabian said rather weakly.

'Funny how you find that so easy to say now that you see your upward financial swing could be at risk.'

'Are you going to do as they say, then?'

Khal could see the barest hint of fear in the slight widening of the other man's eyes. He momentarily contemplated launching into a list of reasons why he would not be discussing his plans with the man who had emotionally blackmailed his own daughter into marrying a stranger, but he found he had suddenly lost all desire to waste his energy a moment longer. He instructed his team to close the meeting on his behalf and quickly excused himself from the room. He knew he should go to Cressida immediately and tell her everything that had been said. But what exactly would he say?

His thoughts took him out into the grounds of the palace, memory directing him to where he knew a small collection of stallions were kept in a paddock. He had spent some time in Monteverre while negotiating the beginning of the marriage deal that would change his life so completely. He chose a large Arabian named Bruno and borrowed a pair of boots from the groomsman. The paddock was not as long as his desert outlands in Zayyar but it served its purpose, giving both him and the horse just enough space in which to race out their excess energy and quiet their minds.

He thought of Cressida's face when she'd spoken of her work, of the life she'd lived in London before he'd come crashing into it. She had told him she felt truly happy in that old life. Would she ever truly feel at peace as Sheikha of Zayyar? She had said time and time again that she was not suited to a public role. That she missed the solitude of her library and the simplicity of a private existence.

Could he really deny her the chance to turn back the hands of time and make a choice based solely on what she wanted to do? These thoughts haunted him even after the sun began to dip low in the sky. Realising he had spent longer than intended out of the palace, he released the stallion to the groomsman and made his way back inside.

They had been assigned a guest suite in the opposite wing to the family; he took the steps up two at a time, eager to get the conversation over with. When he entered the bedroom, however, he found Cressida asleep on the bed. He stood in the doorway for a long while, not wanting to wake her. There was a tightness in his chest that he couldn't understand.

He had no way to be sure what she would decide once he told her of the option to annul their short marriage. He could simply make a phone call and have parliament vote against the whole thing, bury the entire idea as though it had never existed. She would never even know it had been spoken of…

But that would be selfish and he had gained enough self-awareness to know that he could not make this kind of choice for her. Lying to her or withholding information was not protecting her, it was something the old Khal would have done from a place of fear. Regressing was not something that he could justify. She had not been shown much kindness in her life, despite her royal upbringing. She had been used as a pawn in battles between her parents and palmed off as a political sacrifice to a man who was far too broken to ever give her the kind of life she deserved. She deserved to live the life she chose, even if that life did not include him.

Cressida stirred in the bed, a smile brightening her entire face at the same moment that she opened her eyes and saw him. 'What time is it?' she murmured huskily, stretching her arms.

'Almost six,' Khal said, forcing himself to remain still when all he wanted to do was close the distance between them and draw her into his embrace.

'Did the meeting go well? Have you come to an agreement for the press strategy?' she asked, standing up to reveal she wore only one of his T-shirts. She smirked as his gaze darkened. 'Sorry, I couldn't bear the thought of digging through half of the gowns in my case to find my own T-shirt so I stole one of yours.'

This image might very well be imprinted on his brain for ever, he thought with a cruel twist of his lips. She had never looked more tempting than at this moment, wearing one of his white T-shirts. The garment went to her mid-thigh, showcasing her long slim legs. But he was not a barbarian, even though the world claimed he was. Putting his libido firmly in check, he took a few steps away, just as they were interrupted by her assistants arriving to begin preparing her for the evening.

Cressida looked at him uncertainly. 'Is everything all right?' she asked with a frown. 'I can have them come back if you need to talk?'

Khal paused, realising that he had just been about to launch into a very heavy conversation less than an hour before they were due to be seen in public. Cursing his own stupidity, he hastily assured her that everything was okay and excused himself to allow her team to go about their preparations. There was plenty of time to talk tomorrow, he told himself. One more night would not change matters. He went about readying himself, ignoring the niggling feeling that he was simply delaying the inevitable.

Cressida moved to the edge of the party; the air had become uncomfortably warm as more and more guests arrived. She had been told there would be a small gathering of Monteverrian dignitaries and wealthy society favourites in order to show that the royal family stood strong against the scandal. But it seemed half of the kingdom had arrived to get a glimpse of the Sheikh of Zayyar and his scandalous wife.

But as she breathed in the night air, looking at the beautiful ornate fountain and surrounding shrubbery, all lit up in pink and orange lights, she wondered if a husband who was simply understanding would ever be enough. Her mother had said that she and her father had experienced a burning passion in the beginning, then that passion had burnt out, leaving nothing but discontent and resentment in its wake. Without a true emotional connection, would she ever feel secure in her marriage?

'It seems desert life suits you,' a familiar voice came from behind her. Cressida turned to find her middle sister, Olivia, standing in the doorway, her silver gown sparkling like an angel. She couldn't help it; she burst into tears just as Olivia's arms surrounded her in an embrace.

'What are you doing here?' she half choked between sobs.

Olivia wiped one of the tears from her cheek, her classically beautiful features filled with concern. 'We saw the news and we came straight here. Did you know about…the affair?'

Cressida filled her sister in on the entire story, beginning with her mother's version of the affair, leading into her own discovery and Fabian's subsequent emotional blackmail. Once she had finished, they sat in silence for a moment, Olivia shaking her head slightly.

'This family is utterly insane,' Olivia said simply. 'I have never been more grateful for my new distance.'

Cressida smiled, leaning her head against her sister's arm for a moment. Olivia had been the only person she had ever felt a true connection with in her family. Eleanor had always been too busy to entertain her, being the oldest and set to become Queen of Monteverre one day. But Olivia had taught her how to braid her hair and told her the latest gossip from school. She had always envied her sister for her natural beauty and easy elegance. She was talented too, having recently taken the reins of their grandmother's literacy foundation after relinquishing her royal status.

'You seem happy,' Cressida said. 'I'm glad.'

'Roman is wonderful,' Olivia said, a dreamy look crossing her features. 'But I'm also feeling fulfilment from working for the first time in my life.' She smiled widely. 'But I'm sure you know all about that, having had years of freedom in London.'

Cressida thought of that time in her life; it seemed so long ago. 'I do miss it,' she said truthfully. 'I envy you.'

'You could always join forces with me; goodness knows I could use someone with your kind of language skills, Cress.' Olivia's eyes lit up for a moment before she frowned. 'But, of course, you have your own set of responsibilities now. I doubt the Sheikha of a country has time to go travelling around the world teaching children to read?'

The sudden mixture of longing and disappointment that filled her chest took her by surprise. The idea of travelling, seeing the world while at the same time using her knowledge and expertise to teach... She sighed wistfully. But, of course, she had her life in Zayyar and her duties as Sheikha. That should be enough for her. She loved Khal and a small part of her hoped that in time he could come to love her too. But the thought of teaching...

Olivia cleared her throat beside her. 'We could join

forces to do a one off event with the foundation, maybe. It would be great to reconnect and spend time together.'

Cressida opened her mouth to speak, but at the same moment Khal decided to make his appearance on the terrace, followed closely by Roman Lazarov. Olivia's Russian fiancé had once been Khal's Chief of Security and best friend. It wasn't exactly clear how he had come to be engaged to her sister, but it was obvious that it had made things strained between the two men. Khal looked from Cressida to her sister, an unreadable expression crossing his features.

'Olivia was just telling me about her work with the literacy foundation,' Cressida said brightly, covertly trying to swipe away the remnants of her crying episode from her cheeks.

'It's nice to see you again, Sheikh Khalil.' Olivia smiled, nodding politely. 'I was just trying to persuade my sister to put her amazing language skills to good use with the literacy foundation.'

A strange expression crossed Khal's dark features as he looked from Olivia to her. 'Cressida is very talented. She would make an excellent teacher.'

Cressida blushed. She had expected to feel some jealousy with Olivia, considering that her sister had been Khal's original intended bride. But for some reason she did not. Maybe it was the way that Roman and her sister looked at each other, so full of love and happiness. Or maybe it was the fact that she still held out hope that Khal might come to look at her in that same way.

A commotion inside the doorway took their attention and Khal moved aside just in time for the terrace doors to swing open and Queen Aurelia to burst through them.

'I'm done! I want divorce papers drawn up immediately in the morning,' the older woman proclaimed, followed closely by Eleanor and King Fabian. A trio of guards closed the terrace doors, blocking out the scene from the rest of the party.

'Mother, please. At least wait until tomorrow,' Eleanor chided in her best peacekeeping voice as she took her mother by the hand.

'I've waited decades!' Aurelia exclaimed.

Cressida was shocked to realise that her mother was sober; she could tell by the lucidity in her eyes and the hint of colour in her cheeks. She could not remember the last time she had seen her mother look so awake and present.

'Another grand debacle for the entire society to talk about,' King Fabian said, bored. 'I suppose it has been a few months since the last embarrassment.' He looked pointedly towards Roman and Olivia.

Khal moved to Cressida's side, taking her by the hand. 'I think it's best if we go back inside,' he said quietly.

'And leave them like this?'

'They are adults, *habibti*. There is nothing we can do to change whatever is about to transpire. You will only put yourself in the firing line by being present.'

Cressida nodded at his sense, feeling a glow of warmth in the way he stood as her protector. She made to move with him towards the doors, whispering a quiet goodbye to her sisters as her mother continued to berate her father loudly in the background.

'Hold on just a moment,' King Fabian cut across his wife's emotional tirade, his eyes black slits as he took a step towards Cressida. 'As I'm apparently about to suffer an embarrassing and probably expensive divorce, can I at least take it that you two lovebirds have decided to remain married after all?'

Cressida frowned at her father's question—what did he mean, *remain married*? She looked up at Khal, seeing that same stressed expression that he had been wearing all evening.

'This is not the time or the place, Fabian,' Khal gritted.

'I want it in writing that you will not nullify the marriage or the financial transactions that came with it, do you hear me? I want it iron-clad or I will make sure that your kingdom suffers every political roadblock possible.'

'What is he talking about?' Cressida turned to her husband.

'We will speak in private,' Khal gritted, his attention still focused on her father. There was a dangerous glint in his eyes, an awful ruthlessness that she had never witnessed before. It made her recoil slightly, taking a step back from him.

'Cressida,' he said sternly, 'I will not discuss this here.' He reached for her but was blocked by her two sisters, who moved in to stand at her sides.

'What is he talking about…a nullification?' Cressida asked, feeling her hands begin to tremble.

'Parliament have undertaken a motion to dismiss our marriage contract on the grounds of forgery.' Khal's voice was emotionless as he spoke. 'They are saying that because you deliberately withheld the truth of your parentage that I can choose to nullify the contract.'

Cressida felt the ground sway beneath her. 'I see.'

'I did not wish to discuss this with an audience.' He met her eyes. 'I think this is a matter that we should weigh up alone.'

Weigh up? He was discussing the possibility of ending their marriage as though the list of pros and cons was endless. Cressida thought that if she could actually feel her own heart breaking, the pain would be unbearable. As it was, she simply felt numb. 'I don't think we need to weigh up much. If parliament says that my parentage is unacceptable then you need to do what is right for your kingdom. I won't contest any nullification.'

Cressida moved past her sisters and went through the terrace doors, needing to be alone before she let herself completely fall to pieces. She heard the commotion behind her but refused to look back, asking a guard to escort her to her suite. She heard footsteps thundering up the stairs behind them but ignored them, hoping her guard would do his job. Apparently the Zayyari guards only served one ruler, she thought wryly as Khal came striding in the door, slightly out of breath from his sprint.

Khal was silent for a long moment. 'You won't contest it...or you are relieved that it is a possibility?'

'I think if either of us is relieved, it's you. I am hardly the golden bride with political influence that you hoped for. I am steeped in scandal, for goodness' sake. I can hardly make a speech without stuttering.' She shook her head wildly. 'I'm not my sister, Khal. I have tried to measure up as her replacement but I simply can't. Maybe this is best for both of us, to end this now before we go any deeper.'

'How much deeper can we get?' he said, exasperated. 'I know that this marriage did not start out in the most conventional way. I may have chosen your sister first out of convenience, Cressida, but I did not even know that you existed at that time.'

'So if you knew about me, if you could go back and make the choice again, you'd choose me? The awkward, nerdy, antisocial anti-Princess?' she said in complete disbelief.

'I cannot promise that I would have chosen you, given my decision to enter into a loveless marriage. All I cared about was that my bride met criteria.' He moved closer. 'But I would never change you, now that I know the real you. Now that we have begun to share our lives.'

Cressida felt her breath catch in her throat at his words. Surely he didn't mean that he didn't want the annulment? Suddenly she wasn't quite sure exactly who was arguing for or against their marriage any more.

He ran a hand across his jaw, shaking his head. 'What I am offering you now is a real life time machine. A chance to change your future if you want it. Your sister has already offered you a teaching position. If you tell me that you want our marriage annulled, I will honour your request. My conscience would not allow me to hide this from you, much as I may have wanted to.'

'You considered not telling me?'

'God, yes. Why on earth would I want to give you a failsafe chance to walk away from this marriage? Away from me?'

'I just presumed…your plans to have the perfect Sheikha have all gone up in smoke. I'm a walking scandal. Why on earth would you stay weighed down by the burden of me?'

He paused for a moment, the air between them frozen in time. Her heartbeat seemed uncomfortably loud in the silent room and she wondered if he could hear it.

'Yes, you may be a walking scandal. And your family may be utterly insane, and your personality may be better suited to the position of librarian rather than Sheikha...but I promise you, after we have grown closer these past weeks, that you are the woman I would choose over and over again.'

She forgot to breathe, hardly believing what she had just heard. As she watched, he moved closer, coming down on one knee in front of her.

'Cressida... If you truly want to end this marriage, I promise that I will not force you to stay. I have spent so long trying to control everyone and everything around me. Trying to find some sort of peace within myself.' He took her hand, his eyes never leaving hers. 'But I cannot promise that I won't spend every day finding new ways to beg you to come back to me for the rest of my life.'

'Why would you do that?' she breathed.

'Because, while I may have been too afraid to realise my feelings for you before, I know them now. I will not give up on fighting to win your heart. I was afraid to let you all the way in, for fear I would need you too much. It seems laughable now, really, trying to resist my own destiny.'

'You said you don't believe in fate or soulmates.' She felt her insides shake at the look in his eyes, at the sensation that the ground might fall away from under her at any moment.

'Is it not more than coincidence that in a club full of people, in a city with a population twice the size of my entire kingdom...that you would choose me?'

He took a deep breath. 'I realised something today. From the moment I held you in my arms on that dance floor the first night we met, I felt peace. That was what I was running from. I had been so used to feeling at war within myself that feeling your warmth calming me was terrifying. It was as though you took a grip of the darkness in my soul and forced me out into the light again. If that is not love, I don't know what is.'

'I don't know what to say,' Cressida breathed, feeling her hands tremble as he raised one to his lips.

'Say that you will stay by my side. Not just as my Sheikha and my wife, but as my true partner in life. My love.'

It was the romantic proposal she had never received, she realised. She pressed her lips together to stop them from trembling.

'Nothing would make me happier than to stay by your side.' She lowered herself to her knees in front of him, placing one hand on his cheek. 'But I need to be true to myself as well as to my love for you.'

He frowned but she continued quickly, 'I cannot just be a silent figure in a pretty dress by your side. I want to use my skills to help people, to do good in the world.'

A slow smile lit up the darkness in his eyes. 'I will support you in whatever you wish to do with that wonderful brain of yours. You may count on me to stand silently by your side and look pretty in the process.'

She felt the last shred of resistance melt away as she leaned in and pressed her lips to his. He responded by pulling her deep into the circle of his arms, surrounding her with his strength. She felt it in his kiss, the raw power of his love for her. She had not known that this was the missing piece of her heart until he had come into her life and showed her what it meant to be supported and loved for who she was. That she was enough. For Cressida, there could be no greater gift.

EPILOGUE

Six months later...

THE PARISIAN HOTEL ballroom was full to bursting with members of royalty and celebrities alike. Everyone had joined to celebrate the wedding of the year with the most scandalous royal family of the decade. Cressida watched as her sister walked onto the dance floor, accompanied by her handsome new husband for their first dance. 'Olivia looks so happy,' she murmured.

'Roman was never much of a dancer; it appears he has taken lessons.' Khal laughed.

'I will never understand the relationship you two have.' Cressida raised one brow.

'Nor would I expect you to.' He smiled. 'We are both as complicated as each other, but underneath we will always be friends. Brothers now, I suppose.'

'A strange family set-up, if ever I knew one.' She laughed huskily in her throat, gasping as she felt Khal lean in and lay a kiss on the nape of her neck.

'The party is practically over now; surely we can slip away unnoticed?' he murmured playfully, his teeth nipping the side of her ear.

'I am not going anywhere alone with you, Your Highness, not after how little sleep I got last night with you sharing my bed once more.'

Khal had been away for a week while he launched the grand tourism season in the now thriving city of Valar. She had been forced to return early from a trip to South America with the literacy foundation and remain on bed rest at the palace for reasons that they could not yet disclose to the public.

'I hope I did not truly exhaust you?' Genuine concern filled his features as he turned her to look at him. 'You know the doctor said that you needed to rest as much as possible for a couple of weeks.'

Cressida found herself laying one hand across the gentle swell of her stomach in an unconscious show of maternal protection. 'The intense sickness has seemed to ease now that we have got through the first few months. I heard the first trimester is the most difficult.'

Khal nodded, a tight smile crossing his features. His change of heart regarding a family of their own had come as an enormous surprise to Cressida. She had fully intended to respect Khal's wishes to remain without natural heirs, despite knowing that deep down she longed to become a mother some day. But as he had relaxed into the ease of their relationship, she had noticed he tended to worry less and less about things he could not control.

It was not effortless for him. He was a natural protector, after all. It seemed his urge to protect those he loved also included a wish to have children of his own. She had been only too happy to fulfil her wifely duties in that regard, rejoicing when she had fallen pregnant almost immediately. She had not told either of her sisters yet, especially knowing that Olivia's wedding was so close. She did not want to detract from the day.

But as she watched the newlywed couple slow dance

together, she thought she could see a similar glow in her sister's cheeks as Roman's hand slid covertly to her stomach for the briefest of moments. Her eyes met Olivia's across the crowded ballroom, her sister's answering smile telling her all that she needed to know.

'Are you nervous?' Cressida asked a while later as she lay cradled in her husband's arms in the master bedroom of their hotel suite. 'For the baby, I mean.'

Khal moved his powerful body behind her, holding her tight to his chest as he drew lazy circles on her abdomen with one finger. 'Of course I'm nervous. But I think most people are, even if they have not been through a loss. My biggest concern is fighting the urge to place you on permanent bed rest and lock you away for the next six months.'

'Six months in bed?' Cressida pretended to seriously consider that scenario. 'Would you be there too?'

'These hormones have turned you into a sex-crazed hellion,' he scolded, flipping on top of her. 'We have already made love twice today and you still have energy.'

Cressida felt a moment of complete happiness wash over her, looking up into the eyes of the man who loved her. It was almost overwhelming.

'What is it?' Khal asked, a furrow forming in his brow as Cressida's eyes welled up with unshed tears.

'I just realised… I have spent my whole life wanting more and feeling like I would never deserve it. And now here I am with everything that I will ever want or need right here in this bed. I never have to feel alone again.'

'Never,' Khal murmured against her lips, drawing her into his embrace. 'As long as you want me I am yours.'

* * * * *

COMING SOON!

We really hope you enjoyed reading this book. If you're looking for more romance, be sure to head to the shops when new books are available on

Thursday 13th June

To see which titles are coming soon, please visit

millsandboon.co.uk/nextmonth

MILLS & BOON

Coming next month

BOUGHT BRIDE FOR THE ARGENTINIAN
Sharon Kendrick

'You need a wife, Alej. And before you look at me that way, why not? Would-be politicians have been making judicious marriages since the beginning of time. It would be an instant badge of commitment and respectability which would only help your career.'

'But I don't want to get married,' he observed caustically. 'I never did. Not with Colette. Not with anyone.'

She shrugged. 'And that's your dilemma.'

Yes.

His dilemma.

Or maybe not.

From his vantage point on top of the rumpled bedclothes, Alej studied the woman with whom he'd just had the best sex he could remember, and yet here she was calmly discussing his marriage to someone else. A wave of something like bitterness ran through him. Was she so hard-hearted that she could coolly advocate he go and find himself a wife and not really *care*? Did he mean so little to her? *Of course he did. Nothing new there, either.* Yet the irony of the situation didn't escape him because deep down he knew that if she'd displayed sadness and resentment at the thought of him marrying someone else, she wouldn't have seen him for dust.

But maybe *Emily* was exactly what he needed. For now, at least. He'd thought she'd cared for him all those years ago but he'd been wrong, just as he'd been wrong about so many things. But back then she had been barely eighteen with the world at her feet. She must have believed anything was possible and had since discovered that it was not. Because surely it hadn't been her life's ambition to end up running some crummy little business and living in a tiny London apartment. Didn't she miss the riches she had grown up with while she lived in Argentina and the kind of lifestyle which came as part of the whole package?

Even more pertinently, wouldn't she have learnt by now that no other man came close to him when it came to giving her physical pleasure? Her gushing and instant response whenever he touched her would seem to indicate so. Wouldn't marriage add a deliciously dark element to the revenge he was determined to extract from her? Wouldn't it ensure she would never really forget him, because what woman ever forgot the man who slid a golden ring onto her finger?

'I think you could be right, Emily,' he said, easing himself up on the bank of squashed pillows and slanting her a slow smile. 'I need a temporary bride—and you are the obvious candidate.'

Continue reading
BOUGHT BRIDE FOR THE ARGENTINIAN
Sharon Kendrick

Available next month
www.millsandboon.co.uk

JOIN THE
MILLS & BOON
BOOKCLUB

* **FREE** delivery direct to your door

* **EXCLUSIVE** offers every month

* **EXCITING** rewards programme

50% OFF
YOUR FIRST
PARCEL

Join today at
Millsandboon.co.uk/Bookclub